Shared Gardens

A Novel

To Betsy
Hold on to your
dreams—
Anne Biggs

Anne Biggs

PARADIGM
HALL PRESS

HBE PUBLISHING

Dedication

To RL Gandolfo for providing me the tools to survive.

Dan, you know what you did.

Anne

Acknowledgments

To all my writing family who helped me get through and believe
 I could do this.
To our Friday Writers: Gayle, Kara, and Susan,
for every re-write you pushed me through.
To HBEPublishing, who guided this project to reality.
To my family, who has loved me unconditionally.

This is a novel – A work of fiction, based on real life events.

When your face
appeared over my crumpled life
at first I understood
only the poverty of what I have.
Then its particular light
on woods, on rivers, on the sea,
became my beginning in the colored world
in which I had not yet had my beginning....

... Fear hems me in.
I am conscious that these minutes are short
and that the colors in my eyes will vanish
when your face sets.

– Colours – Yevgeny Yevtushenko –

Shared Gardens

Slow-moving clouds hid the late afternoon sun. The wind came up just past four, bending the low hanging branches to scratch against the classroom windows. I finished my day, cleaning chalkboards, returning books to their places, straightening chairs. Keeping an eye on the clouds, hoping to get home before the storm.

A young girl in ragged jeans and a flimsy t-shirt stood in the doorway, her hand over a rounded belly. Her pants soaked. "Mrs. Hamilton?"

"Rachel? You're all wet, let me get you a towel."

"You remember me?" as her fingers ran across her smudged face.

"Of course, I do. What's wrong?"

She began to cry. "I think my water just broke. I'm scared..." she dropped her head into her hands.

"Oh, Dear Lord, sit down. Have your contractions started?"

"I think so."

"How far apart?"

"I don't know, they just come."

"We need to get you to the hospital." I placed my coat around her shoulders and felt her entire body shake. "I'll call 911."

"I can't go to the hospital. They'll want money.... I can't pay."

"Listen, Rachel," I took hold of her chin, and looked directly into her eyes. "You have to go to the hospital."

"Then you take me."

"I don't think that would be safe."

I tried to stay calm. "Tell me, when are you due?"

"Before Christmas sometime. I'm not sure."

"I'm going to call an ambulance."

"If you call, I swear, I'll leave."

"There is nowhere for you to go."

She got up from the chair and moved across the room. Stopping abruptly and turned back.

"I'm bleeding." She stood still, legs apart. Blood began to slowly leak through her jeans.

"Okay, stay here. I'll get my car." I took a deep breath. "I'll be right back." I grabbed my keys off the desk and ran through the door to the back of the campus.

I pulled my car up on the sidewalk next to the door and went inside. "Come on." I wrapped my arm around her waist, guiding her to the door. "Are you okay?"

"I'll stain your seats."

"Don't worry about that. It will wash off." The clouds let loose as I pulled from the parking lot.

"What did the doctor say?" I asked, patting her knee.

"I haven't seen one."

"Oh, Rachel...." I shook my head.

"The clinic said I was pregnant, but they asked too many questions. I never went back."

"And the father?"

"Gone." She choked back the tears.

"Does he know?"

"Of course. As soon as I told him, he left for California. Said he was going to find work." She rested her head against the window. "I begged him to take me, but he said no. Said he'd be back, but he stopped calling and never sent any money. When I couldn't pay the rent, the landlord threw me out." She leaned back and took a deep breath.

"Once you get to the hospital, they'll help. They'll even help you and the baby find a place to live."

"You think I'm keeping it?" she asked, looking at me.

"You don't have to think about it, now." I didn't look at her. I couldn't begin to imagine what she must've felt.

"Yes, I do." She turned toward me, running her fingers through her hair. "I can't take care of a baby. I'm a mess. I have no choice."

"They'll help you get into a women's center. You'll have a home for a while... until you can get back on your feet."

"Mrs. Hamilton, you're not listening. I'm not keeping the baby."

I tried to swallow, but my throat tightened. She was right, I wasn't listening.

"I made the decision when I got kicked out of the apartment. What do I have to offer a baby? Anyone, for that matter?"

"There are services..."

"And when the services run out? What then?" She turned back to the window.

"Rachel..."

I turned off Elm Avenue into the emergency entrance. An orderly came up with a wheel chair as I helped her from the car.

"Her water broke and she's bleeding." I watched as he gently took her from my arms and settled her into the chair.

"We'll take it from here," he said, moving toward the nurse waiting at the doors.

"Mrs. Hamilton, please don't leave me," Rachel cried as they wheeled her down the corridor, her arms reaching back.

"I won't. I'm right here." I walked over to the admittance desk, as they turned the corner. Once again, she called out my name.

"Can I go with her?" I asked the nurse.

"Not right now. We'll let you know how she's doing. We need to get her signed in. Is she your daughter?"

"No. Her name is Rachel Stevens. She was one of my students. I'm pretty sure she's homeless."

"How far along is she?"

"She's due around Christmas, her water just broke."

"Do you have an address? Family contact?"

"No. She's been in foster care most of her life."

The questions kept coming like bullets. I did my best to answer, but there was too much I didn't know.

"Will she be all right?" I asked.

"I'm sure the doctors will do everything they can. There is nothing you can do. Go home. You can call in the morning."

"I should stay."

"She's in good hands."

I drove down Highway 30 with the street lights reflecting off the wet pavement. With my thoughts on the young mother, the eight miles home passed in a blur until a familiar driveway appeared on the right.

I gathered my coat and purse and looked at the small pool of blood on the vinyl seat. I pulled a towel from the back seat and wiped at the stain. Over and over, her words rumbling in my head.

"I'm not keeping the baby."
I have no choice.

I brushed my tears away and opened the door.

* * * * *

In the quiet of a sleeping home, I gazed through the sliding glass door of our family room. The rain had turned to drizzle as the clouds shifted over the moon, its beams flickering on the wet patio.

Walking to the far corner of the yard, I inhaled the aroma of rain on the garden.

I loved this place ... my place.

The smell of jasmine, honeysuckle and lavender afforded me warmth, like the feel of a favorite sweater. I took a seat on the granite bench. The closed buds of jasmine hung like delicate ornaments on a Christmas tree. The garden stored my memories and mended my broken pieces.

I leaned my head back, closed my eyes, and saw Rachel's baby wrapped tight in a pink blanket, with no idea her mother would leave and go on with her life. The child would have no memory.

In shattered fragments, I heard my own story, different from Rachel's. They said she died. I never had a memory of a face, or a moment I could call mine. Years later, placed in a home where I knew no one, I could claim nothing but the clothes on my back and the Miraculous Mary medal around my neck. The one thing that was mine. I still had it, hid away for safekeeping as people do with secrets.

I locked the sliding door, and went down the narrow hallway, looked in and found our children safely wrapped in their dreams. In our room Carl was tucked into bed, his head against the headboard, absorbed in a movie.

"Hey you're late." He turned on the bedside lamp. "And you're wet."

"I know. Sorry, I should have called. There was an incident at school," I said as I opened the top drawer of the dresser.

"Is everything okay?"

"One of my students came by, she was pregnant. Her water broke and I took her to the hospital. I didn't have time to call, sorry." I dug down in the drawer and found the small silver box and lifted it out.

"What are you doing?"

"I just wanted to see something."

"What?"

"The medal that I wore when I left the orphanage." I turned toward Carl, holding it up. "Mom said the medal was tied around my neck when I came off the plane. She never knew where it came from. She gave it to me when I was older."

I rubbed the medal, clearing smudges of tarnish. "You never really talked about it before."

I returned everything back to its place. "I never thought about it much, but after Rachel... I can't stop thinking about it. I just needed to reconnect, I guess."

"What is it about Rachel?"

"She's signing the baby away, it makes me sad."

"That's her choice, Claire."

I slipped out of my clothes, leaving them on the bathroom floor and grabbed a towel for my hair. "I guess it's because she does have a choice..., so many girls don't. My mother didn't."

"Is this about Rachel or your mother?"

"My mother, I guess. I just wonder what she was like? What her name was?" I took my robe from the hanger on the bathroom door. "I feel sad."

"For who?" he asked.

"For us all. Really Carl, what if she hadn't died? Things would have been so different."

"Yeah... you would have never come to Oregon. You would have met some Irish farmer and gone off to the country to have babies and raise chickens. You would be stuck mucking out the barn and slopping the pigs."

"I still wonder..."

"You wouldn't have married me and we wouldn't have made these kids."

"I'd miss that..."

"Which part? The kids or the making?" He ducked as I threw the towel.

"Would she have given me away, or would she have fought for me?"

"Claire, don't do this," he said. "You have no idea. No one was given a choice. It was a different time."

"I just wonder.... Why can't I remember?" I pulled my robe closed.

"Sometimes it is best we don't remember."

"I could never have imagined giving Devon or Adam away."

He sat up. "How could you even begin to compare the circumstances?"

He was right, there was no comparison.

Carl had pulled the covers around him, "Are you coming to bed?"

I shook my head, "I'm going to sit up a bit."

"Don't make it too late."

I went down the hall, stopping first in Devon's room. I picked up her scattered clothes and put them in the hamper. In Adam's room, I moved the He-Man castle against the wall, scooped up the action figures and placed them on his desk.

In the kitchen I took a glass from the cupboard, and filled it from the open bottle of wine and went into the living room. I curled up in Carl's chair, took a sip, laid my head back, and closed my eyes.

It had been a long day.

I drank the white wine slowly, methodically, letting it settle in, capturing its essence. I pulled Carl's afghan around my shoulders, holding tight to my glass with another sip.

With the click of a pen the baby would never know her mother.

2

"Claire, are you ready?"

"I need a few more minutes." I didn't want to go, but owed Carl an evening out, and though I hated to admit, I looked forward to being someplace else.

I had called the hospital in the afternoon to check on Rachel. She was doing well, and would be released in a few days. They said nothing about the baby. I wasn't family, they told me. I was glad I hadn't gone to see her. I would have upset things, said something I would have regretted.

Tonight, was for Carl, and I'd promised to leave my drama at home. He came up behind me and wrapped his arms around me, and started to nuzzle my neck. "Okay, I know where your mind is, let me go, I need to finish. I'm still not sure what to wear."

I tugged on my jeans, then pulled a flirty shirt over my head. I wrapped my hair into a knot, letting a few strands hang down below my ears, pretending I felt sexy. Slipped on dangly earrings, dabbed on lipstick, and went out into the living room, where I found Carl watching television.

"How do I look?"

"You look great, but you do know it's casual?"

He got up from his chair and I moved toward him, reaching up and wrapping my arms around him. "We could stay here, you know," I ran my tongue across my lips.

"You had your chance... come on, Claire, how would we explain ourselves?"

"Really? You're worried about explaining our absence?"

"Come on, let's go," he pulled away.

"Okay, but you don't know what you're missing. I nudged him with my hip and laughed.

He looked at me, ran his hand down my thigh and kissed me. "We'll have plenty of time when we get home. We don't have to stay too long."

I grabbed the bottle of wine from the counter and paused in the doorway before stepping out, I pulled the clip from my hair and let the curls fall around my face.

As he drove across town, we were silent for a while. At the light he looked over at me, "I missed you coming to bed last night."

"Sorry I must have fallen asleep."

"Or passed out? You went through the whole bottle."

"It was only half full. Are you mad?" I looked over at him.

"No, just worried. It's not the first time."

"What are you implying?" I pulled my hand from his lap and leaned closer to the door.

"Nothing. I just worry, Claire."

I reached over and touched his shoulder. "Carl, I'm fine. There wasn't that much in there. You don't have to worry." I kissed him quickly, as he pulled up to the curb. "Come on, let's just have a good time. You know, let our hair down. I promise I won't fall asleep in the living room tonight."

He patted my behind, and took hold of my hand as we walked up to the front door. We stepped inside, immediately greeted by Carl's friends. I stood back as they shook hands, looking around the room, trying to find a place I could feel comfortable, or a face that I knew.

I put on a big smile as Carole came toward me with a glass of wine.

"Hey, we thought you guys weren't coming." Carole said, giving me a hug like we were the best of friends. I hugged her back.

"Just a late start."

Carole and I became friends when Carl began working for the same firm as her husband. We met for coffee a few times, and mostly talked about our kids and work. She had told me about her parent's divorce, and I told her about being adopted. It was safe and we were comfortable with each other.

"I like the new cut," I said motioning to her hair, which was now in a short bob compared to the longer style a few weeks earlier.

I took a seat at the bar and watched a few women in the corner, huddled deep in conversation. One looked up at me, but quickly returned to her friends. I could hear bits and pieces of what they were saying. They were talking about Rachel. *Why would they be talking about her?*

I looked over at Carole. "Who are they?" I recognized Cindy, she was Carl's boss' wife, but not the other two.

"They're the wives of the new partners," she motioned.

"Well, you're quite the hero, I hear," Cindy said, as she pushed her tight red sweater to the island where Carole and I stood. Two of her friends followed. "It's all over town how you saved that poor, wretched girl."

"I didn't save anyone," I said, irritated that they would think of gossiping about something they obviously knew nothing about. "I was no hero. I drove her to the hospital. That was all."

"So glad she's giving up the baby, you know she couldn't possibly keep it. Why, of any one, you'd understand, wouldn't you Claire?" Cindy quipped.

"Was she on drugs?" Another woman asked. "Oh, that poor baby. It's a good thing. They'll find a good home for it. It's such a disgrace."

I paused, biting my tongue before I could answer.

"I'm not really comfortable talking about her." I took a sip. "And just to clarify, she wasn't on drugs, just alone and scared. She came to a place she thought she'd be safe."

"Well, if she gives it up, it would be best for everyone," the woman continued. "There's no way she should keep the baby. It will be so much better with a family that can love it."

"You're so right," Heather, another woman piped in. I looked back and forth between the women who had been talking. Cindy smoothed her lipstick and adjusted the spikes to her hairdo. I didn't know Cindy that well, except for Carl's work parties. She knew nothing about me.

"Well you would know better than anyone, wouldn't you Claire, being adopted and all," Cindy said.

"Excuse me, but my life is none of your business."

"Whoa, Claire, don't get upset," Cindy continued. "I'm just saying. She has no family, right?" Cindy took a sip of her wine as if she were talking about the weather.

"So, now it's because she doesn't have a family, she shouldn't be able to keep her baby." I lowered my voice. "Wow, poor and single, that would make her a terrible mother by any one's standards, wouldn't it?"

"No, of course that isn't what she said," Carole broke in. "Come on ladies, this is not a night for politics."

"No, let's see where this goes," I said, almost baiting a fight.

"Well actually, yes, I am. There are so many families that would do anything to have a healthy baby, and they could love it so much better than her. You know... giving it everything. Really, don't you think it's the best thing she could do?"

"I know this young lady, and there is nothing that would make me believe she would be a bad mother. Do you have any idea how hard this decision was for her?"

"I didn't mean anything personal, just that with her youth against her, it would be better for the infant to be raised by people who could give her what she needed, you know, love her more?"

"Love her more?"

"You were adopted, weren't you?" Cindy continued. "You've had a much better life, than you could have, if you had stayed with your mother."

"Oh my God, tell me you're kidding?" I looked at the women gathered at the counter. *Should I tell her she was full of shit or that my life was not her business?*

"What's wrong?" Cindy asked, looking around as she took a sip of wine.

"My adoption has nothing to do with this girl giving up her baby." I took a drink, and braced myself for what was to come.

"You must have been so grateful to your adoptive family when you learned what they did for you," Cindy continued, "that's all I'm saying."

"My mother died. I spent four years in an orphanage. The circumstances are entirely different. I don't know what you expect me to say."

"They did so much for you. They gave you everything and made you who you are today."

"Don't we do that for our children?" I asked. "I don't understand what your point is." I could feel my chest tighten. I brushed loose strands of hair from my face. "I do everything I can for my children. I don't expect them to be grateful. That's my responsibility to them, not theirs to me."

"Well of course. Just that, well you know, you were so lucky to be chosen over everyone else."

"Yes, you're right, I was chosen, if that is what you want to call it. I was picked from pictures. That's how it happened. Like mail order."

"I bet you're glad that you were given away. You had such a better life."

"You did hear me say my mother died? It wasn't a matter of choice."

"But...."

"My God, just stop. You have no idea what you're talking about. I wasn't chosen — I wasn't grateful. It had nothing to do with me, but you obviously don't understand that."

"Cindy," Carole broke in, "I think you've said enough. She was Claire's student; of course, she would do everything she could for her."

"Well of course," Cindy said. "That is why she's our new hero."

"You're making things a little too personal," Carole added, as she looked around the room. "Let's get another glass of wine."

I saw Carl looking at me, somehow sensing that something wasn't right. I saw his concern but shook him off.

"Besides, I've heard most agencies tell the orphans their mothers died. It's easier. You know, so they don't waste their time looking? It's better for everyone."

"Cindy, you have no idea what you're talking about, so keep your fucking mouth shut."

The room fell silent, I started toward the door, but turned back. "And you know what? Fuck all of you for letting her talk like that."

Carl put his hand in the small of my back and guided me past the couch and out the front door.

"Holy shit," he said closing the car door. "What was that all about?"

"I just needed to remind them of their place."

Once in the car I let myself relax. My head leaned against Carl's arm, our fingers entwined, like high school lovers, as we drove back across town.

"What if she didn't die?"

"What are you saying?"

"What if they lied. What if she was forced to sign me away, and they just told me she died, so I wouldn't ask."

"That is pretty outlandish, don't you think?"

"If she was dead, I'd never go looking, but if she was alive, there would still be a chance."

What if she didn't die?

Monday morning, I got a call from the social worker at the hospital. She told me everything had been completed. Rachel and the baby were gone.

3

I pulled to the curb and stared at the house. I couldn't see her through the window, so I figured she might be puttering in the garden. I walked up the long drive, feeling the past unfold before me. The house looked no different than it had when I was a child, lush, manicured lawn. The rose garden stood bare in the late autumn sun.

"Claire, I'm over here," she called from the breezeway. "Come on back. Do you want to come inside?" she asked, stepping on the two-step porch, dropping her work gloves to the ground. She pulled her sweater across her chest. "It's a bit chilly."

"Yes. That would be fine." I followed her inside still holding my keys and took a seat at the table where I'd eaten dinner every Sunday of my childhood.

"Do you want anything? Coffee, tea?"

"No, I'm good. I came over to ask you something."

"Sure. What is it?"

"It's about my adoption." I gently laid my keys on the table and leaned forward in the chair. "Mom, did I ever ask you... I mean... was I born with the name Claire?"

"Claire was your middle name. We changed it. I told you that a long time ago."

"I don't remember. Could you tell me again?"

"We thought people would make fun of you with such an odd name." She cleared her throat, "besides..., we didn't really like it. It was so foreign sounding. And the spelling was absolutely ridiculous." She looked up, tying her apron around her waist. "Why are you asking now?"

There had been another name. They had taken it from me. By choice.

"What was it?"

"What was what?" She looked at me with her mouth twisted at an angle.

"My name. My birth name?"

"Oh..., Finnouala Claire Brennan."

Just like that, the name fell from her lips like something she said every day. I had moments I couldn't remember the names of people I saw every day, but after all those years, she recited a name she had probably never said out loud.

"How did you know? I mean, who told you?" I asked, still processing the words. My name. My birth-name. *Why was I so stunned?* Tears welled in my eyes. I brushed them away, I couldn't let her see my whole world was shattering.

I suddenly felt broken. I leaned forward and dropped my elbows on the table.

"We had all your papers. They were sent along with you," she said. "They had your name, birth place, the town, even your mother's name."

What had she just said? My mother's name? The town? I wanted to throw up. This happened too fast. It was too simple. One question and she spilled it out like marbles on a playground.

"Why didn't you ever tell me?"

"You never asked," she said. "We didn't think it was that big of a deal."

That big of a deal? How could someone's name not be a big deal? The one thing most people hold in such high regard. The one thing that identifies who they are, how people see them?

"We could never call you Finnouala." Another shock.

"Why would you change my given name?" I asked.

"I told you. We thought people would make fun of you. It was so odd. You know different. I don't understand, why you're asking about it now?"

"You said you know her name?"

"Whose name?" she asked, seeming to have no idea.

"My birth-mother, in Ireland. You know her name?"

"Oh, yes, her name was/is Alice Brennan. I imagine she's still alive."

"Alice? You said, Alice? And she's still alive?" *I couldn't breathe.*

"I don't understand all the fuss." The words sounded incidental, unimportant. Just a winter afternoon chat.

"Mom?" She looked at me in shock.

"What?" She finally noticed. "Why are you so upset?"

"I asked you so many times when I was growing up about my history, and you never told me." I took a deep breath, believing in my heart she had to know what was coming. "You said she didn't die?"

"Who?" She said, still looking perplexed.

I wanted to scream. "My mother."

"No, of course not."

I thought I was going to fall out of the chair, right there. Everything drained from me. It took thirty years to find out, that my birth mother had not died in childbirth. Why did it take so long?

I got up from the chair and walked into the kitchen, then into the dining room and turned back toward her. "Oh my God. You told me she died." She still sat at the table, sipping her coffee, as if no earthquake had just shaken the world to its core. I came back to the dinette and sat back down in the chair.

"We would never have told you that." And then out of nowhere she began to laugh, not the deep in your belly laugh, but the silly frivolous laugh that makes people feel foolish.

"But you did, every time I asked. You told me she was dead."

"I'm sure you're mistaken. When you got older, you were always asking about her, wanting to know everything. It was such a nuisance. One day, I looked for the papers, so I'd be ready the next time you asked. You never did."

"Mom, I think I would have remembered if you had told me she was alive. And you sure as hell, never told me her name." We went back and forth.

"Yes, I'm sure we did. Her name, was/is Alice Brennan, just turned 15 when you were born. We were told she had been raped, but you know how that goes. I think her family just wanted to cover it up. The records were destroyed after the adoption. I believe Sister wrote there had been a fire."

"So, you're saying she didn't die? And her name is Alice Brennan?"

"What is going on?" She seemed stunned by my confrontation "Who in the world told you she died?"

"Oh my God, are you kidding?" I tried to stay calm, but my insides were churning. "You did."

"Why would we do such a thing?"

"Mom." I stood in front of her so she could see my face. "You told me repeatedly that there was no reason to search for her. She was dead. You told me to stop asking."

There was a long pause. My mother got up from her chair, and went over to the stove, poured herself another cup of coffee. "You sure you don't want one?"

"Jesus, Mom, I'm fine. Tell me I'm not going insane. Please tell me the truth."

"Fine." She took a sip of her coffee. "At first we told you she was dead because we thought it would be easier for you. You were ours. You were starting a new life. We didn't want you to think about where you came from. Oregon was your home. We thought it was best that you not be connected to Ireland any more. It was the past, we wanted you to forget it ever happened."

"Then why did you take me to those damn St. Patrick's parties, if you wanted me to forget?"

She shrugged, "We had to. The church arranged them. You never had a good time. You always stood off in the corner. You were such a moper."

"Because, I hated them."

"We wanted this to be your home. We were your parents. You stopped asking after a while. We thought that you had forgotten the whole thing."

"But why? I can see as a child maybe, but don't you think when I became an adult, I should have learned the truth so I could make my own choices? Before I had children." I paused, then continued. "It's my history."

I stepped away from the table and leaned against the sink, looking out through the yellow gingham curtains at the familiar gray sky. "Do you have any idea what it was like to always wonder how things may have been? Why I didn't look like you? And for the record, I never forgot about Ireland. It was in my head all the time, and by "killing her," you made her even bigger."

"Don't you think you're being a bit over-dramatic?"

"No. I think finding out that I had a different name and that my birth-mother didn't die is a pretty big deal."

"Like I told you, I thought you knew."

"Were you afraid I'd have looked for her?" I brushed the tears away, pulled my hair back, then turned toward her. "Searching for her wouldn't have meant I didn't love you and Dad. You know that, don't you? I just needed to know. It was mine to know."

"We didn't know anything about her. What was the point?"

"I have to go. I can't stay here."

"I'm sorry you're so upset." She reached out and touched my arm. "Claire, just leave things alone."

"I'll call you later."

In the span of a half hour, the missing pieces of my life were laid out in front of me. I had my birth mother's name... my name, the name she had given me.

My mind spun in circles. I had waited years for this information, and now that I had it, I didn't know what to do with it. I took a pen and notepad from my purse and wrote it down. *Alice Brennan. Finnouala Claire Brennan.*

This was mine.

She was only fifteen when I was born, she could still be alive. I put my hand to my mouth to hold in the laugh. I had a place to begin.

Finnouala Claire Brennan.

4

From the car, I stared at the princess porch with oval shaped castle windows on three sides. You could sit on any of the ledges and look out at the houses that lined our block.

I remember our swing-set that stood tarnished, with rusted edges. The girls across the street had a brand new one. Slides adorned each side, a teeter-totter, and a double swing. With its fire engine red, and sunshine stained colors, it was Disneyland right there in their front yard.

On summer nights we danced through sprinklers, while our parents watered their lawns. The boundaries of our block protected us from the world outside. This was the life I knew, not an orphanage, from a country far away.

I started the engine, still staring at the yard, watching my mother peek through the curtains. She would wonder what I was doing, but she'd never come out to ask.

I drove down two blocks and pulled to the curb and looked at the little cottage across the street.

Nothing had changed about Sally's house. Ivy still climbed the walls and wildflowers grew in every patch of dirt, and my mother still couldn't bear to even say her name.

There she stood outside her gate surveying her vines, just like the first day we met.

Sally, with her long gray hair tied back, her brown eyes like milk chocolate, cheeks with deep dimples, and flowing skirts that swirled around her legs.
"Good morning, Claire Fischer."
"How do you know my name?"
"I've seen you before, on your bike. I've lived here a long time. People don't talk to me much, but I see what goes on."
"Do you know my mother?"
"I've never talked to her, but yes our paths have crossed."
"I know. Do you know anything about me?"
"I know you love to ride your bike. Is there more I should know?"
I laughed. "No, I guess not."
Her voice soothed me. I continued to pet the kitten as she talked about her cats, her flowers and the garden.
"Would you like to come in and have some lemonade?"
"I guess it would be ok. Ok, for just a little bit, I guess."
"Bring Simon with you. He hates to be left alone." The black and white cat had settled in my arms. She noticed that I couldn't take me eyes off her flowers.
She smiled. "I've always loved gardening."
"They're amazing. I have never seen so many. My dad has a rose garden, but you have everything. I mean he just has roses, and they're all in a row, but you, you have everything, all just growing together."
"Come sit down and have some cake and lemonade."

And that was Sally.
"What are you doing in this neck of the woods?" she called from the gate.

"Just driving by."

"You never just drive by. And what is that look on your face? I know you too well. Come in, sit down, Tell me all about it."

It had been awhile since I visited. She guided me through the gate, back around the patio and into the kitchen. I took a seat at her glass table, where the cat immediately jumped into my lap. It was Chloe, her calico head rubbing against my chin.

"Here," she said, handing me a steaming mug, as she took a parting glance at Chloe.

"Thanks, by the way, the patio looks fabulous. And so do you, of course."

"You can tell the difference?"

We both laughed, and she took a seat across from me. "So how are you?"

"I just left my mother's house."

"How is your mom? I don't see her much."

"Come on now, Sally. You don't see her at all. Her neighbors don't even see her."

"You look very disconcerting. Is your mother sick?" She blew the steam from her mug but looked on intently.

"No, not at all. I don't even know where to start?"

"The beginning would be nice."

For the first time that day, I laughed out loud. I took a sip of my coffee and stroked Chloe.

"I went over to ask her about my adoption, you know if there was anything she hadn't told me."

"Was there?" she asked, reaching down to stroke yet another of her cats.

"Yes." I let Chloe jump off my lap, then I got up from the chair and walked over to the bay window, leaning against the counter. "Sally, she told me my name, like she talked about the weather."

"What name?"

"My birth name and my mother's. And she never died, at least not then."

"Wait a minute, back up. One fact at a time. She gave you a name?"

"Finnouala Claire Brennan. That was my real name. And her name is…was Alice Brennan."

She stared at me, still holding her mug.

"Sally, say something." Here was the one woman who knew my secrets. I had trusted her with everything, and now I told her the one thing I had waited a lifetime for. "Tell me what you're thinking?"

"That you can finally do it."

"Do what?"

"Find her." She picked one of the blooming flowers and handed it to me.

"How would I do that?"

"Don't tell me that wasn't the first thing that came into your mind when she told you?"

"Oh my God. I really could." I set the cup on the table. I had thought about her so much. *How could you find a dead person?* But knowing she might be alive changed everything.

"When did you find out?"

"I just left her house, and when I drove by and you were outside, it seemed like the right thing to do… to tell you."

She got up and came toward me. She took hold of my hand and squeezed it so tight. I just looked at her. I didn't know what to say.

I took another sip from the cooling mug, then got up from the chair and stood in the doorway.

"What if I do it and can't find her?"

"You'll know that you did everything you could.

Then you can let it go," she said, patting my shoulder.

"I don't want to hurt my mother."

"How would searching for your birth-mother hurt her?"

"She would think I didn't love her?"

In that moment, I saw her face as she told me my history, as if it meant nothing. She wasn't telling me with pleasure or joy, not even as a responsibility, just common knowledge, like the weather, the time of day.

"Claire, do you really believe that?"

"I don't know what to believe."

"What do you want to do?"

I sat there for a moment, then looked up. "Before I can do anything, I have to bury a ghost."

"And what ghost might that be?"

"Teresa…, I need to find her." I got up and moved across the pond.

"She'll be glad to meet you." Sally sat back and smiled at me.

5

Just past nine, I watched as Ms. Wile unlocked the doors of the library. I fiddled with my nails, as people rushed off to work, wrapped up in their worlds. I didn't tell Carl about coming here, instead I told him I needed to go to school to prepare upcoming lessons. I felt guilty not telling him I had decided to dig up the past; to learn the truth — my truth.

I hurried from the car to get out of the bitter wind that picked up overnight. Ms. Wile greeted me as she adjusted the buttons on her cardigan.

"Good morning, Claire. How are you this blustery morning?"

"Morning, Ms. Wile. Doing good, I was wondering if you could help me find some family history? Doing some research for my mom."

"Sure, what are you looking for?"

"Mom talks about this friend of hers that passed away a long time ago. Something about her wedding in 1953. She said she was a distant cousin, but I can find no mention of her in Mom's notes."

"A wedding? You should check the old newspapers. We have The Chronicle on microfiche. The machines are right over here. Have a seat and I'll pull the films. You said 1953?"

"Yes. Sometime in the latter half of the year, but she wasn't sure."

"Great. I'll pull from June '50 to June '55. That way we'll be sure to catch it. Have a seat, I'll be right back."

"Thanks," I said, taking a seat in front of the odd shaped machine.

After a few minutes, she returned with several little pieces of plastic in paper sleeves. "Here you go. If you find anything, there is a print button right there," she said, pointing to the red button on the side. "Good luck." She pushed the cart down the aisle between the stacks.

As I whirled through the news articles, I learned the day to day happenings of St. Helen's; an accident where the county sheriff rescued children from a car that landed in the lake. In 1951, the town's Christmas tree fell over in the hurricane style winds that lasted the entire winter. Then I found it. The obituary dated November 7, 1953. It read like a love letter. Instead of writing about the accident, her father wrote about her smile, her friends, and her sass.

Reading the obituary made my stomach turn. I could only imagine how his heart broke, when she died. So many pieces, he'd never find them all.

For her, he had planted a rose garden. He had no idea what my favorite flower was, or the books I read. He had never talked to me with anything more than courtesy. In his love letter, I found the words he'd never be able to say to me.

From the news reports, a week after the accident, they buried Teresa at St. Matthew's Cemetery after a Mass at St. John's Church. The entire parish attended.

He had asked that flowers be omitted and donations to be made to St. Benedicts Hospital in her name. Nobody listened. The casket had been draped in white and pink roses. White sprays of baby's breath, covered the altar. The picture in the paper had been nothing like the one I found in the closet when I first learned about her.

She lay like remnants of winter, hidden on the floor of the closet. Shoeboxes tied with ribbons, stuffed full of pictures I had never seen. After sorting through I understood the reasons for their silence.

Once opened, I engrossed myself in the overflowing pictures. A girl with the blonde ringlets beamed from every picture. There, with the man I thought was my father, laughing under the Christmas tree, lounging in shorts on the lawn, wrapped in a winter coat with a mink collar, Dad in hat and gloves, his lapel pulled up around his neck. I saw them walking in the rose garden, at church with her in her Easter bonnet. I slipped them back into the box. All but one. A snapshot of her playing in the sprinklers. That one I hid under my pillow.

I turned on the small bedroom light and held a picture up for my sister to see. "Who is this?" I asked.

"Where did you find that?" She sat up in bed and reached for the picture.

"In Dad's closet," terrified that I had revealed my secret. "You're in a few, but mostly they're of Dad and a little girl. Who is she?"

"You better put that back before she finds out."

"Who finds out?"

"Mom, who do you think?"

"Then who is it?" I asked again.

She handed the picture back to me and turned the light off. I held on to it in the dark, then slipped it under my pillow. I turned away and closed my eyes. Only our breathing filled the room.

"Her name was Teresa. She was my sister. She died. You can't ever talk about her." Her words were cold, no excitement or fear, just blunt.

In the darkness I thought about what she said. I knew the story of my adoption. I had been told about Ireland and my mother dying in childbirth, but I had never been told about the girl in the pictures.

"Do you remember her?" I asked, breaking the silence.

"Of course, I do. She was my sister. All I know is, she was here, then one day she was gone. Then you were here." Her words were cold and stiff.

"I'm sorry." Another long silence took over, then her voice cracked, and I imagined the tears streaming down her face.

"She took me everywhere. She bought me presents, tucked me in bed with her long-eared-bunny, and read my favorite stories until I fell asleep. I loved her so much."

"What happened?"

"There was an accident. Don't bother asking, they never told me anything"

I heard the rustle of her blankets. I turned to see if I could see her. I saw the reflection of her eyes in the shadows against the darkest sky. Susan continued to bring her memories to life.

"Everyone was sad for a long time and after a while they just stopped talking about her. Teresa was gone, then Mom became so sad she never came out of her room. Dad spent all his time working, and when he wasn't at work, he was at church." The sorrow in her voice was clear. "When they brought you here, I was so mad. You were sick all the time. I hated you."

"I'm sorry I made you mad."
"That's ok," she said.
We never talked about Teresa again, but she lived on the surface of everything we did.

It didn't take long to drive across town to St. Matthew's Cemetery, just outside of town, Teresa's home since the day the white metal casket left the church, and they placed her somewhere beneath the grounds.

I pulled into the empty parking lot and stared from my car into the front office. Through the window I saw an older woman, with too much make-up and bright red lipstick, flipping through papers. She looked up from behind the counter, as the bell hanging in the entrance chimed as I walked through the door.

"Morning, love. Can I help you with something? Planning a funeral, are you?"

"No, I'm trying to find someone buried here in November of 1953, Teresa Fischer is her name."

"Well, let's see what I can find," said the short, wrinkled-faced woman with a nametag that read Edna Morris. "I've been processing names here for forty years, since 1942. If she's laid to rest with us, I'll find her. Take a seat, while I find the book."

"Thank you," I said, sitting down on the old tweed couch. I grabbed one of the National Geographic's dating back to 1965, from the scratched coffee table. Edna slipped behind the closed door and after a few minutes returned, placing a large black book on the counter.

"Okay, love, this book holds the names of all the people resting here from 1947 to 1962. If she is buried at St. Matthew's, then she's in this book. Come on over and we'll look for her."

I walked over to the counter as Edna turned the book around for both of us to see. She flipped to 1953, and then to the month of November.

"Do you have an exact date?"

"She died November 22, but I believe she was buried on the 30th."

"Well let's start at the 20th. You said Teresa Fischer?"

"Yes, ma'am."

She slowly turned the pages. Her painted nails slid down the old parched paper as she passed each hand-written name. My eyes fell on the only name posted for November 22. "Deceased, Teresa Fischer, Daughter of Charles and Marie Fischer, died November 22, 1953, Lane 79, Row 20, Space 11. Here she is. And yes, she was buried on the 30th."

I ran my fingers across her name. I felt myself go numb. "Can you show me where she is? I mean how to find her plot?"

"I'll take you in my car. It's quite a ways from here."

"That would be nice, thank you," I said, as I went to the couch to collect my purse and keys. "Wait, can I go to my car to grab the flowers that I brought."

"Sure, sweetie. While you get your flowers, I'll lock up. If anyone comes, they'll just have to wait. I'd better put a sign on the door," she said, as she went back to the desk.

Coming back, she grabbed her keys, locked the door and pointed to her car.

"Isn't she beautiful," she said.

"Excuse me?"

"I just love her. My husband did it, a perfectly refinished 1955, Buick."

She opened the door for me and I got into the front seat. She patted the dashboard with unabashed affection before she started her baby.

"She is lovely." I looked around and watched as she admired each sparking gadget.

"Let's go and find your burial site. Is she family?" Edna asked, as she pulled from the driveway, turning right at the corner. She looked over and saw my face, then reached over and patted my arm. "It is a tough time. I just thought you might want..." Her voice faded in the car.

"Yes, a cousin," I lied, with no reason to go into details.

"It's about a quarter of a mile down, then another quarter mile in. I can wait while you place your flowers," she said, running her forefinger across her lips.

"No, I can walk back, thank you," I said, staring out the window, looking around at the varied crosses and marble stones that identified lives long lost. As we drove further in, I noticed fewer gravestones, and the bouquets were withered and worn from the weather.

"This is an older part of the cemetery. A lot of the plots in this area are unmarked," she said.

"What do you mean unmarked?"

"No headstones. Your Teresa doesn't have one. A lot of people couldn't afford them in the 50s. Her gravesite is marked with a brick, the plot number engraved on top."

"It's so stark. Don't they come out and clean up the debris?"

"Not in the winter. They'll clean up, come spring," she said.

Besides dried flowers, the only elements of life were the brown lawn and dried leaves that covered the sacred ground.

"I had no idea." I really thought there would be a massive stone, with a picture, or an angel, or a rose, something to identify her. I stood over the tiny square marker classifying the Lane, Row, and Space.

"I'm sorry love, I need to get back. You going to be all right?"

"I'm fine, thank you. I'll find my way back."

"You sure now, love?"

"Yes, you go on ahead. Thank you."

"I'm sorry," Edna said, as she turned to go back to her car.

"She's my sister," I whispered. "I never met her."

"I'm even more sorry for you, dear. You take as long as you need."

I held the yellow roses close to my chest, and the smell of them weaved through the air. The aroma calmed my senses. I knelt down amongst the debris around the small slab that had built up over the winter. Setting the roses to the side, I brushed away remnants of wind-blown leaves and small branches. I rolled the spindly weeds into the bed of brown lawn that grew above her.

The sun moved and hung behind the clouds. As the sky changed shape, rain began to fall. I took the yellow roses and placed them over the marker. *Why would they have left her grave unmarked? She'd been so vital to their lives?*

"You never knew me. I came after you. You left your mother so broken, she could barely move. He thought I would save her, but she never loved anyone but you." I whispered to the marker.

The words spilled out before I had a chance to catch them. I didn't want to leave. She had been alone far too long. The rain continued, but I couldn't pull myself away. I watched the rain drench the roses and trickle into the ground.

"I found you again," I said out loud. *"First, hiding in your father's closet, then the archives of the library. Now hiding among markers with no names. I was so angry. Because of you, I came second in everything, but had you survived I wouldn't be here."* I half expected her to sit up beside me and say she was sorry. Nothing happened, the ground didn't open up, above me the naked branches were still. There was no sign she had heard me. No magic changed our worlds.

"I brought your favorite," I said, gently petting the roses. I'm sorry no one ever came to see you. I'd have come, if I had understood better, but it was her you would have wanted.

"I resented living in your shadows." Oblivious to the rain I rambled on. I couldn't explain the feelings rushing through me, then it all came together, the anger, the sadness. I spread the roses across the dried grass.

I walked back the same way Edna had driven. Taking each remembered turn, I found my way back to the parking lot in front of her office door. I watched her through the window as she applied her lipstick, gazing at the ledger. She never looked up, and I never bothered.

I sat in the car, feeling the cold from my shirt seeping through to my skin. I started the engine and pulled from the driveway. I found her and now I'd let her go.

6

Carl sat in his recliner shuffling through the Sunday paper. The comic section first, then he spent most of the morning combing through the sports section. Usually, I liked the Parade section, it kept me up to date with the celebrity gossip, but this morning I sat at the kitchen table stirring my coffee, my mind a thousand miles from the latest insights on the pages in front of me. Today was not a day for mindless gossip.

He came into the kitchen to refill his coffee. "Can we talk?" I asked.

"Okay, that's not good," he said as he filled his cup, leaning against the counter.

"No, no it's not bad," I said.

"We've been together long enough to know that when you say, 'can we talk,' it's not good."

He adjusted the buttons to his flannel shirt, pushed up his glasses. "What's up?"

Shit, did I really want to do this?

"I talked to my mom a few weeks back, I asked her about my adoption."

He looked at me up over his glasses and rubbed his chin. "What did she tell you?"

"My real name, for one thing."

"Your real name? I thought Claire was your real name."

"Claire is my middle name, the full name was... is Finnouala Claire Brennan, then she told me my mother's name, Alice Brennan."

"What? She said she never knew."

"I know. That's what she said all along. And you know what else?" I didn't wait for him to ask. "She didn't die."

"What do you mean?"

"For years when I was growing up, Mom told me that she died during childbirth." I took a sip of coffee, then another breath to slow myself down. "She didn't die." I waited for Carl to respond, to say something, to show me he understood.

"Claire?" He rubbed the bridge of his nose and took a breath.

"What?" I watched the spoon stir my coffee, afraid to meet his gaze.

He leaned forward. "I know you, what else?"

"What if I could find her? ...I want to find her." I took another sip.

"You mean go to Ireland?" he asked, leaning closer.

"No, not yet."

He moved to the table and sat down "Okay, what then?" He shook his head. "I don't get it. She gave you up. Why would you want to find her?"

I shrugged my shoulders and leaned back in the chair. "Maybe she didn't have any choice, they said she *was* only a teenager."

"Don't you think, after all this time, if she wanted to, she would have done everything in the world to find you?"

The words stung as they filtered into my head. What he said made sense. Why should I look for someone who gave me up? I could feel wetness on my cheeks and I bit my lip. "I want to meet her, touch her face, hear her voice, everything that children never give a second thought to."

"I don't even know if I'll find her."

His jaw tightened, he stared at me from across the table. Things were getting tense, "Why would you even consider doing this?"

"To learn about my past. I don't want to change the world. I just want to find out what happened."

"Is that what you were doing at the library a few weeks ago?"

"How do you know?"

"The kids told me. You said you were going to school, but the kids said you were doing some research at the library."

I emptied my cup. "I was just looking to see what I could find out about Ireland's hall of records. I wanted to find out where to order documents, like my birth certificate, a copy of my passport."

"What did you find?" He sat back.

"There are two places where I can send for my legal records."

He turned away from me and opened the kitchen door for the dog to go out and stood at the counter.

"What else?"

"What are you talking about?"

"You don't think I've noticed the changes over the past few months?"

I was surprised. "What are you talking about?"

"The second glass of wine you need every night? The library research? Is there anything else you need to tell me?'"

"You don't get it."

"You're right, I don't." He adjusted his glasses and

continued. "I thought the kids and I were enough. Don't we have a good life? Aren't you happy with what we have created? Why do you need more?"

"My wanting to look for my mother has nothing to do with the life we have. Of course, I love our life; I love you. I love our kids, but I need this."

He just stared at me, like he was waiting for me to erupt with more secrets I'd been holding from him.

"What?" I asked.

"Is this over? I mean I don't want you holding back, then saying I didn't give you a chance to explain. Have you said everything you wanted to?" He leaned back against the counter and folded his arms, steeling himself against what I was going to say.

"Okay, okay...." I pulled my hair into a tighter ponytail. "I'll try. You know those baby pictures that hang in your mom's house? The ones of you and your brothers?"

"Yeah," he said, looking at me more perplexed than ever. "Everybody has those."

"No, they don't. I never did. See, you take them for granted."

"I don't take anything for granted," he said, cocking his head, narrowing his eyes.

"Yes, you do. You look at those pictures and you know they're there, but you don't see them. Why would you? You know your history. You know the story of your birth." I paused, "YOU... have it all."

"Pictures don't mean anything."

"If you have them, they don't. My life in pictures began with a passport photo. That's when my life started. Four years old. No one can tell me about the first hour or the first day — my first year, no one except her."

"Just because you don't have pictures? You have a history. It may not be documented, like normal, but it doesn't make you less of a person."

"There, you said it. 'Like normal.'"

"Claire, come on." He banged his coffee cup on the counter and rubbed his forehead.

"Claire...."

I was doing a terrible job of telling him how I felt about everything. I moved to him and placed my hands on his hips. "Babe... let me try again. I need to know... when Mom said she didn't die, it took everything out of me. My whole life was thrown against the wall. Everything I knew as true was shattered into a million pieces." I took his hands, kissing his fingers.

"Let me try again, okay?"

"I'm listening."

"Our kids look at their pictures," I said, gesturing toward the wall, "and they ask me about the day they were born because of those pictures." I paused, then couldn't stop myself. "They know they were each born on a rainy Tuesday morning, and they know I cried when I held them. Devon knows she had a headful of hair, and Adam knows he had a scab on his nose. Those pictures mean something."

"I understand that. What I don't understand is what their pictures have to do with your memories?"

"Jesus, Carl, that's the whole point. I don't have any. No pictures... no memories... I don't have anything."

"Okay, Claire I get it."

"No, you don't." I pushed away from him and bowed my head. "You don't get it at all," I whispered.

I was too embarrassed to look up. I brushed my

hair away and tried to continue. "These stories mean something to them. I'm looking for something for me. Something that will tell me who I am."

He shook his head, "Fine. Do what you have to. Just don't lie to me anymore."

"What the fuck are you talking about? I've never lied to you."

"Really, Claire? What do you call it, then? You tell me you're going to work, then you go do research. You sneak around doing who knows what... I have to hear about it from Ted." He leaned against the wall.

"What?"

"Why were you at the cemetery? Was there a funeral you didn't tell me about?"

"Jesus, Carl, what the hell?"

"Ted said he saw you out there, cleaning off a gravesite while a lady stood watching you. She left, and he said it looked like you were talking to someone? Were you?"

I flung myself to the couch. "I can't believe this. After all we've been through... fifteen years of marriage... what the fuck, Carl, it was Teresa."

"Teresa... your sister Teresa? She died a long time ago and you've never even mentioned her, let alone gone to visit her grave. What were you doing? Who were you talking to?"

"I really don't need this shit, Carl. After I learned about my name, I decided I needed to find her."

"You don't even know her." He turned to stare out the window. "Jeez, Claire, it's like I don't know you anymore."

"She's always been such an unspoken force, that I thought if I was going to do this, I needed to put her to rest. I went to the cemetery and that lady helped me find her. I don't know how to explain it. It even sounds stupid as I say it out loud."

"Talking to dead people is a little strange, even you have to admit that."

"It was something I needed to do."

"I want to understand, I want to know what is going on, but you're scaring me, Claire."

"Why? I didn't do anything wrong."

"You're researching a past you'll never have, you're talking to dead people…, and you're falling asleep in my chair at night with an empty bottle of wine next to you. Something is definitely going on."

"God damn you." It was too much. I started to cry. "You don't understand."

He brushed back his thinning hair. "I'm trying pretty damn hard to. You're not making it easy."

"You're making too big of a deal out of this." I jerked away and went into the lkit.

He followed. "I like our life Claire, even the chaos. You are my world, but sometimes…." He stopped and touched my cheek. "You scare the shit out of me."

I couldn't stop the tears. He sounded so normal. I sounded like a raving lunatic. Maybe it had been Rachel, or it had been simmering in me all along. Maybe I was crazy, or I was losing a sense of what was really important. He wrapped his arms around me.

"Look Babe, if you need to do this, I'm okay with it." He took my face in his hands. "Just don't leave me in the dark. Don't expect me to understand things I don't know anything about."

I let go of him and turned away, embarrassed that he had so much more insight into me than I could ever have.

"Are you all right?" He asked, following me.

"Do I look all right?" I stopped and turned toward him, my cheeks burning crimson.

He grabbed my hips, pulling me closer. "No, you look pretty beat up."

I wiped the tears from my cheeks. "I need to do this," I finally said.

"I know, but you don't have to do it alone. Why don't you get some help?"

"What kind of help?"

"Frank told me about his sister-in-law who had some trouble dealing with post-partum, or something like that... she called a doctor..."

"Therapy?" I pulled away from him. "You want me to get therapy?"

"You need someone who is not so close to you, that can have a neutral ear. I don't want to see you get hurt."

I took a deep breath. "I'm not going to get hurt."

"I love you more than anything, but I don't know how to do this, and to be honest, I'm really afraid for you."

"You don't think I can do this?"

"No. Not alone. This is way over our head. There is too much going on."

"I don't need therapy. I'll go slowly. I'll cut back on the drinking. I promise."

I didn't wait for him to say anything else. I went to the fridge, got my bottle of wine and emptied it in to the sink. "There."

I cleared off the counters still hearing his words, telling me how broken I was, but trying to drown them out. Then I froze. I saw my reflection in the window. He was right... right about everything.

I didn't want him to be right about anything.

7

The next morning, I found the business card Carl had left on the kitchen counter.

Dr. Benning, PHD
Individual, Family, Marriage Counselor

I put it out of sight and closed the drawer.

He had made himself clear.

He wouldn't talk about therapy, or about the nights I drank too much and fell asleep in his chair, but his opinion was clear.

I tried to make sure he didn't know. I hid the evidence before he got up. I mended the headache with aspirin, went to work, and stood tall, but he knew. He knew me better than I knew myself.

It wasn't that I didn't want to go to therapy, actually it sounded like a reasonable idea, but I needed to decide my path; go in Carl's direction, methodical, with a therapist to guide the way, or I could do it my way, barrel through, crash against the wall and let pieces fall.

Mrs. Henderson came as an image, crème pearls adorned her neck, tailored suits, teased hair doused in Aqua Net to keep it in place. A flowery perfume lingered, even after she left the room. I remember as a child, thinking her rouged cheeks and lips marked her as a clown from the circus.

She was our liberator. A super-hero, complete with invisible cape. In her arms, we were whisked away to strange new families we would call our own. Never to be reminded of where we came from.

We'd be forever grateful to Mrs. Henderson. Her goal kept us from the poverty and the sadness we had known through our small lives.

I touched the letters painted on the glass of the newest building in St. Helen's, built by the richest woman in town.

As they wiped out our history, they erased our existence, then implanted their own version of the facts.

I took a deep breath and pushed against the double doors. A young neon pink-lipped girl with matching nails sat at the reception desk flipping through the pages of a magazine lying on the immaculately clean desk. I waited for an acknowledgment. After what seemed like an eternity, I tapped my keys on the glass. She finally raised her head.

"Can I help you?" she asked, as she closed her magazine and folded her arms across the desk.

"I have an appointment with Mrs. Henderson."

"Your name?" She opened the appointment book that hid beneath her magazine.

"Claire Hamilton. No wait; tell her Claire Fischer."

"Which is it?" She asked, as if I had given her too much to think about.

"Hamilton," I said.

"Let me see." She ran her painted nail down the edges of the paper. "Yes, there you are. Let me ring her."

I watched her face as she used her nails to push down the buttons on the phone, informing Mrs. Henderson that her appointment had arrived.

I should have dressed up I thought, a skirt at least, but I wore jeans and a cable sweater, with a scarf and jacket slipped over my shoulders. She came to the door and tapped on it. I heard a faint "come in," and the receptionist motioned me to come through.

Mrs. Henderson sat behind her own glass-topped desk with an open file spread in front of her. She looked up, then back at the papers on her desk but didn't acknowledge me.

"I came to talk about my mother," I said. The pearls had been replaced with a large pendant, hanging down to the center of her silk shirt. She still had the ratted hair and the tailored suit but seemed much older. Her hands were clouded with splotches of dark skin, her fingers, long and spindly, were covered in diamond rings.

She finally looked up, closed the file and placed the pen on top.

"You're not the first."

"Do you remember me?"

She leaned back in her large leather chair, still seeming to look past me. "Of course, I remember. You were quite hard to forget."

"My mother told me I was your last trip." I searched her eyes for some sense of safety.

"Yes." She looked up from the file, her pen barely inside her lips. "I never went back because you broke my heart."

My breath caught up in my throat. "How did I do that?"

"I'm sure you know your story..."

"They told me I was sick."

"I brought home strong, pink-cheeked babies, and when we arrived news photographers took pictures, and wrote stories about saving them from poverty. Then you..." she paused, looked away from me, as if she were talking to the window. "You were so lost and alone. I saw it in your eyes. You could barely lift your head."

"I don't remember."

"A blessing."

I had taken her back in that moment she had seen us lined up, touched our shoulders, stroked our chins. She was back in the orphanage.

"You had the saddest eyes I had ever seen. I thought this would be good for you. I had taken you away from poverty." She stood up and moved to the window, her sadness reflected in the window's image of her. "Enough of that. What can I do for you?"

"I want to find my birth mother."

"Why on earth would you want to do that?" She asked, turning toward me. "You were left in an orphanage. She gave you up, gave you away. Why would you want to meet her?"

"My husband asked the same thing... I didn't have an answer for him either. I don't know how to explain it. I need to find out where I came from, who she was, and what the first five years of my life were like."

"If you love your adoptive mother, you won't do this."

"It's not about her."

"It's always about her. Do you love her?"

"Of course."

"Then why are you searching?"

"It doesn't mean I don't love her. This is for me. I need to find my roots."

"Your roots are right here… in St. Helen's. You have nothing in Ireland. I don't mean to be harsh, but why on earth would you want to meet someone who gave you away? Someone who left you alone in an orphanage for almost five years, and never came for you."

"Maybe she didn't have a choice."

"Everyone has a choice." She moved back to her leather chair and opened the file in front of her. She took a seat and adjusted the collar on her silk blouse.

"What happened to her?" I asked.

"I don't know, but she got herself in trouble. You babies were the price paid. I took you away from all of that." She looked up. "I did my part."

"But what if it wasn't that way?"

"Honey, all the girls had their stories. They were on the streets, the boys took advantage of them."

She stared at me but said nothing. "You have all the answers. Why was I left behind?"

"Because healthy babies were a high commodity, sick babies were not."

"Look, I hoped you would help me, give me some place to start. Some place I could learn…, or get back my history."

"Go home, Claire." She came around to the front of the desk, folded her hands, as if she had the final word. "Do you have children?"

"Yes. Please don't make this about them. They have nothing to do with any of this."

"They have everything to do with it. Kiss them,

hug them, and be grateful for the life you have."

"God, I am so tired of being told to be grateful. Looking for her has nothing to do with being grateful. I was a child. I didn't know what was happening. I didn't ask for any of this."

"You're not listening. It has everything to do with it." She stepped back around her desk and took her seat and picked up the receiver and began to tap the numbers.

"Thank you, Mrs. Henderson. I hoped you might help, but I see you have your mind set."

She looked up.

"I am helping you. You just don't know it."

I turned toward the door, grabbed hold of the knob, then turned back. "I will find a way to go back. I'll find her with or without you."

"Claire, if you try to go back, I promise, you will regret it."

I turned and gently closed the door. I walked past the young woman buried in her magazine. "I'll do this with or without you." This time I whispered the words to myself and went out the double doors.

I didn't go to my car right away, instead I walked around the block, then crossed the street to a park. Parks filled St. Helen's.

An empty bench beneath a tree called to me, I sat down staring at the small pond. Ducks swirled in front of me, but I barely noticed.

I saw both sides. I understood it all, yet because it was my life, it was different. I could forget it all. Promise Carl I'd cut back on drinking and throw myself back into my life... let it all go. Or, I could take a different road; turn left instead of right. That road was foggy.

"Claire?" She stood in front of me, adjusting her wool coat. "I don't agree with any of this, but I understand." She handed me a card, before I had a chance to read it she turned back. "Don't call me again."

I turned over the card and stared at the name and address.

Dr. Barnados
45 Crossroads
Black Rock,
Dublin, Ireland

I watched Mrs. Henderson step off the curb. I held the card, turning it over as if I had just been gifted a secret. So sacred, it burned my fingertips.

I should be happy. I had a direction, but the sadness in her eyes burned into my mind.

I felt like a traitor.

8

The more I thought about her, the stronger the turmoil gouged at my heart. What was I thinking... maybe she was right. Didn't my mother deserve a doting daughter? Don't my kids and Carl have a right to my attention? Why should they have to deal with my selfishness?

That's what it was. Selfishness. None of it was necessary.

I was standing at the sink when Carl came in the kitchen door from work. "Hey, Sexy," he said as he squeezed my behind, walking by.

"I'll give you exactly three hours to stop that," I said, wiggling my hips.

"You're in a good mood... I think I like." He raised his eyebrows. "What's got you so ... what's the word I'm looking for?"

"Playful?" I said with a smile.

"Playful is a good word," he sputtered. "What's got you so playful? Me, I hope."

I slapped him with the towel. "Of course, it's you. It's always been you."

"Uh oh, what happened? What do you want?"

"All I want is you. As for what happened...

nothing...yet." I moved closer, draping my arms around his neck.

He looked around and took a deep breath, "What did you have in mind?"

"I thought we could order in. Do you remember, before the kids, when we used to have pizza in bed?"

"I remember what it led to." He pulled me closer.

"Now, you're getting the picture." I caressed his ear with the tip of my tongue.

He pushed me back, holding my shoulders, "Who are you and what have you done with my sweet, innocent Claire?"

"I just thought it would be nice if we could forget about things for a bit. I love you, and I don't want you to ever forget it.... It's been a while."

"Oh Babe, you show me every day. I love you, too." He pulled me back to him, kissing me, holding me tight.

"Let's forget about dinner." I pulled him to the bedroom by his belt and pushed him down on the bed. "I've been thinking about this all afternoon."

I stood over him, fumbling the buttons of my blouse. I could feel a flush spread across my skin. "Let me," he worked the buttons like a tailor.

"You're good at this."

"I'm inspired." He rested his hands on my hips, holding me, then pulled me to the bed and kissed me.

"Stop!" I said laughing, pushing him back and falling into his arms. "I love you so much."

Carl stroked my arm as we cuddled, my head resting in the crook of his arm. "You want to tell me what's going on."

"Your hair is tickling my nose."

"Not that. What happened today? Why the shift in attitude?"

I lay against his chest, running my fingers across his skin.

"Claire? You still there?"

"Yeah, just trying to find the words."

"What? C'mon Babe, what's going on?"

"I went to see Mrs. Henderson today."

"Henderson... isn't she the one who brought all the babies here for the Church?"

"Yes. She said I was the last one. She said I broke her heart."

"What's that supposed to mean? You weren't even five."

"That doesn't matter. She also said I was hurting Mom, you and the kids. She said if I really loved you, I wouldn't push trying to find my birth mother. It kind of makes sense. I mean, look at the way I've been treating everyone. How long has it been since we've even done this? Carl, I can't lose you. I won't drive you away. She said I was hurting everyone."

"Son of a bitch... she said you were hurting us? Pushing us away?"

"Well. Not in so many words, but...."

"Christ, why can't they just mind their own fucking business?" Carl sat up, shaking his head.

"Claire, you need to forget everything she said, she's just an old woman who thinks her opinion matters, just because she's rich. Your mom didn't act hurt, did she?"

"No."

"And I can tell you right out, you're never going to get rid of me and the kids. You're stuck with us. We're family and that is never going to change. I told you when we got engaged, I would love you forever. I promised I would stay with you till the end of time.

"I'll be damned if I'm going to let some crazy old bitch shut you down."

"But ...."

"But nothing. I told you I was OK with you doing this, I just wanted you to be careful. I love you, Claire. I just don't want to see you hurt." He leaned in and kissed me again.

At that moment, I wanted to lay forever, in his arms.

9

I slipped in behind his chair and put the card in his open hand, patted his chest and went into the kitchen.

"You called?" He asked, getting up from the chair and following.

"Yep."

"And?" He turned me toward him.

"I made an appointment. But if he has a pipe or patches on his jacket, I'm out of there."

"What does that mean?"

"Long story.... I didn't like the way you did it, kind of sneaky — but yes, I made an appointment."

"I didn't know how else to do it," he said. "I just worry about you." He squeezed my hands. "I mean I think it will really help."

"It's okay, I get it, but no promises," I said, tugging his ear. I moved over to the counter so I could start dinner.

We didn't talk about the card or Dr. Benning again that night.

Dr. Benning's office was on the other side of town, close to the high school. There would have been time to take the wrong turn, go for coffee, sit in the mall for an hour.

No. I wouldn't do that. I was terrified, my knuckles turned blotchy red as I gripped the steering wheel. But as long as it wasn't the therapist from college who everyone called 'The Professor', I'd be good. At least for the first appointment.

In a patched wool jacket, he leaned back in a rickety office chair. He stared at me like I was someone he was considering sleeping with, then pulled a pipe from the inside of his jacket and lit it. I waited as he drew in the smoke, releasing it in little puffs. It wavered around his face making his complexion look splotchy.
   "So, you can't keep a man."
   "I don't sleep with them, if that's what you mean."
   He relit the pipe. I rubbed my fingers along the seams of the chair.
   "You're a good-looking girl. Stop being a teasing bitch. Sleep with one of them. You might get a second date."

I never went back. He never called to find out why.

I stood in the foyer of the main office, looked around at the second-hand chairs, the JC Penney paintings, and the worn carpet. I took a seat in the corner. I could do this, I told myself as I flipped through the Fish and Game magazine. I could tell a stranger about my life, and it wouldn't bother me a bit.
   Shit... I was such a bad liar. I could barely find the strength to tell Carl. How could I tell a stranger my deepest fears?

The glass window to the receptionist opened and a man peeked out. He had salt and pepper hair, with a pale blue shirt and dark blue tie. Blue must have been his color.

"I'm Dr. Benning," he said opening the door. "You must be Claire." His smile was soft and kind. I eased up reluctantly, and unclenched my fists.

"That's me." *So far, so good, I thought. No sign of a pipe or patched jacket.*

"My office is down the hall." He pointed, still smiling.

He guided me through the door, again, blue everywhere. The variety of shades were soothing. Inside, two wing-backed chairs, much more comfortable than those in the entry. "Have a seat," he said, motioning to the wing-backs. I picked the chair closest to the floor-to-ceiling window where a Ficus stood. He sat in a leather armchair, he pulled from behind the desk.

The plant stood limp and uncared for. Leaves that should have been green, were limp and streaked with yellow. In places, long brown leaves hung drooping, amidst the yellow. It had been neglected. On an impulse, I grabbed a leaf and began to rub it between my thumb and forefinger, then looked down at my watch. *Not even five minutes.*

"I'm not good with plants," he said.

"It just needs a little more water and a little less sun." *I had learned that from Sally.*

"I'll have to find a new spot."

"It would do really good in that corner, where it can get morning sun."

He smiled and took his yellow pad and pen from the desk and placed them in his lap.

"I'm sorry. I have a friend who has taught me a great deal about plants."

"Don't be sorry, I've always been impressed by green thumbs."

"That's not what she calls it." We had said enough about plants and green thumbs. I sat back and kept my wallet and keys in my lap.

"On the phone, you gave me a little background. Can you tell me, what brings you here today?"

I fiddled with the keys, tossing them back and forth. "I guess. Well... I've been..."

He leaned back and crossed his legs. His smile disappeared. "That might be a harder question than it seems. Why don't you tell me a little more about yourself?"

Ok, that's easier I thought. I could do that. I put my keys on the side-table next to me and folded my hands in my lap.

"I'm a high school teacher. History," I said.

He gave a small smile, more with his eyes, like he was trying to tell me not to be nervous.

"I loved history," he said, as he wrote on the yellow pad.

"Most people don't," I said. "Kids don't like the past." I couldn't take my eyes off the pad, as the pen moved across the page.

I looked up and he must have seen the sheer panic spread across my face.

"Oh, don't worry about this," he said, holding up the pad. "I have an awful memory." This time it wasn't his eyes, but he gave a broad smile that covered his face. I took a deep breath.

"I just get nervous." I continued rubbing the leaf between my fingers, thankful the dead leaves hung so close to my reach.

"That's okay." He looked at my hands, his jaw

tightened just a bit. "Sorry about the plant. I've never been very good with them, but every spring it seems to come back, so I keep it."

"It gives me something to do," I said, holding up the leaf. This time, I smiled back.

"Okay, tell me a little bit about your family."

"Well, like I told you on the phone, my kids are in elementary school."

"What do you do when you aren't working or with your family?"

"I like old movies and I read a lot..., and I have a garden that I love."

"Now, I'm really embarrassed," he said looking over the wilting tree.

"Don't be. Maybe a little fertilizer every other month might keep the leaves from dying." The ice had been broken and I let my shoulders drop.

He continued to take notes that I tried to eavesdrop on, but his handwriting was awful, a shorthand that I couldn't read, neither printing nor cursive. He looked up, smiled, and when he folded his hands across his lap, they were relaxed..., something about that eased me as well. I tucked my leg under myself.

He was formal in his questioning, like these were the things he asked every new patient. I looked around the room as we talked, and I wondered what it would be like being in here all day, but I figured it was no different than where I stayed all day. Made me love my garden even more. I did notice, his office wasn't very personal. It could have been anyone's. He must have done that on purpose, to keep his life private, so patients couldn't learn too much, become attached, or find connections.

I rested my elbows on the arms of the chair and tried to pretend I was fine, but still, I was anxious. *Maybe this was a bad idea... maybe I didn't belong here? But he was nice.*

"Claire?" He sat back and re-crossed his leg, which seemed to be a comfortable position for him. "Can you tell me about your family when you were growing up?"

I dropped my leg and crossed them in front of me, mirroring his image. "Well, there were my parents, and I had a sister."

"How were things growing up?"

"Like everybody else, not too exciting. We got along, got by."

"Tell me a little bit about them."

"My dad sold insurance, my mom stayed home, and my sister and I went to school."

"Was there anything that set your family apart, let's say from others in the neighborhood?"

"I was adopted."

"And how was that?"

"People had a hard time with it. It wasn't as accepted, as it is now."

"What do you mean?" He loosened his tie, just enough to unbutton his shirt.

"My mother's family was not too accepting. They thought that family meant blood." I had to be careful of what I said. People still had very different opinions.

"Is this one of the reasons you came?"

I looked around the room a little. I didn't feel like I had an answer. "No, not really. It was my husband's idea."

"Okay. Can you tell me a little more?"

He moved the pad back to his desk. He must have noticed that I kept moving around on the chair, or that I had picked another leaf from the tree.

I wasn't about to mention the drinking, at least not yet. I didn't believe that Carl had wanted me to come for just that. I watched him and realized I could do one of two things. I could lie, and he would see right through me, as most good therapists would do, or I could just suck it up and be as real as possible.

"I found out some news that was a little unsettling. A few weeks ago, my adoptive mother told me that my birth-mother never died. I also learned my birth-name." I took a breath and sat back, still stroking the yellow leaf.

His voice softened. "Do you realize the whole tone of your voice just changed?"

"Did it get anxious?"

"No, you've been a little tense, but the minute you talked about your birth-mother your voice softened and became endearing. Can you tell me more about what happened?"

"I kinda made my birth-mother out to be this hero who died in childbirth. I always wondered what she would have been like, you know... the color of her hair? Did she have freckles, like me? What it would have been like...."

"Then I found out she didn't die." I stared out the window, distracting myself. I eyed a black cat under the bushes, lying on its side, stretching in the late afternoon light. I looked at my watch, checking to see how long I had to sit there.

"Do you know anything about her?"

"No."

"You don't know where she lives?"

"I think she probably still lives in Ireland?"

He looked surprised. "Ireland?"

"Yes. I was five, when I was brought over."

"So, it was an international adoption?"

"Yes, it was done through the church."

"You think she might be alive?"

"When I was little, my mother said she had died in childbirth, that they didn't know anything about my past."

I pulled another leaf from the Ficus. *The adoption part had come out sooner than I expected. We were barely done with the first session.* I looked down at my watch. *Still fifteen minutes.*

"Do you mind if I ask you a few questions about your adoption?"

"No. I'm okay with it. Just please, don't ask me if I'm grateful?"

"Why not?"

"Because every time I tell someone I'm adopted, they tell me how grateful I must be. I hate that word."

"I can understand that. I won't ask, but it might come up in our discussion. Will that offend you?"

"No. I get it. It will be part of you getting to know me better."

"You said you hate that word. Why?"

"Because it makes me feel guilty."

"Can you explain that? I'm a little confused."

I looked up. "Throughout my whole life my parents told me to be grateful, because without them, I'd have nothing."

"Were you?"

"Oh my, God, yes. Every minute of every day." I dropped my head, embarrassed to admit that fact.

"What's wrong?"

"I just don't like to talk about it." I looked at my watch. "Are we almost done?"

He smiled again, the same as when he opened the

sliding glass window. "We still have a few minutes. But it might be a good time to ask.

"Do you think you want to come back?"

I stared out the window, the cat was now asleep. I brushed my hair back and held the crumpled leaf in my hand. I looked up again, away from the cat and the mud stained window. "Well, you're better than I thought you'd be. My experience in therapy has not gone well, but you've been okay."

"Glad I'm okay," he said. "So, do you want to come back?"

"Sure."

"Good." He placed the pad and pen back on the desk. "I think there might be a lot of things that came to the surface when you found out your birth-mother might be alive. I think you have feelings that you've never admitted. I don't think this is really about Carl wanting you to come, but we can talk about that, too."

"I'm not sure. I do know that, for a few minutes today I felt safe."

"I'm glad." He didn't really smile, but the wrinkles on his forehead disappeared. "When's a good time?" he asked, taking his planner from the corner of his desk.

"I like this time of day, if it's all right."

"Perfect." He wrote down what I thought was my name, then handed me a card. "You can call, you know, if anything comes up."

"Thanks, I think I'll be okay until next week." I gathered my things and followed him to the door.

He opened it and I shadowed him down the hall. I slipped my check through the window and closed the door behind me. I didn't go to my car right away, but instead walked the two blocks to the center of town. I decided to get coffee. I wasn't ready to go home.

Dr. Benning was a kind man. If I was smart, I'd listen to him. He didn't make me feel stupid, but I wasn't too sure what he knew about adoption. I was relieved that he wasn't condescending, and he didn't have a patch on his sleeve or a pipe in his pocket.

I ordered a cup of coffee and sat outside. I watched the kids at the park across the street, move from the teeter-totter, to the slide, back to the swings.

It wasn't quite spring, but the buds had taken hold in the late afternoon. I let the coffee go cold, as I stared into the playground. After a few minutes I tossed my cup in the trash and walked back toward my car.

I called Carl from the booth at the end of the block.

"Hey, I just got done."

"How was he?"

"I like him. Hey, I want you to know that I'll agree to continue seeing him, but I want to search for her."

"Okay...." I could hear the hesitation in his voice.

"I just want you to know there may be some days when I'm anxious, and others when I'll be sad."

"Okay."

I hung up the phone and walked back to the car just as the rain began to fall. It felt refreshing to finally have someone to talk to who wouldn't judge me, not that Carl really had, but lately every word felt like an attack.

10

Seeing Dr. Benning gave me a strength I didn't know I had. I didn't realize how comforting it was to talk to someone and not be judged. Even though I questioned everything that came out of my mouth, I kept talking. I'd had three visits with Dr. Benning, when I finally got the nerve to send the first letter. It wasn't the name from Mrs. Henderson, but what I had found in the library.

It began with a simple request to a stranger, with my name and birthdate, and her name. That was all I knew about her. Sending her name in a letter like it was mine, gave me ownership.

> *January 10, 1987*
> *Joyce House*
> *To Whom It May Concern;*
>
> *I am writing in hopes of gaining background about my past.*
>
> *This is what I know:*
> *My mother's name was Alice Brennan*
> *My name was Finnouala Claire Brennan. I was born somewhere in Ireland, November*

*20, 1949. Somewhere between that date
and June of 1953, I was brought to an
orphanage near Dublin. I don't know the
name of the orphanage nor do I know the
town. Any information that you might be
able to provide me would be appreciated.
I know this letter must seem very
confusing, but it is my only hope of finding
my past. I live in Oregon now, but the
state can't help me since it was a foreign
adoption. If you are not able to help, please
try to point me in the right direction.
Please contact me as soon as possible. If
there is no information, I would appreciate
you informing me of that as well, so that I
may try other routes.
Thank you for your time and consideration.
Enclosed, you will find a self-addressed,
stamped envelope.
Sincerely,
Claire Hamilton
(Finnouala Brennan)*

I had told Carl, in passing, about Mrs. Henderson
and the letters, trying not to make a big deal of any of
it. Of them all, Devon was the most excited, but as the
weeks went by, even she forgot, getting wrapped up in
her world. In time, I forgot as well.

I checked the mail every day after work, but I'd
return to the house empty-handed. Winter faded and
blossoms filled the trees and rain fell every other day.
Life went on with little regard to secrets.

I saw Dr. Benning on Thursdays. We talked about
work, family, and I even told him about the letters and

beginning a search across the world. It didn't take long before I told him about Sally, how she had been my savior, my respite, all those years growing up. It was like once I got started, I couldn't stop. But the words weren't intimate, not about me, not deep as he might have thought it should have been. It was informational, except when I was talking about Sally. There were times I took deep breaths to hold back my emotions for her.

I was getting the handle of therapy. Answer his questions, don't sulk, and to the best of your ability, be truthful, but I still kept my guard up. I didn't talk about my mother or father. So many times, I couldn't believe what I said really happened. After experiencing her reaction, I couldn't help but think maybe my life had somehow been a lie. *What if I said something and it never happened?*

Late at night when everyone was in bed, I stayed up, grading papers, drinking wine. When my thoughts became blurred between reality and truth, I wrote make-believe letters to my mother, writing her name…, signing mine as if we were dear friends. It had been over six weeks and no response. I had sent four letters.

Who was I kidding? It wasn't going to happen. Too much time had passed, too much distance. Even if I found her, how would I ever get across the world to see her?

I had to get back to my life.

I waited at the ballfields behind the school. Cars lined up, waiting to pick up their kids from practice. I watched as they finished up, Devon in softball and Adam had baseball across the lot.

The kids hopped in the car and we drove home. They chatted on about their day, practice, and homework. Their chatter was just what I needed.

Once in the house, I prepared dinner, had Devon get the mail and Adam set the table.

"Mom, this is for you. It has all kinds of postage on it."

There it was. It had been six weeks... something finally arrived. I set it on the table and went back to the kitchen.

"Aren't you going to open it?" Devon asked.

"I will. After dinner, when everything is cleaned up."

"Mom! Come on. It's from Ireland. You've been waiting for this!"

I dropped the spatula and took the envelope from her, retrieved a knife from the drawer and slowly ran it under the flap. I could tell there wasn't much there.

"Come on. Hurry," Devon said, hanging over my shoulder.

Adam responded with a "cool," while Devon got all jumpy about finally getting mail from a foreign country.

I slipped the single folded paper out.

March 27th 1986
(From Joyce House)
A Chara,
I wish to refer to your recent inquiry.
The General Register Office is the
central authority, which holds records
of registration of Births, Deaths and
Marriages and can only provide certified
copies of these events. Unfortunately, we
have no means of knowing people's current

addresses or tracing relatives.
It is suggested however that the Garda
Siochana, missing Persons Section,
Phoenix Park, Dublin 8 may be able to
assist. The Salvation Army, Social Services
Investigation Department, 105/109
Jodd Street, King's Cross, London WC1M
9TS also operates a tracing service.
Advertisements in national newspapers
may prove fruitful. The following are
national daily papers.
The Irish Independent, Middle Abbey
Street, Dublin 1
The Irish Press, Tara House, Tara Street,
Dublin 2
The Cork Examiner, 95 Patrick Street, Cork
Mise le meas
John O'Connell
General Register Office
If you contact"Dr. Barnardos"
244 Harold Cross Road
Dublin 6, Ireland
They may be able to assist you better than
we can.

I read it over twice, and it made no sense. What was it saying? Then I looked at the name he had added that I might want to write to. It was the same name Mrs. Henderson gave me, weeks before. I had held off sending to that address for reasons I could not explain. I knew who I would write next.

"Mom, what does it say? Does it tell you anything?" She asked, still jumping around behind me.

"No, it doesn't sweetie, but it does give me another address to write to. So, I'll try that."

"Are you sad?" she asked, as she watched me slip it into my desk drawer.

"It is only the first one. There will be a lot more. I'll be okay." I hugged her and kissed the top of her head. "Can you set the table?"

"Sorry Mom," when Adam saw me come back into the kitchen.

"I'm fine. Come on, Dad will be home soon."

I didn't think I would share it with Carl, at least not yet, and hopefully the kids would forget by the time he came home. I went about putting the finishing touches on dinner, when Carl came in through the back door.

"Dad," Devon jumped all over him.

Too late, I thought to myself. I'd have to share whether I wanted to or not.

"What's going on?" He asked, trying to get through the back door.

"Mom got a letter from Ireland."

He looked at me, and I nodded and went on placing dinner on the table. I didn't want to show any particular emotion. I didn't want Carl to think I might fall apart at the possibility of bad news. It wasn't bad news... it was basically, no news at all.

After dinner I showed him the letter.

"Are you okay?"

"Don't do this, please. I'm fine. It was good, now I have another place to write. I knew from the beginning it would take time."

"Will you tell Dr. Benning?"

"Of course." I patted his chest and kissed his cheek. "I'm fine. We don't need to talk about it. Don't worry, I'm not going to fall apart."

I cleaned up the kitchen, flipped off the light, and watched as Carl tucked into his recliner to read the paper, but he didn't notice I was watching. I went into the room I called my office and sat down in front of my new computer, my Christmas gift from Carl. I slipped in a disk and went to the file labeled *Letters to Ireland.*

I typed in my second letter. This time to Dr. Barnados, saying pretty much the same as I did with the first, but Dr. Barnados was no doctor.

11

I made it just in time for my appointment. I pulled into the parking lot, slid a pale shade of lipstick across my lips, brushed back my hair, and tried to make myself look like it was more like ten o'clock in the morning, instead of four in the afternoon. I shook my head as if clearing it of the cobwebs. I sat in the parking lot, anxious about the hour coming up. We would talk about whatever came to his mind. I wasn't good at bringing up topics, so he would start with the family, and I'd tell him how I went to go see my mother every weekend. I might begin with Rachel today, and how I couldn't help her, and how thinking of her reminded me of my mother. No, I wouldn't have the nerve to bring that up, maybe another day, when I understood my mother better.

Walking into his office, I thought about Dr. Benning as a real person. He was a tough cookie— just telling stories were not enough. He dug deeper. He hacked away at the feeling I had buried, the feelings that had kept me awake at night. Sometimes I sat there for ten minutes without saying a word. He was patient. He adjusted his tie, took hold of his pen and wrote a few lines on the yellow pad, then changed his position in the chair, but he always waited for the words to come from me.

I thought a long time about why the words were so hard to come by. Why, even though I knew what they were, I couldn't say them out loud. I continued to dig deeper with Dr. Benning, but as we did, the depression took an even stronger hold. Sadness took on a shape and filled a space in my life that I couldn't control. I couldn't get around it, or past it, so there were times I let it drown me.

"Let's talk about the depression," he said. The sun came through the window and the cat slept on the damp ground.

"So, it shows, does it?"

"What's going on?"

"It takes hold of me and I can't breathe. I can barely get out of bed. But I do— Everyday. I do everything I'm supposed to do, but I don't tell anyone."

"If you get through the day so well, what do you do at night in the dark?"

"I sit outside in my garden. My sleep is pretty erratic."

Now it was my chance to speak up, tell him what was really going on when the lights went out. How after everyone goes to bed, I went to the kitchen, took the bottle of wine and a glass to the garden. I laid down in the lounge chair, pulled the blanket around me, then with my pen in hand I wrote in my journal in the dark. The words were such a smear that I couldn't read any of it the next day.

Do I tell him I lay there in the dark and drink so I can stop the pain? Do I tell him that I don't crawl back to bed until awakened by the dog licking at my feet, or the rain?

I hide the evidence by staggering to the trash, throwing the bottle away, washing my glass in the sink and using mouthwash to hide the taste. I stumble down the hall and fall into bed, pulling the covers up tight. I roll over to the back of my husband, reach around him, and kiss the nape of his neck and fall asleep, for a while forgetting the sadness.

Do I tell him those things? No, not yet. I look up at him and finally respond.

"I think."

"And what do you think about in the dark?"

"I'm scared that people will find out."

"What are they going to find out?"

"That I'm a lie. That I don't belong here."

"Why shouldn't you belong here?" he asks, really believing I'll give him an honest answer.

"I don't mean to be alive, I mean at work, or get-togethers, places where people notice you."

"That doesn't make sense," he said, perplexed.

I could tell he was confused, his eyebrow went up just on the edge, and his mouth tightened.

"I feel invisible. And when I do show up, people will know I don't belong."

"You know in your heart, that isn't true, don't you?"

For the first time in the session, I looked up at him and held his glance, "No," I said, firm with resolve. "It's true." I believed it with all my heart.

"What does the sadness feel like?"

"It feels like a huge heavy coat that I have to wear, and every day it gets heavier. After a while I can't stand up any more. It's hard to move."

"So, what do you do?"

"I hug it tighter."

"What does that mean?"

"I guess it means if I embrace it, then I give up."

"Why?"

"Because it's too hard."

"You don't seem like someone who gives up because something is too hard," he said. "Look what you've accomplished. You finished your degree, got a good job. You're talking about things you wouldn't have talked about even six months ago. You're searching for your birth mother. In case you don't realize, those are not things that people who give up, even think about doing. You still have a lot to deal with, but no, I think you're wrong. You have gotten stronger over the months, not weaker."

I recoiled at his words. They took me deeper into myself. If he knew the truth, he wouldn't be saying those things. He would show me the door. Suddenly, without even thinking about it, I got up from the chair and moved to the couch against the wall. I curled up, pulling my feet under me. I made myself as small as I could.

"You don't understand." I mumbled.

"I think I do," He rearranged himself and turned the chair in my direction. "Why did you move to the couch?" he asked.

"So I could get smaller."

"Are you a child?"

"No. I just want to be invisible."

"I've been thinking Claire, maybe it's time. I think we need some help, here."

"What do you mean? I don't want to see anyone else. I just got used to you."

"Well, thank you," he grinned. "No, I think it might be time for some medication." He said it matter-of-factly, as he folded his hands in his lap.

"You mean an anti-depressant?"

"Yes. I think your depression has gotten bigger than you. This will help you take the edge off, feel more comfortable when things are difficult."

"What would the side effects be?"

"Everyone is different. You might get headaches, dry mouth, maybe gain, or lose weight. We'll see how it goes. You'll let me know, and we can adjust."

"I already get migraines really bad. I can't imagine them getting worse." I knew if I was to go on meds I'd have to tell him about the drinking because I couldn't do both. I wasn't ready. "I don't think the meds are a good idea."

"Why not?" He sat back. His eyes grew bigger. I could tell he wasn't expecting that response.

"I can't take the meds because I've been drinking. A lot." I took a deep breath and looked away.

"Oh." He paused, looked toward the window, then back at me. "Yes, that does change things," he said.

"I should have told you, but, well..." I slouched over on the couch.

"How much is a lot?"

"Maybe three or four glasses a night?"

"Wine glass size?"

"No. Bigger." I hid my head.

"I promised Carl I'd cut back, and I have, but not enough. If I start taking anti-depressants...."

"Have you missed work because of it?"

"No."

Surprisingly, I hadn't missed a beat in my life. I went to work, did everything at home, even went to every one of the kids' events. Maybe that was why I was so tired.

"How often do you drink?" He asked.

"Pretty much every night."

"For how long?"

"I go in spurts. Sometimes I go a long time and don't drink at all, but then there are others when it is way more than it should be."

"Why?"

"Why does anyone drink?"

"No. I asked why are *you* drinking?"

I sat up straight, put my feet on the floor, rubbed my hands down my slacks, but still couldn't look at him. I was saying too much, but I had to, I couldn't take meds and drink the way I was. He needed to know, but he was asking questions that went past the drinking.

"I'm trying to stop the pain."

"Is it working?" He sat back.

"It does for a while, then it goes away."

"Does Carl know you're drinking this much?"

"That's one of the reasons I'm here. I told him I'd back off, but I haven't, at least not as much as I should."

"Did you try?"

I started picking at my nails, "Sort of."

"Define sort of." He had his pen ready to take notes on this one.

"I never really had a plan."

"I do," he said, leaning forward. "How many glasses do you have a night?" He asked, entwining his fingers together.

"I guess maybe four."

"Okay, then just have three."

"You mean you don't want me to quit cold turkey?"

"No, not right now, just cut back, but monitor it. Do you think you can do that?"

"I-I don't know."

"Keep track, write it down. Don't take the bottle with you. Leave it in the refrigerator. It takes too much trouble to get up if you're comfortable in your chair."

"Okay. I guess I can try."

"That's all I'm asking."

I squirmed on the couch, wanting to leave, embarrassed that I had brought up the drinking, but knowing if I kept playing with the facts we weren't going to get anywhere. Dr. Benning stood up and opened the door.

"I can't promise anything."

"You can promise to try."

I left his office and walked outside. I needed to go home and start dinner, get back to my life. Being with Dr. Benning was a little like a fairy tale, it took me away from reality for a while. When I was behind those doors I was in a separate world, and as hard as it was for me, there was a safety I hadn't known for a long time. I had told him about the drinking and there were other things to tell. Maybe if I told them I could stop drinking all together.

I found my way home, started dinner and got the kids settled at the table doing their homework. It would still be awhile before Carl came home. I opened the refrigerator and took out the bottle of wine that I had bought the day before. I opened it up and emptied it in the sink. I ran hot water down along with it, then sprayed the room so the smell of wine wouldn't linger. I'd show Dr. Benning I could do it, forget about cutting back. I'd just stop, then I could take the medication and maybe feel better, maybe stop the depression. I knew I would buy another bottle, but for now..., there wouldn't be any wine tonight.

I didn't tell the kids or Carl what I did; there was no point. I cleaned up after dinner, we all sat in the living room to watch TV. Carl in his chair, I had the couch with the dog, and the kids took over the floor. In a few minutes Adam came and cuddled next to me. I wrapped my arm around him, kissed his forehead and settled in for the night. I wasn't thinking about Carl, or even Adam. I was thinking about the bottle I had thrown in the trash.

The bottle that would have kept me up.

* * * * * *

Every night for the next week I was in bed by ten. The kids were tucked in. I checked each door, but one night, Adam called out my name.

"Mom?"

"Yea, baby? What do you want?"

"Are you coming to my baseball game tomorrow?"

"I sure am. I'll be there by three."

"I might be pitching."

"Good for you."

I brushed his hair back and kissed his forehead. I turned the fan down to the lowest it would go and closed the door.

Devon didn't move when I looked in on her. I closed her door and went to our room. Carl and I made love, but I didn't fall asleep after. I lay in his arms and followed the shadows around the room, fighting the sadness that had taken over.

12

"Can I tell you something?" I asked Dr. Benning, getting anxious, knowing that if I waited too long, I'd never say it. He looked tired, not as professional as usual, like he had something on his mind that had nothing to do with me.

"Always," he said, finally looking up at me.

"You all right?" I asked.

"Yes, just a lot on my mind. Sorry, I need to pay attention."

"I guess it wouldn't be appropriate for you to talk to me about it."

He laughed and sat up straighter. He put his pad on the desk and folded his hands in his lap.

"No, it wouldn't. I'm fine, a lot going on at the university and some deadlines. I didn't think it was showing."

"Over time, I've just gotten to know you pretty well."

"Yes, you have. I need to hide myself better." He laughed.

It wasn't like him to let anything show. He was stoic, but there had been a few times when he let me see through him. I paused and stared at the cat who for all I knew had never been touched, but who had found a way to lounge in front of the window for everyone to watch.

I got up and walked over to the couch, but I didn't curl up like I had before. I sat straight and folded one leg over the other. I could see the cat better and him. If I went to the couch, he was always straight in front of me.

"I know why I don't trust you," I said.

"I thought you did. Did I do something wrong?"

"No, but I've been trying with all my heart, but maybe it's not such a good idea. There would be no reason to tell it now."

"I'm not sure what that means?" he asked, adjusting his tie, and fumbling around in his chair.

"I'm going to tell you something, and I can't explain why, maybe it's a test, but I'm not sure who the test is for."

"I don't like tests."

"I know, and I don't mean for it to be that way. Actually, I think it is a test more for me, now that I think about it.

"Something happened to me a long time ago. I never told anyone, ever, but I know it affected every part of my life."

"Did someone hurt you?"

"Not physically. I mean I was never hit or anything, it was different. No one talked about it back then, and I never totally understood, when it was happening, but I think it has a lot to do with my dad."

"You've really never talked about your dad before, except that you try to please him a lot."

"Yea, I've spent my whole life trying to please him and I've never seemed to be able to do it. I've always felt invisible to him and I couldn't figure out why."

"Did he show you any attention?"

"No. I pretty much felt invisible."

"How does this event connect to your dad?"

"I had a teacher who took an interest in me, not like a crush or anything, well I didn't think it was, but as I look at it now, it was perverted. He was obviously much older, fatherly. He had short coarse gray hair, with wrinkles that folded into his face, creating deep creases. He had an old-world accent, like 'Zorba the Greek'. Do you remember that movie?"

"Yes, go on. I'm still trying to connect the dots."

"He wore a white long sleeve shirt, with a different paisley tie every day. He was the only teacher I knew who wore a suit and tie every day, with brogue shoes."

"Do I really need to know what he looks like?"

"No, I guess not..." I stopped and looked away from the center of the room. I stared out the window, but the cat was gone. I still put myself in the garden.

"Why are you telling me about him?"

"I guess I thought it was important. I wanted you to be able to see his face, his stature."

"Why?"

"He assaulted me."

Dr. Benning didn't say anything. He wrapped his hands into each other, his knuckles red from the tightness of his fist.

"Do you want to tell me about him?"

"No, but I think I should."

"Okay, however you want to do this," he said sitting back.

"I guess slowly."

"Or you could treat it like a band-aid, rip it off really fast so it doesn't hurt."

"Maybe a little of both. Can you just bear with me?"

"How about I ask you a few questions and it might make it easier."

"Okay, you start." I took a deep breath, determined that I wouldn't bolt for the door.

"How did it start?"

"He told me to come to his room after school to talk about my progress in his class."

"How did you feel about that?" he asked, fiddling with the pen he had picked up from the desk.

Even as I talked, I couldn't figure out why I decided to tell him about these feelings, because once it came out, it would surely all be my fault.

"Scared, more than anything else."

"What happened?"

"At first he asked about school. You know general questions, homework, activities."

"Did that bother you?"

"No. I was surprised it was not more specific."

"Then what?"

"After a while he started asking questions about how I felt about myself and boys."

"How did you feel about that?"

"Awkward. My dad never even asked about that."

"How often did you go to his room?"

"Twice a week."

"When did things change?"

"It was like he was trying to read into my soul, but at the same time, I was excited that someone paid any attention to me at all. He told me I didn't look very happy."

"Were you?"

"Hell, I don't know. I was a teenager."

"Did you tell anyone?"

I almost laughed out loud, tucking my feet under me. "God no, I was too embarrassed."

"Not even your girl friends?"

"I was afraid they'd make fun of me. I mean he was old, not like some of the younger teachers that we all had crushes on."

"You said things changed. So, what happened?"

"One day he pulled down the shades, locked the door, then walked up to me and ran his hand down the center of my face, to my chin, then down the front of my shirt. He stopped as quickly as he started and then just stared at me. I didn't know what to say. It wasn't about school anymore."

"Did you ask him to stop?"

"No. I was too scared."

"How did he make you feel?"

"Terrified."

"If you were so uncomfortable why didn't you leave?"

"I was afraid. He kind of threatened me." As the weeks went on, things changed. I thought about telling someone, but I was too scared they'd think I was lying."

"So, you never told anyone?"

"There wasn't anyone to tell, and the one teacher I trusted, well, I was too embarrassed to mention it. I kept thinking that maybe I was leading him on in a way."

"When you think about it now, were you?"

"No, I don't think so. You have to understand no one ever paid so much attention to me."

"Did you like what was happening?"

"In a way, not the touching, but the way he was talking. No one had ever shown me such consideration."

"Was there something wrong with his attention?"

"I knew the touching was wrong. He patted my face, and shoulders without saying a word, but not like a father might do to a child. It was more intimate."

"What went through your mind when he did it?"

"I was so caught up. I was afraid to go, but I was terrified not to go. One day he had me unbutton my blouse and he touched my skin. He ran his finger between my breasts. I should have pushed him away, but I didn't. I froze. I felt worse than I had ever felt in my life, but he didn't stop, and I didn't stop him. He told me I couldn't tell anyone. He said it would be our secret."

I stopped talking and looked away trying to hide my face. It was the first time I had spoken about this out loud and hearing it made me nauseous. I could feel the bile move up. It settled in my throat, like a lump. It made it hard for me to swallow.

"What's wrong?"

"I'm feeling sick."

"You can stop, if you want." He sat up. "Do you want some water?"

"No."

"You okay?"

"I think so."

"Let me get you some. You look a little flushed."

I brushed my hair from my face and wiped my eyes. I couldn't believe I had told him. He came back and handed me a mug of water, then sat back down in his chair. He didn't look up at me but took notes.

"How about if I ask you a few questions, then you might be more comfortable answering than just saying it on your own."

"Okay, sure."

"Why do you think he wanted to keep it a secret?"

"Then… I didn't know, but looking back, he knew it was wrong. He never had to worry that I would tell. Who would have believed me anyway? Who would believe that a teacher with such a good reputation would do something like that? Would I believe it if someone told me?"

"Would you have?"

"No. Everybody thought he was incredible."

"What happened after that?"

"I kept going back." I brushed a tear away so he couldn't see.

"Are you all right?"

"I feel stupid. I let him touch me and that was wrong. I should have stopped him."

"What happened the last time you went?"

"He acted really anxious. When I came in, the blinds were already closed. He immediately locked the door as he always did, turned toward me. Then we had the weirdest conversation. I remember every minute of it.

"Do you want to tell me about it?"

"No. But I've told you this much, and I'm kind of regretting it."

He adjusted himself in the chair again. "We can stop. But you said it had something to do with your dad."

"I never really had a relationship with my dad. We just never connected. I think he played on that. I think he somehow knew I was disconnected."

"What makes you think that?"

"He asked me if I was nervous about coming to his room."

"What did you say?"

"Nothing."

"He unbuttoned my shirt, and I let him because I couldn't say no. He told me to sit down on his lap. I knew it wasn't right. He seemed to get mad and said, 'Do you really think I'm going to hurt you?'"

Dr. Benning watched me. He stopped taking notes, even put the pad back on his desk. He straightened his posture and watched me.

"Do you want to go on?"

"He told me to think of him as my dad."

Dr. Benning folded his hands in his lap and titled his head. "Did you?"

"I told him that wasn't right. I asked him why he was doing this?"

"And?" Dr. Benning leaned forward.

"He said I care about you. I want you to get your self-confidence back."

"Did you believe him?"

"I didn't know what to believe. I was barely making it from day to day, then someone started paying attention. In a sick way he made me feel good."

"Did you sit on his lap?"

"Yes. He put his hand between my legs and moved it up and down like he was kneading bread. I got off his lap then he told me to pull my skirt up. He knelt down and looked up at me, then he said I had a space between my legs because I was still maturing. He touched my thighs.

"What did he say to you?"

"He told me I was pretty. That I should hold my head up and walk tall. He said to wear make-up, so my cheek bones stood out. Then the conversation completely changed," I continued. "His whole tone changed."

"What happened?"

"He told me he'd turn me over his knee and spank me if I ever told anyone about our meetings, or that he locked the door, or that he opened my blouse, or touched me. *'It's our secret, and you must remember that.'* Like he was trying to convince himself it was true, like it was his job, his responsibility to be sure I remembered."

"Do you remember what you were thinking then?" Dr. Benning asked.

I could see the angle on Dr. Benning's face change. He was mad at something. I thought it was me for what I allowed to happen. Staring at him, I regretted even telling him.

"Are you mad at me?"

"God, no. I just can't believe he thought it was okay to terrify you the way he did. You were a child. He threatened you. I'm disgusted, that's all."

"At me?"

"Claire, you were a child. I mean, I know you were a teenager, but he had no right to do that. You didn't do anything wrong. Even now you have to know that. Especially now, as you tell this for the first time."

"I never pushed him away. I should have. I should have run out of the room kicking and screaming, but I liked what he said. I mean I didn't like the words, but the attention." I paused and looked out the window, looking for the cat, looking for something to distract me. "It made me feel special and I didn't feel that way very often, but I knew there was something very wrong about it."

I gave an awkward smile as I finally looked up at Dr. Benning. I felt the flush in my cheeks, yet I also felt relieved. I had come out of it whole. I didn't break into pieces. I survived.

"I'm sorry that happened to you, but I have to ask you a question."

"Okay, what?" The smile dropped from my face.

"The whole time you were telling me this story, you were smiling."

"No. I wasn't."

"Yes. You tell me something so terribly tragic, that it would bring anyone to tears, and you smiled through it."

"I didn't realize I was doing that."

"You don't have to be brave. What he did was wrong. Whether you told him to stop or not, he was wrong. Not you."

"I always thought it was me, that I was to blame. That's why I never told anyone."

"You said you haven't told anyone. Will you tell Carl about it?"

"I don't know."

"Why not?"

"I'm not ready."

"It's been twenty years and you know you didn't do anything wrong."

"There are some things you just keep to yourself. You bury them... you bury them so deep you can't find them. Even though I've said them out loud, I don't think I'm ready to do it again. I couldn't stand it if he judged me. You know how people always seem to blame the people caught up in this. You know my mom even blamed my birthmother for what happened to her. People just do it without thinking."

"Can I make a recommendation?"

"I already know what you're going to say."

"Okay, I won't say it, just think about it."

We ended our session. I stood up and wiped away the tears.

"Claire, you've come a long way, and I know this was hard for you. Think about what I didn't say, and when you're ready, you'll know it."

I wanted him to hug me, to wrap me up like I had never known. Someone had taken advantage of me because I hadn't been given the confidence to say no. Slowly Dr. Benning was giving me back that confidence without touching me. Maybe I really would come out of this a whole person.

13

Even since starting therapy, I still spent a great deal of time alone at night. I curled up in Carl's recliner, drinking, journal writing, and pondering.

I had promised him and Dr. Benning that I'd stop, or at least slow down on the drinking, and for a while I did. I made sure I hid my feelings during the day.

But in the darkness, when I was alone and the memories flooded my mind, I fought to put everything together, to understand my feelings. But I grew sadder every day.

If Carl had thought my drinking was a problem before, now there was no doubt. Even the promise I made Dr. Benning didn't change things. Not as much as I had hoped.

The only thing that had changed was that I was hiding it better. I didn't drink during dinner, or even while watching TV. But after, when everyone was tucked in, the lights had been dimmed for the night, I got up and found my way to the living room and the bottle, then out to the patio. No matter the weather.

And then it happened.

I had sent out letters in April and it was now September. The envelopes came. I balanced each one in front of me. Then I took the smallest one, from Dr. Barnardos. I opened his first. He was not a doctor at all. 'He' was an organization that provided assistance to organizations and individuals like me, searching out their past.

I scanned the letter a number of times to see what would be helpful. A woman named Evelyn had signed the letter. I was glad to be dealing with a woman. She might understand better, might even be a mother. Maybe offer some suggestions for a newcomer. Once passed all the pleasantries, it was down to the meat of things.

(1) Castlepollard Co. Westmeath has closed, but the records are held by Sr. Sarto, Sacred heart Convent, Blackrock Co. Cork. You could write to her.

(2) St. Patrick's Infant Hospital, at Temple Hill, Blackrock Co. Dublin has also closed. St. Patrick's Guild 82 Haddington Road, Dublin 4 holds all their records, and you can direct your letter to Sr. Helen Marie.

(3) If you have your "full" original birth cert. from Register of Births at Joyce House this may give your mother's home address at the time of your birth, which could be helpful. If not, have you tried to get your mother's birth cert.? The registry of births can do a five-year search, as her name is very uncommon; it should not be too difficult. If Joyce House can't help further you could consider employing a family researcher or genealogist to check records. I cannot recommend anybody, but I have enclosed a list furnished by our National Library.

(4) Do you know which agency in Ireland was involved in arranging your adoption if not, those mentioned?

(5) In which country was your legal order granted? If in America, you can write to the Court or Government agency involved to see if they have records. If you were legally adopted in Ireland, you would write to the Adoption Board, Hawkins House, Hawkins St. Dublin 2 to Ms. Evans, Senior Social Worker.

I had sent letters to Joyce House and the General Registry Office six weeks earlier. Finally, the answers.

The first envelope was from the Registry office, and clearly held documents of some sort. It looked official, yet it felt very private. Like something that needed to be hidden. The other was from Joyce House. It didn't look official, but still…

I hid them in my dresser, sliding them beneath my underwear.

I didn't open either one.

It was Monday, I was alone in the house and Carl had promised to pick up the kids. I placed the envelope on the counter and stared at it, as if it were going to jump off the table and run out the door.

I thought about waiting, but if these were my certificates, I needed to see them now, and if they carried bad news, I didn't want to have to share.

I poured a glass of wine and sat on the patio. Turning it over and over, inspecting every little crease. I was amazed it had made it so far. Thousand of miles from Ireland, across the Atlantic to the West Coast of America. It was a different world.

My world.

I slid my finger across the backside. Nothing else was in the envelope, no note explaining why the decision was made to send it, or who made the decision, only a single, double folded parchment paper. I unfolded it and stared at it.

There it was.

Alice Brennan, born in Westmeath, April 4, 1934, her mother's name was Julia and her father was James.

They had lived in the same county, they were my grandparents, my blood.

My mother's family had never really accepted me. They made sure their definition of family was understood. Family was blood, nothing more nothing less. Since I wasn't blood, I was a stranger, with no right to anything considered family.

My dad didn't have any relatives, at least none that I ever met. He was raised on the east coast. Boston, a million miles away.

It felt odd to read her history... my history, even as random as it was.

She had been barely fifteen when I was born. *Did this one piece of paper explain it all? Why she signed me away? Was she too young?*

As a kid I asked about her, Mom said she had died in childbirth. It made me sad. She said she deserved what happened, she may well have been a whore.

At ten, I didn't know what a whore was, but from the tone my mother used, it was not something to be proud of.

But I dreamt of her and held her close in my

heart. I imagined freckles, red hair, high cheekbones, with green eyes and a smile that told me everything I needed, though I had neither red hair, green eyes, or high cheek bones. I cut pictures out of magazines of women I thought she might look like.

She couldn't be sinful, or wicked, or cruel. None of the things my mother implied.

I always hoped there had been someone. I couldn't talk about her, I could only dream.

Seeing the certificate helped me realize she was real. She wasn't a dream or a piece of my imagination.

I didn't know what she looked like, but I knew she was fifty-two years old, she had a mother and father and that she was loved.

And her daughter was searching for her.

I opened the second envelope with the same anticipation. My name and then my mother's, the date, but the father's line left blank. My real birth certificate looked nothing like the amended one from the state of Oregon, the one I had known my whole life. This one was parchment, hand written with an Irish seal. Someone had copied it off the original that was held somewhere in the Registry Office.

Finnouala Claire Brennan. *There it was, my name.* For the first time, I saw it in writing. Alice Brennan's name was listed as *Mother*. I said her name out loud. Even though I had known it, being able to read it, made it more real.

I lay back in the chair, closed my eyes, and let memories float through my mind, looking for something to grasp. Anything that would connect me to her world.

There was nothing to remember. But now, I had

something that was really mine. I'd never had that before.

Lying back, I searched the memories of my childhood. Grammar school, dinners at the kitchen table, summertime in the yard, on the swing, bike riding through the neighborhood.

I saw the room, the yellow gingham curtains, yellow paint on the wall. Mom stood over the sink, I watched as she glided her hands through the water, bubbles floating over her hands.

"I have a surprise for you. Let me finish up and I'll get it."

She had never surprised me before. She left the room, and when she came back, she placed a black box on the yellow tablecloth.

"This is for you. Go ahead. Open it."

I lifted the lid, inside a silver band, with a purple stone.

"Whose is it?" I asked.

"Yours."

"Really? Are you sure?" I had never seen anything so beautiful. I was afraid to even touch it.

"Yes."

"But what about Susan? Shouldn't she have it?"

"She has her own birthstone. This is for you."

"Is it my birthstone?"

"No, not exactly," she said.

I was confused. Why I would get someone else's? I was grateful, but I didn't understand.

"It belonged to Teresa."

I stared at the light purple stone. I remembered her from the pictures, the girl no one would talk about.

"What's wrong? You don't like it?"

"No, it's beautiful. Why would you give it to me?"

Her face changed in that moment. Her eyes narrowed, her lips closed, she got up from the table and went over to the sink and began to wipe down a perfectly immaculate sink. The simple idea of asking her a question had made her angry. I wasn't being grateful enough.

"I thought you'd like it. We bought it for Teresa when she turned twelve, and well, you're twelve now, so..."

I felt cheated.

"Let's see how it looks," she said, reaching for my hand. "Do you like it?"

"Of course, I do. Thank you." I smiled on the outside, but inside my stomach tumbled like a pebble rolling down a hill.

"Let's not say anything to your sister," my mother said, closing the box.

After she left the room, I held my hand up to examine the stone. All I could think was that it wasn't mine.

I never wore that ring in public. I hid it away, too. I went back into the bedroom, opened the jewelry box and took out the ring that had never been mine. The stone was dirty, and the silver tarnished. I dropped it back into the jewelry box.

It would always be Teresa's.

I put the envelopes in the drawer, under my clothes, not ready to share with anyone. They would stay hidden, at least for now.

14

I kept the birth certificates buried in the drawer for the next few weeks. I busied myself with anything and everything that would keep my mind cluttered. Randomly I'd go to the drawer, pull them out and read the name that had been taken from me.

Such an odd name, *Finnouala Claire*.

My adopted name was *Claire Jane*. Compared to Finnoula Claire, Jane seemed... plain.

I remember how my parents couldn't wait to get rid of it, *"too awkward, they'll make fun of it. We don't like it. Too foreign."*

I researched Finnoula and learned it had been a name from a children's legend. I wondered what made it special, why she picked that name, in particular.

Besides the birth certificates, I took the ring from the jewelry box and slipped it on my finger. Holding it up to the light, I wished she had given me something that could have been mine, instead of a hand-me-down. I kept it on as I gathered everything I'd need to take to Sally's.

The kids piled in the car and we headed to the respective practices. Adam, to the elementary field, while Devon would be across the street at the junior high.

With the promise to pick them up in two hours, I headed across town to the quiet street corner where I had grown up.

I drove past the house. There was a stillness over it, even the leaves didn't move. Shadows danced around in the breeze, but it was easier to leave the silence undisturbed, than ruffle the feathers of the past.

I parked in front of the neighborhood jungle, opened the gate, and followed the worn path to her kitchen. I saw Sally through the open French doors, bent over the sink, her head dipped into the crevice of her arm.

I ran through the open doors and dropped the envelopes on the table.

"Are you all right?"

"Don't be fussing with me. You'll spoil me."

"What happened?"

"Just catching my breath. I worked too hard in the yard today."

She was covering up something. I put my arm around her chunky waist, pulled her up as best I could and led her to the chair at the kitchen table.

"It's back isn't it?"

"Don't be silly. I'm fine."

"No. You're not fine. I've seen this before. You need to call the doctor."

"Just let me be."

"Sally.... Let me get you some water."

I balanced her in the chair and waited for her to be steady. She put both elbows on the table and held her head high. I watched her for a few moments, then got a glass of water. She drank slowly, setting it on the mosaic table, brushing strands of hair from her face. I sat down and waited. We said nothing.

I had been with Sally when she became sick. She did a good job of hiding things, but when the body breaks down it is hard to hide. She had a quick recovery, with just a short hospital stay and an adjustment of meds, but it would always be there. She shouldn't go through the bouts alone.

"I'm not leaving you alone."

"Yes, you will. I just got over-winded. If you could make some tea, I would be very grateful."

I went to the stove, checked the water in the kettle and turned on the burner.

As the water heated, I studied her. Her complexion was pale, her breathing labored. "It's back, isn't it? Do you want me to call the doctor?"

"No. You're making such a fuss. I'll be up and about in no time."

"Sally, don't make me worry."

"Like I can stop you? Tell me, what brings you?"

"You're changing the subject."

"My subject to change. What's going on?"

"Well, I have some news."

"Tell me. It'll get your mind off me. Come on, spill it."

"I received some answers, more specifically, our birth certificates."

"That's wonderful."

"I learned a little more than I had."

"And?"

"I don't know how to explain it. I had to let it settle for a while. It was a big deal, seeing our names together."

"Of course, it was. That's why you should be shouting from the rooftops."

"I don't want to hurt my mother here."

"I don't think you are Claire. She had to know this day would come and you'd find out the truth."

I nodded.

"Honey, your mama's pain has nothing to do with you." She patted my hand, like she knew a secret.

I unfolded the envelope and placed it on the table in front of her. "I was born in Castlepollard."

"Where's that?"

"I looked it up. It's right in the middle of Ireland. It was a mother baby home, run by the Sisters of the Sacred Heart. But it really wasn't a town, more like a convent or a hospital. I think the place came first and the town followed."

Sally had regained herself and turned the documents over as if they were something fragile. "Do you know anything about her?" she asked, handing the documents back to me.

"Born in Westmeath. I can only hope she's still alive."

"Have you shown these to Carl yet?"

"No. I wanted to keep it just for me for a while. I thought about showing him last night after the kids went to bed, but he was talking about work and the kids and it just didn't seem the right time."

"What are you afraid of?" She asked, taking a sip of her tea, wiping her forehead with her hand.

"I don't know."

"I think you do."

She was right. I watched her fill another cup, then looked up at me. She knew as well as I did that the fear was mine and no one else's. I took the envelopes and moved them to the side, and stretched my arms across the table to take her hands.

"When you were little, you were always afraid, too terrified to even speak. Do you remember how long it took you to tell me about your life?"

"Forever?"

"Almost. You'd talk about the flowers, the plants, the fish in the pond, even the cats as they twirled at your feet, but to tell me about you? You were terrified. Then one day your fears seemed to melt away. You started to talk. You let me in."

"This is different," I said, knowing in my heart there was none.

"Claire, there is nothing wrong with sharing what you've learned with Carl. He's your partner. If you love him, then tell him everything. This is your heritage. There is nothing shameful about it."

"You didn't share Grace with any one."

"There's no comparison." She picked up her tea and leaned back. "There was no one to tell. No one I was close to. I can tell you now, if I'd had someone who loves me the way Carl loves you, I damn sure, would have told them."

She looked at me like she always did when she was calling my bluff. Like she was saying 'Come on girl, get your head out of your ass,' without saying a word.

She knew me too well. She could see the hesitation and she was a good enough friend, to call me on it.

I let out a sigh. "Fine. I will, I promise, but I have to write one more letter, then I can tell him."

"Just don't wait too long."

* * * * * *

I didn't know what I would say, but if I had a chance of finding her I would take it. I waited until the house was empty, the following Saturday. I sat in front of the computer and it spilled out.

April 23, 1989
Dear Sr. Helen

I was given your name by Evelyn Johnson, from Dr. Barnardos Adoption Advice Service. My name is Claire Hamilton, I was born Finnouala Claire Brennan on November 20, 1949, in Castlepollard, Delvin, Ireland. At the time Mrs. Henderson brought a number of children from the St. Patrick's Orphanage in Dublin back to the states. She herself adopted five children from St. Patrick's.
Ms. Johnson informed me that the records from St. Patrick's might be with you. I have enclosed a passport picture taken just before I left for America.
At the time of my adoption, I was in poor health. I had rickets and malnutrition. I could barely walk and was only able to speak a few words. I was told the nuns took care of us in the orphanage, but that I might have spent some time in foster care. If I did, how would that work? I was also told I might want to consider placing a "personals" in an Irish paper. Would that be a good idea? If you could tell me anything, I'd really appreciate it.
I do not have the means to come to Ireland

right now. I am 40 years old with a family of
my own. I just hope I'm not too late. Anything
that you can do would be appreciated. I look
forward to hearing from you.
Thank you so much and God bless.
Sincerely,
Claire Hamilton

Weeks went by and I continued pretending my life was fine. Counseling always came right to the edge, then backed off. After six months I was still not ready to betray my true feelings about being adopted. If I couldn't put them into order, how could I display them for anyone else? Maybe I could do all of this without going into the depths of my soul — without feeling ripped apart.

Before I started the search, I felt guilty, that I had no right to pieces of my life. Odd, how someone can come to feel that her life didn't belong to her. I had a past that I had no memory of and somehow people were making me feel that I had no right to it. It was something to be forgotten. How do you forget? How can you pretend the first five years of your life don't mean anything?

I printed out Sr. Helen's letter, folded it into an envelope.

Adam was in the kitchen pounding his action figures into new identities. "Hey, want to go to the post office with me?"

"Can I?"

"If your chores are done."

"I just have the trash left and I can do that before we leave."

"Good. Get to it and don't forget your jacket. Maybe we can stop for ice cream after."

"Really? That would be cool. Just you and me or does Devon have to come, too." I knew the ice cream would grab his interest.

"Just you and me. It's been awhile since we've been on a date." His grin lit up the room.

"Why can't you just put regular stamps on your envelopes?" He asked, sliding the envelope between his fingers.

"It's going out of the country, so it requires different postage."

"Why are you sending it so far away?"

"That's where the people live that I want to write to. It wouldn't do any good to send the letter to San Francisco would it?"

He laughed. "No, I guess not."

We pulled up to the post office and walked in together, hand in hand. We waited our turn, and in a few minutes the letter was on its way.

"So what kind of ice cream?" I asked.

"Can we go to Sherman's? They got the best Blue Medal Chip."

"Sherman's it is."

We drove the few blocks and before long we pulled into the parking lot. Adam found a table while I ordered the ice cream. In a few minutes, both of us were enjoying our favorite dessert.

"Why are you sending so many things to Ireland?" He asked.

"I guess it's time to tell you. You know how sometimes you ask about the day you were born, and I tell you every moment I can remember? And you smile and hug me."

"Yea, I don't do that so much anymore. But I do like the pictures."

"I know, so do I."

"Mommy doesn't have any pictures like that," I said. "I was born in a very different place, and I didn't get to stay with my mother."

"I thought Grandma was your mother?"

"She is, but not my birthmother. I didn't come from her tummy, like you came from mine."

"I don't understand," he said.

"My mother couldn't keep me, so she had to let me go. She was too young and couldn't take care of me. I lived in an orphanage until someone wanted to take me home."

"How long did you stay?" He asked, licking the bottom of his ice cream cone.

"A pretty long time, then someone found me and took me to Grandma and Grandpa's to live."

"Are you looking for her now?"

"Yes, baby, I am. I want to meet her, and someday I'd like you and Devon and Daddy to meet her, too."

"What can I do to help?"

"What would you like to do?"

"I don't know. What could I do?"

I wiped away the tears that were staining my cheeks. I reached for his hand and squeezed it tight.

"What's wrong? Why are you crying?"

"They're happy tears. I'm so glad you're in my life. I couldn't imagine going on without you."

"Well, you don't have to," he said, smiling and squeezing my hand back.

I stared at my baby, on the verge of young adulthood, though still a child. He, like Devon deserved to be a part of the journey, but not like Sally, or Dr.

Benning, or even Carl. They needed to see the signs of hope, that it wasn't a sad journey, one to be dreaded. It was joyous and each letter, even if it was a setback, would move us forward.

* * * * * *

Fall slipped away and the letters remained tucked away in my drawer.

I had told Carl only what I wanted him to know. He knew she was alive and that I had the birth certificates. That was enough for now. He watched my face to decide how he should react. I could tell he was looking for a smile, or a frown, something to give him direction. I smiled, then shrugged. He did the same.

"So are you any closer to finding her?"

"No. The Sisters keep saying they find an 'Alice,' but she ends up being the wrong one. Reverend Mother keeps writing that I need to help pay for their travels, that they keep going on wild-goose chases trying to find her. I told her I would, but she hasn't responded."

"Claire, if they found her, would you want to go back? To Ireland, I mean?" He asked it sheepishly like it wasn't even a question.

I looked at him and leaned forward. "Honestly?"

"Of course," he said, keeping his stare on me.

"I'd sell my soul to go." I sat back and folded my arms across my chest. "There. I can't help it. I don't remember anything as a kid. I feel like I have lost so much."

"I wish you could go, too." Looking at him, I actually believed him.

"Someday, maybe."

He left the kitchen for his recliner and even after the heavy rains, I decided to go out into the garden. I took the clippings Sally had given me and repotted them. I pulled up the rows of zinnias that had died away, leaving only the seeds which I shook into the ground for next year's planting and trimmed back the bougainvillea's growing along the trellis.

Being in the garden brought me great comfort. It took my mind off everything and allowed me a freedom that nothing else could. I understood in those moments why Sally's garden brought her such pleasure. When the world got too big, too hard to handle.

15

My dad hovered just at the edge of therapy. I kept pushing him back.

Seeing him every Sunday, bringing him a present, pipe tobacco, a magazine, was enough. He didn't belong on the couch next to me.

Dr. Benning decided otherwise.

Every week, he gave me a topic and asked me to journal it. This week was my Dad.

I spent the week thinking about our relationship, making notes. It was a struggle to put anything down at all.

I realized I couldn't remember the first time he entered my life. I remembered the exact moment with my mother in the dining room, watching the rain, Sally in her garden, even Carl coming down the stairs from the plane, decked out in his dress blues.

With my dad, there was no one moment, no one occasion that screamed his name. He was just there; at the dinner table, in his car driving to work, in the living room with his pipe and paper.

I couldn't remember a time when his attention was just on me, a time we shared moments.

The week was over, and the day had come.

"I mentioned last week, I thought we should talk

about your dad. Are you ready?" He paused and looked down at my lap. "I see you came prepared."

"I wrote a few things down," I said, "but I really don't know him."

"You don't know your father?"

"Not really. I don't know his favorite color, or his favorite ice cream.

"I do know he watches the news and reads the paper."

"What did you write down?"

I opened the journal and read my checklist. "He never reads books or goes to movies. He loves being at church. He cherishes his pipes, he keeps them in a little rack on the coffee table.

"He expects dinner at six and is in bed right after the news."

"What else?"

"I remember the night before my wedding he came home after ten because he had set up the church for someone else's wedding. He stayed to watch."

"He didn't come to my wedding."

"I'm sorry."

I looked up and brushed a strand of hair from my face. I smiled. I couldn't tell him how I really felt.

"Did you say anything to him about not coming?"

"We saw him after the ceremony. He had to work." I looked away and wiped my face.

"What did you say?"

"What was there to say? He made his choice. I wasn't it." I felt a smile form, though I tried to push it back. I pinched my fingers together, rubbing them together to distract myself.

"What does your dad look like?"

I pictured him in my mind, then opened the paper

and looked at the blurred lines. I hadn't written a description. I thought about when I saw him hunched over his chair reading the paper.

"He's balding, and shorter than you might expect. He has a Hemmingway beard that dignifies him, and spotless, trimmed nails. Each morning he dresses in a suit with matching tie, and goes off to sell cars."

"Okay, that's the outside. What about the inside?"

"He's never been very loving. I've never seen any kindness, except when he talks to strangers."

"What do you mean?"

"He just seems more comfortable with strangers. I never understood it."

"What was it like when you two spent time together?"

"We never have."

"Why not?"

"It always seemed he didn't have time for me, between work and church."

"No, what was it like when it was just the four of you? At home."

I can't remember those times. How would I tell him that nothing connected us? I could watch him, at the dinner table, or in the living room when he watched TV, but I didn't really know anything about him.

"Do you mean with just the two of us, when he actually paid attention to me?"

"Yes."

"I don't have too many of those."

"Tell me about just one."

"My dad has a rose garden. God, he loves that garden. Every Sunday after church he goes out and putters for hours. He has the most amazing roses."

"How do you feel about his garden?"

"The garden?" I asked, smiling as I recalled it in full bloom. "I don't think much about it."

That was a lie, that garden was a work of art, seventy-two rose bushes, pink, red, yellow, white, every color possible. I think he loved that garden more than he loved me.

"I have a feeling there are some things you're not telling me."

I smiled up at him, knowing that he knew me better than I wanted to admit, but wasn't ready to tell him my truth.

"Why are you smiling?"

"What's wrong with that."

"With smiling? Nothing, but when you hide your feelings behind a smile, there's a problem."

I didn't have the words for him, or the explanation of what I tried to hide. I've hidden things my entire life, mostly my feelings. I hid them with smiles, though I knew I would never tell him that I didn't know how to be.

"Do you love him?"

"Of course. I don't know where I'd be if they hadn't taken me in."

"No. I mean do you love him with your heart?"

I brushed strands of hair from my face but refused to look at him. I ran my hand along the ribbing of the couch. I looked up into his eyes, the eyes that didn't judge me.

I realized I'd never thought about loving my father, not how I loved my children or my husband, or even my friends. I had moments I hated him, like when I turned around at my wedding and he wasn't sitting in the last row of the church.

I hated him then.

How could a man care for a garden of love and not

find any time for me? Maybe he didn't have enough. He used it all up on her.

Can someone do that?

Could I love my son more than my daughter? Could I not have enough?

I couldn't see that.

"Where did you go?" He asked, moving forward in his chair. "You were gone?"

I looked at him.

"When I asked if you loved him with your heart, you disappeared."

Did I love him? The idea crossed my mind and I couldn't help but smile, though I felt self-conscious, now that he had pointed it out.

Did I have memory of loving him?

One of the few memories slipped through my head, *wheeling the wheelbarrow around in his garden, cutting the dead roses, while leaving the new buds. One by one I completed the tasks he had set for me. By the end of the afternoon everything was done. Would he love me for that? Those were my memories, trying to make him love me.*

"Where are you?"

"In the garden, cleaning it for him."

"Did he appreciate it?"

"He said I missed some dead flowers in the corner."

"Did you?"

"Yes." I felt a blush cross my face. "They were way back behind the bush. I didn't see them. But you know what bothered me the most? It wasn't missing a pile of dead flowers, but when he said, 'I expected better of you,' then he just walked back to the house, like I wasn't even there."

"And?"

"He left me there."

"How did it make you feel?"

I smiled and covered my face with my hands.

I hated when he asked how I felt. I was terrified around my father, afraid I'd do something wrong. Wasn't everyone? What was the point in this, I wanted to ask him. No matter what we said it didn't change how I felt, but I had promised Carl, so I needed to be as honest as I could.

"He made me feel stupid." I tried to laugh it off.

"Does this bother you?"

"No." I kept smiling "I just don't get it."

"What?"

"How is this helping? I remember so little about him, how could it be important? What's the point in analyzing them?"

"Why don't you tell me what you think?"

"No. That was my question to you. How does talking about him help me? Please explain it."

"I think you blame yourself for the relationship. Maybe if you talk about it, you might come to realize it wasn't your fault."

I sat still for a while, looking away from him. *It was always my fault. Then it hit me. I could barely talk to the man. I couldn't even look him straight in the eye. What would Dr. Benning do with that if he knew?*

I looked back at him, smiled and pulled my knees up tight to my chest.

"Claire did you ever have a moment with him that you could say was good?"

"It might not seem so to anyone else, but it was important to me. We had never really been alone together. There were no emotions involved. It didn't involve flowers, or anger, just silence and a T.V."

"Tell me about it."

"It was 1968. Bobby Kennedy had just been shot. I had marched against Vietnam, read Emerson's poetry, and debated Thoreau's essays from Walden Pond. He was going to change the world."

"What happened with your father?"

"Sorry." I smiled up at him. "I was curled up in the chair doing my homework, watching Kennedy give his acceptance speech. As they wrapped up the coverage, I went to turn off the light and go to bed. Suddenly a lot of commotion came from the television. Bobby had just been shot."

"What did you do?"

"I went to my parent's bedroom to wake my dad, I tapped his shoulder, and told him."

"What did he do?"

"He followed me into the living room. I watched, stunned at what came from the television. He took his usual chair, lit his pipe, and sat back. I looked over as he leaned back in the chair. He didn't avert his attention from the television. It was like I wasn't even there."

"Was this the first time you had been alone together?"

I nodded. "This may sound crazy, but there we were, sitting together; watching the same television. But I know I was invisible. I'd never been alone with him like that. We sat there for almost two hours watching the news, repeatedly hearing the gunshots, watching Kennedy go down. Together, we listened to the commentators talk about the unanimous vote Kennedy had attained. They talked about the difference he would have made for America, about his honor, but as they talked, I watched my father. He never even looked at me."

"It wasn't about Kennedy at all, was it?"

I felt my throat tighten. The words could barely slip out.

"No, it wasn't." I wrapped my hands around the back of my head. "He was sitting in the room with just me. No one else." I closed my eyes.

"He'd never done that. I wanted to say things, to ask him questions, but when I looked over, I lost my nerve. Then he stood up and said, 'I'm going back to bed, and you should too. I think we have seen all that we can tonight.'"

"What did you do?"

"I walked over and pushed the off button on the TV. He turned off the light and walked out of the room. We shared the space which meant everything to me, but then nothing else. It made me sad."

"What would you have wanted him to say?"

I couldn't answer his question. "I don't know."

"You just wanted your father to acknowledge you."

How did he know what I was thinking? Was I that transparent, that desperate?

I'd have done anything for a cigarette, but I licked my lips and leaned against the couch.

"That must have been hard."

"Sort of... I don't know." *How would I answer that? It embarrassed me to think I was so vulnerable. I'd never had that before. And I never had it again.*

"What happened after that?"

"The next morning, he didn't say anything about our few hours together, but I remembered it. Every minute. It was the one and only time we'd ever had together."

"How did you feel over the next few days?"

God, there it was again.

"I can't do this anymore, not about him, not today."

"Do you regret talking about him?"

"I don't know. I'm not his daughter. He didn't want me. I was never part of their plan."

"Is it possible that none of this was about you? Perhaps he didn't know how to love you after his daughter died."

"Are we done?" I asked, wiping away the tears that embarrassed me.

"There's still time. Do you want to talk about your feelings?"

I smiled at him. "Not anymore."

"You shouldn't leave this upset."

"I'm fine. I'm not upset."

I wiped the tears away, brushed back my hair and straightened my sweater. *I'm just fine*, I thought, then I looked up at him.

"Do you think he loves me and I just can't see it?" I asked.

"Do you think you could forget someone loving you?"

I sat back and let the memories float back. The garden, the living room, in his chair staring at me in my gown. I dropped my head in to my hands and let out a sigh.

"What if I've got it all wrong?" I asked, pulling myself back up on the couch. Why can't I remember anything good?"

"Maybe the good never happened, Claire."

He adjusted his tie and straightened his jacket. I knew our time was almost up.

I wanted so much, to remember something happy. But it wasn't there.

I just wasn't there.

"Claire, you can stop smiling anytime you want."

16

I stopped smiling and walked out the door.
         He didn't know that I couldn't stop smiling
because that was the only thing I could hide behind.
Shit, I had to stop blaming myself for everything.
It exhausted me. The rain beat against the wall, but
instead of waiting for the storm to subside, I was sick
of it. I wasn't going back I told myself, kicking at the
puddles as they puddled in the parking lot. *I would*
figure this shit out on my own and be done with it.

I dug my hands deep into the pockets of my jeans.
I hadn't grabbed a jacket because the sun was out when
I left the house. A sweatshirt sufficed. I forgot how
the clouds could just open up and a beautiful morning
could turn into a stormy afternoon.

I sat in the car for a while, then put the key in
the ignition. I didn't turn it. I dropped my head down
toward the steering wheel and let it rest there.

I wasn't getting better. I was worse. Okay, I
wouldn't tell anyone that late at night I curl up in the
chair, and drink. I write rambling incomprehensible
pages in a journal. I write letters I'll never send to Alice,
letters to my father to tell him how much it hurt that he
couldn't let me in. I huddle in the chair with the knife
and a glass of wine. I'd never tell him about the knife

*moving up and down my arm, pushing a little harder
each time, edging the pain closer to a reality.*

*If I could just find a way to get better, I wouldn't
have to tell.*

When the afternoon thunder came, I looked up
and watched the skies, as they parted. It would rain all
day I thought. I had the whole day to myself. I should
go home and clean up the house, have a nice dinner
ready and pretend the world was in its place.

My feelings about my dad connected to finding
Alice, besides it could all be over in a minute. I could
get a letter from one of the Sisters, find out that she
was nowhere in Ireland and that I could give it up. I
didn't know how to deal with any of it, but I also didn't
want to go back and admit that I had failed.

When I arrived home, turned on the stereo
and lost myself in the tasks of stripping the beds,
vacuuming, and dusting the knick-knacks that
identified our family. I showered and changed into
a warm sweat suit, made a thick soup that would be
perfect for dinner, along with French bread and let it
simmer on the stove for the next few hours. I brought
in the mail and found a letter from Sr. Helen, but didn't
open it. I slipped it into the drawer and went back to
the living room. The rain was still coming down. It was
an unusual storm for spring, so I grabbed a paperback
and curled up in Carl's chair. *Loose Change* was the
title, by Sara Davidson, about the hippie generation and
women's movement. I held my steaming cup of tea, and
threw myself into the world of Sara and her sorority
sisters. I didn't come out until just past four when the
phone rang.

"Claire, this is Dr. Benning. I need to change our
appointment for next week."

When I first heard his voice I thought he was calling to cancel me entirely. Tell me to never come back. Ever.

"Oh, okay. That would be fine."

"You were planning on coming in?"

I paused. "I'm sorry about today."

"No reason to apologize. I understand that what we're doing is very hard. You don't have to be brave."

"I wasn't trying to be brave."

"How about Friday at five o'clock?"

That would work. I could get things done and not have to bring them home for the weekend I thought. "Sure. I'll be back. And again...."

"Please, stop. You didn't do anything wrong. I'll see you Friday."

* * * * * *

I arrived on time, but empty-handed. I didn't bring any notes because I had made a decision. In the week that had gone by, I had decided. Like the storm that lasted for two days, then disappeared. I would disappear as well. I would stop therapy. It wouldn't be something that I'd tell Carl. I went back to my regular chair and sat straight, reserved. I refused to let myself fall apart again. I'd never fall apart again. If this was to be my last session, there would be nothing that we couldn't talk about and I would have control.

"I worried about you this week."

"I told you I was sorry about rushing off like I did, but I've made a decision."

"What kind?" He looked at me like he knew what I was about to say.

"No, I get it now." I adjusted myself in the chair.

"I've been thinking about it and decided, this will be my last session."

"Okay." He sat back in his big leather chair. "What brought you to this decision?" He looked calmer than I had expected.

"I received a letter from Sr. Helen and," I pulled a leaf from the tree. "They told me not to come."

"Does that change things for you?"

"Why would I go if they can't find her?"

"You still have time Claire. It doesn't mean they won't find her, but what does this have to do with you stopping therapy?"

"Okay, I was going to tell you. I have a better understanding of my depression and why I'm drinking, so I think I'm good."

"What about your dad?"

"What about him?"

"You were really upset, by what happened last week."

"No, I'm good, really," I said, looking away from him.

Then he smiled, adjusted his tie, and stared at me.

"You've been coming here for a few years now, and have told me some incredible things about yourself."

"I made too big of a deal of them. Everybody goes through shit, and they come out the other end. Right?"

He shook his head and slipped the pen back and forth through his fingers.

"Please tell me that is not your reason for quitting?"

"Why not. I get it. I just need to relax."

"Do you really think it's that easy?" I asked.

"I didn't say it was easy."

"I don't think you made a big deal of anything."

I stopped listening to him. He and his words became a blur that I couldn't understand. I didn't want to understand. I had made a decision, and he was not going to talk me out of it.

"You didn't make a big deal of things."

"Well, I've decided I don't need to keep talking things out. Sometimes you can just wear yourself out trying to figure things out. I think I have a handle on things."

"Well, we have this time right? You're not going to leave before the hour are you?"

"No. I'll stay."

I knew I didn't want to leave. I wanted him to tell me to stay. Inside that door I was safe from the world, even from myself. For an hour each week I felt cherished, but he wasn't the real world, and that was where I lived for all the other hours.

"Back to your dad."

"No, I don't want to talk about him."

"Why?"

I tucked my leg under me, "Because, there is no point."

"Did you see him?"

"Yes." I felt exasperated. *Shit, he doesn't get it.*

"How did it go?"

"Like it does all the time." My hands slipped under my legs so they wouldn't fly about. There was too much to control in this moment to keep the words from falling out. I looked over and watched the cat.

"Why does it feel like you're lying to me?"

"Why would you say that?"

I became angry I was not a better liar. If I told him the truth, he'd be convinced I needed more therapy. He'd ask me to stay. It wasn't so much the therapy I needed. I needed this office, the blue chairs and the blue couch. And the cat who rolls in the dirt. I needed to feel cared about. He had no idea what he meant to me, more than he could ever imagine, but I knew what I was doing. I was replacing him for my father, replacing him for anyone I thought should have loved me. All the feelings I couldn't tell my world I was putting on Dr. Benning.

"I'm not lying. You did give me a better understanding of everything, that none of his feelings were my fault."

"Are you saying that because you believe it, or because it's what you think you should say?"

"No. I get it. Really. To put it simply, he has his own shit to deal with, and it's not about me. It's not my fault."

I sat up straight and crossed one leg over the other. I pulled my hands from under my legs and placed them in my lap. He wasn't taking notes, instead, he stared at me, like he was waiting for something. I didn't know what to say. I rubbed my hands together and took a deep breath, but I felt it catch up in my throat.

I looked back at him, smiled and slipped my hands under my legs, again, after taking them out over impatience.

"Claire was there ever a moment with him, your father, that you could say was good?" Now he pulled out his notepad, and laid it in his lap.

"Yes…, the night Kennedy was shot. As I said last week, that was the only time. It wasn't much, just a TV and a tragic moment in history. There were no words, conversation…. But we were together. That means something, doesn't it?"

"It does."

"It was one of those days when you knew exactly where you were. I don't know if I remember it because it was Robert Kennedy or because for two hours I was with my dad. It wasn't a time when people talked as they watched."

"Did you try to talk?"

"Times were different then. People didn't talk while they watched TV. Besides, it was history."

"This wasn't about Kennedy at all, was it?"

I felt my throat tighten. The words could barely slip out.

"No... it wasn't." I wrapped my hands around the back of my head. "He was sitting in the same room with me. We'd never done that, not alone, anyway. I wanted to say something, ask him why, but I lost my nerve."

"What did you want to say?"

"I don't know. It wasn't really the time to say anything. There were no words. In that one moment, history was made. My sadness didn't matter."

"You didn't answer the question. What did you want?"

I looked up. "Nothing... everything.... Just that we were together seemed to be enough."

"Really? Just sitting there?" He asked.

"What do you want me to say?"

"Tell me what you wanted him to say to you." He leaned forward.

I was puzzled. He was asking me something I couldn't answer.

"Maybe, that he was sorry he couldn't love me. That if he could, it would change everything."

"Is that what you wanted?"

"I don't know. Something, I guess. Something that

would have shown some kind of feeling toward me."

"Maybe he couldn't do that. Maybe you were right. He loved Teresa so much, he had nothing left."

"Maybe because I wasn't blood."

"Did you believe that?"

"Someone told me that once. They said he couldn't love me because we weren't related."

"How did they know?"

"I don't know. It made it sound so simple."

"And it made sense?"

"I wasn't his daughter."

"Claire, think about it. Do you love people you aren't related to?"

"Of course, but everyone is different. Maybe he couldn't."

God, I wanted a cigarette.

"Are you all right?"

"Sort of. I don't know." *How would I answer that? It embarrassed me to be so vulnerable.*

"So, are we done for today?"

"You shouldn't leave this upset."

"I'm fine."

I wiped the tears, brushed back my hair and straightened my sweater. I was just fine, I thought, then I looked up at him.

"Do you think he loved me and I just couldn't see it?" I asked.

"What do you think?"

I sat back. "Shit. Don't say that. Just give me an answer."

"I don't have an answer. Maybe losing Teresa had been too much."

I let my mind float back to my memories: the garden, the living room, in his chair staring at me in my wedding gown. I dropped my head in my hands and let out a sigh.

"What if I've got it all wrong?" I asked. Why can't I remember anything good?"

"Maybe this *was* the good, Claire."

* * * * * *

On the way to Sally's house, I still didn't feel any better about him, or myself. There was something I was missing and I couldn't figure it out. Sally greeted me at the gate, with a look of concern on her face.

"What happened?" she asked as I got out of the car.

"I need to ask you something about love."

I followed her through the gate and picked up the kitten that swirled between my feet. "Would you like some tea?" she asked, moving past me toward the open doors.

"No. Could you just sit down for a minute? I'm really torn about something."

She took a seat, and I went over to the bench still holding the kitten. "He's new, isn't he?"

"He was dropped off last week, in the middle of the night, I heard the car."

I let him curl up in my lap, then looked up at Sally.

"What has you going on so?"

"We talked about my dad again. I feel so foolish, I'm a grown woman and I still go on about him.

"Could I have done more to make him love me?"

"Oh, sweet girl, there's nothing you could have done. His heart ached. It happens that way, sometimes."

"The rose garden— that was for her.... I should have known."

She came over to my side and brushed my hair. "Oh girl, after all these years, you have it all wrong. Those roses make a statement about both of their lives. Claire, he loved her, that means he is capable of loving you, but you have to understand that kind of loss doesn't just go away; it lingers like winter colds. Some days it's better than others, and some days it's unbearable. The point is, he loved."

"I get all that, I know he loved her, but that has been the problem, it all went to her, there was nothing left for me or anyone. I know that I saw it every day. I admire and love him for it, but I hate him at the same time, because I get nothing, nothing from him. We are invisible to each other."

"Maybe one day, he'll let you in."

"How long will that take?"

"How long will it take for you to get over me, when the time comes?"

"That's different."

"How?"

"You say you love me?"

"Of course I do."

"Will you ever let someone replace me in your life? A year? Five years? Ten years?"

"Sally no one could ever replace you."

"Don't you see? We have known each other since you were all of ten years old. He had her for 14 years, and you want him to let go of her?"

"No, I just want him to let me in the way you have."

"Claire that may never happen, but it isn't because he doesn't want to—he can't. Can you forget your mother?"

"Of course not!"

"Imagine that, and you've never met her."

"I know Sally, I just want to belong somewhere, know that I am important."

"You have to be important to yourself, really nobody matters after that. Everyone who comes into your life and loves you, will be a bonus."

17

I didn't stop counseling. I returned every week and spilled my secrets. As the letters came, I shared them, still wondering if I was doing the right thing. I waited a while before taking the certificates to Dr. Benning, but finally decided it was time. I held them on my lap as we reviewed the week. I wasn't in the mood to talk about Alice or the idea of meeting her. I had even debated for the thousandth time about even coming back, but I had documents, it was real.

As I got deeper into the search, I found that the depression consumed me and I couldn't get a handle on it.

I knew it took over and I I fought it with everything I had, but I failed. Each night I drank. I dug a knife deeper into my skin and watched it draw blood.

Who in the hell did that, at my age? What the hell? I pulled the sleeves to my sweater down, even past my knuckles. I could never show the cuts.

It didn't take long for him to notice the envelope. "You have something to share?"

"Yes..." I paused, fondling the envelope as one might a puppy. "They came, both of them." I waved it around like an extra ticket.

"You don't seem too happy about it?"

"I don't know. I feel more sad, than anything."

"Can I see them?"

"Of course." I handed him the envelope, watched as he took the parchments out and unfolded them. He examined each one, turned them over and handed the envelope back to me.

"So, what's wrong? Isn't this what you've been waiting for? Your history?"

"It is. I know it doesn't make sense. I should be thrilled, but I don't know how to be."

"It means you can start. You aren't just reaching out for random information, any more. You have a direction."

"I didn't tell you about another letter I received."

He didn't say anything, just watched me, like he usually did. He was not quick to question anything. He waited with a patience I had not been blessed with.

"Dr. Barnados sent me a response. He's not a real doctor, not like I thought. It's an organization that helps people like me, connect to their families. A social worker wrote back. She gave me the name and address of two Sisters who might have information about my records."

"Why didn't you say anything earlier?"

"I don't know."

"Did you share them with Carl?"

I dropped my head, like a guilty child.

"Why?"

I didn't even shrug or anything. I was empty. I had nothing.

"What's going on, Claire?"

I didn't have an answer for that either. I couldn't even give myself an answer. Part of me regretted that I even started this thing in the first place, and another part was buried in absolute terror. Maybe I would be too late, she'd say no, or worst of all, there was no one out there.

"I think I'm scared I'll really find her."

"It's okay to be scared. Nothing gets done when you're not scared."

I finally looked up. "You do know that platitude shit isn't working, don't you?"

He gave me a weak smile. "Really?"

"I know everything you're saying, and I know I don't usually give up, but this? This isn't a paper I have to write, or a lesson to plan, it's real. She gave me away forty years ago. She must have had a reason. Right?"

"Everybody has a reason for the things they do, but it doesn't mean she didn't love you. You can't know that. She was a child herself."

"So, how *does* a child get pregnant?"

"Do you really want the answer to that question?"

I moved from the chair to the couch, and slid onto the floor, my favorite place in his office. I pulled my knees up and leaned my head down.

"I have to do this, don't I?"

He straightened himself in the chair. "Actually, no you don't. You don't have to do anything...."

"You're doing it again."

"What I hoped to say, is... No, you don't have to do it, but you will always wonder. Do you want that?"

I said it barely loud enough for either of us to hear. "No...."

"There is one other thing while we are on the topic."

"What? Pretty much thought we covered it."

"You have to share it with Carl."

"Why can't this just be mine?" I asked.

"It is yours, but telling him keeps it from being a secret, and you, young lady are pretty good at keeping secrets."

I didn't respond and he didn't push it.

We spent the hour talking about the possibility of Ireland, the kids and finally my moods. It was a day when he did most of the talking, guiding me back and forth, somehow knowing that I'd lost my strength.

I left the office with the thought of telling Carl and wondering why I broke to pieces. I didn't have an answer, but even thinking about it created a depression that was so big.... Much bigger than me.

After dinner the kids and Carl watched television, I hid out in the main bathroom, drew a steaming bath, and stepped in. I slid down in the water and laid my head against the porcelain. I knew what happened, but I didn't know how to stop it. I thought about showing Carl the envelope after the kids went to bed, but I was drained. I could barely pull myself from the tub. I wrapped the towel around me, went to our bedroom and closed the door.

Dr, Benning was right... I was good at keeping secrets. I pulled the letters from their hiding place and left them on the nightstand. I could see them in the mirror, waiting for Carl, as I brushed out my hair. They screamed as I pulled on a tee shirt and crawled into bed. I could barely breathe.

* * * * * *

The house began to look a lot like Christmas, red and green lights glimmered off the fireplace, and the tree against the window reflected the season. I took a seat at my desk, staring at the window back into the room, then decided to clean things up. I put boxes in the far corner, stuffed the ribbons in plastic bags, and sat back looking at my handy work.

"What are you doing?" Carl asked, patting me on the behind.

"Just trying to clean up after the mass decoration. The kids tried to do a good job, but they stopped short when it came to putting things away."

"It looks great. They did a nice job."

"We all did a nice job." Carl wrapped his arms around me. I turned to kiss him, felt his lips, warm and tender. He stood back and stared down at me. "Can we talk for a few minutes?" Carl asked.

"Okay, sure." I immediately felt defensive, almost jumping out of my skin. "Hey, I've been trying really hard. I haven't missed an appointment, and I've cut back on drinking as much as I could."

"Slow down. I'm not here to criticize."

"I'm sorry. I'm a little wary of everything. I'm so caught up in the letters, it just scares me."

"What are you talking about, why would they scare you? Did you get something I haven't seen?"

"No. nothing more. They just seem to contradict each other. And therapy has been pretty intense, and then the holidays coming. I've been a little overwhelmed."

"How has therapy been? I mean if you want to talk about it." He looked sheepish asking about something so private. I hadn't really shared anything with him. It was the one thing that was mine, so I held it close.

I sat down on the couch and stared at the brightly colored lights from the tree. "We've talked about my dad for the last few weeks. I really struggle with memories of him. Actually, I'm struggling with memories about everyone."

"What does Dr. Benning say?"

"Not too much. He makes me try to figure things out on my own. He tells me not to take it personally."

"How's that going?"

"Well, since I take things personally all the time, not so well."

"I am glad that Dr. Benning is helping. I want to give you something... something that might make it easier." He handed me an envelope. "This is for you."

"But it's not Christmas?"

"Well, I wanted to give it to you." He kissed me on the forehead.

"What is it?"

"Just open it."

I took the envelope from his hand, slipped my finger under the flap, and pulled out the paper.

"No." I almost dropped the paper from my hands. "You can't do this," I said. "I can't accept it."

"It is too late. Done deal."

"You've been saving up for so long. I won't take that from you. You promised the guys. You were all going to go in on the boat, together."

"I'm giving it to you. They're getting close, and you need to find her. It might not happen next week, next month, even next year, but I want you to know it's there for you."

"I can't take it. I'd be too selfish."

"No. This is for you."

I sat back and tried to figure it out. I mean I knew Carl gave me his bonus check to go back to Ireland, but I couldn't figure out why.

"This should go for the kids if you aren't going to share it with the guys."

"I've already talked with the guys and the kids

totally agree. Actually, they want to go with you, but they want you to have it. When the time comes, you need to make the trip."

"I don't think they're going to find her," I said. "I think they're going to end up telling me I'm out of luck."

"Knowing you, you'll find another way?"

"Carl, I can't take this. You've been working overtime and saving for a long time."

"I have. I've been saving for something special. I personally, can't think of anything more important. You're pretty special, don't you think?" He asked.

How does he do this? Bring me back from the edge? I didn't know what to say. I felt a tear slide from my eye. "I love you," I whispered.

"You better... I'm giving up a drift boat for you."

"Stop it and kiss me, foolish boy." I slapped his arm and pulled him to my lips.

"I mean it, Claire. Don't forget we love you. You are our world."

"I know that, and you're mine. It's just that sometimes...." He patted my behind again and gave me a squeeze.

"So, what's going on with the Sisters?"

"They're telling me she's not where they think she should be. Every time they locate her, she seems to disappear. I think they're playing with me."

"Didn't they offer to do everything they could?"

"They did, but it doesn't seem like it. Then again, what if they find her and she won't see me?"

"Settle down, Babe, You're a little scattered. You can't think about that right now."

"I think about it all the time."

"What does the doctor say?"

"He just wants to know how I feel. I get so frustrated." He looked at me like I was scaring him.

"Promise me you'll stay with him through this. It won't be easy, and I don't have any answers. Things could go very wrong."

"You don't think I haven't thought about it? That's all I think about. She might very well be dead."

"That's why I'm asking you to stay with Dr. Benning to get through this."

"Why are you so concerned about Dr. Benning?"

"I'm not, I'm concerned about you. He'll get you through this, especially if you make the trip. You'll go to Ireland, find out what you can, then when you come home, you can let it go."

"Wait? What are you asking me to do?"

"I'm asking that you search everything out, learn what you can, then let it go. Come home and be the wife and mother we need for you to be."

"And if I can't? What if I can't let go?"

"It consumes you, it takes you away from us."

"Takes me away from what?"

"I don't mean it that way."

"Carl, I can't promise anything. I don't know what will happen if I ever get the chance to go to Ireland. If you make me promise this…"

"Jeez, no, I don't mean that." He got up from the couch and moved to the tree. "I'd never give you an ultimatum. Just promise me you won't lose sight."

"I told you I'd go for as long as I thought I needed him."

"I don't want to lose you, Claire."

"I'm not going anywhere."

Carl backed away from the tree. "Are you coming to bed?"

"No, I'm going to do the dishes, so I don't have to in the morning."

I went to him and wrapped my arms around him. We didn't have any more to say. We would put the money away and if the time came where the Sisters found her and everything came together, I'd go, but for now we'd go on with our lives.

"Can't that wait until tomorrow?"

"I'll be there in no time."

I went down the hall and looked in on the kids. No surprise, they were asleep together on Devon's double bed, and the new puppy Carl had promised them lay at the foot of the bed. Chelsea's shaggy head looked up when I stepped into the doorway. As I headed down the hall, I heard the gentle tapping of her feet behind me.

I went into the kitchen and stared at the check I had placed on the door of the refrigerator. I took the wine from the refrigerator and poured a glass. I took the paring knife, it felt right in my hand.

Grief took over me. My husband supported a trip, my kids had a new dog. I looked down at my feet where she had curled up. We'd named her, Chelsea. I shook my head at the lump of fur at my feet...

I took a sip of wine and watched the Christmas lights glisten. *Such a happy time of year.* I covered myself with the afghan and shifted the blade.

I pushed the knife hard against my skin, finally little red drops popped up, like the lights shining on the tree.

I felt the rush and for a second, I forgot. There was no explanation. I watched the blood well on my arm. I didn't feel the physical pain, everything was numb. I felt the guilt; I had no right to do this, and if anybody knew I'd be shamed.

I was always shamed.

18

The holidays were a blur. Between work and the kids, it was a new decade before I knew it. 1990. Maybe a new start was what I needed, a change of pace, of direction. A new outlook.

Then it happened, she was alive.

The Sisters found her living near Dublin. She had married and had a daughter living at home.

She wouldn't see me.

Sr. Helen had spoken with her and told her about me. That I was looking for her.

It didn't matter, my mother couldn't possibly allow me to meet with her. It would ruin her life. I was a secret that needed to stay a secret.

There it was, spelled out in Sr. Helen's elegant handwriting. The trip would never materialize, there was no point. She had a life that had nothing to do with me. A husband and children who knew nothing about what had happened to her.

I put the letter in my nightstand drawer, refusing to look at it. I didn't need to read it again. I didn't tell Dr. Benning, Carl or the kids. I didn't tell anyone. I went on with my life as she went on with hers.

I pulled myself up on the pillow, leaned over and patted the bed as Carl walked into the bedroom. He moved next to me and sat on the edge.

"What have you got there?"

I handed him the letter from Sr. Helen. I don't know what I expected. He surely wasn't going to jump up and down, and tell me how great it was, or maybe he was. He read the words, then looked over at me, a bit of the same way that Dr. Benning might.

"When did you get this?"

"A while ago."

"And you kept it from me?"

"I was scared."

"Of what?"

"Looking foolish."

"Because she won't see you?"

"Yes. Sr. Helen is the nun who was with her in the Home and she located her. It's over."

"How's that, Claire? They found her. That's what's important."

"We read the same letter, didn't we?"

"Yes, I know, it said she won't see you. That doesn't matter."

I started to cry. Everything was falling apart.

He handed me the envelope, and I put it back in the nightstand. He wrapped his arms around me and held me until we fell asleep. I dreamed of a red-headed girl and woke with a start.

Did she miss me? Did she remember I had come from her?

"I would have remembered." I heard myself say out loud, brushing the tears away. Why couldn't she love me enough?

* * * * * *

The winter rain beat down as I sat on the patio. Devon came in with the mail and dumped it in my lap as I sat under the patio reading.

I flipped through the bills, telephone, garbage, electricity, and then it was there, another letter from Ireland. This time from Sr. Bridget, in Dublin. I fumbled as I opened it, turning it in every direction but upright. Finally, I gently slipped my finger into the envelope and tore it open.

> *2, January 1990*
>> *Dear Claire,*
>> *I need to let you know that your records here were not destroyed, thank God. We found them buried behind a stack with a later date.*
>>> *Your birth weight was 6lbs. 6ozs. You were admitted to our Nursery St. Patrick's Infant Hospital. Temple Hill, Blackrock, Co. Dublin on 29th November 1949. There were no legal adoptions in Ireland at that time. You were fostered in the county between December 1950 and 30th January 1953. During the period of fostering you developed rickets and were re-admitted to St. Patricks for some months. You were placed for adoption in the USA in May 1954.*
>>> *She was Alice Brennan and came from the Midlands. She was 14 ½ years at the time. She was admitted to Castlepollard on the 7th July 1949, It was reported that she may have been assaulted thereby causing*

her pregnancy. They discharged her to the convent on the 27th November 1949.
Baby D/O/B 20/11/49
Baptized 24-11-49
Baptismal name: Finnouala Claire Brennan.
Baby discharged: 29-11-49.
Once we were able to find her, we called and she would not speak with us. A day later, she rang Sr. Helen and asked that we not call again.
She will not see or talk to you. We don't know if you were thinking of coming to Dublin, but we would recommend that you not come. It might be too difficult
If we can be of any further assistance, please feel free to contact us.

> *With every good wish,*
> *Yours Sincerely,*
> *Sr. Bridget*

She had been raped. I couldn't imagine what she must have gone through—and then to get pregnant. God, she must have hated me.

In three paragraphs my life was laid out before me. My first four years spent being shuffled between random foster homes.

It explained so much. There were still questions, but it finally made sense.

It was over.

I left the letter on Carl's nightstand.

* * * * *

Saturday morning, I was up early, fixed breakfast and sent the kids off for a day with their friends.

I spent the morning cleaning the house.

Carl worked for half the day, but was home by one, carrying a large Burger King bag and two sodas.

"Hey, what are you doing?"

"I brought lunch and I wanted to talk."

"Thanks. I wondered what I would do for lunch."

"Come on then, sit down."

"What's going on?"

"I've been thinking... I think you should go to Ireland."

"Why?" What's the point? She won't see me. The Sisters made that clear."

"Even more the reason for you to go. They each have different pieces of your history, correct? From different parts of Ireland?"

"Yes. Sr. Helen's in Cork, and Sr. Bridget's in Dublin."

"Go find out what they know, in person.

"We have the money.... Go and get your answers."

"Are you sure?"

"Yes. Take time off. Go over St. Patrick's Day. See the parade. Do all that, then come home. You never know, she might change her mind."

"I can't believe you want me to go."

"I want you to find your answers." He reached over and kissed me.

I was going to Ireland.

19

I made the appointment with Dr. Benning for Wednesday, two days before my flight.

I waited in the familiar waiting room, flipping through outdated magazines, bouncing my leg as it hung over my knee. He popped his head out and I followed him back to the office.

Today would be light and easy. I grabbed a leaf from the Ficus, and waited for him to settle into his leather chair.

"I'm glad you came, I thought you might not," he said.

"Of course, I'd come. I need to hear that I'll be okay," I said, staring out the window.

"You know I can't tell you that."

"I know, wishful thinking." I looked over and smiled at him.

"So, are you all set?"

"As ready as I can ever be. I'm packed. I have all my documents. There's not too much else to do."

"If it's like any of my trips, you'll forget something." He tapped his pen on the pad. "I always wake up in the middle of the night going over my lists."

"I've been doing that for weeks." I rubbed my palms against my jeans. "She doesn't want to see me you know."

"Who?"

"Alice. I got a letter from Sr. Helen. She's talked to her. She won't see me if I come."

He didn't say anything, just looked out the window. "I don't know what to say."

"There's nothing to say. Carl said I should go meet with the Sisters, anyway. Learn as much as I can about her, her family and her life. He thinks it will help me let go."

"Will you be able to?"

"I don't know if there is really anything to hang on to. I mean she didn't want me then, she doesn't want me now." I could feel the tears building. "I can't believe Carl."

"You have to know by now that he supports you."

"I know..., it was his idea that I still go."

Suddenly, he slapped the pen against the pad. "You know what? He's right. You need to go, meet with them. Learn everything you can. You never know, she may change her mind."

"I don't think so. Sr. Helen made it pretty clear." I brushed away a tear and pulled another leaf from the tree. "I'm afraid I'm making a mistake."

"Claire, we all make mistakes. That's the nature of being human. We have to allow that from each other."

"Mistakes are good, I guess. We learn from them."

"Claire, I don't think it's a mistake..., it's not wrong. It will be hard, but you've done hard things before."

We spent most of the next hour talking about Ireland, and how I might talk to the Sisters, and all the things I would see. The hour slipped by and I didn't want to leave. I was safe there, but my time ran out.

"Wait, can I ask you something?" I turned toward him.

"Of course."

"Can I have a hug? Just a little one?"

"You don't even have to ask." He got up from his chair and I stepped into his embrace.

I buried my head in his chest, and holding me tight, he whispered. "You're going to do just fine. I'm proud of you. Now go face the world." I smiled and looked up at him.

He grinned. I had been coming to him for almost five years. He made me feel safe, cared for. With his help, I had grown into who I was supposed to be, I just hadn't met her yet.

"Thank you for everything. I'll see you when I get back."

I went out of the office and stood in the late winter sun. In my years of coming to this office, I was often too afraid to even breathe, but not today.

Today... this moment in time, was a victory.

Finally... I was headed to Ireland.

20

When I packed my suitcases, I tucked in scarves and sweaters to subdue the closing of winter. Along with everything else, I made sure to pack every hope I had of finding my mother.

I crammed in books, journals, and a teddy bear, from Devon to remember her, while away from home.

I had left Carl a list of chores, along with an envelope stuffed with cash for everyone to continue their lives while I was gone.

I had folded all the clothes, filled the refrigerator and pantry to over-flowing with snacks. Everything they would need to make it the ten days without me.

I did my best to plan for every unexpected thing. He could order pizza Friday night and Sunday he'd take the kids to McDonalds.

If he played his cards right, he'd be the "best dad ever."

"I'm going to miss you," he said. He'd come up behind me in the doorway, wrapping his arms around my waist. I turned and kissed him, I saw sadness in his eyes.

"I'll be back in ten days," I said, whispering into his ear.

Carl put my suitcases in the trunk while the kids stood on the sidewalk and watched. Devon dug her s deep into her pockets and Adam bounced a basketball while I said good-bye.

"Do what needs to be done, then come back to us." The quiver in his voce made me almost go and pull the suitcases out of the trunk and say to hell with it all, but I didn't. As he had done, I hid my fears behind my eyes and took a deep breath.

"I promise," I said, closing the door, settling into the driver's seat. The wind had settled in for the early days of March, but a storm was due a world away.

* * * * * *

I had decided to fly out of Seattle instead of Portland. There would be a lay-over in Boston, then on to Dublin. Much easier than sleeping in an airport somewhere.

As I drove down the gray highway, I tried to focus on what lay ahead and the excitement of my first trip out of the country. I tried to squash the conflicting emotions threatening to drown me.

Focus Claire, no matter what happens, it's an adventure. You'll survive.

The radio helped set the pace, as cars flew by me. I was in no hurry, I had given myself plenty of time, for a tangle on the freeway, or backup over the bridge, but with no trouble and tons of country songs, I guided myself toward the entry of the hotel a little before five.

I had completed the first leg, my first step. All I had to do was keep putting one foot before the other.

I went down stairs for an early dinner and found a small restaurant around the corner. I garnered myself a booth in the back of the room.

While I waited for my food, I watched the comings and goings of people caught up in their own worlds. A man sat reading Stephen King, turning the pages between bites of his sandwich. A couple sat holding hands, smiling in their conversation.

My waitress brought my wine and a few minutes later, a waiter brought my dinner. I stared at the grilled chicken and vegetables and realized I wasn't as hungry as I'd thought. Food didn't seem to be the answer, at least for now. I took another sip of wine. The taste was sweet and cool. It relaxed every part of me.

As I nibbled my dinner, I wrote a list of questions on the napkin. Things I'd ask the Sisters, if given the chance.

"Would you like another glass of wine, ma'am?"

"Yes, thank you...." Then I paused. "On second thought, no I'm fine, I have water."

I really did want another glass, more than anything, but I'd been working really hard to cut back. I knew a million reasons why another glass would be a mistake. I needed to be clear-headed when I boarded the plane, and that meant being free of even a simple headache.

As I sat there, everything swirled in my head, the letters, the Sisters, the customers here in the restaurant. The next ten days would be spent returning to a past I couldn't know.

Early morning travelers packed the airport. I found a seat near the gate, waiting for the trip of my life. Strangely, I was calm. After the rush of getting ready, the three-hour drive, I guess I was worn out.

Whatever happens, happens.

21

Cabs lined the curb, as I stepped into the early morning drizzle of Dublin. Drivers stood just outside their cabs, vying for the attention of arriving passengers.

An older gentleman, in jeans and a heavy woolen jacket leaned casually against an old Mercedes, caught my eye. He stepped up when I waved to him and loaded my bags into the trunk. "Dublin Hotel, on O'Connell Street," I said.

He nodded, "Know exactly where to go," he replied and pulled from the curb.

I spent the forty minutes, marveling at city. The architecture; the cobblestones; the river.

* * * * * *

Once in my room, I put my belongings in the bureau, hung my clothes in the closet, and laid on the bed, wondering what my next move would be. It would be a few days before I could meet with the Sisters.

Late afternoon, I went down to the lobby to get my bearings for the next day and talk to the concierge for some tips on seeing the city. After, I took a stool at the bar, which gave a full view of the lobby.

A group of teenage girls were streaming out of a large conference room, followed by a smaller group of adults. The girl's chatter filled the lobby with energy. The laughter and giggling made me smile.

"You mind if I take this stool?" A woman with a gray bob asked.

"Oh, of course, have a seat. I'm just watching the crowd."

"I'm glad to get away from the madness. We just got back from a tour and I need to get away from the chaos of teenagers. Too much chatter."

"I can totally understand, I'm a high school teacher."

"I'm Ruth Tanner. I run the tours for the hotel, may I join you?"

"Nice to meet you, Ruth. I'm Claire Hamilton from Oregon. Here for a visit."

"All by your lonesome or do you also have a pack of wild animals in tow?" I had to laugh. I knew exactly what she was talking about.

"I'm by myself. I don't know if I could handle the excitement with a flock of teenagers."

Ruth had crimson checks and dressed in a tailored black pantsuit. While I looked around, Ruth took a pack of cigarettes from her purse.

"Would you like one?" she asked.

"No thanks."

"So, tell me what makes you come to Ireland?"

"I was born here."

"Oh my, a fellow countryman. What county?"

"Castlepollard. Not sure exactly where that is. The Midlands, I was told." I asked turning it into a question.

"A mother/baby home?"

I nodded. "You know anything about them?"

As the waitress brought our drinks, Ruth paused, as if she had to decide about answering my question. She straightened the napkin, then looked up.

"Mostly gossip. When girls were sent there, people talked. Most of us didn't know much about them. They were pretty secretive."

"I'm finding that out."

"Had a cousin who went to a home. We were always reminded what kind of girls were sent there. I don't think as a youngster, I totally understood what happened."

"I haven't been able to find out that much either, but from what I learned my mother was there for my delivery. I was sent off to an orphanage and she was sent off to a convent."

"That's not how it usually worked. More than likely, she was sent to the Magdalene's."

"I don't understand."

"She was most likely sent to the Laundries."

"Are the Laundries and Magdalenes the same?"

She nodded. "One and the same, they named it after Mary Magdalene, for her sins. The irony is that all girls were considered sinners regardless of their circumstance.

"Why wouldn't she be sent to a convent? What's the difference?"

"A convent means that she might have been sent to school. I know for sure she wasn't sent to school."

She stopped me in my tracks. I remembered the word "convent" in the letter, saying she'd been released to a convent. I had never heard of the Laundries.

"I still don't understand. What were the Laundries?"

"No place you ever wanted to be." She took a drag from her cigarette and stared at her glass.

"I'm just hoping to find my birth-mother. The Sisters said she was still alive but doesn't want to meet me."

"I'm not surprised. In the 40s, 50s, and 60s, oh hell, whenever a girl got into trouble, regardless of how, the humiliation was too great. They were told to forget what happened to them."

"So that's why she won't see me?"

"If she's married and has children, my guess is, she has never told any of them. She'll never tell them, let them see her shame. She may be your Mum, but she'll never tell her secrets. And if your Mum went to the Laundries, she'll never get over that."

"So, you're telling me I'll never meet her?"

"Not as long as her family is still here. If she hasn't by now, she'll never tell her husband."

I heard the words as if Alice's story could have been any woman's in Ireland.

"You understand, don't you? These women went on with their lives and tried to forget. There was no room for a bastard child who would never be accepted...."

She paused and looked up. "Claire, I am sorry I was so brash. I go beyond myself at times. But in all honesty, it's unlikely she'll see you."

I brushed my hair back, broken by the bluntness of her words. "It's OK. I need a dose of truth, now and again. I hoped in every way they'd be wrong."

"That's why she gave you away, and probably why she may never meet with you." Ruth spoke soft and clear. Her words were precise. I wiped the tears from my eyes.

"Oh, dear girl, look what I've done, gone and broken your heart."

"I couldn't imagine signing my daughter away, and then when given the chance, not try to meet her. I'm sorry...I don't understand."

"Oh Claire, it's not about understanding. It was a different time back then. These women would do anything to forget their pasts."

I didn't see any emotion in her face. Her eyes didn't tear up, and her jaw didn't tighten.

I took a sip from my glass. "I just want to see my mother." Tears streamed down my checks and the muscles in my neck tightened as I fought to justify why she wouldn't want to see me.

"Oh, you dear thing. She's not being heartless. She's just trying to survive. You were not a teenager, under the control of a prideful father, living in a country where men are always right. These girls lived in religious homes and the shame was unbearable. They didn't have a choice." She took another long sip and smiled.

"You have to understand the only thing some of these men had were their names. If their child disgraced them; no matter how, they would not stand for it. This was the Irish way."

"I'm getting quite the history lesson."

We both had a second drink and in changing the subject, she asked about life in Oregon.

"We get a lot of rain, like you do here, and we're a small town just outside of the mountains by the coast. It actually reminds me a lot of Ireland."

She laughed and took a drink. In the light, I saw the rosiness of her cheeks and the tiny lines that furrowed on her brow.

"How long have you done this, being a guide, I mean?" I asked, taking my own drink.

"I started after my children left home. I didn't have much to do, and I love traveling. I know the country well and I like meeting new people. Plus it allows me to be home almost every night."

"You live in Dublin?"

"Yes, on the other side of Stephen's Green."

"Stephen's Green?"

"A section of Dublin, farther north."

"Maybe you could give me some tips, then, about the countryside."

"You know what? I can do better than that. How long are you here?"

"Ten days. I have appointments with two Sisters, one in Cork and then back here in Dublin."

"When do you go to Cork?"

"In a few days."

"Let me do my job. Let me take you around Ireland?"

"I couldn't do that."

"No, it would be my pleasure. I have a few days off this week, and next week as well. I can help you understand our country, so you don't feel so alone."

"Why would you do this?"

"Because, when you're given the chance to do something that can make a difference, you need to do it. I'm being given this chance now. Please let me do my part."

I sat back and looked at Ruth. I saw someone I felt connected to. "You're sure? I can be a handful."

"Nonsense, you saw how I handled myself with that mad group of pixies. If I can deal with thirty-two teenagers, I can deal with a single American sweetheart."

"Thank you," I said yawning. "Sorry, I think everything's catching up with me."

"Go get some rest. I'll see you in the morning." I put my money on the bar, but Ruth grabbed it back and stashed it in my purse. "This was my treat tonight. You can buy dinner in a few days." Ruth pulled her scarf tight around her neck.

"Let yourself relax a bit. You'll be having a grand time."

We parted in the lobby and she reached over and kissed my cheek. I watched as Ruth went through the glass door. I went up to my room, flipped on the TV, and ordered a small dinner from room service and thought about everything she'd said.

22

Ruth and I spent two days going up and down the coast of Ireland. On the third day, she went back to her tours and I took the early morning train to Cork. I was filled with more anticipation than I could have imagined. From reading her letters, meeting Sr. Helen terrified me.

At the station, I gave the driver my destination, Leland Road. I stood outside the brick building with the blue door. I was early, so I walked up the street, then turned and came back and stood in front of the two-story building with chipped paint.

The sun came out while the rain stopped, perhaps to take a rest. After two more trips to the end of the block, I arrived at the front door at exactly eleven o'clock. It didn't look like a convent, more like a house in disrepair. It once had a lovely garden, but had been abandoned. The wind and rain had weathered the buildings, flaked stucco lay at the base of the wall.

I felt like the cowardly lion. How would I stand up to the symbol of my past—the Sisters? They controlled everything. In their eyes, I was wrong, most of all in trying to find her.

They had written repeatedly, that I should be happy with my life. It was best Alice not see me.

Sr. Helen greeted me without a smile.

"You're late." Her jaw was set, her face pale, almost white. There was nothing kind or gentle about her. Nothing that told me, no matter how this ended, I would be okay.

As I walked through the doorway, I could feel my strength ebbing. Along the long hall, hung pictures of Jesus and Mary, the kind I remembered seeing at Woolworth's where I worked during high school.

"I can't promise you anything. I wrote you she said no. I'm still not sure why you came all this way," she said, opening her office door.

The room was lined with chipped and splintered end tables placed against the walls. Sacred crosses covered holes in the plaster. It smelled stale, like mold, and was damp. In the middle of the room, was a folding table with plastic chairs.

The card table was old, with a piece of folded cardboard underneath a shortened leg. The metal had pulled away from the side and there was a jagged edge on the corner. A manila file sat in front of her. She thumbed through it like she had dropped something in the garbage and had to dig it out. It was not personal, not to her. It was a job.

That file held a lifetime—Alice's lifetime and mine. Here was the future that would tell my past.

"I came because I can't give up. I've been lied to so many times, I had to come see for myself. Besides, Ireland is my home."

"No." She interrupted me. "Your home is with your family."

"She's my family. Don't you get it? She is my mother."

She gave me half a smile, giving the first sign that behind the habit, she might be human. "No. She gave birth to you, but she's not your mother. She left you. She didn't raise you."

What was she saying? How could she be so cruel?

"You're right. No one did. I was in an orphanage for almost five years. I didn't have any one. Up to the time I was adopted, I was left completely alone. No one knew me."

"Your adoptive mother loves you. If you do this, it will only hurt her. Do you want that?"

"I don't want to hurt anyone, but this isn't about her."

"Alice doesn't want to know you." Though still seated, her presence filled the room. This was what she'd been waiting to say.

I was the little girl sitting in the third row of a schoolroom. The one who grabbed the pen with her left hand, but quickly dropped it because it was the wrong hand to use. It was second grade all over again, Sr. Thomas towering in front of us with a ruler in her hand. Sr. Helen telling me what to believe.

"I'm here for only one reason. Can you call her, please? Let her know that I am in Ireland, that I'd do anything to see her."

She tapped the pen against the folder. "I don't see the sense in it. But since you're here, maybe we can get it over with and you will forget this nonsense. I'll call her, but you have to make me a promise. You just sit there and don't say a word. You have to abide with her wishes. If you can't promise that, then we'll have to stop here. I won't even make the call."

"I promise, I'll let you do whatever you have to do and I won't do a thing."

As she dialed the phone, I couldn't breathe and my throat tightened.

She started speaking as if she were giving out a recipe. It had to be Alice.

"She's here now," I heard her say, automatically motioning to me. "Yes. She came from the States and arrived just a few days ago. She asked me to call you. I understand from our last conversation that you don't want to see her, but she was adamant that I speak with you again."

There was a long pause, like maybe she thought of giving a different answer. I reached my arm up to touch her sleeve, but she pulled away quickly.

"Shush!"

A Sister shushed me.

"Yes, I understand. I'll tell her."

Another long pause, I looked away, unable to watch. I stared at the Woolworth pictures across the wall. I'd have prayed to them if I thought it would do any good. Though Sr. Helen said nothing that I didn't expect, the look of her face dug into me like a splinter. I couldn't bear what her face was saying, what her words had said to Alice.

"Alice," she said, "she wants to meet with you privately, wherever you think it might be safe." She shifted the papers in the file. I held my breath. I looked for the picture of Jesus, so I didn't have to watch her expressions.

"I understand, Alice."

"..."

"Yes, thank you. No, I won't bother you again."

"..."

"Yes I understand."

She replaced the receiver and I sat silently waiting.

It was over. She leaned back in the chair and folded her arms across her chest.

"I warned you, Claire. She will do anything to keep her family protected. She never told her husband... you can see why."

"What exactly is she protecting them from?" I leaned forward in the plastic chair.

"The shame she brought her family."

"She brought her family? It happened. She didn't ask for it. How could anyone blame her?"

"You don't understand."

"You're right, I don't."

"My dear," she paused and placed her hands on the desk. "You could destroy her life as she knows it. Her husband could leave her... her children could disown her."

"Don't you think you're being a little dramatic?"

"We're done here. You need to leave. We are closing at three."

"I'm sorry." I sat back and took my hands off the table. "I don't want to destroy anything. I just wanted to see her, that is all I've wanted since I found out about her."

She shook her head. "You really are a silly girl. She had a child out of wedlock and never told her husband."

"She was raped. You said so yourself. How is that her fault? She didn't do anything." I suddenly realized Sr. Helen was right. I had no idea. We could go around in circles for hours and it would do no good. "Could I have her number? Maybe I could call her later?"

"No. I promised I wouldn't give you any information. I can't tell you anymore."

I pulled myself up from the plastic chair. I reached into my purse and pulled out a card. "Here is the number to the hotel. I'll be there until the 18th. If things change… and a letter." I stopped and dug back down inside my purse, pulling out a white envelope where I had written *Alice Brennen* "Could you see that she gets this? All you would have to do is put her address on it and mail it."

"I'll put it in her file, but I'll have to ask her. It will be most unlikely." She stood and placed the letter in the file.

"Can I ask you? Did you know her? Were you ever in the Home with her?"

She picked up the file and walked toward the door without a word.

"Sr. Helen? Did you know her?"

She didn't turn around and her voice dropped to a whisper. "No, I don't believe I did."

I didn't believe her. I couldn't identify it, but I had a feeling she knew Alice far better than I could ever imagine.

"You said you were in the orphanage on Navan Road? We have the beds that were there. We are still using them. Would you like to see the nursery before you leave?"

The conversation was over. There was nothing more to say. She wanted to show me baby things.

I wanted my mother not the relics of cribs.

She called a cab, then we walked through the vegetable garden. She spoke of how the orphanage in Dublin had been closed and that only a few girls stayed here in Cork, with their babies.

She went on to say that since adoption was legal, it allowed them time to find homes in Ireland and the children were no longer sent to the US.

We moved through the garden and down a long hall as she rambled on. We entered a room lined with cribs. I froze. I could feel the hairs on the back of my neck stand at attention. I had just walked through a time warp.

The painted white metal cribs were chipped from years of use. The thin blankets lay rumpled.

If I touched one I'd be thrown back in time, I'd see myself lying there, waiting for someone to come and pick me up, to take away the loneliness.

I took a deep breath. I wondered which crib was mine— how many helpless babies had cried there, after me. Another connection to the past... it had nothing to do with someone's face. I pulled my coat around me. It would be a long time before I could give up this memory.

Sr. Helen may have thought I left empty handed, but I didn't. I had this picture. My days in the orphanage were painted before me, crying alone in a tiny metal crib, waiting for someone to come.

"Thank you for coming, Claire. I'm sorry, but I have some place to be. Can you find yourself out?"

I found the door and stood outside waiting for the taxi, trying to figure out what just happened.

23

I had decided to stay in Dublin Center for the day to see the sights I had missed so far. The next morning, coming out of the elevator, a tall girl behind the counter stopped me.

"Are you Claire Hamilton?"

"Yes."

"I have a message for you." She handed me an envelope, with a sticky note attached. *"Have a wonderful day! Ruth."* Inside the envelope was a letter and a train ticket to Meadow's Glen.

> *Claire,*
> *I have been thinking about you a lot in the last few days. I am sorry I couldn't go with you to Cork.*
> *I knew when you told me your mother had come from Meadows Glen, there was something I could do. So, take the ticket and see as much as you can.*
> *It may not do anything, but you'll know you've walked down the same streets she has. You may even look at people who knew her. I can only hope this ticket will bring you some peace. Here is my number,*

012-762431. Ring me when you get back.
Perhaps we can have dinner before you
return to the States.
Ruth

I had never thought about going back to where she lived, walking the same streets, maybe even going into her church, finding her school.

I went back upstairs, changed clothes and grabbed a cab to the train station.

I boarded the train to Meadow's Glen at 10:00 o'clock. The countryside was just like the pictures in the travel books. It was like I'd stepped back in time. The true Ireland passed by as we rolled through the landscape. It was like nothing I'd ever seen. The greens were beyond imagination. And the sheep seemed to be color-coded, in every color of the rainbow.

Once in Meadow's Glen, I took a cab to Main Street, stepped out and followed the narrow, cobbled streets until I reached the courthouse. There was a café across the street, so I took a table outside. People passed by, not bothering to look me in the eye, but did greet me with a smile, even a wave at times. I couldn't help but wonder if a relative had passed, as I watched people hurry by. Just past 1:00 o'clock, I saw some of the shops had closed for dinner.

Tourists could easily be identified carrying bags of souvenirs from Carroll's. I didn't want to look like a tourist. I wanted to be considered country folk, but the townspeople all had a singular look of familiarity. They could have been my relatives, I thought, watching them buy flowers, talk to their neighbors, or get groceries for dinner.

I walked up one side and down the other, taking in the shops and the people when something stopped me. Down a side street was the backside of a building with the name "BRENNAN" painted in massive black letters, against a solid gray background. I had remembered seeing the name in books of Irish sir names, but now it had more meaning. It was mine.

I went inside the shop and an old woman with a loose bun tied back, stood behind the counter. I wanted to ask if her name was Julia, if she had a daughter named Alice, but my mouth couldn't open.

I couldn't breathe, I could barely say "good afternoon." She was sorrowful looking, like she had lost something that might be gone forever. Did she lose Alice, or just her keys? A man, even older, walked in and went behind the counter, kissed the old woman softly on the forehead and patted her shoulder.

It was evident he was her husband. The love in his eyes, the way he patted her hair, touched her cheek. He knew her well.

Finally turning toward me, he asked, "Do you need some help, Miss?"

"No, just looking."

"You're quite a ways from the City. Do you have family here?"

"Ah, no, I'm from the States."

"I thought so, I could tell by your accent."

"That's funny, I don't have an accent. I'm from Oregon." *It's interesting how an accent is determined by what you're used to hearing.*

"Now what are you doing all the way out here, Miss?"

"I had a few hours, and someone said the train ride was beautiful and that I could see Meadow's Glen and be back in one afternoon. I didn't want to go home thinking I had missed something."

"Oh yes, Miss, this is the heart of Ireland. You can see big things in the city, but you can't see the real country until you visit a town like ours. We are the heart of the country."

The old couple talked quietly to each other. I didn't want to interrupt, so I slipped out the half door. I would probably never see these people again, but I turned and gave a wave. She looked over and waved back.

Walking back to where I would pick up the taxi, I found myself questioning my behavior. *How could I have been so shy in not asking?*

They probably would have said, "No sorry, we don't know any Julia or Alice Brennan." Now I'll never know.

Once again, I took the safe direction, and took no action what so ever.

If I kept this up, I'd never learn anything.

When the taxi came for me, we went straight to the address I gave him, 5113 Port Road. He stopped at the edge of the gate, then asked if I was getting out. I just sat there staring out at the meadows that surrounded the house and barn. The cows grazed, never raising their heads at the taxi sitting outside the fence.

"Do you know anyone with the last name of "Brennan?" I asked the driver.

"Sure, they're all over town, Miss. Did you go in the store? Brennan's don't own it anymore, but the new owners kept the same name."

"Who was the couple inside the store?"

"Mr. and Mrs. Donleavy. They've lived in this town their entire lives, raised their children and kept that store open every day, even if only for an hour or two.

They could tell you more about who you are looking for than anyone in town. Do you want to meet any of them?"

I felt something twist inside. I was as close as I could have been to a connection and I walked out the door.

"No, I don't think I should. I mean they don't know me and well, we may not even be related. It's probably best to just leave them alone."

"Well I bet they would be excited to meet someone from the States. There were some Brennans who left town about 30 years ago and went to America, but they never wrote, so no one knew what happened to them. They would love to see some relatives."

"No, I'm a little embarrassed, besides there's a good chance I'm not even related."

"Well if you're going to be in town tonight, stop by O'Leary's Pub by the train depot. You're sure to meet some of the Brennan's. They go there every night."

"No, I have to get back to Dublin late this afternoon."

"Are you sure you don't want to go up the walkway?"

I shook my head. "No, I better get back; I don't want to miss my train. Thanks anyway."

I rode back to the depot in silence. Every now and again the driver would ask a question about Oregon or California. The questions were pretty silly, mostly about movie stars, but I remained cordial and answered him politely. Peter O'Toole was famous in America also, and no I'd never been to the Oscars, but yes, I had been to a professional baseball game.

The humming of the track took me back to the conversation with the driver. I had missed another chance.

Why did I even bother to come? I needed to be aggressive, get something accomplished. Meeting someone, learning something. It might be my only chance.

I was exhausted. I closed my eyes, the vibration from the floorboard was soothing.

What the hell was I so afraid of? Of course, I knew what the answer was. I might actually find her.

"Hello Miss, you mind if I have a seat?"

"No, go ahead."

"Having a nice ride?" He asked.

"Yes, it's lovely."

"Where did you come from?"

An average size man sort of the Alan Bates type—rugged, Irish-looking with an incredible accent that was almost indistinguishable to me, took the seat next to mine.

"I was in Dublin and just wanted to take a train ride to Meadow's Glen."

"No, I mean you have an accent, and it isn't from here. I would say California?"

"Close. I'm from Oregon."

"That is a long way. What brought you here?"

"Research."

"Hope you've had some time to play and enjoy."

"Oh yes. I've done some tours. I love this country."

"Most people do. I think it is the rain. It cleanses the soul."

"Yes, it does. This has all been very exciting. I don't want to think about having to go home."

"Well don't, enjoy every minute."

I couldn't take my eyes away from his gentle ruggedness. The hidden smile behind his manicured salt-pepper beard, and his blue eyes spoke volumes. We had never met before today, but I felt this incredible urge to tell him everything, right away.

"I'm here to research some family history."

"Well, my, my. Would you like to tell me about it, or is it too personal?"

"Well yes, it is very personal. I've been looking for my birth-mother. I started searching for her in 1985. It took four years of "snail mail" to track down the Sisters who knew anything about my mother. A month before the trip, they wrote and told me they found her. Then a week before I was to leave, she wrote, saying she wouldn't see me."

"What happened?"

"I met with the Sisters, they even called her, but she still wouldn't see me, so I came out to see where she lived. I know it's foolish, but sometimes there are things you have to do no matter what the outcome."

I gazed out the window at the immensely wet green countryside. I touched the window as the rain pelted down. I had said all of this out loud to strangers, but here on the train, away from everyone, I felt the need to cry.

I told him my whole story. It flowed out of me, like a waterfall, the words streaming over a cliff. He let me get it all out without saying a word. Then he asked me something I was not expecting.

"Are you willing to do something bold?" he asked.

"Concerning my mother? I've been told not to be so bold."

"Let me introduce myself. My name is Thomas Malone. I have a radio talk show and since Mother's Day, here in Ireland, is March 22, we are doing a special. You could use the radio to search for her," he said calmly, as if he were ordering a sandwich.

"How would I reach her on the radio?" I asked.

"Mother's Day is two weeks away. I could call you in the states and we could tape the interview. You could say something personal and maybe if she was listening, she might call into the radio anonymously. I could call you later if she did, then send the tape with the information. My show talks about everything from the price of eggs to abortion. You could send out a personal plea to her. Even if she didn't call in, she might hear you. You don't have to use real names, nothing personal, just a story of an American girl coming here to search her heritage."

"I don't know if that would be a good idea."

He looked up as people began moving toward the doors. "Here's my card, keep it. I think you have an amazing story. People need to hear it. My name and phone number are on the back."

For the rest of the ride I continued staring out of the window, then back at his card, and out the window again. What if she listened to the show and heard my voice and in some strange way knew it was me? I had a new excitement. Everything else had failed, so why not this? Why not be bold as he suggested?

I sat back and took my journal from my backpack. I had at least another hour and a half before I'd be back in Dublin. I opened the journal and wrote the notes from Mr. Malone, still wondering if all of this could be real, and if it was something I should even consider doing. I had already been warned about advertisements in the paper. Would this be comparable to that?

Then my mind wandered back to the streets and the people I had met. I wrote for a while without looking up. The words poured out, even as I held back the tears. It seemed a while before I looked up at the rain.

A Moment

I looked through random faces into eyes
for a sign, some glimmer of recognition.
How could she let me leave and not know
the color of my hair, the touch of my cheek?
I was you, born from a violent hate,
then nestled to sleep in cold metal beds,
lined along the walls like coffins.
At night when sleep huddles in the corner
I am left fitful with dreams,
your face streaks across the shadows,
slipping in and out of consciousness.
I didn't expect kinship, just a nod, a brief acceptance,
a moment that would have replaced our last memory.
A time we could have shared, not a lifetime; just a
moment.
March/1990

24

I had an hour to kill before meeting Sr. Bridget, so I took a seat at a café down the street from her office. The idea of meeting her terrified me. I only knew her through letters, which had started out kind, but as it came closer to my departure, her words turned heartless.

Don't come. She doesn't want to see you.

The waitress brought a glass of water and my coffee, while I watched Dubliners go about their day.

Sr. Bridget was the key. She'd given me a list of reasons not to come, that I'd go home empty-handed, but she had everything I needed. She knew everything of Castlepollard, my mother — and me.

If I couldn't meet Alice, I had to learn whatever I could—learn what happened to her and why seeing me would be so devastating.

It was a bright green door, with bold, black numbers to the side, 1153 Paddington Road. Flowerpots filled with geraniums stood on the steps, while heather grew in the gardens surrounding the brick building; very different from the house in Cork that lay in poor repair.

I introduced myself to the woman who answered

my knock. She stood as round as she was tall, leaning on a cane. She stepped back and looked at me from head to toe. "Well, look at you, very nice to meet you Claire. Come in, come in. Let's sit in here."

I followed her to a long oak table that sat in what looked to be a formal dining room. She placed her cane on the corner of the chair and took a seat. With the drop of her hand she motioned for me to sit down. "I have your correspondence here." She grasped the file in her hands and waved it around, like a stray paper.

"You understand that I can't let you see it. I can tell you about it, let you know minor details, but nothing about your mother. Are we clear?" She placed it back on the table to be sure I had acknowledged her statement.

I adjusted the chair and placed my purse on the floor. "No, Sister, I'm not clear at all. You sent me the basic information. I need you to tell me what I don't know, about my mother, and my time in the orphanage and what happened to me.

"I lost four years of my life." I leaned forward but kept my hands in my lap. I didn't want her to think me too aggressive. "Why can't I see what concerns me?"

"Your mother was very clear when she spoke to Sr. Helen. You were not to be given any information on her whereabouts. She doesn't want you showing up at her doorstep. The papers she signed relinquish her of any responsibility."

Sr. Bridget flipped through the pages of the file, though reading upside down, I could see medical records, letters on Castlepollard letterhead, a letter signed by Monsignor Matthew. I saw the letters my adoptive mother had sent along with her donations to the orphanage.

"What papers did Alice sign?"

"Papers that awarded you to the state. Upon your release from Castlepollard, you were placed in an orphanage."

"She was fourteen years old, her signature would have meant nothing. She was a minor."

She adjusted her habit, pushed her unframed glasses up over her nose. "It doesn't matter how old she was, or even who might have signed her name. By Irish law the signature transferred all responsibility of the infant and in turn protected her privacy."

"Sr. Bridget," I tried to stay calm. "I don't want to know her address, but there must be more you can tell me. With all due respect..." I paused, taking hold of one of the buttons on my sweater. "There is no one else who can help me."

"I'm afraid I've provided you with everything I can."

"No. You told me how much I weighed, and that I was fostered out. What happened? Where was I? What four-year-old can't walk or talk? Or has rickets and is malnourished? What happened?" I heard the rise in my voice, so I covered my mouth and waited.

Her jaw tightened and her eyes narrowed. She folded her hands on the desk. I could barely breathe, the hair on my arms stood up, and a chill came over me.

"Please Sr. Bridget, I've come a long way. You are the only one who can help me. Don't send me home with nothing."

"I'm sorry." She finally looked up, taking her glasses in hand. "I can tell you when you left the orphanage. I can tell you your physical condition at the time. I can even tell you who picked you up."

I got up from the chair and moved to the window. "I already know those things. How can I make you understand? I need my history."

She got up and came over next to me, placing her arm around my shoulders. "You should have gone to Boston, but you were too sick. By the time you were ready, the family no longer wanted to adopt." I could feel the warmth of her body. She continued. "You were fostered out to a woman in Athlone. There were no new requests for older children."

"I was left in foster care? Is that when I got sick?"

"No one knows."

"I don't believe you." I brushed away tears. "And my mother?"

"Your mother was raped. Her family was poor. She was sent to Castlepollard when she was five months past."

I leaned against the wall and listened. She spoke as if it had happened yesterday.

"You were with her for nine days."

Nine days. I let a smile cross my face. *Nine days together.*

"She took very good care of you."

"So, we were together."

"Yes, then she was sent to the Laundries, while you... well you know."

"Could you open a window or something? I need some fresh air."

"Would you like some water?"

"Yes, please."

She left the room, and in a few minutes came back with a glass. I took a small sip, then another. She sat back down at the table and motioned for me to return.

"I know everyone has the best intentions, but it's

my life, and no one wants to tell me the truth. Please let me go home with some sense of dignity."

Without a word she opened the file and paged through it. I sat silent, knowing it would do no good to interrupt her. "It was harder to adopt out the older babies. You may well have been fostered when some of the adoptions were taking place. The healthy babies brought more money."

"You had to hide the sickly poor babies. God forbid anyone know the truth."

"I'm not saying what happened was right, but it was done. What more do you want me to say?"

"You're right. Nothing will change." I didn't know what else to say.

"I'm sorry about your mother, but I think it would be best, if you forget this quest, go back to your family." Her shoulders rounded and she took on a slouch in the chair, not looking as stern. "Claire, you have children, correct?"

I nodded.

"They need you. Go home, be the best mother you can be. I can't give you any more."

"Why I'm searching has nothing to do with my family. I love them, but I need this."

"She doesn't want to see you. I don't know how to say this any more clearly. You need to let her go."

There it was, Sr. Bridget had put it out there, very clear and very simple. I leaned over and picked up my purse, placing it on the table. "I have something I'd like for you to give her." I pulled out an envelope.

"No, I can't take that," she said, pulling away.

"It's a letter."

"I know what it is. I can't be responsible for it."

"You have her address. You could mail it to her?"

"No." Her sternness returned.

"Why?"

"No letter will be posted to her, not by me, or anyone else. It would violate privacy laws."

The frustration came back. "I'm not violating anything."

Her cheeks flushed as I laid the envelope on the table. "In case she calls you, or comes here, please, give it to her."

She took the letter and put it into the file. "I can't guarantee anything."

"Sister, I lost four years. I thought I might find them here, but you chose otherwise. That is as simple as I can make it." I took a deep breath and stood up. I would not let my eyes lose hold of her.

"I'm sorry, I'm bound by Irish law."

"You've made that very clear. I just thought you might find it in your heart, just this once, to make an exception."

"I'm sorry. I have to hold my ground."

"I can't say I understand. Thank you for your time."

I watched her fingers move across the file in front of her. She was hiding something, something personal. Her eyes betrayed her.

"You knew her, didn't you? You were there."

"You're mistaken."

I shook my head. "No. I can see it, you're trying to hide it, but you knew her."

Suddenly everything about the old Sister changed. She laid her glasses on the table and lowered her face into her hands. It took a while for her to say anything, to even move.

"I had only been there a few weeks, when Alice

came. I was only sixteen." She raised her head and I saw redness in her eyes.

"Did you ever talk to her?"

"Yes... nothing personal. We weren't allowed."

I saw her going back in time. She was face to face with a teenager like herself, but she was the one in charge. I couldn't help but wonder what it must have been like. I waited for her to continue.

"We were to oversee them, make sure they did their jobs." She began to flip through the file, her jaw twitched. I thought for a moment she might cry.

"The only reason any of the girls were there, was their parents couldn't, or wouldn't, reimburse the convent for the cost of room and board. The standard payment was 90 pounds. If payment wasn't made, the girls worked it off in the laundries.

"Some were barely teenagers, frail, frightened from giving birth. It was our job to be make sure that they obeyed the rules. Any girl who broke a rule was reported to Reverend Mother Michael. She handled things."

"Handled things?"

"The girls had to be disciplined."

"And my mother?"

"It was a long time ago." She pulled her hands away.

"I don't believe you. Something about my mother stuck out. What did she do?"

"Gardening." She raised her head and looked at me. "She was out there, rain or shine."

"There must have been more than the gardens?" I asked, clasping my hands in front of me on the table.

"She was a frail thing, always terrified, so young. But she had gardening. And she had Jonathan."

"Who was Jonathan?"

"The groundskeeper. He taught her everything she needed to know." She removed her glasses and cleaned them with her sleeve, working to regain her composure.

"He helped her escape. No one ever proved it. He came back the next Monday like nothing happened, but we knew he was behind it."

"Why are you telling me this?"

She got up from her chair, and with her cane, walked to the bureau and opened a drawer. She placed the file inside. "I wasn't going to tell you anything about her..." She moved back to the table. "I've had other babies come back, but I never knew their mothers. I knew Alice. We were the same, but I wore the habit. I had the power. She had nothing."

I saw true sadness in her face, but I found it hard to find any sympathy. Before me stood an old woman who remained in the convent and watched it happen time and again. I couldn't forgive her.

"Your mother endured a great deal."

"What else?" I had to keep her talking. I had to hear it all, every detail.

"I'm surprised she survived."

"What was done to her?"

"There was a priest." She placed her cane on the edge of the table. "Monsignor Matthew was his name, I believe."

"I saw his name in the file."

She nodded. "He had an office next to the chapel and said Mass every Sunday."

"What else?"

"He took a liking to some of the girls." She paused. "He did favors for them."

"What kind of favors?"

She closed her eyes. "He liked Alice. He was the one who allowed her to work in the garden. He gave her time in the reading room, too. Some days, she even missed Mass. In turn, she delivered meals to his room."

All of a sudden it became very clear. This Monsignor Matthew had done favors for Alice. If he did favors for them, he surely expected favors in return.

"He raped her, didn't he? That's what you've been trying to say all along."

"No one ever knew for sure. She went to his room a lot, but we never questioned his requests."

I moved back to the window. "You knew about it, and said nothing?"

"No one knew for sure. There was really no point in saying anything. No one would have listened. He was a priest. We were nothing."

"So, he got to do whatever he wanted?"

"We never questioned him."

"Did you ever see her again?"

"Reverend Mother Michael did. Alice came back when she was an adult, looking for you, to find out where they sent you. Reverend Mother sent her away."

"You knew all this?"

Then everything changed. She straightened up and took to her feet. "We're done here, Claire. I told you more than I should have. To be honest, I'm not sure any of it is true. Might be nothing more than hearsay."

"You know it's not."

She adjusted her glasses and took her cane. "You know your way out?"

I walked toward the door, now able to realize why she didn't want to see me. It would bring it all back.

The pain, the shame, she would relive it over and over again.

I stepped outside the green door, closing it behind me. I knew I'd never see Sr. Bridget again.

25

I met Ruth in the lobby when I got back from Sr. Bridget. It was the first time I had seen her since before Meadows Glen.

As we took a seat next to the window she asked, "how was your train ride?"

"Oh Ruth, it was amazing. Thank you so much. The countryside was beautiful. I can't remember ever seeing anything like it."

"Yes." She smiled and nodded. "Did you find anyone?"

"No, I found a store that had her maiden name painted on the building, but it had been sold years before. I was too afraid to ask if anyone knew her. I walked around town staring at faces. I don't know what I was hoping for, someone to recognize me, maybe? That sounds stupid, doesn't it?"

"No, not stupid. A little desperate maybe." She laughed. "Don't be so hard on yourself."

"I just thought it would be easier. I came so far... I feel like I'm walking away empty-handed."

"Well, if it makes you feel any better, the Irish are very friendly to outsiders, but when it comes to their friends and families, they're extremely private. I doubt they would have said anything, even if you had asked."

I knew, when I looked into her eyes, Ruth was saying the truth. I was looking into the heart of an Irish woman. If anyone knew how they thought; their beliefs; their history, it was Ruth.

I wished everything she said was soothing, but it wasn't. Meadows Glen was another failure. Another wild-goose chase.

"Do you mind one more walk in the rain?" She asked.

"No. The rain is just the thing I need to clear my head."

She entwined her arm around mine as we headed out the double doors toward O'Connell Street. The crowds had thinned from the parade, but there were still plenty of people cruising in and out of the pubs.

Having Ruth encircle me, I didn't feel so alone. Before long, we dropped into a pub where we found an empty table, outside, under the canopy.

"Are you ready to go home?"

"Oh God, yes. I miss my family very much."

"How are you feeling about your mum, and everything that happened?"

I didn't have an answer for her. The visit with Sr. Bridget was something I'd keep to myself. Ruth was a godsend, but some things were best kept private. "The Sisters wouldn't tell me anything I didn't already know."

"You really don't have to be sad about this. Look what you've accomplished. So many others can't say the same. You came and you fought for her, for yourself. You faced your demons."

I watched her adjust her woolen coat, unwrapping her scarf. She had no idea. She had good intentions, but she knew nothing of what I was feeling.

"You make it sound so simple," I said.

"I know what you did wasn't easy. It must have broken your heart."

"Ruth, can we not talk about it? I'm tired, confused, completely broken to be honest."

"I understand. You must be overwhelmed."

"No, Ruth, no disrespect, but I don't think you do. I know you've talked to people and done research, but you've never lost anyone."

"That's true, but...."

"I'm just a bit fragile right now, but you have to know I'm so thankful for you... getting me to Meadow's Glen, showing me around Ireland..., everything. It's meant a great deal to me."

Ruth fell silent and went up to the counter to place an order. She returned with a huge smile. "You're right. It's your last night, let's celebrate. Tell me about your children."

Just as I started to tell her, the waitress brought two glasses of wine to the table, with a plate of house bread and muffins.

"They're my life, so amazing. Devon my girl, she takes after me, I guess. She's quiet, kind of shy, loves animals and wants to be a marine biologist, and for twelve is a very good pitcher. And Adam, he got every one of his genes from his father. He loves sports, football, baseball, and basketball. He is a loner at times, will play for hours in his room, making up football plays."

"And your man?"

"Carl. He tries so hard. He's an amazing dad, funny,

loves old movies, and doesn't like to go out and about much. Like Adam, a real homebody."

"You're a lucky woman."

"I know."

We drank and broke the bread apart, then I asked Ruth to tell me of her life.

"Nowhere else I'd rather be. Kids are close, but far enough to be on their own, not a grandma yet. Simon, my husband passed. Well I told you that. I do what I want, when I want." She grinned and took a bite of the bread.

"Yes, I remember. You're lucky as well. Living your life, the way you please. Not all women get to do that."

"Simon and I had a good life and he left me very comfortable, you might say."

We finished our wine in silence, grabbed our coats, and took one more cruise around Dublin Center. Without too much conversation, weaving in and out of the crowds.

How was it that she came into my life? Was she placed on my path on purpose, to give directions; to give me strength?

She had, in a way. The way she carried herself, the very nature of her grace.

We parted at the hotel.

"Thank you, for everything," I whispered. She had given me something no one else could. I was thankful for that. I would think of her often.

I hugged Ruth and put her in a cab, promising we'd keep in touch. I waved as she drove away. It's amazing how you can find solace in a stranger's kindness.

Everything Ruth had said echoed the words of the Sisters. It explained a lot. My foolish selfishness could ruin everything for Alice.

* * * * * *

The plane arrived at Logan International at three o'clock in the morning. I walked through the airport, returning the same way I had come.

The layover would keep me in Boston for almost nine hours. Carl was an early riser, but one in the morning was ridiculous. I waited till six Oregon time, to call and let him know I was back on American soil. We had talked randomly while I was in Ireland, but usually about the kids, the weather, and how I missed him. I hadn't talked about the daily heartbreak or the setbacks.

"How did it go?" His voice, quiet in the early morning.

"She wouldn't see me." I slid down the airport wall. After hearing Carl's voice and saying the words out loud, I cried. I cried because I had failed. And because I finally understood why she wouldn't see me. It all came crashing down. I couldn't hold on any more.

I never cried in front of Ruth. I had held everything in out of embarrassment, shame, I didn't know what to call it. "I really can't talk about it over the phone. I'll tell you everything when I get home. I miss you. I love you. Give the kids my love."

"Claire?"

"Don't. Not now. I don't think I can bear it. I'll see you soon."

I don't know how long I sat there. I found myself frozen in the moment. Finally the tears stopped and

I looked around. Nobody was paying attention, they were all too busy with their own dramas. They didn't notice, if they did, they never let on. I stood, replaced the receiver back on the cradle, and gathered my belongings.

After yet another delay for weather, I boarded the plane for Seattle at seven in the evening, took my window seat and disappeared into the clouds.

When I arrived in Seattle, I called Carl again. He suggested I spend the night, but I wanted to sleep in my own bed, wake up to my kids. I'd find the strength to pretend how much I loved the trip, I'd find the answers to their questions.

Carl must have heard the garage door open, because I found him leaning against the washer. I pulled in all the way to the edge of the step. I got out, hugged him so tight, then kissed him tenderly on the lips, leaning back against the washer in the dim light. I was home.

"Come on, I'll get your things later. I'm so glad you're home."

We walked down the hall and stopped at Adam's room. I kissed his cheek, brushed his hair from his face, and kissed his cheek again.

"Mom, is that you?" He said, barely opening his eyes.

"Yeah, Honey. I'm home."

"I'm glad you're back," he rolled over as if I had been a vision from a dream.

I went into Devon's room, and kissed her as well. She opened her eyes and smiled.

"You're back." She sat up, hugged me tight, then fell back on her pillow.

I went into the bedroom and sat down on the bed, Carl came over and knelt by my side.

"Was it that bad?"

"No. It was amazing, the countryside, the people, everything about it was great." I paused.

"No, I mean the Sisters, the reason you went."

"That's a long story. It was an experience."

"What were they like?"

"They were fine. How do I describe it? They treated me like a child. Like I had no right to be there.

"Sr. Helen even called her in front of me, but she covered her mouth and whispered. Everything was such a secret." I could feel my breath catch.

"Sr. Bridget dangled a file in front of me like it was a carrot. Every time I reached for it; she'd pull it away. I was so pissed." I flopped back on the bed.

"She was raped, Carl, then carted off like some kind of criminal."

"I'm sorry." He lay next to me and stroked my hair. "Maybe that's why she couldn't see you. It was just too hard. You never know what will happen, maybe in time she'll come around."

"I left the letter, but Sr. Bridget said she wouldn't send it to her, she couldn't. Something about it being against the law."

"Well, you're home now, safe and sound. And you have us." He kissed my forehead. "I missed you."

"I've missed you, too."

I kissed him back, pulling him closer. He unbuttoned my shirt, sending chills as he kissed the crevice between my breasts. I had missed him.

"Don't stop," I whispered. We laid together fondling, groping like teenagers. He slid my zipper down and ran his hand across the small of my back. I kicked my jeans to the floor.

"Lay with me until I'm asleep?" I asked.

He flipped off the light and went around to his side of the bed, and crawled in next to me. I felt his body mold to me. He wrapped his arms around me and filled me with his warmth. In his arms the pain finally stopped. I closed my eyes and listened to the rhythm of his breathing, the beat of his heart.

I felt broken. I had believed this trip would change everything. That it would make me whole.

That's what I had thought... what I had wished for.

I fell asleep in his arms.

26

I sat in the outer office for about ten minutes before Dr. Benning came out. I flipped a green worry stone over in my fingers. It was my souvenir for him, from Dublin, something small, but something he could keep in his office. When he looked at it, he could think of me.

As I waited, I tried to decide what I would tell him. I knew I'd tell Carl more, but it was too soon. Was it too soon for Dr. Benning? Was this the place I would let it go?

He had no idea how things had gone. Should I spill it all out in the office, even what Sr. Bridget had said, or would that be what I held on to? He paused as he opened the door, maybe trying to catch a clue before he even asked his first question. My face hid nothing.

"Okay, what happened? No wait, don't tell me anything until we get inside."

"Here, this is for you," I said, dropping it in the palm of his hand. He flipped it over. "It's a worry stone," I said.

"Thank you, I guess you figure I worry a lot?" He said, as he turned and moved down the hall.

"No, but your patients do. When they get fidgety, they can hold it. Maybe it will help them relax, a little."

He took a seat in his high back leather chair, while I curled up in the blue winged chair. I grabbed a leaf from the Ficus. I felt safe here, maybe I could tell him everything I had learned about Alice.

"What happened?" He crossed his legs and settled in.

"She wouldn't see me."

"I saw that in your face."

"The country was really wonderful, and I met this amazing woman who took me all over the place. She even bought me a train ticket so I could go back to Meadow's Glen. Her name was Ruth, an amazing woman."

"That's good, you had a guide. What about the Sisters?"

I grinned, then ran my hand across my mouth, like I was trying to erase it. "Well they were everything I remember from the fifth grade, minus the ruler."

"Wow, that bad?"

"No. That's not fair, they weren't that bad. They did their job. They protected her and kept us apart."

"What did they say?" His face was softer today. He wasn't being a counselor, or if he was, he wasn't showing it. He sat back and listened.

"They said everything they'd said in their letters, that I should have stayed home."

"What did you say to them?"

I dropped my head. "What was there to say? I knew what they were doing, but I felt so ashamed. Even though she called while I was in the room, Alice still said no. I just thought once I was there, she couldn't possibly say no."

"Did they give you any explanation?"

"That it was Irish law, and that there were privacy

laws that must be respected. I tried to give Sr. Bridget a letter to give to her, but she said she couldn't mail it."

"Was there anything else they told you?"

I moved over to the couch and slipped down on the floor.

"What's going on? You usually don't sit on the floor unless you're really upset."

"Okay you have to let me talk, don't ask questions, just listen. I'm not sure I can get through this."

"That's fine, take your time."

I straightened up but remained sitting on the floor. "Sr. Bridget, the nun in Dublin, who had the adoption file, knew her. They were almost the same age. She remembered when she was in the Laundries. That was where Alice was sent because her father wouldn't pay the 90 pounds."

I brushed away the tears and retied my hair. "She loved gardening." I smiled, so did Dr. Benning. "A priest, where she was, raped her. Repeatedly." The tears came down, but I didn't brush them away. I took a deep breath.

"She escaped with the help of a caretaker, the same one who let her work in the garden." I looked up at Dr. Benning. "I get it now. I didn't before, I thought it was me, I mean it was, but not what I thought."

"I'm sorry, Claire."

I pulled my knees up close. "I understand why she wouldn't see me. It wasn't just the shame of my birth, but her continued abuse at their hands."

"Are you okay?"

"I don't know. I get it all now, but sitting there with that woman, just made my heart sick, to be so betrayed by someone she trusted."

"But you, how are you feeling about this?"

I looked at him and realized I didn't have any answer. I got back up on the couch and tucked my feet under my thighs. I had told him all there was to tell about my ten days.

"Did you tell Carl all this?"

"Some of it, not everything. We didn't really talk too much about the trip. We were just glad to be together."

"Claire, you faced everyone you intended to face. You did everything you could. What else could you have done?" he asked.

"I could have been stronger." I walked across the room to the picture window and watched the black cat that settled below the tree during our sessions. For five years Dr. Benning had been the strength behind almost every decision I made, but maybe, this time he had been wrong. I flopped into the chair, pulled another dead leaf from the Ficus tree, and stared out the window.

"They made me feel like a fool." I didn't even try to stop the tears. It would have been impossible. So, I let them come, not even brushing them away

"You didn't get the response you wanted. I'll agree, but it doesn't mean that you did anything wrong."

"It means she wouldn't see me."

"Claire, you knew that before you left. Now you understand it better."

"Yeah, and I was stupid enough to go anyway."

He rubbed his eyebrows. "You did it. That was the success. That will always be a success."

"It doesn't feel like one."

"It will, maybe it's too soon. Let this settle in for a while. Get your life back on track. The ball is in their court, let them make the first move. You have a life to get back to."

I looked at the clock and knew my time was over. He got up from his chair and like two weeks earlier he wrapped me in his arms. This time I cried, again. Maybe if I cried enough, I could flush it out.

I stepped back, wiped my eyes and smiled.

"I'll be okay. It isn't that big of a deal."

"Yes, it is. Don't diminish it. It's a very big deal. You did something amazing. Something a lot of people wouldn't have the guts to. You did it."

"You can stop now," I said patting his arm.

"Wait, why did you say that?"

"Because I feel like you're just trying to make me feel better."

"And if I am?"

"It's not real."

"Everything I said is true, now it is up to you to deal with it. I can't control what happens next. Let yourself mourn, then move on."

··*·*·*·*

The days and weeks passed. Good along with the bad. Devon's softball team went to division finals and Adam's baseball team took second in the City tournament. And I was finally accepted into the graduate program for Creative Writing. Something I had been waiting years for.

Life went on, but I wasn't at the top of my game. My broken pieces were held together with extra sturdy band-aides of wine and tears. I thought I could make it past not being able to meet Alice, but each day it ate away at me a little bit more.

I never let it show during the day, but at night, sleep just wouldn't come; I sank further and further into depression.

After a while, I stopped fighting it. In the dark, I couldn't control the spiral.

While everyone renewed their strength for the new day, I wallowed in distractions and self-judgement. I brought out the alcohol and drank. It wasn't the sorrows, I didn't even know what they were, anymore.

I worked while I drank; graded papers, kept my journals, even continued to write to Ireland. But it was of little use. I slid further and further into the rabbit hole.

I got up every morning and greeted the day as if it was fresh and new; that it held something I could believe in.

But when dinner was finished, the dishes done, the kids in bed, I'd kiss Carl goodnight and dig myself a little deeper.

I had no choice.

I hid the bottles under papers when I took the recyclables to the curb and hid my wounds beneath long sleeves and pantyhose. Each day it got harder and harder to face, I couldn't find the answers, so I wallowed in my sorrow. I became rather good at it.

I continued my counseling, but still hid a great deal from Dr. Benning.

Every now and again I came in ready to tear off the facade, but by the next week I had it built back up. I think I was doing everything I could to jeopardize my relationship with him, if he turned me away, it would be universal. I was unlovable.

27

Friday, October 30, 1992, at almost exactly three o'clock in the afternoon, in the week of witches, goblins, and ghosts, I dropped to the floor as I was heading out for the weekend. A teacher saw the event and called the office, immediately causing quite an uproar.

Or so I heard.

With no memory of the fall, I had bruised my knuckles, hit my head and found myself in and out of consciousness. People moved past in a blur. Teachers — the principal — paramedics.

I woke up in an emergency room, my husband on one side and a doctor at the foot of the bed, looking at me.

"What am I doing here?" I asked

Carl spoke first, "Claire you had a seizure at school. They brought you in an ambulance and they're going to take a few tests to make sure you can go home."

"A what? That's not possible."

I started to cry. I lay on the bed, under warm blankets, but suddenly became very cold. I rubbed my knuckles where the bruises were starting to show and

I felt the burning on my cheek where I had hit the edge of my desk.

The doctor moved to the side of the bed and checked the dilation in my eyes. "We're trying to find out what caused it. I've ordered a full gambit of tests, now that you're awake, we can get things started. Your blood work is inconclusive." He scribbled something on his pad. "Try to get some rest, you're going to be here a couple of hours."

By the time I was released, he simply told me nothing came back positive and that I should make an appointment with a neurologist as soon as possible.

That night at dinner, we told the kids what had happened.

"I'm going to be taking a few days off work," I said, looking back and forth between them.

"Why? What happened?" Devon asked.

I looked over at Carl, and he nodded. "I had a seizure today as I left school. I fell and hit the tables when I went down."

"I don't understand," Adam said.

"I don't exactly know how to explain it. I just need to take some time off and rest. I don't..."

"She's going to need your help — you know around the house and all. She won't be able to do much, so we need to pitch in — all of us," Carl continued.

"How long will you be sick?" Devon asked.

"I'm not really sick, I just need to take it easy. I hope to go back to work next week sometime."

"I can help with dinner," Devon said. "And I can wash the clothes," Adam piped in.

"No, I think I can do those things. I'll just need to rest... and I might not be able to go to all your games, like I have been. I mean I'll try, but I'll have to take it day-by-day."

I thought we had done a pretty good job explaining, but Adam grew more and more uneasy. He didn't understand, I could see his confusion. His life was being turned upside down and there was nothing I could do about it.

"Who'll pick me up after school? Who'll take me to my games? What was happening to my mother? What was happening to my life?" He never said those things out loud but as we sat there, I saw his fears.

Devon tried to come across like she did. She was fourteen. If I couldn't be the mother, she would. At least as best she could. Her worries were of a different nature. She never said it, but there was fear in her eyes, too. I think she worried, if this could happen to me, the same would happen to her.

"She just needs extra naps during the day," Devon said, looking at Adam, holding her composure.

We had dinner, and together as a family watched TV, where they both fell asleep. Carl woke them and got them into bed. I turned out the lights, sat in his chair and closed my eyes. I didn't say it either, but I felt like Adam: *What was happening to my life?*

I slept off and on most of the weekend. One four-and-a-half-minute seizure had drained me of my very life. I was exhausted. I wanted to go back to work on Monday, but Carl reminded me that I had the week to recover, besides I had a doctor's appointment to make.

My week off work seemed more stressful than it should have been. My injuries became more apparent, from hitting the tables and desk, as I went down, I had bruises on my head, around my eyes and on my jaw. My hands were also scratched and bruised. I didn't know where they came from until I found out I fought the paramedics as they tried to get me on the gurney. I'd been having continual headaches since the fall. Tylenol wasn't helping.

I called Dr. Benning on Saturday night and told him what had happened. He changed my appointment, so it would be easier to get a ride. I must have looked awfully pale because when I came in, he stepped back. I had rested all weekend, but I still must have looked weary.

He opened the door and waited for me to walk past. "How are you feeling?" He asked.

"Still a little shell-shocked," I said.

"Do you understand what happened?"

"Well, I did some research and it looks like I may or may not have had them before, but I never remember anything specific. I remember fazing out and falling, a lot."

He went on to explain the medical details of them and what he knew. He was more reassuring than the other doctor, but then again, maybe I was just hearing what I wanted to hear.

"How does it feel having people take care of you?"

"I hate it. I'm a burden."

"There is nothing wrong in letting people help you."

"So, what happens now?"

"You take it easy so you can get your life back. It was likely brought on by stress."

"But I had two more over the weekend. I didn't tell Carl. What if I can't go back to work?"

"Slow down. Let's take one seizure at a time."

"The doctor in the hospital said I may have been

having these my whole life and just didn't know it. He said it was unlikely that they just popped up out of the blue. I fell a lot when I was a kid, breaking bones, tripping over absolutely nothing. They kept calling me clumsy, and then they laughed."

"Do you remember the first time?"

I let out a small laugh. "Like it was yesterday."

"Tell me about it. Just talk as you remember. I won't interrupt you. When you get it all out, we can talk about it."

I sat back, closed my eyes and allowed myself to go to that time.

I was about seven, I remember walking along a side street, excited to get back to the activities of summer camp at the playground. I had rested for over an hour, but as I walked along my body began to ache. Randomly, when I looked up, I saw stars floating in and out of my vision. Just as I reached the chain-linked fence, I stumbled and fell. I didn't remember the gravel under my feet or crossing the street to the playground. I tried to open my eyes, literally pushing my lids apart, but an unimaginable weight held them down. It shut out the world.

When my eyes finally opened, I stood at the gate, not remembering where I was. I looked at my scraped and bloody knees and wondered how the gravel had gotten itself so deep into my skin. When I looked up, Andi, the camp counselor stood in front of me.

"What happened?" she asked.

"I don't know," I looked around, still unsure where I was.

"You have blood on your leg."

I stared at my legs.

"Come on, let's get you cleaned up. Your sister can help you."

"No. Please don't tell her."

"Do you want me to call your mother, have her come get you?"

"No. Don't do that either." I stood silent, too scared to look up.

I walked away from Andi but could feel her eyes on me. Once in the lavatory, I took a paper towel and soaked it in the basin. I folded it into fours, cleaned the blood and gravel from my leg, then folded it back the other way. I rubbed it down my elbows and brushed away the dirt. I stared at the girl in the mirror, searching for what my mind wouldn't let me remember. I had no idea what happened.

I went back into the clubhouse and slipped onto the bench before my sister could see anything. Later in the day I saw Andi talking to her.

I finished my potholder, and in the next hour glued the pinecones together. At five o'clock Andi locked the door and waved as we walked home. As I had done in the morning, I followed behind my sister and prayed that nothing had been said.

"Andi told me you fell today," she said, slowing up and waiting for me.

"Are you going to tell?" I asked, almost frozen in my steps.

"It's no big deal. Just stop being so clumsy."

After everyone turned up their driveways, she slowed down and put her arm around my shoulder.

"Don't worry. I won't tell."

"Claire, look at me. Why didn't you want to tell your mother?"

I focused on Dr. Benning. "I was afraid she'd be mad, then I wouldn't be able to go to the playground anymore. I had learned to keep secrets when I was young, and this was a secret I was too terrified to tell anyone."

"Why were you so terrified all the time, I mean of your mother finding things out about you? You were a kid. Kids do that. They fall. They get dirty."

"I remember them telling me that they could send me back."

Dr. Benning didn't say anything. He didn't write anything down, he just stared at me.

"Send you back?" I saw his confusion. I smiled.

"I know it sounds ridiculous, even to say it out loud."

"Where would they have sent you?"

"I guess back to the orphanage. They never told me that part."

"I am so sorry. You should never have been told that. Not ever."

"Oh, trust me, I was a really good kid." I laughed.

"I bet you were."

He adjusted his chair and brought his pad back down to his lap. "When do you see the neurologist?"

"Wednesday."

"Call me when you get more details. I may want you to come in twice a week until you can get past all of this."

The hour was gone, but I didn't remember most of it, except for Dr. Benning telling me he was sorry. I thought about the next few days when the seizures might return. Would I be walking down the hall, in the grocery store? Would the kids be with me? I stood up to leave, wobbly from the conversation and the unknown, even though today Dr. Benning had only given me words of reassurance.

"Claire, you will get through this."

"Really? I don't know. I think this might be the apple that I'll choke on."

He laughed. This time I didn't, I didn't even smile. I just looked at him.

"I'm really scared, this time."

28

The next morning, I woke up around 5:30, with an eerie dream lingering in my head. I was with an old woman, in a beautiful garden with a small pond. Both of us carried a basket. My basket held two swans. Hers had pots of flowers, ready to be planted.

She said we couldn't go anywhere because we were waiting for the swans to die. Instead of the swans dying, the old woman died. As soon as she passed, the swans flew into the water. I just stood there and watched.

The dream reminded me of Sally's garden, but the old woman wasn't Sally. I had never seen her before and hoped I never saw her again. I had no idea what the dream meant, but I sure hoped I was one of the swans.

I got up and took a shower, letting the steaming water fall around me. I closed my eyes, balanced myself by putting my hands against the wall. For a few minutes I reveled in the peace. The water came down like a storm, warm, soothing, and for just a minute I let myself forget.

I pulled on my jeans and sweatshirt, then some sandals. I braided my long hair and brushed back the bangs. I put on a dash of lipstick and blush and went into the living room. I can do this I told myself.

Dr. Benning had said I was resilient. The day passed quickly getting the kids out the door, things picked up, and random puttering in the garden.

Carl came through the door ready to take me to my two o'clock appointment with Dr. Turner. We drove to the appointment saying nothing. I knew Carl. He felt guilty because he couldn't fix things. He would stew until he could figure it out, then be right as rain.

I had another seizure earlier in the day, hitting my shoulder as I fell down the hallway. I didn't tell him. I picked myself up and vowed that I would be stronger.

Once in the doctor's office, we filled out all the emergency papers and waited to be called in. It took longer than we had expected, but finally a nurse called us back. Carl took my hand and we followed her to the last door on the left.

Dr. Turner stood up when we walked in and reached out his hand to both of us. We took a seat and for the next hour he asked me questions I couldn't have imagined. I gave him every piece of history I could think of. I told him about the falls when I was a kid, the black-outs in college.

"They called me clumsy," I laughed.

"I don't think you were clumsy," he said, not smiling. "But I don't know what's causing them. It could be stress, or there could be a tumor, or very simply you could have epilepsy. I won't know until we run specific tests, but I'm going to give you a prescription to try to control them, for the time being. Do you have any questions?"

"What are the side effects of the meds?"

"A lot, I'm afraid," he said. "You might need to take more time off than you had expected."

"How long will the side effects last?"

"Ten days, maybe more," Dr. Turner adjusted his papers.

"Shit," I said under my breath.

"I am sorry Claire, but you need to take the stress off. I'm going to make a recommendation you aren't going to like."

"You want me to quit my graduate program, don't you?" I asked.

"Yes. I'm afraid if you don't, these won't stop. You can't quit your family. You can't quit your job, but you can take some of the extra stressors off. I think that might be one of them."

"I really wanted this." I tried not to let it show, but I dropped my head so he wouldn't see. I'd worked so hard, and now it was gone, just like that. For three years I had tried to get into this program and had been rejected, finally, I was there. Now I had to quit.

"You can always go back when you're feeling better. I'm going to schedule some tests, then I want to see you in two weeks. I don't think you should drive for a while, at least until we get these under control." I listened to his words, and pretty soon they all mushed together. All I heard was that everything in my life had changed.

We stood up, shook his hand again, and walked out to the nurse's station. She handed Carl a sheet with the names and places for the tests they had scheduled. I sat in the car and didn't say anything. What was there to say?

"Are you okay?"

I looked over at Carl. "No, I'm terrified. Everything is going to shit. I can't drive. I won't be able to go anywhere. I'm losing everything I worked so hard for."

"It's just for a little bit, until they can get a handle on what's going on."

"Can we just go home?"

We stopped at the pharmacy, then went home. I took the capsules as he directed. He said the headaches should stop within a few days.

The next morning, I woke with the same headache, but forced myself up to get everyone off to school. I went back to our bedroom, closed the shades, flipped on the television, and watched a movie without paying attention. After a while I covered my head with the pillow. Even with the new meds, nothing stopped the pain, but I felt grateful I hadn't had a seizure going down the hall. It didn't take long for the side effects to begin. The rash started on my arm around my wrist, then traveled up and around to my shoulder. It didn't take long to become familiar with every part of me.

I closed my eyes and didn't open them until after five in the afternoon. I didn't hear any noise coming from the kitchen. I didn't hear Carl fixing dinner for the kids, and I didn't hear them open the door to come in and talk to me, then leave, when I wouldn't wake up.

At seven, I got up to take medicine and go to the bathroom. I looked in the mirror and realized that after sleeping all day, I truly looked like shit. My face was swollen, even my tongue. I went back to bed and fell back asleep.

I woke up again at nine. When I flipped on the light, and looked into the mirror, everything was worse. I immediately called the exchange, who connected me to Dr. Turner. He said I needed to hang on for ten days. If the side effects hadn't diminished by Monday, I was to stay home. It was Wednesday. I stayed in most of the week. Carl took the kids shopping when they got home from school on Thursday and fixed them dinner.

I slept through it. I slept through everything.

When the house was empty and I found a little energy on Friday, I went out to the garden. Dr. Benning called, and we talked for a while, but I really had nothing to say except to complain about the meds and their side effects. He rescheduled my appointment. By Friday at three, things were not looking any better, so I called the office at school and talked to the secretary, letting them know my absence was indefinite.

"Claire don't worry about anything," she said.

"I have lesson plans, and papers." I heard myself crying into the phone.

"You don't need to worry about any of that. Rest and come back to us. Everything will be fine. Joan is helping your sub. Don't worry, she knows your books."

I hated this new life. It was not mine. This was not who I was, or how I spent my days. I tried to stay awake to be in the garden, hoping the sun would make me feel better but the pills were draining me of every ounce of energy.

After coming back from therapy, on Monday afternoon, I forced myself to stay in the garden. I picked up a book and allowed myself to fall into it. I heard a tap at the door. I ignored it, and went on reading, but then the bell kept coming back in unison, like a song, or a message. I got up to peek, but forgot I had left the front door unlocked, and in the hallway there Sally stood. Her hair tied back, with strands falling over her face. She wore a wide brimmed hat, and one of her long flowing dresses.

"So, when were you going to tell me?"

"Tell you that my life's a mess, and that things will never be the same?"

"No, tell me you were sick and that you needed help, like you would have expected from me."

She hugged me and I tried to cover my face, but she noticed the swelling right away.

"No need to hide. I've seen worse."

"I'm sorry. I should have called." I pulled Chelsea back so Sally could walk through. Sally bent down, petted her, then followed me through the entry hall. "I was in the garden. Can I get you anything to drink? Tea? Lemonade?"

"You go on and sit down. Let me get you something. What do you want?"

"I have water on the stove, tea would be good. I'll help."

"Find me the cups and then go outside. I'll do the rest."

I pulled two over-sized mugs from the cupboard and placed them on the counter. I grabbed two tea bags, along with the sugar bowl, and set them in front of her. I stood and watched.

"You go on, sit, I'll be there before you know it."

I left the kitchen and went out the sliding doors. I fluffed up the pillows, took a seat, and waited. This was nothing like Sally's garden, but in time the jasmine would fill in the trellis, and the lavender and orange blossom together would fill the air.

"Okay, here I come." Sally carried the two mugs, leaned forward and handed me a steaming mug.

"It's hot."

"Yes, I noticed."

Sally took a seat and looked out around the garden. "It's nice. You're doing a very good job. You've come a long way. I'm impressed."

We sat together on the swing. Chelsea took her place under the chair. I watched as Sally settled in, reaching down to scratch behind the dog's ears.

"Okay, tell me what's going on? When I called, Carl gave me some details, but I need to hear it from you."

"I went down at school, and now I'm on meds that make me swell up like a friggin' balloon. Look at them." I held my hands out for her to see.

Sally leaned forward and took them in hers. "It'll go down soon."

"I don't think so. I've been taking the medicine since last Monday. A week. Nothing has changed."

"Carl said you'd be off work for a while. Do you know how long?"

"At least another week. I'm hoping once the swelling goes down, the meds will take hold."

"Have you had any more?"

"Four, since the first one. They make me so tired."

"You better pay attention to the way you're feeling. How are you sleeping?"

"That is all I'm doing. I have no energy. The doctor did say it was partially because of the pills. I sleep all the time." Chelsea nudged my hand.

"They don't want me back at work," I said, feeling the depression take over me.

"How do you know that?"

"A parent already called the school to have their kid taken out of my class because…" I paused.

"What did they say?"

"That I was an epileptic."

"Shame on them. That doesn't mean anything."

"It means everything."

"Are you going to let them get to you?"

"They already did."

"Then shame on you."

I turned and looked at Sally a bit shocked by her response. "Me?"

"You're better than any of them. Get rested, get better, and go back and show them."

"Sally, I'm fighting migraines, I'm exhausted, and I'm afraid to go outside. The depression is... I'm not strong enough to fight all of it."

"Well no shit. Not all together, no one is," Sally said. "You have to handle one thing at a time. For example, do one thing productive each day, maybe wash the dishes, or read some from your book. Hell, clean your bathroom. If you can do one thing each day, you will have accomplished something."

"And the headaches?"

"I have some tea that might help relax you a bit. I'll bring it by. If all else fails, tell your doctor you're not getting any better and you need meds for it. No point in suffering when you shouldn't."

"I already have meds, remember?"

"You need to give it time."

"I don't have time."

"That's all you have." Sally let Chelsea rub against her legs, and she rubbed her neck.

"And the depression? What do I do about that?"

"What are you doing now?"

I raised the sleeve to my shirt and showed her the marks on my arm. She reached over and ran her hands across the red marks. She looked up at me with the saddest of eyes, then wiped my tears away.

"Oh baby, you can't be doing this. You got to promise you'll stop. Did you tell your doctors?"

"No. Well, Dr. Benning knew, but I told him I'd stopped."

"You better tell both doctors."

"No, I won't do it any more." I looked straight into Sally's eyes. "I promise."

"You can't promise anything, not where you are right now. You have to tell them."

"Carl is struggling with the whole idea of my being sick. He wants so much to help me, to fix everything, but there doesn't seem to be anything to fix. I'm not a radio he can take apart and put back together."

"Claire, you know there's no magic formula, no pill that will make this better. No super glue to make things whole."

"Sally, I don't know if I can get through this."

"When is your doctor appointment?"

"Three," I said. "Why?"

"I'll take you. You need someone with you if you are having those tests, especially the MRI."

"Where's Carl? He said he'd take off work to come."

"I told him I'd take care of you, this afternoon. You also have a prescription that needs to be picked up. The doctor ordered it for the depression."

"How do you know all this stuff?"

"Carl is taking good care of you, I'm just trying to give him a break."

Sally stayed all afternoon. She held my hand through the MRI as I slipped inside the tube, and she wiped the tears when I came out. I waited in the car as she went into the drug store. I took the new medicine right away, and after a few more errands we were done.

"You ready to go home?"

"Yes. I need to get dinner going."

"No. We're stopping on the way home to get some pizza. No cooking for you tonight."

Instead of pizza she stopped at a deli, and picked up enough food for a few nights, meat, pilaf, vegetables, then drove me home. "Thank you," I reached out and hugged her. I held on so tight, I was afraid if I let her go, she'd melt right into the floor.

I finally let go and watched from the door as she walked back to her car. I went into the kitchen when she had gone and put the dinners on plates, covered them in foil, and placed them in the oven to keep warm. As much as I wanted to eat with them, I couldn't. I left a note for Carl.

Dinner is in the oven. I'm in the bedroom. Wake me when you're home.

I took the bag of medicines with me and dropped them on the bed.

I read each label carefully, then placed them on the counter in the bathroom. I slipped out of my clothes and pulled one of Carl's shirts from the drawer and pulled it over my head. I set the alarm, so I'd wake up enough to take the pills as needed. I fell asleep buried deep beneath the covers.

* * * * * *

I returned to work, and took it minute by minute. The side effects were getting worse. Over the weeks my hair began to fall out, and I started having tremors. My arms shook, and my legs bounced up and down. I couldn't control them. I couldn't keep my feet flush to the floor, or my hands flat on a table.

I never knew if my loss of balance was because of the seizures, or because of the medicine. I was supposed to be gaining weight, but I had such an upset stomach from the meds, I lost weight. But of everything, I couldn't remember the things that I had once known. I forgot names of friends, authors, characters in books even family. Everything that I had known and had been second nature, slipped away and I couldn't do anything to get it back.

I couldn't make sense of anything.

The doctor visits increased and every two weeks the seizure meds were changed. Nothing worked. It was almost Christmas and I had been off work for over a month. I was a zombie, but worst of all, the seizures continued at an unruly pace.

* * * * * *

Carl came with me as I went in to meet with another new doctor. I stepped in and took a seat. I first noticed his glasses, which he took off the minute he looked up.

"I'm Dr. Clarkson. Dr. Turner sent all your reports over."

"So what did you learn about me?"

"Good news and bad news."

"Give me the good first."

"No tumors."

I fell back into the chair relieved, and grabbed hold of Carl's hand "Okay, the bad news."

"I don't know what's causing all of this. I think it might be stress, but Dr. Turner said you had a fall as a child, down some stairs?"

"I wasn't given a lot of details, but yes. I have a scar, right here." I pointed at it, placing my finger to my forehead.

"It could have caused some damage, I would need more extensive tests. But for now, to lower your stress, we need to monitor the seizures. How are they doing?"

"Terrible. I've had six drops, and about ten petti mals, you know, I kinda just space out." Carl looked over at me. I hadn't told him about the drops, and looking at him that moment, filled me with guilt. He squeezed my hand.

"Let's still stay on those meds for now. It hasn't been that long yet."

"What about the headaches?" I asked.

"Migraines?"

"They're getting more and more out of control. The more I take the meds for the seizures; the more the headaches go into full cycle."

"I have something that might help, but they're shots."

I cringed. "Seriously? I hate shots."

"They'll get rid of your headaches. Is that reason enough?"

It was all coming together. The one accident, or fall, whatever it was, in the orphanage, might have changed everything. It impacted everything in my life.

When I approached my mother, she had a broken memory about the seizures, only that I fell all the time, sometimes breaking bones, others, just popping up, like nothing had happened.

In college I didn't connect the falls or the migraines to anything, only that I just seemed to have a tougher time than everyone else. I had no idea what the future would hold.

29

I didn't feel the wall crack when I slammed into it. It was solid, but like Humpty Dumpty, I splattered into pieces to the floor. The headaches continued, even with the shots they changed, but never really stopped. They moved across my forehead and affected my vision.

Toward the end of April, I pulled into the school parking lot. I had been back to work for four months and I was no better. I sat in the car for the longest time, finally I heard a tap on the window. I looked up and saw a fellow teacher. I rolled down the window.

"Claire, are you okay?"

"I can't do this anymore."

"Do what?"

"Come to work every day and pretend I'm not going crazy."

"What do you mean?"

"I see how they look at me, like I'm going to crumble any minute."

"No one is doing that."

"Yes, they are. I see it every day." I laid my head back on the headrest, closing my eyes, unable to even focus.

"What are you going to do?"

"Can you take me home? The headaches, the stares, everything. I can't do it anymore."

"Ok, wait here. I'll be right back."

So I waited. Then without even realizing it, I started to cry. I pressed the palms of my hands against my forehead. When I opened my eyes, I saw her coming from the main office, but she wasn't alone. The principal came toward the car.

"What do you need me to do?" He asked, bending down toward the window.

"I've really tried," I blurt it out. "I really tried, but I can't."

"Ok, we're going to drive you home now. Will that be all right?"

"Yes."

"I'll call Carl and he'll meet you at home. Everything is going to be fine."

"I don't know when I'll come back."

"There is little over a month left. Don't worry about that. We'll have everything taken care of. You just need to get better."

I slipped over to the passenger seat, and Judy jumped in the car, without a word, she started the engine, and pulled out of the driveway. I dropped my head, as I didn't want anyone to see me.

"I didn't know it was that bad. I should have realized what you were going through," Judy said, as she stopped at the light.

"How could you? I never told anyone. I was so sure I could handle it on my own. I'm sorry."

"Don't be sorry. You've been through a lot. You just need some rest."

"Carl's going to be upset."

"Oh honey, no he isn't. He loves you."

When we pulled to the curb, Carl stood in the driveway. Judy helped me out of the car and Carl took me in his arms.

"Come on, let's go lie down."

"Okay. I'm just so tired."

"I called Dr. Benning and told him what happened. He thinks you should take the rest of the school year off. So do I."

"I can't do that."

"Yes. Claire, this is wearing you out. You can't even think any more. The headaches are so bad, most of the time, you don't even know where you are."

I lay down and closed my eyes, but I could hear Carl and Judy down the hall. Their voices melded together, Chelsea had jumped on the bed, laying her head across my stomach. With the lights out and the shades drawn I slept through the afternoon, past dinner and into the next day.

I spent the next month going to therapy, going for walks, reading when I could, but mostly sleeping. I had been given my license back, so I drove myself to wherever I needed to go. My time in therapy became more intense. I spent much of the time crying, but not really understanding what I cried about.

When I wasn't crying, I was sullen and wouldn't talk, many times leaving a session where I had barely said anything. I left letters for Dr. Benning, but never seemed to have the strength to talk about them. I continued cutting myself, even though I had told him I'd stop.

Late at night the blood came quicker, streams of droplets sat on the top of my leg. It didn't stop the pain on the inside, but it stopped me from thinking about anything.

"So how are you handling the depression?" Dr. Benning asked during one of our sessions.

"I thought I would be handling it better, but…."

"No, really Claire how are you doing. I have a feeling you are trying to fool me."

I sat back in the chair, staring at him. He knew something wasn't right. I pulled up the sleeve to my sweater and put my hand on my knee.

"What's this?" He didn't move his eyes from my arm.

"This is how I've been handling the depression."

"I thought you stopped?"

"I tried. When I went to Ireland, I did. And when I got home, I was okay, but then the seizures and everything, I just fell apart. I don't have a reason. I did stop drinking."

I felt bad looking at the expression on his face. I had done it. I had fooled him, or at least I thought I had.

"So, all this time when I thought you were pulling it together?"

"I'm sorry. I should have told you, but I was embarrassed. And…" I paused.

"What?" He perched his chin under his hand and leaned forward, his jaw tight.

"It sounds stupid, but it was the only thing I felt I could control. Everything has been out of reach: my family, my job, even my house. I'm taking a shit load of pills. I'm a mess. They're sending me to Portland to have the seizures monitored."

"Claire, are you cutting anywhere else?"

"On my legs."

"Oh Claire." He shook his head and leaned back.

"So, that's how I'm dealing with it."

"Why did you pick that route?"

"I never saw it as a choice."

"You had me the whole time. You had someone to talk to. Why wouldn't you tell me?" He asked, his eyes sad, his expression broken.

"You don't get the embarrassed part? What I said?"

"If you keep doing this, I'm not going to be able to trust you."

"I know I'm sorry. Are you mad?"

"I'm not mad, just disappointed. I wasn't able to give you the strength to tell me."

"Now, now, Dr. Benning, you aren't that powerful, as you would say to me."

"Okay, so what are we going to do about this? Are you going to stop?" He asked.

"You mean can I promise you that I won't hurt myself anymore?"

"Yes, that's exactly what I mean."

"No, I can't do that. You probably won't understand, but I get a satisfaction from it. I don't mean that in a weird way."

"Not taken in a weird way, but you know you can't keep doing this, right?" Dr. Benning put his pen down and crossed his arms over his chest.

"I don't want to keep doing it, but at night when I can't handle the pain... and no one is there. I can't guarantee anything."

He leaned down and opened his drawer and pulled out a sheet a paper and placed it on his desk.

"I need you to read this, and then sign it."

"What am I signing?"

"A contract that you won't hurt yourself."

"I don't know if I can do that?"

"If you can't I can't let you leave," he said, saddened by what was to come. "I'd have to call in a 5150."

"You'd do that?"

"You leave me no choice."

"Jesus, I'm not trying to kill myself. I'm never going to cut any deeper."

"You don't know that. You could get so caught up, that before you know it, it would be too late."

"That's bullshit, and you know it. I explained what it was like. Does that sound suicidal?"

I sat back in the chair and stared at him. I felt betrayed by the one person I had trusted for years. Our eyes locked and he wouldn't look away.

"I thought you cared about me?"

"More than you'll ever know, but I have to know you will be safe."

"Fine, Doctor... I'll sign it."

"Why are you signing it?" He asked.

"I get it...." He touched my hand as I was about to sign. "No. Really, I promise, I won't cut myself, and if I think about it I'll call you no matter what time. I know what this means."

I felt the tears building up deep inside, but nothing came. I remained stoic. I got up, went to his desk and signed his document. He took hold of my hand and squeezed. I looked up.

"Please don't make me act on this or regret my decision."

"I know, I won't. I promise."

We ran out of time talking about whether I would consider continuing to hurt myself, but the session ended with Dr. Benning asking me to contact Dr. Jensen, a new psychiatrist. I knew what she was going to suggest, and I didn't want to hear it. She would recommend that I enter a psych ward, especially since I had been so reluctant to tell Dr. Benning that I would not stop cutting.

My first meeting with Dr. Jensen came three days after signing the contract. I did everything in my power to stay focused. I didn't want to go to Willow Creek, to leave my family. I took my meds, but the headaches woke me up at random hours of the night. The seizures came at random. I forced myself to stay in bed, but one of those nights, I was drawn out to the garden. I left the wine in the kitchen and took a paring knife. My rationale was if I could hold the knife and not use it...

I thought about Alice and Sr. Bridget. I thought of what it must have felt like to be raped. I pulled my legs up tight on the chair and held my ankles. I thought about Sally and my kids, maybe they would be better off without me.

Shit, that would be awful, but what was I to them? Always sick? I couldn't work, couldn't go to their events out of fear of what might happen. Maybe it would be better, Carl could meet someone who was everything I wasn't. I was being ridiculous... was I? The pain was more than I could handle, I wasn't strong enough. What if I didn't get better?

I didn't even realize what I was doing, the first cut was small, just above my ankle bone, where a bracelet would have sat. There was no blood, so I went deeper. The cut was white, like a chalk mark. I did it a third time and a tiny trickle sat on top of the edge of the cut. I stared at it. I had broken my promise.

I was afraid the pain would never stop.

I met Dr. Jensen on a Friday afternoon at her office. I had made it a point to dress nicer than when I went to see Dr. Benning. I didn't want her to think I was crazy. I wore slacks and my red cashmere sweater set. I had cut my hair a few weeks earlier, so I was sure that my newly shaped bob looked relaxed, but stylish.

Her outside office was very different from Dr. Benning. She had plants in every corner, and cushioned chairs. A secretary called me in and took me down the hall. She was at her desk, but stood the minute I entered the room.

"My name's Jennifer, won't you have a seat."

She was beautiful, couldn't have been over thirty-five. She had on stilettos and a pencil skirt, with a matching jacket, very formal, business like.

"And you're Claire?"

"Yes." I took a seat and watched as she crossed her legs and clasped her hands around her knees.

"I've been talking to Dr. Benning, it seems you've been having a rough time of it."

"I've been sick with seizures and headaches. I'm a little overwhelmed."

"Why don't you tell me about it."

I rubbed my shoulder and arched my back. *Would I tell her about the night before, about the blood, and the headaches?*

"I have a lot of side effects from the medicine and they can't seem to get them under control." I looked out the window and took a deep breath. She didn't try to interrupt me or put words in my mouth. I liked that. "I hate that I had to quit work."

I paused, and she watched me, then waited.

"Tell me about the depression."

"That it overtakes me? That I feel like I can't breathe? Is that what you want to know?"

She gave me a faint smile. "Yes, tell me about that."

I fell silent. I moved in my chair, I adjusted my purse. I dropped my keys to the floor and picked them up, but I said nothing.

"Is this how it feels?"

I felt the tears coming down. I couldn't talk about it. I was afraid if I said the wrong thing, she would see that I needed to be sent away.

"I'm scared, all the time." That was the only truth I knew.

"Do you ever try to hurt yourself?" She asked.

"Don't you already know the answer to that? You said you talked to Dr. Benning. He knows what I've done."

"Can you tell me about it?"

"Yes. I can tell you that I wake up in the middle of the night and I go outside in my garden. I try to find some peace, but it doesn't come, so I cut myself to know that I am alive."

"When is the last time you did it?"

"Last night."

"Do you do it to harm yourself?" She didn't have a yellow pad anywhere on her desk. She just sat there, with her arms clasped around her knees.

"I don't want to die, not really, but I can't seem to help myself."

She got up and moved over to her desk. I knew what she was getting. It was the contract that I signed with Dr. Benning. She brought it over to her chair with a pen and set it on the coffee table between us.

"Can you sign this?" She asked, holding out the paper.

My eyes blurred, and I wiped the tears away.

"Yes," I said, sitting up straight. "But it won't mean anything, not right now."

She set the pen on the contract and went to her desk. I watched her pick up the phone, dial a number, and wait. She turned away from me. I signed the contract. In a few minutes she hung up the phone. I don't know who she called, or what was said. I did know that it wasn't good.

"I'm worried about you. You can't seem to get a handle on the depression. You say you don't want to hurt yourself, but how can I know that something won't happen that will set off a trigger."

"You don't, and I don't either, but here," I handed her the paper. "I signed your contract. I don't want to be sent away. I have my children to think about."

"But I have to know that you're safe. You need some help, some structure. You can get that in a hospital."

This time I didn't stop the tears. *What was the point?*

"My secretary is making arrangements for Monday. I will give you the weekend to settle things with your family. You are to report by noon. It won't be that bad. You'll get the tools you need to get stronger. Dr. Benning will come and see you as well."

"How long?" I asked.

"Two weeks?"

"Fuck." I fell back in the chair. I didn't care anymore.

"I don't want anyone coming to see you until after the first week. Your husband can come the second week, but I don't want your children to come, at all. It might scare them. You can talk to them on the phone."

"I have to go two weeks and not see my kids? I've never done that before."

"Claire, I know this is hard, but you'll be surprised what can happen in two weeks."

"I'll fall deeper, you know," I said through my tears.

"I know it will get worse before it gets better, but you will turn this around. Dr. Benning tells me you are a strong woman. You won't let this keep you down."

"I've been trying for so long."

And so to finish out the hour we continued to talk, mostly me, telling her things I had already told Dr. Benning, but no secrets. I wouldn't give those up.

"Please don't make me regret this, but I'm going to let you go home to your family for the weekend. Dr. Benning will call you tomorrow to check in. I've let him know everything."

She reached out and shook my hand. Her skin was soft, her nails manicured. I don't know why I noticed that, maybe because mine weren't. I headed toward the door.

"Claire?" I turned toward her. "Don't make me regret this."

Shit, why was everyone saying that to me?

30

Late on a sunny spring Monday, I kissed the kids before they left for baseball and softball practice. I made promises I knew I couldn't keep, but I had to give them hope. *I had to give myself hope.*

Carl dropped me off at the double door, I got out and he came around with my suitcase. He wasn't allowed to come in, so we kissed and hugged at the door. I was so torn about saying good-bye to him for two weeks. In a way I knew I needed it, but in another I just wanted to pretend I was normal. I wanted to get back in the car and go have dinner somewhere, then go home and fall asleep in his arms. I even thought of suggesting it, but I knew I had to get well. I had to stop cutting myself and I had to find a way out of the hole I'd put myself in.

First, I checked in my belongings. I wasn't allowed any bottles of mouth wash or perfume. I couldn't have a belt. They did allow me a pen for writing, which surprised me because of my last actions. A girl took me to my room at the end of the hall but had to come out for a group meeting at seven o'clock. Some of the meetings weren't mandatory, but they took role in others.

My roommate's name was Cindy. I thought it would have been more appropriate to have someone closer to my age, but she was going home in three days, then I'd have the room to myself for the rest of the time. There were moments I remember very clearly, meeting Jenny, taking a walk every day around the grounds that were hidden behind a six-foot brick wall. I could hear the cars on the other side, and every now and then sirens, or the screech of tires, but it was peaceful, and being spring, all the flowers were in bloom. We had a set time to do everything and unless you got sick or were in therapy you had to go by the schedule they posted throughout the hallways.

Breakfast 7:00 – 8:00
Groups 8:30 – 9:30
Individual therapy 10:00 – 11:00
Lunch 11:30 to 12:45
Arts and Craft 1:00 – 3:00
Groups 4:00 – 5:00
Dinner 5:15 – 6:15
Meditation/Calming groups 7:00 – 8:00
Groups 8:00 – 9:00
Free time 9:00 - 10:00
Lights Out 11:00

It could make for a long day, with every minute accounted for. Sometimes the groups weren't groups, but team building activities. I was not much of a team player, so I usually dreaded those activities.

Dr. Benning came every other day at 10:00. When he wasn't there I had to see the house therapist. There were three of them and they saw patients throughout the day. I felt so special that Dr. Benning, who actually drove across town to spend time with me, but he also made sure I talked to the other therapist.

We'd meet in a small conference room, the chairs weren't very comfortable, and it was always cold.

"How is it going?"

"Well I haven't cut myself if that's what you want to know." To this day, I never understood my sarcasm to him, but he chuckled and asked again.

"It has been two days, how are you?"

"I'm sorry. I'm good, really. I lose my roommate today. I've really been trying to focus on the groups. I've taken them very serious, except the team building crap. I hate that. You know, falling back and having to trust someone is going to catch you?"

"Don't you trust anyone?"

"I don't know anyone."

"It will get better."

"No, it won't. Once I start to trust someone, they leave and someone new comes in and it starts all over again. I'm just not good at that."

"Have you been sleeping? Any bad dreams?"

"I've done okay. I know I've been dreaming, but when I wake up I can't remember anything. They started new meds and I keep waking up because I'm thirsty, then I have to pee."

"Did you call Carl?"

"I can't, remember? No family calls the first week."

"I could arrange for it. Do you want to?"

"No. What would I say?"

"Why don't you tell him how you're feeling?"

"I'm not ready. I want to call him when I can say I feel great and I'm ready to come home."

We continued until the hour expired. We talked about the counselors and activities, and what I needed to do to get better. Without my having to even ask, he hugged me before he left, whispering, "You're going to be just fine. You'll get through this, like you have everything else."

"Thanks. I am really trying, you know?"

"I know that," he said, looking down at me. "You always have."

I watched him go through the locked double doors and knew I had to show some signs of improvement before he came back in two days, not because I was on a timeline, but because I wanted him to know that I understood why this was so important. For both of us. I went back to my room and decided I had some time before lunch and wanted to take a shower and read.

The hot water flowed over me, down my face, my arms, my legs. I was lost in the steam, my mind seemed to spasm. I found myself down on the floor, curled in a ball. There was blood on my leg and a pen lay on the floor next to me. Then I felt the sobs heave up. The blood fled down the drain. Suddenly the shower door swung open and a woman in a pair of jeans stood over me.

"Oh my God, Claire, what have you done?"

I didn't even look up, as she helped me up and wrapped a towel around me.

"Please don't tell."

"Claire, look at your leg. What were you trying to do?"

"I don't remember doing anything. Honest. I never meant to do anything."

"We can't let this be ignored, but I'll tell you this. I won't tell, but you must," she said, slipping the pen in her pocket.

She took a tee shirt from one of my drawers

and pulled it over my head and helped me to bed. Embarrassed, I hid my head under the blankets. I couldn't explain what I'd done. And worse, I couldn't remember doing it.

Diane didn't come in right away, no one did. I fell into a deep sleep. When I woke up the room was dark, the shades down. I looked over and all of Jenny's things were gone. There was a tray on the nightstand, but I turned away, still hiding under the covers. After a longer than usual time, I heard the door open. She tapped my shoulder and pulled me toward her. I saw the short blonde hair, and bright red lips.

"What happened?"

"I don't know," I said, "I don't remember anything."

"Did you intend to hurt yourself?"

"No," I said, sitting up and leaning against the pillow.

"What were you thinking?"

"I just met with Dr. Benning and we had a good session. I decided to take a shower, change clothes, then do some reading. I feel really good, honest."

"Well something happened. Let me see your leg," she said, pulling the covers back.

She stared down at the jagged red mark against the white skin. It was still bright red. I touched it, pulling my finger away quickly."

"I don't remember doing this, I swear," I said. I started to cry.

"Okay, I want you to get up, brush your teeth, comb you hair and be in my office in ten minutes."

"Are you going to call him?"

"I don't know yet. We'll talk about it."

"Please, it won't happen again, I promise. I'll tell him on my own."

"I'll see you in a few minutes. Oh, by the way, I'm taking all your pens. You can write, but it will have to be in the rec room."

I pulled myself out of bed and slipped my jeans delicately over the open cut on my thigh. I combed my hair, brushed my teeth, and headed out the door. Janet and Diane were both sitting on the over-stuffed couch. I took a seat on the chair and folded my legs under me.

Diane looked nothing like Janet, except that they both wore bright make-up and flashy clothes, but her hair was long and brown, and she wore stilettoes, while Janet had short unmanageable blonde hair, she also wore flats. Her shoes distracted me, a bright Dodger blue, which matched her dress.

Diane and Janet were staff social workers. They ran the groups, did private sessions and monitored everyone's behavior on the ward. They got to know each of us just enough to figure out what was wrong with us, but they kept their distance, never weaving in too close. I didn't know them until the Monday I walked in, and didn't really trust telling them my deepest secrets

"Okay, so what do we do about this incident?" Janet asked.

"I'm sorry." I heard my voice begging. "I don't remember any of it happening, but it obviously did. We had a really good session, and I feel very positive."

"When was the last time you did something like this?"

"The other night. I woke up in the middle of the night, feeling funny, so I got up and went into the living room."

"Do you always cut yourself when you're feeling funny?"

"No. It was just such a desperate feeling." *Shit I kept saying the same thing.* "I don't know how to explain it," I said.

I could tell they were trying to figure out what happened, but the more I talked the more they looked at me in confusion and I couldn't blame them. *Why couldn't I remember? Why would I take a pen into a shower? And why cut myself now when things were looking up? Maybe everyone was right, I did belong in a hospital.*

"Look, I don't have any answers. I wish I did. I wish I could explain why I did that, but I can't. I want to get better. I really do."

They continued to ask questions, that I did my best to answer. "You know what, go down and get some dinner. You must be starved. You missed lunch as well."

"I'm really not hungry, more worried."

"Why?"

"You have to ask? I did something that I don't remember doing, and it was something that could change everything for me, if I can't figure it out."

"What do you mean?"

I got up from the chair and walked across the room. "I came here thinking I was dealing with depression and in a week or so, I'd be better, but I'm not getting better. And if I can't remember this, what else has happened that I don't remember?"

"Claire sometimes you have to get worse, before you get better. Maybe this is what's happening now. You have to face your fears, overcome them, and then you can come out the other side."

"What if things don't change for me?"

"If you work hard and do what you need to do, you'll find your way."

"You know, that seriously sounds like such bullshit. I don't mean to be rude or anything, but you have to admit..."

"What do you want me to say? It is all up to you. Use the tools you're getting here and from your therapist and you'll do it."

I left the office but didn't go to the cafeteria. I was hungry, but afraid I'd throw up if I tried to eat. I decided to go into the rec room and watch some TV, so I didn't have to think. I was tired of thinking through every second of my life.

On Thursday at ten o'clock I stood outside the office and waited. He was late. I knew that we were scheduled, because the nurse had told me on Wednesday that he would be there at ten. I slid down the wall and waited. I could feel my new scar through my jeans, but still, as hard as I tried, I couldn't remember the details.

When he came around the corner, I stood up to greet him. He unlocked the door and went inside. He took the chair in the far corner and I took the seat next to him.

"How are you doing?"

"We need to talk," I said, jumping right into it. "Something happened."

"Are you all right?"

"No, I'm not. I cut myself, but I don't remember doing it. I don't remember any of it."

"Okay, slow down, a little bit at a time."

"After our session last week, I went back to my room to read for a while before lunch, but then decided to take a shower. The next thing I knew, there was blood everywhere. Someone came in and helped me up and pointed out that I had cut myself on my thigh."

He didn't say anything as I relayed my story. He stared, seemingly like I wasn't there. Then he looked up and I saw it in his eyes.

"I'm sorry."

"No, it's just that it worries me."

"What?"

"That you don't remember any of it."

"I don't know what to say."

"You have been very honest, but you seem more depressed than when we suggested you come here."

I didn't want to cry in front of him. I wanted him to think I had gotten better and in the last few days I had gotten over feeling so sad, but I finally realized this sadness wasn't something that was just going to go away. No matter what Diane and Janet said, it was going to take more than just believing in myself.

"Are you taking your meds?"

"Yes. She comes in every morning with them, then she brings something in at night."

"They've increased your antidepressants. What about the headaches? Did you have a headache before you took a shower?"

"I don't think so. I can't remember any of it. I am so embarrassed."

"Don't be. How are the groups going?"

"I don't know, I missed everything yesterday."

"I don't want you to be alone. Go to the groups, stay busy, maybe even spend time outside. I want you to keep busy."

"Will that help how I'm feeling?"

"It can't make it worse. How have you been feeling?"

"Obviously, after what I did, you have to ask?"

"Come on." He ran his fingers through his hair.

"I've just been really struggling with everything. I thought with all this "therapy"...." I made quote marks with my fingers. "that I'd be doing better. I'd get it all out there, but I just keep hearing everyone else's story. It gets a little boring...." I looked up. "That's rude isn't it? I'm sorry."

"Sometimes it's just good to know that people are going through things like you are and if they can make it, so can you." He rubbed his chin, like he wanted to say something.

"I don't see how listening to their stories is making it any better."

"I know, I get it, but you might be surprised over time."

"Fine, I'll pay more attention."

"Have you met anyone?"

"Yes, I met a girl in the rec room. She's much younger than I am. Her name is Cindy. She said she's bi-polar."

"Don't get caught up in her issues."

"I don't get it. You tell me to meet people, then you tell me to watch out for them."

"I'm sure she's very nice, but sometimes it's easy to get caught up in other people's problems. Just be careful, that's all."

"Are you mad at me?" I watched him, as he kept moving around in his chair.

"No. I'm not. Just worried. I want you to get better, and I was hoping this might be the place, but maybe I was wrong."

"No. You weren't wrong." I leaned over and patted his hand. "I hate it here, but if it helps me get better, I have to do what they ask. I moved over to another chair and sat down.

"Have you had any seizures?"

"I don't think so. I mean I haven't fallen or anything, unless that's what happened in the shower, but that doesn't explain the pen."

"Okay, we have a few more minutes. Here is what I want you to do. I want you to participate in as many events as possible. Do the groups. Go outside and write if you can."

"She took my pens."

"I know, but they have pens in the rec room and you can write there, better to do it with people around, even bring your books out, read outside. And when you get that feeling, go tell someone, or call me."

"When will you be back?"

"Next week, probably Tuesday."

"What if it happens again?"

"Tell someone about your feelings. Tell Janet, call a nurse."

When he stood up I moved toward the door, opening it for him. I watched him go as I had done a few days earlier. As he turned the corner, he waved, and I waved back. I had to find a way to get through to Tuesday so I wouldn't do anything that would make things worse.

I survived the first week and actually began to participate in the events. I did everything Dr. Benning recommended and I only had to call him once, on Saturday night, when Cindy went on a manic rage and had to be restrained.

I was anxious to tell Dr. Benning about the incident, but that wouldn't happen. After dinner one of the nurses came into the rec room and handed me a message.

Claire,

I can't come to our appointment on Tuesday. I will try to be there on Wednesday afternoon. If you have an emergency tell one of the other doctors or call me.

Dr. B.

I couldn't help but feel abandoned. I felt better, but I couldn't share it with anyone. I didn't have any interest in telling Janet that I felt better because she was too wrapped up in her groups.

I didn't cut myself the rest of the time I stayed at Willow Creek. I went to every counseling session, every group session, but still stayed clear of the trust activities, I couldn't allow myself to fall into anyone's arms.

I said good-bye to everyone on Sunday afternoon, gathered my belongings, minus my pen, and went back to my life. I knew I wasn't cured of anything. I knew at any minute I might tumble down the hallway or take a knife to my leg. But I also knew, I had to find a way to put everything behind me.

31

I made it through the end of March, then the headaches came back, and the seizures broke through. I attempted to wake up each morning and pretended it was a new day. I looked at myself in the mirror and said, "this will not happen again."

And I knew that was bullshit.

For three weeks I had at least two or three seizures a day. I was exhausted, unable to sleep, so I stayed up at night in a quiet house, with my dog by my side. She couldn't prevent my seizures and she couldn't prevent me from hurting myself, but she was there. I hadn't stopped the cutting, instead I extended my range, now I remembered every move. I started slow, but each time I had a fresh place to cut and no one could see. For a while it replaced the high from the wine.

Even as I did it, I knew it was ridiculous. It accomplished nothing, but somehow it gave me the peace I had been missing. The pain on the outside diminished, while the pain on the inside wasn't getting any better. When I cut on my legs, I kept it from Dr. Benning, but there was more to my sadness than cutting my thighs. It didn't take long for things to fall apart.

* * * * * *

I sat in the car just outside Portland University Hospital watching people go through the revolving doors. I looked over at Carl, waiting. I couldn't move. Getting out of the car meant I agreed to everything. I didn't want to agree to any of it. Because of massive grand mal seizures, I was set to go through a final round of diagnostic tests to find out if I qualified for brain surgery. Most of the tests had been done locally, but for the last round we went to Portland.

"I don't think I can to do this," I said, watching Carl rub his hands across the steering wheel. He looked over at me, pulled me close to him, then kissed my eye lids.

"Do you want me to take you home?" He whispered into my neck.

"No. I want you to make the seizures go away. Can you do that?"

"No. I can't."

"Then what can you do?" I asked.

"I can walk you through the door. I'll call you every night, take care of the kids, but I can't guarantee you anything else."

I watched him get out of the car, come around to my side, and pause, staring through the window. He didn't have any answers either. He took my hand as I stepped out of the car. I brushed away the tears that collected in the ridge of my nose. He took hold of my purse and suitcase, as I held onto his hand. He guided me up the sidewalk. Once inside the revolving doors, the nurse came and greeted us.

"Good afternoon, Mr. and Mrs. Hamilton, my name

is Jenny, I'll be taking you upstairs, Mrs. Hamilton. I'll give you a few minutes. When you are ready, I'll be at the desk."

Carl let go of my hand and pulled me close, taking hold of my chin so I could see his eyes. He kissed each cheek, and I dropped my head, nuzzling in his shoulder.

"Can't we just leave?" I whispered into his chest.

"No. You have to do this. I'll call you tonight," he said, handing me my purse.

It physically hurt to let go of his hand, like a burn going through my entire body. I knew what I was to experience before I'd see him again. I dreaded every minute of what was to come. I watched him go back out the doors.

"Let's go upstairs, Claire." I followed her to the elevator. "As I told you, I'll be your nurse while you're here."

"Where are you taking me?"

"You'll be on the psych ward while you get through your initial testing."

"What testing is that?" I asked. I expected to be adorned in my new headgear.

"You will be given a psychological evaluation to see about the surgery. Didn't the doctor tell you?"

"I guess I didn't understand."

"Based on your previous testing you might qualify for the epilepsy surgery, but it is quite extensive, and they need to do a psychological work-up to see if you're ready for it emotionally."

"I'm ready for the seizures to stop so I can go back to work."

"Did your doctor explain how the testing would go?"

"Yes, but I didn't realize there were evaluations to go along with it."

"Are you okay with them?"

"Sure. Can you tell me how long the testing will take?" I asked as the elevator closed.

"Just a day or two, then they'll transfer you to the seizure ward. Taylor will be administering your psychological evaluations."

As we entered the room, she motioned for me to put my suitcase in the closet. I laid my purse down when I noticed the girl in the far bed, leaning against the wall, holding a pillow across her chest and watching us. She waved at Jenny who had already left the room.

"Don't worry, she'll be back in a few minutes."

I turned toward the girl on the bed.

"I'm Donna. Welcome to Crazyville."

"My name is Claire. I don't think we're crazy." I lowered my head.

"You will be by the time you leave. The bathroom's over there," she said, pointing across the room. "If you need it before you start your testing."

In a few minutes Jenny came back and guided me down the hall.

"Understand, you can stop at any time if you become uncomfortable, or tired, or need something to drink. She is very informal, so please don't be nervous about it."

"How long will these tests take?"

"Like I said, it will take a few days."

Taylor had an oval, cheerful face, with a broad smile that streamed across her face. She looked much too young to be a doctor, wearing a small pink diamond on her left hand. I adjusted my sweater and brushed back my hair. I took a seat as Jenny left the office, closing the door.

I sat at the far end of the table while Dr. Addams flipped through the pictures, read the sentences, and asked the questions. We had been going for over two hours when things began to blur together. I had taken my shot for the headaches just before we left the house, but it was wearing off, getting harder to distinguish the pictures.

The room spun around. I couldn't focus on anything. I knew I had to get through this. I had to make her believe there were no problems, but as she continued, every picture, every question, made it harder to stay focused. I stared at the pink nail polish that matched her full lips.

"Can we stop, for just a minute?" I asked.

I slid my tongue across my teeth and over my dry lips, then brushed my hair from my eyes, holding it away from my face.

"Are you all right?"

"Yes. Could I get some water?" I stared at the young engaged doctor, who seemed to have no idea of what I was going through.

She went over to the small refrigerator in the corner of the office and pulled out two frosty bottles of water. She came back and placed both of them on the table.

I placed the bottle against my forehead and took a deep breath. I opened the bottle and took a drink, then watched her move folders around. She didn't seem to notice anything, more engrossed in her testing and what the results might be. My throat tightened as I sat there, and I could feel the sweat running down my arms and sticking to my sweater. She became a blob right in front of me, even as I rubbed my eyes to make things clearer.

"What's wrong?" She sat back, twirling her pen, then tapped it on the desk.

"Nothing. Could we take a small break? I just need a change of scenery for a few minutes."

"There is really no place to go, but there is a restroom down the hall."

"Yes, would that be all right?"

"Take all the time you need."

I came back in what seemed like only a few minutes, but I could see the frustration on her face. It tightened. The delay had inconvenienced her. She kept looking at her watch. There must have been a schedule, another appointment to get to. I, on the other hand, had nowhere to go, except back to the seizure ward to be fitted for my monitoring device and wait out my sentence.

"If at all possible we really need to finish these sections today." She positioned the cards face down on the table.

"Are you afraid of the surgery?" she asked, reaching across the table for my trembling hand.

I stared at the woman. "I am terrified. The meds can't stop the seizures, and every time I fall I break something. I never know when it's going to happen. I've stopped going outside except when I have to."

She put her pen on the table and leaned forward. "Claire, what are you feeling right now?"

"I'm feeling terrified, anxious, nervous. How is that?"

"I know this is hard."

"How could you know that?" I was being rude, and immediately apologized. "I'm sorry, I'm just having a hard time."

"You're right. I don't know. I'm sorry."

She fiddled with a single strand of blonde hair that had fallen on her neck, then stood up. I watched and waited. She held my future with the tip of her pen.

I stared through the window out into a garden that didn't seem to have an entrance. There was a bench and overgrown shrubs everywhere. Two apple trees in bloom, along with streaming roses, a lilac tree filled the crowded space. I wanted to inhale the sweet scent of the season. The breeze would have wrapped itself around me, and mingled in my hair, and calmed me for a few seconds.

In a few days I'd have the wire slid through my skull, the tabs glued to my head to monitor my every move, and the loss of all privacy for at least the next week. Cameras watching my every move, waiting for me to collapse on the floor, land against the wall, all so the lines could move up and down telling them I had seized.

Had I been in the garden, I'd have stroked the flowers, as if they were my pets keeping me company. I looked up at her, as she twirled the pen between her fingers. I turned away from the flowers, took another sip of water, and sat up straight.

"Are you ready?" She asked.

"Yes, thank you."

I felt confident. We'd completed two more tests, before the blurriness came back. I couldn't remember the words on the list.

"Do you want to try the memory tests again?" She asked.

"Yes, please."

"You sure?"

I could see her doubt. She began to read the words from her list. I had twenty-five seconds to repeat them;

"door," "tree," "bike," "fence." I knew the words, but in my mind they had disappeared. I couldn't remember the order, and that was the whole point of the test.

"Claire, what's wrong?"

"I should be able to remember. Why can't I?"

"I don't know. Do you need to stop again?"

"No. I want to finish, but I can't remember."

"I think we should stop." She went to the far end of the room and picked up the phone. I watched her polished nails hit three numbers. I couldn't hear what she said, but as quickly as she had picked up the receiver, she put it back down.

"What's wrong?" I asked, leaning forward in my chair.

"I'm going to stop now."

"No. I'll be okay. We can finish."

"No, Claire, I don't think you are, we need to stop."

I didn't know what to say.

"Tell me how you're feeling right now," she asked, closing the file.

"I don't know."

"Just tell me what comes to mind." She folded her hands across my file as the pen rolled off the desk.

"Okay, what comes to mind? Let me see. My kids, my husband, my life. I feel like I'm losing everything, and I can't get it back."

"Tell me what it's been like for you," she reached for the pen, and turned to a blank paper in the file.

"Do you know what it is like to just fall to the ground for no particular reason, or have regenerative migraines for fifteen days at a time, because of the meds you're taking? To have seizures when you're taking 3600 milligrams of Neurontin? Do you know what it is like to have your hair fall out? To not remember the names of your students? Or to repeat the same word thirty times in a row and not stop until someone touches you? Do you want me to keep going?"

"No." She gave me a half smile. "I have no idea what that's like. I'm sorry you're going through this."

"Please, don't patronize me."

"I'm not. I just want you to know I'm trying to understand." She leaned back in her chair, twirling her pen, seemingly to give her hands something to do.

"No, that's the whole point, with all due respect, everyone says they understand, but unless you've even had a few medical issues, you don't understand anything."

I began to sweat, not the kind when you're working out, or in the heat, but where goose bumps run up and down your arm, and it feels like sticky snow falling on top of you. My body shut down, my fingers numb, my toes twitching, and everything else out of control. I trembled when she asked the question I dreaded, but also after our conversation, it was almost expected.

"Claire, how often do you feel this way?"

"Do you have a scale? Once a week? Once a day?"

"Can you describe your depression?"

"Sometimes I can't breathe, and I want to crawl inside my chest."

"Have you ever tried to hurt yourself?"

I paused for a moment, looked at all four walls, then raised the sleeve of my sweater. "Yes."

"How long have you been doing this?"

"Off and on for a year or so."

I watched her staring back at me. She couldn't take her eyes off my arm, but somehow, I felt she had no idea why anyone would cut themselves. I asked myself that every time I let the knife run across my skin.

"Claire, I need to ask you something."

"I think I know what it is. I've been asked before."

"When you go back to your room can you promise me that you won't hurt yourself, I mean like try to cut yourself."

I had a choice. I could lie, or I could tell her the truth.

"I can't promise you anything right now."

32

In the room, while I waited, Donna rambled on, almost in a daze as she leaned against the wall with her pillow wrapped tight around her. Her spikey hair, obviously cut in a moment of rage, stuck out on all sides. In an odd way, it looked good on her, maybe her youth, or the shape of her face.

"So how are you liking it so far?" she asked peering out behind the pillow, like a child, playing hide and seek.

"I don't think I've been here long enough to really know."

"Well it won't take long. The food is awful, the orderlies are bitchy, and Dr. Henderson... Is he your doctor? Well...."

"No."

"Well, he's an asshole." She sat up straighter in bed, like she had something important to say.

"I don't know him," I said, wishing she'd stop talking.

Suddenly she jumped off the bed and took a seat on the dresser that divided the room. She wore torn jeans, and a USC sweatshirt. I sat back on my bed, and watched her every move.

"Do you have any money?"

"No. They told me not to bring any."

"Too bad." She twisted her nose, like a child not getting her way. "I trade with the orderlies."

As quickly as she had taken a seat on the dresser, she moved over to my bed and began picking through my clothes in my open suitcase.

"What are you doing?" I closed the suitcase, almost catching her fingers, but she must have seen it coming.

"Just looking. Don't worry I'm not going to steal anything. God, old people are so bitchy."

"No. we just don't like people going through our things. Would you like me to go through yours?" I said, hoping that would quiet her down.

"Oh hell, I don't care. Do whatever you want."

My psychology had not worked, she even lifted the cover to my suitcase. This time I got up from the bed, took the suitcase, zipped it and put it out of her reach.

"Nothing personal Donna, but I would appreciate it if you would leave my things alone."

"I'm bored. I have an appointment in fifteen minutes and I have nothing else to do."

"Perhaps you could read or something, maybe go for a walk?"

"I hate reading and I can't leave the room alone. So, there, that takes care of that." She moved back over to her bed, grabbed the pillow and sat on the edge, still watching me.

She pulled herself back on the bed and sat in the corner, again grabbing hold of the pillow to cover her, I suppose.

"Calm down," she said pulling the pillow tighter across her chest. "I'm not going to hurt you. Just trying to pass the time."

I wanted to be nice, but I had a thing with personal space. It was hard for me to be pleasant when I felt invaded. Suddenly she curled into a ball and pulled the pillow over her head, and rolled to her side.

"I'm, sorry. I just don't like people going through my things."

"I wasn't going to steal anything." She jumbled her words and sounded childlike, but I understood what she was saying, even through the pillow.

"I know. I didn't mean to imply that you were."

Then without any notice, she popped up. "I gotta go."

She threw the pillow on the floor, jumped off the bed, and left the room without another word. I felt relieved for her to be gone. I picked up the pillow and placed it against her headboard. I thought about putting my clothes in the dresser, since we both had one, but I'd be leaving in no time.

A tap on the door startled me. I turned and saw Jenny who had escorted me between wards.

"You've met Donna."

"You could have given me fair warning." I smiled.

"Well, she does take a bit of getting used to. She's not so bad. She's been here a number of times, and yes, I should have told you, she likes to go through people's belongings."

"Thanks." I nodded. "Do you know when I'll be moved?" I asked.

"That's what I came to tell you. I'm afraid there won't be a bed on the ward for two more days."

"Are you kidding? I have to stay here for two days?"

"You're free to move around if you like. You can go downstairs to the gift shop and the library. And you will have your appointments with Dr. Morris. Dr. Taylor will also be finishing up on a few things, so you will be busy."

"Donna said no one can leave the room without an escort."

"She can't leave the room. She has a history of taking off. Once we found her on the third floor."

"Oh my."

"You won't need to worry about her, she will be out of her room attending group, and individual sessions most of the day."

"I was just hoping we could get this over, so I could go home."

"If anything comes up, you are the first on the list. Things change around here all the time."

Jenny left, and I lay down on the bed. It had been a long morning, and from my newfound information it would be a long two days to come. I faced the wall and imagined the kids at home. They'd be at school, then in a short time off to practice. Soon, before realizing anything, I fell asleep.

"Hey, you'll miss dinner if you don't wake up."

I felt the jerk on the bed before I heard her voice. I sat up and turned around. Donna had plopped down next to me. She had changed from the USC sweatshirt to a Disney tee shirt.

"I'm really not hungry right now."

"You better eat, they won't bring anything to the room, and the kitchen closes at seven o'clock."

I got up, went into the bathroom and washed my face. I looked into the mirror and noticed sheet marks on my face. I finger-combed my hair and pulled it back into a half ponytail.

"Are you coming?" Donna called out, "I'm going to leave without you."

"I'll be out in a minute. You can go ahead if you want."

I hoped when I came out that she'd be gone, but there she sat. She got up the minute I came out. I couldn't imagine having to stay in a psych ward more than once, but here I was, my second time, but I was not here because I was crazy.

"Great, let's go."

Donna went on to the rec room after dinner, while I went back to our room. I preferred to read. I had my books. I had started *A Woman of Independent Means*, and hoped to have it finished before I got home. I also brought *Joanna's Husband and David's Wife*, in case I had more time than I thought. I had become a big fan of Elizabeth Forsythe Haley, and her take on women's lives.

I took a shower, slipped into a nightshirt, and crawled into my small single bed. I flipped on the light and called Carl. Everyone was fine, but practices had been cancelled because of rain. They were caught up on their homework and were settled in watching a movie. I smiled as the kids told me how great they were, but then each added before sending kisses, that they missed me.

"Carl, I miss you so much."

"You'll be fine."

"I know I just wanted to get things started. I have to wait two more days. My other testing didn't go too well. I kinda had a meltdown."

"It was probably just nerves."

"Probably." I choked up but held back the tears.

"Are you okay?"

"I just need to stay calm. Oh, I forgot, I have a roommate."

"I thought you'd be by yourself?"

"Me too, but in this ward you get what comes to you."

"How is she?"

"I don't think I'll be bringing her home for dinner any time soon. But I feel sorry for her."

"What's wrong?"

"I don't know, but she has already gone through my things and she hops around like a rabbit. Reminds me of some of my students. I think she is here for depression, suicide watch. She hasn't really said, and I didn't ask."

"Can you just keep to yourself?"

"Hey, I gotta go. I think she's coming. We'll talk tomorrow. Love you."

I opened my book and lost myself in Bess's letters. The noise I heard from down the hall, disappeared. I was alone. After about forty-five minutes I heard her voice but didn't look up.

"Hey, you missed a good show."

"I don't like TV that much. I enjoy reading."

She plopped down on my bed, and actually took my book from my hand.

"Donna, could you not do that?" I asked, taking it back from her.

"Calm down, I just want to see what you're reading."

She got up and went to her side of the room. She dug through the bureau and from the mirror I could see her taking out clothes, then she went into the bathroom, but left the clothes on the dresser.

I had to decide if I wanted to continue reading when she came out, or turn off the light and pretend to be asleep. I mulled it over in my mind. What was I thinking? I had every right to be reading. *Come on Claire, get some backbone. Don't let her dictate your actions.*

I sat up in bed and continued reading, turning away from the center of the room. I heard the water go on, and then after a while it finally went off. I leaned back on the pillow. Donna came out wrapped in a towel. In a few minutes she dropped it to the floor, standing naked, her back to me. She looked almost goddess-like, the curves, and her rounded backside. She walked over to the dresser, stepped into her underwear, then pulled a nightshirt over her head. I watched in the mirror as she spiked her hair and put some cream on her face.

She really was a pretty girl. Except for the blonde hair she reminded me of Rachel, fragile and almost broken. *It had been a long time since I had thought of Rachel. What could have happened to her..., and Olivia?*

"Do you want the light on?" she asked, nothing near the same tone she had used earlier in the evening.

"Go ahead," I said. "I'll turn mine off when I'm ready."

"God, I wish they had TVs in these rooms."

I didn't answer because I didn't know what to say. I only hoped she would roll over and go to sleep, but she didn't.

"So how many times?" She asked, pulling herself up in bed.

"How many times what?" I asked, still holding up my book.

"Did you try to off yourself?"

I wasn't expecting her bluntness, and I had no plans of telling her anything. I wasn't ready to talk to her about my life or mental state.

"I've never really tried, not that it is any of your business."

"Then why are you here?" She watched me, peeking her eyes around the same pillow she had hid behind earlier in the day.

"I told you, I'm only up here for psych testing, and they are transferring me to the seizure ward as soon as a bed is available."

Suddenly she popped up on the bed, holding the pillow as a shield.

"Sure, keep telling yourself that."

"Excuse me?"

"Come on, it had to be pretty bad to put you up here. This place has a reputation."

"Donna, I am here for testing, nothing more, and to be honest, I prefer not to discuss my private life with you."

"Well, aren't you a big shit?"

"I didn't say that."

"Didn't have to," she said, her eyes narrowing. "You guys really get me, thinking you are better than everyone. We all have the same shit going on. We are all just a little bit crazy. So quit acting like you're all high and mighty."

I didn't know what to say. I sat motionless, then Jenny came in the room. "What's going on here?" She looked around at both of us.

"Nothing," I said.

"She was all being just tough shit," Donna blurted out.

Jenny went over to Donna's bed and pulled the

covers back, then tucked in her legs. "Donna, it's been a long day, why don't you turn off the light and try to sleep."

"I'm too nervous."

"I'll bring you something to help you sleep."

As Jenny left the room, she nodded toward me. "Don't worry," she whispered. "She'll be fine. She has a hard time at night."

After Jenny left there was a long silence, and I went back to my book.

"Oh, I've done it so many times I can't count."

I didn't know if I should respond or not, but now I was feeling sorry for her more than I was angry at her.

"Why?" I asked.

She pulled herself up, adjusted her pillow, and pulled her knees up tight to her chest. "To show everybody," she whispered.

"What would you show them?"

"That they were wrong about me."

"You confuse me. How would killing yourself make people see they were wrong?"

"I guess I thought I could make them pay attention to me. I'd show them. I know, it was stupid. I'm working on it, but I've got my demons."

"Don't we all?"

"The depression takes over, almost strangles me. I can't see any daylight." Her voice changed from sarcasm to sadness.

"I'm sorry, that must be really hard." For the first time, I totally understood what she was saying.

"I started running away when I was thirteen, even ended up in juvie one weekend."

I realized at that moment that she wasn't rambling incoherently. She needed to talk. Maybe me being a stranger changed things for her? Maybe she felt safe? It didn't matter anymore. I had the same feelings in my 20s. But I wondered, why didn't I end up in a psych ward? Why did I work so hard? And, why did I feel like I was giving up now?

"I tried the first time at sixteen, then again at eighteen."

"How old are you?"

She brushed the tears from her cheeks. "I'm twenty-two."

"Are you here for that now?"

"Yes, see." Even from across the room I could see the red marks. "I just can't seem to figure out the right way to do it, I guess."

She slid down and pulled the sheet tight around her neck. I waited a few minutes to see if she would pop back up. I could hear her breathing. I got up and put her blanket over her and turned off her light.

She reached out and took hold of my fingers. "Thank you."

"You'll get through this." I patted her shoulder and went to bed.

All the anger I had felt toward her earlier in the evening had melted away. She was a child. I realized watching Donna, she was a blessing for me. I knew she was on the edge of her life, but desperately wanted it back. So did I. I had a life and was frantic to hold on to it. I lay down. Images floated around when I closed my eyes, but my last thought in the silence.

Oh please God, don't let that be me.

* * * * * *

I lay alone in the bed, listening to sounds of the

psych ward. It was an unsettled silence, lights flashed, and bells rang. I lay entangled with my demons. Donna's words danced around in my head, bumping into each other, like in a storm. If I cooperated, I'd find my life, like it had been lost somewhere and, with patience, I'd get it back.

The next day I was told that I'd be seeing another doctor, Dr. Morris since I had signed a contract not to hurt myself. I'd see him the first thing in the morning. I didn't hear anything until I felt a nudge by my bed.

"Wake up, sleepy head."

"What time is it?"

"Eight-thirty. They'll be coming for you soon. You ready for it?"

"I'm ready to go home."

"That won't be happening for a while. You're on the psych ward, honey."

"I'm only here for testing."

"So what did ol' Blue Eyes ask you?"

"Who are you talking about?"

"Dr. Morris, who do you think?"

"I haven't seen him yet." I went into the bathroom for a quick once over. I put on clean clothes and even some make-up. I wanted to look fresher than I had the day before.

"Well, here she comes. Good luck."

The red shoe-laced nurse stood in the entryway, motioning for me. I smiled at Jenny and followed her down the hall to the elevator.

"Are you doing okay?"

"It was a tough day, yesterday."

She squeezed my hand as she opened the door to Dr. Morris's office. He sat in his short-sleeve shirt, hovering over the light from his desk. The blinds were drawn and darkness filled the room. I pulled my sweater tight over my shoulders and as he looked up I took the chair in front of him.

"Looks like today is a big day for you."

"Hoping someone tells me I get to go home pretty soon."

"All the reports are in, but they still haven't decided about the surgery. Dr. Hanson will be meeting with you later today to give you the alternatives to surgery and then work with you on what they have decided."

"What do you mean? What alternatives?"

"...."

"You're not doing the surgery are you?"

"I don't think so. It looks like your seizures are originating from too many different places. We can't guarantee it will be effective."

"I don't understand."

"You're having too many different types of seizures. Some are caused by stress, happening because part of your brain just shuts down, like a light switch. You've had gran mal seizures, petit mal, and drop seizures. Some are barely noticeable by anyone from the outside. We don't know why, but we can say you do have epilepsy. The doctors want to stabilize you as much as possible."

"So, it's not me? I mean I'm not making this up."

He tipped his glasses down and smiled. "No, not at all. You can't control what's happening. I do know the meds aren't working because of the break-through seizures."

"I'm taking so many drugs, with side effects especially from Neurontin."

I finally felt someone was engaged with me and

what I might be going through. I felt like he listened.

"What are your side-effects?"

"Regenerative migraines, depression, tremors. I've had hair loss, balance and sleeping issues. My memory is sporadic. The bottom line is," I paused. "I'm a mess. I feel drugged all the time."

"They're going to do another round of monitoring for a few days to be sure they know what's going on. I'm pretty sure they'll change your meds because of the break-throughs."

"I hoped the medication would help, but they seem to be worse than the seizures. I mean once I had a seizure then it was over, but the side-effects go on forever. I can barely function anymore."

"We're going to try to change that for you. We are going to transfer you up to the seizure ward hopefully this afternoon and get you started."

"How long do I have to wear the head gear?"

"Maybe just a few days, but at the most, a week. I'll come to see you while you're upstairs. I've also talked to Dr. Benning and he'll be calling you."

"Well at least we seem to have a game plan. I get really nervous when I don't know what's going on."

"How are you feeling now?"

"I'm feeling a little more clear-headed since I stopped the meds yesterday."

"Well, hopefully you'll have one while we're monitoring you."

"Wow, you want me to have a seizure. Never heard that before. I'd laugh, but it isn't funny."

"If we can get it figured out, your life will be so much better."

"God, I hope so."

"Tell me, how've you been feeling since yesterday?"

"Better. I just got overwhelmed with the testing. I was really anxious."

"Well let's try to get you back on track."

"That sounds good."

"I won't overwhelm you with questions. I'll let you relax for a while. We won't be doing any more of the psych testing. Is there anything you'd like to talk about before the transfer?"

"Yes. Am I going to get better?"

"We'll do everything we can for you. You also have amazing support when you get home. You have great doctors. We are all on the same page."

"Thank you." I could feel the blush cross my face.

I wasn't allowed to leave until Jenny could escort me back, so I watched Dr. Morris make the call.

"Are you ready for me?" Jenny asked, as she tapped on the open door.

"Yes." I followed her down the hall and we stood silently at the elevator. I looked back around, realizing I was on the seizure ward. It looked exactly like the psych ward. Someone could get lost, I thought.

The room was empty. I lay down on the bed to process everything that Dr. Morris had said. They were going to do everything to make me better. I couldn't ask for anything else. The tears came with an immense sense of relief.

33

I was jarred awake, when I felt a gentle nudge on my shoulder.

"Claire, my name is Celeste. It is time for your procedure."

"Oh shit." I looked up and saw the bluest of eyes staring back at me. "I'm sorry. I just dread this more than anything in the world."

I had been through this twice before since my seizures started. Neither test had brought any concrete results; and the pain had been unbearable. The idea of inserting a wire into someone's skull to monitor brain activity was not something I ever imagined would happen to me, now I was back for a third time.

"I know. Everyone does, but they do have some new procedures since your last one. I can give you a pill that will help you relax. You won't go to sleep, but it will calm your nerves."

"Will it still hurt, like before?'

She didn't have to answer, I saw the look on her face. "I promise I will make it as comfortable as I can for you."

"So yes, it will?"

If I could I would have willed myself to be anywhere but here, instead I took a deep breath and lifted myself from the bed.

She handed me the pill and I placed it on my tongue and waited as it slid to the back of my mouth.

"It'll melt, then in a few minutes hopefully you'll feel more relaxed. It doesn't work the same for everyone."

I could feel it dissolve, I didn't really feel anything, at least nothing physical. While I waited, I folded my hands in my lap, as she ran a cool washcloth over my face, making sure she had brushed my hair back. In a few minutes an orderly rolled in a cart, with two nurses following behind him.

"How are you Claire?"

"Nervous."

"I know. My name is Tom. I'll be handling your procedure, doing everything I can to get you through it. Did Celeste give you the pill?"

"Yes."

"How do you feel?"

I didn't say anything, just looked up at him, already starting to tear up at just the thought. He patted my shoulder. Celeste pulled a chair up in front of me. For the first time I noticed a simple gold cross hanging from her neck. I kept my eyes focused on the cross.

"I'll be right here." I know she meant for that to be consoling, but it wasn't.

He rubbed alcohol around my temples. It was cold, and I felt a shiver.

"Don't move. Just squeeze my hands." I was sure I dug my nails in, but Celeste didn't make a noise. I held on, staring at the cross, and then in a soft voice he began to talk to me.

"I'm starting," he said in a low growl. "The first prick was like catching your finger on the thorn of a rose bush, then he pushed harder, the fish-line wire went deeper and the memory came back. It caught my breath, and I gasped, like a nail going through my skull. I cried out, but Celeste held on harder to my hands.

"Okay, it is in. I'm going to guide it down your temple. Take small breaths," he murmured.

The initial throbbing stopped, but the pain was immediate, stabbing through my scalp. I felt the tears right away, but Celeste wiped them away. I attempted to move my arm, but she held it down. "Not yet. You can't move through the procedure."

"The wire is now moving along the skull," Tom said. "I can see it in the camera. Not too much longer."

I smiled. I didn't take my eyes off her cross. I had to keep focused I was glad I couldn't see anything. Even as I felt it move inside my head, the thought of it made me nauseous. I felt more tears on my cheeks. Celeste wiped them away. I didn't know if it was her or the pill, but I felt myself relax. I softened my grip on her hand.

While he moved the wire, the two nurses began to part my hair and attach what looked like round band-aides to my scalp. "Now we're attaching the wires, one-by-one. We'll have to glue them to your scalp, so you might lose some hair when we take them off."

I closed my eyes and took myself away from the moment when the word seizure had never been a part of my vocabulary. I felt my toes and counted my breaths. I let the sensation move up my body, through my legs, my thighs, even up to my chest.

When the technician finished, the nurses wrapped additional gauze around my head to cover the wires. He waited while they cleaned up the remaining fragments left behind.

"You all right?"

"I think so."

"You're quite a trooper. I can't begin to imagine how difficult this is." No, he couldn't, no one could, but I had to get through it. If they approved the surgery, it would be so much worse. I would be awake though the whole process, so they would know that all my senses and nerves were still working. As much as I wanted the seizures to end, I just wanted to go home.

"I've been through this before."

"From my understanding you will be monitored for at least five days. Every morning they will review the printouts." He wheeled his cart out of the room.

"Be careful when you lay down," Celeste said.

"I know the protocol." Even still, she showed me how to adjust my head, so the contraption wouldn't slip.

"Thank you." I touched it on both sides. I wasn't going to look in the mirror. God forbid, I looked like a monster.

"I'll be in a few times each day to check and make sure things are in order. Ring me if you need anything, or if you think it might be slipping, or if a headache develops. Can I get you anything before I go?" she asked.

"No, I'm good, I have my books, and journal, and I think I'll just take a nap."

I lay back and adjusted myself as she showed me. I called Sally and told her about the antics of my very worrisome roommate, and the handsome technician who set up my contraption. I told her also about the loneliness and the depression that I was fighting.

When I called Dr. Benning, I didn't tell him anything about Donna or the procedure, instead, I asked him to walk me through a self-hypnosis so I could do everything in my power to stay focused. After dinner, I called Carl and talked to the kids.

"Mom, you doing okay?" Adam asked in a tense voice, unusual for him.

"I'm great baby. I'll be home in no time."

We talked as if I were sitting next to him, ready to kiss him goodnight. Then Devon came on. "Mom, what's it like there?"

"Well, it's a hospital, but everyone's been very nice."

We chatted like we did when we went for ice cream on summer nights.

"I'm so ready to come home, Carl."

"How did it go?"

"Tedious, it hurt so much."

"You'll be home in no time. I love you." Just as I was ready to say good-bye Celeste came back in. "Hey, I have company, I gotta go. I'll call you tomorrow night."

"I just wanted you to know my shift is over. Nancy will be coming in to check on you, if you need anything."

"Thank you." I pulled myself up to see her better.

As she turned toward the door, I asked her to flip off the light and I closed my eyes. The phone rang, and unthinking I picked it up.

"It's me. What's going on?"

"Donna?"

"Yea, you ready for some company?"

"No. You can't come right now."

"Why?"

"They just finished putting on the monitor and they want me to rest." I hung up before I could hear her say anything else. I closed my eyes and before long drifted off. I awoke with a start, but no one was in the room. Then I remembered Donna had called. I couldn't have her calling all hours of the day and night I thought.

I rang the desk and in a few minutes Nancy opened the door.

"What can I do for you?"

"Is there any way I can have my calls blocked, or stopped?"

"I can call the switchboard and ask them not to put calls through for you."

"Thank you."

"Is everything all right?"

"I've just been getting calls from someone on the fourth floor, but I don't feel like talking to anyone while I'm here. I'll make any necessary calls I need."

"No problem. I can call down and request that she stop calling you."

The phone didn't ring for two days. I was relieved for the silence.

On the third day, when it did ring, I had forgotten about Donna. Not thinking about anything, I reached over and answered it.

"Hello." *Oh God, it was Donna. Shit. Why did I answer?*

"Why haven't you picked up?"

"Donna, I really don't want to talk to anyone."

"Can I come see you?" She asked, like she wasn't even listening.

"No. Please don't. Besides, you're not allowed to leave the ward on your own."

"I do whatever I want. I'll be there shortly."

"No...."

She'd already hung up. I rang the nurses' station,

hoping they could ward her off, but no one answered.

Dinner had just been brought in, but I pushed it aside, and rolled over. I heard the door open and heard the one voice I recognized.

"Hey girl, here I am," Donna said.

"I asked you not to come," I said pulling myself up on the bed.

"Wow, look at you. An alien from outer space. What is that thing?"

Donna plopped on the bed. I decided to get it over with, so I could go back to being alone. The minute I saw her, I knew something was different. Her wide eyes stared blankly. She was looking, but she didn't see me.

"You look like you're from outer space." She stared at my head.

"I can say the same about you. What's going on?"

"Just having some candy." She reached deep into her sweatpants and pulled out a handful of what looked to be pills, or candy.

"Can I touch it?" She reached up moving her hand closer. I pushed it away. "That's crazy."

"No. Leave it alone. What are you doing with those pills?"

"Kidding. They aren't pills, they're just candy."

"Why are you here?" I watched her every move, prancing around the room.

"I had to get out of there. I'm sick of group. I decided to come see you."

I didn't know much about being high, but this girl was over the moon. Her pupils consumed her eyes. Her words spilled out so fast, I couldn't keep up with them. She jumped from the bed to the window seat and back again.

"How did you get out of the ward?"

She smiled, then began picking at the dinner, on the tray. "I snuck out."

"The doors are locked Donna. You don't just sneak out."

She dropped her smile, "I do. After all the times I've been in these places, I've learned to figure things out... like escaping." She laughed.

She got up from the bed and walked around, staring at my head. "How do you handle that thing? I'd go insane." She ran her fingers through her hair. "Hey, do I look like you?" She held on to the spikes of her hair and danced around.

"Donna you need to leave. I'm going to call the nurses station and let them know you're here."

"Oh, come on, don't do that. I just need to be free."

I pushed the tray away and swung my legs over to the floor. She continued to finger the dinner plate, picking up a french fry.

"Donna, you have to stop."

"You are so dull. I just want to have some fun."

"Not now."

"So, what does all that stuff feel like? She gestured to the wires around me.

"I have a headache, and I'm really tired. You have to go." I heard myself pleading.

The door opened and Celeste stepped through. "I'm sorry, I didn't know you had a visitor."

"Celeste, this is Donna, she came from the fourth floor." She had to know by looking at her sweats, that she didn't just come from her car. I lowered my eyes, then realized the nurse understood everything that Donna was doing.

She gave me a quick nod and adjusted the door, so it was half open. She watched for a few minutes then left us alone.

Suddenly Donna's whole tone changed, her voice became almost inaudible. She dropped her head and slid down the wall.

"Do you miss your family?" She asked, now almost crying.

"Of course."

"I don't miss anyone," she blurted out. "It does no good to miss people. They only hurt you and don't really care." I could tell she was spiraling down. Her tone turned to melancholy. She began to jab at her arm, like there was a scratch, but there was nothing there. Then she pulled herself up and came back to my dinner plate, taking another french fry.

"You know I could do anything I wanted in this place, and they'd never know." She dipped her hands in her sweat pocket and pulled the pills again. "See, I got these, they didn't even miss them." Without another word, she slipped the pills back in her pocket.

Suddenly two orderlies walked in. "There you are. We've been looking for you, Donna. It's almost dinner. Time to go back to your room."

"You mean my cage." She grabbed the glass of water from my tray and drank it all, then with a quick wink she patted her thigh where she had dropped the pills. "Like candy," she laughed.

"Come on now. We aren't that mean." Both the orderlies stood between her, taking hold of her arm.

"Oh Fred, you are such a stick in the mud. A party-pooper." She laughed and stumbled toward his arms.

"It's time to go home. This is not your room."

Donna grabbed one more french fry while they escorted her out the door. "I'll be back," I heard her words echo off the walls down the hall.

I grabbed the orderly's sleeve and pulled him back. "She has some pills, in her sweats. She said they were her candy. You need to get them from her before she does anything."

"I'll let the doctor know."

"But, she has pills."

"She does this all the time. We're used to her."

When I woke up, my room was dark, except for the lights coming from the monitor. I sat up, relieved I was alone, then the door opened. It was Jenny. I had not seen her since I left the psych ward.

"Am I interrupting?" She asked.

I immediately drew my hands up to my head to cover the monstrosity "No." I looked around, still a little confused. "What time is it?" I asked.

"It's about noon." She leaned against the closed door behind her.

"It can't be. I just fell asleep."

She went to the window and opened the shades.

"Yep, already midday." She smiled and took a seat on the edge of the bed. "I need to speak with you."

"Did something happen?"

"Yes." Her face was tight and drawn. Her usual smile was nowhere in sight. She rubbed her chin, then clasped her hands together. "Donna came to see you yesterday, didn't she?"

"Yes, but I got Celeste to call the orderlies and they came and took her back to her room. Why? Did something happen?"

"Yes, as a matter of fact. They found her this morning in her bed, nonresponsive."

"What are you saying?"

"Donna overdosed last night and didn't survive."

"No, that can't be. I told the orderlies about the pills she had. She called them candy. Didn't they take them from her?"

"They found an empty bottle between her mattresses. She had been stowing away pills for quite a while. That was why she'd been so erratic."

I heard the words and knew what they meant, but they didn't register.

"Are you all right?"

"I told her to leave. I told her I was tired, but I think she just needed to talk. I shouldn't have sent her away. I should have listened."

"It's not your fault."

"I know that, but in my mind, I can't help but think I should have done more for her. I was being so selfish, just thinking about myself, and this stupid headgear."

"It is not your fault. She knew exactly what she was doing. You couldn't have changed anything, no matter how long you talked to her."

I held back the tears. I didn't know if I cried for her or me. I didn't even know what I felt, except guilt.

"I'm sorry. Are you okay?"

"I don't know."

"Do you want to talk about it?"

"I don't know exactly what to say."

Jenny sat for a few minutes and watched me. She didn't say anything, didn't try to make it better.

"I've been going through a lot with these seizures and having to be away from my family. To do this, again." I pointed to my head. "I've been really depressed, and..." *Should I tell her what was going on? Let her know my demons were no different than Donna's? I didn't need to tell her. I knew the fears, I woke up with them every day. Donna just brought them front and center.*

"What can I do for you?"

"Nothing really. I think I need to be alone for a while."

"Are you sure you're all right?"

"Yes. I just have a lot to sort out."

"Dr. Morris will be in to see you in a few minutes. Are you ready, or do you want to cancel?"

"No. I'm good. I think I need to see him."

Jenny left and I went into the bathroom to wash my face. I heard the door open and still holding the towel stepped over by the bed. The door remained open and I took a seat in the chair, looking out the window, down at the trees and roses. I ran the towel over my face again.

"I'm sure you heard about Donna?"

"Yes, I guess everyone has."

"Do you want to talk about her?"

"No."

"What are you thinking?"

I looked up into the soft face of the old man who had taken Dr. Benning's place. I was sure he already knew what I was thinking.

"I was thinking I don't want to end up like her, and that you're afraid I will."

He smiled, but I kept my eyes on him.

"No, actually I was worried that you might be blaming yourself. You are very fragile right now. You came in very distraught a few days ago. You certainly didn't need to add this to your plate."

"I'm not the one who's dead, Doctor Morris."

Then a french fry, on the floor, caught my eye. It must have fallen, or maybe Donna had knocked it off and hadn't noticed. I reached down and picked it up, setting it on the window sill.

"What's that?" he asked.

"A french fry. She was picking off my plate before she was taken back to her room. I will not end up like Donna," I said. "I will not let this beat me."

34

The memories of Donna were left in Portland, finally ready to start over in every way I knew how. I was not going to end up like Donna. Though her memory still haunted my dreams.

Recovering from my time in Portland took longer than I expected. I thought about Donna every night when I closed my eyes. I went back to reading and working in my garden, buying random flowers and trailing vines that I replanted between the jasmine and honeysuckle. I deadheaded the roses that had bloomed while I was gone. I felt cleansed as I dug my hands deep in the soil. Not a day went by that I was not outside, finding the peace I needed to heal.

Every night I made dinner and our family sat down, like we were whole again. We laughed, talked and for the first time in so long, I found the serenity I feared I had lost forever. Even with setbacks I was becoming whole again. I called Sally three days in a row, leaving messages, finally on a day that lay free ahead of me, I went to see her.

There was no one else I wanted to see more. I had freed myself from my demons. My head was straight, and by hell or high water, I was moving forward.

I lingered in Sally's garden just past the gate. I

didn't call to her, but wandered, eyeing new blooms I might have missed. What was it about the garden that made me love it so? I knew it held my secrets and those secrets kept me safe. She had kept them all, like in a box, locked away, or buried.

She greeted me as I came around the corner. She had changed. The time since I had seen her had taken a toll as it had done on me.

"You're here." She pulled me into a hug.

"Why didn't you answer the phone? I called for almost a week."

"I had things to take care of..."

"That you couldn't answer your phone?"

"I hope you're ready for dinner?"

"You're ignoring me. What's going on?"

"Let's have dinner, and we'll talk about it. Come on." She took my hand, like I was a little girl. Without her I might get lost.

"No, I'm not expecting you to feed me. I've just missed you. The last six months or so have been insane. Talking to you on the phone has not been enough."

"For both of us." She let go of my hand when we reached the french doors.

I took a seat at the fully set table. She went to the counter, opened the cupboard and took out another setting.

"It will be nice to have someone here." She sat down and began to serve the meatloaf and mashed potatoes. Cut blooms of wild heather sat in a vase on the table.

"This is beautiful. I've missed them so."

"Now tell me, how you are, my darling?" She reached across the table.

"I survived. I'll be going back in September, pretend it never happened," I laughed.

"Oh no, don't do that. I hope your doctor told you to remember it every day, so that you can see your progress, because every day will be better, and you have survived it all."

"I won't forget. I'm moving forward. You know Sally, maybe all the stuff in the orphanage, whatever it was, prepared me to get through all of this." I patted her hand.

"I'm proud of you, coming out on the other side."

"It has been all about me for the last year. How are you? You look different." Maybe it had been age, or the stress with her brother, but I could tell the difference. Sally was different in a way that worried me. Her once massive braid was nothing more than clumps of strands pulled away from her face. She had dropped weight, and there was a translucency to her skin, especially in her hands. She looked old. She poured two glasses of white wine and then began to talk in a way I knew I couldn't interrupt.

"I need to tell you something. It might be hard, but I have made some decisions, and I won't be swayed."

"Okay. You never have been one to bounce back and forth, so what is this decision?" I took a bite and she began.

"I'm going away, but I don't exactly know when." She said it so slowly I thought I was going to have to drag the words from her mouth, like pulling someone out of a hole.

"Where are you going? In all the years I've known you, I can count the times you've left town."

"I'm not leaving town, per se." She took a deep

breath, then took a drink of her wine. "I don't know how to say this. I never thought it would happen, at least not like this."

"Come on, Sally, you've never been like this before. What's going on?"

"I'm sick."

"Okay, this is way too somber for the flu. What are you talking about?"

"Claire, I'm dying. I've refused any surgery that would prolong things. I've had all the tests they could run. I'm now left with time."

"Why would you refuse surgery?"

"Because I'm at the end, and I know it. I want the last year to be mine. I don't want needles or therapy. I want to be who I am through all of this."

"What is *this*?"

"Nothing you need to be concerned with, for now."

"You're not going to tell me?"

"No. I'm not. You're going to have to trust me on this one. I'm keeping it to myself, and that is done."

"I want every minute I can with you. I don't care what it's like, or how you are." I watched her slowly lift the fork, as if the simple act caused her pain.

"I do. I want to be sane. I want to remember everything. I'd rather have that than time."

"What about meds? Would you agree to them?"

"I know the meds can make things better, but not forever."

The words didn't make sense, it was like listening to a foreign language and having to ask someone what was just said. Or someone whispering and missing every other word.

"How long have you known?"

"For a while. I just never told anyone because there

were no signs, and I could keep it to myself," she said, sipping her wine.

"Why now? Why not just never tell anyone, and when the time came, we would just think it was natural causes?"

"Because for the time I have, there will be signs you will notice and I don't want you to hover. There will be good days that we can spend in the garden and then other days that I will send you away."

"Every day I'll wonder."

"I guess that will be your burden, as this is mine. It can't be too much to ask."

"No...." I paused. "I just never thought about you not being here. How will I go on?"

"Heavens girl, you don't need to worry about that. Enjoy the days we have. Don't think about the future."

I stood up and moved away from the table, then turned toward her. "Why tell me this at all?"

"Because you would never forgive me if I didn't."

"You're right."

"Did I make a mistake?"

"No, of course not. Have you told Paul yet?"

"No, because he would have sold my house and sent me into a home. I'm never leaving here."

"Why didn't you tell me sooner? I could have been there for you."

"No. It would have changed everything. I didn't even want to tell you now, but I felt that I owed it to you. I don't want you to act any different. Do you hear me?"

"I wouldn't have treated you differently, really."

"Yes, you would have, not on purpose, of course. You probably wouldn't have even known you were doing it, but I would've, and it would have changed things for us."

"Things will never change between us."

"So, what are we talking about here—be blunt. I'm not the same girl you met years ago. I can handle it now."

"The doctor says I have about a year—two at the most if the meds continue to work. Things will start to happen when it gets worse. I'll lose balance, there'll be headaches. He says I might not get too sick, more like the flu, but toward the end. Then he said that, one day, I just wouldn't wake up. I hope your face is the last I see."

"No, Sally, you have family, a daughter, you want her to be with you, not me. We should call her. Bring her here to be with you."

"Why would I want that? If she didn't want to be around me in the good times, why would I want her here now? I want someone who loves me, and cares about me, and that is you."

"You would want her because she is your daughter. I could only hope, if my mother were in your shoes, she would want me. But then, she didn't even want to see me. Don't shut your daughter out of this."

My dearest friend in all the world was dying, and she wanted me to be the last face she saw on this earth. I took a seat at the table, but I couldn't eat. I drank the wine, pretending I hadn't heard any of it, but knew I would be haunted by this day for years to come.

"So, tell me how you are. Home from Portland, what was that like?"

"It opened my eyes."

"What does that mean?"

"A girl I met there…" I thought about telling her, but under the circumstances, there was no need. I knew how Donna had changed me, that was something I could keep to myself, as Sally needed to keep her own secrets.

"What did she do?"

"She helped me realize I had to be willing to fight harder, to not give up."

"And are you?"

"Everyday." I couldn't tell her about the cutting, so I didn't. I kept it hidden, buried deep. Then I realized why she couldn't tell me about her dying. We were both the same, recovering in our own way.

She was right, but in different ways. She had accepted her fate, and fought, in her own special way, to do just what she wanted. I was fighting for my survival, to move forward every day.

We resumed dinner in silence as if none of the conversation had happened. I drank the wine, and sat back as Mittens jumped in my lap. I replaced the fork and snuggled with the cat as I watched Sally. Though she looked more frail, she didn't look like she was dying.

Suddenly, Sally went outside and took a seat in the rocker. I left her alone, cleared off the table, even took the food and put everything into containers. I cleaned up the kitchen and brought her glass of wine out and sat at the table.

"Could you help me to my room. It's been a long day."

I moved over to her rocker. I kissed her softly on the forehead and helped her to her room. I wouldn't ask if there was pain, or what caused it. I would do everything she wished for from now on.

I pulled back the covers while she went into the bathroom. I mulled around the small room. It was neat and tidy, everything in order. I had never been in this room before, usually only the kitchen or the living room. I looked around at the simple lace curtains and closed them. I smelled her perfume, then moved to the edge of the bed and waited for her to come out of the bathroom.

The door opened and she stepped out in a long flannel gown, her hair loosely tied back in a ribbon. She had washed her face as I could see soft fluffs of hair by her ears. She sat down on the bed and lifted her legs over, then lay down. I adjusted the covers, sat down and took her hand.

"I can stay for a while, if you like?"

"No, you need to go home. I'll sleep now until morning."

"Call me tomorrow."

"I won't be letting you check up on me."

"I won't be doing that."

"Wait before you go, could you get Milo for me. I can't sleep if he isn't on the bed with me."

I went out to the garden and called for Milo who was asleep under the bench. I picked him up and snuggled him close to my chest as I walked down the hall. I placed him on the bed with her. She closed her eyes as I kissed her cheek.

"Tomorrow, my friend."

I locked everything up, making sure she was safe. As I went through the garden, I had a melancholy sense that after today things would be different.

35

It had been three years since my last trip to Portland. My visits to Dr. Benning had been cut down to every other week. I had not missed a day of school for three years and life was back on track. Devon was in college and Adam would leave next year.

The conversations with Dr. Benning were not as intense. I was no longer a little girl growing up in the confines of his office. I had reached my maturity. I was ready to face the world, but I held back from making the final bold statement. I always found something to talk about, some little thing that would take me back to the days I had been so sick, on the edge of my life.

I wasn't there anymore. It was time and I knew it. I had to let go of him so I could be free of the past. My appointment was at four o'clock. A few months ago he had moved into a new office, much farther across town. He was on the edge of retirement and wanted a smaller place.

He didn't have the usual window that he could slide across and stick his head out, so I tapped on the door to let him know I had arrived. He opened it and told me he would need a few minutes, but I could go back to his office.

Though the building was different, everything was in place.

I was telling him good-bye today. I had come to the end of my road.

"So, how are you?"

"I'm good. Actually, really good. I have something I need to talk to you about."

"You said you were good? Is there a problem?"

"No, not at all. Remember a while ago I told you that I could never live without you?"

"Yes, and I remember telling you that a day would come when you'd be ready to let go."

He looked over at me with a sweet smile. "So, this is what you want to talk about?"

"Yes, I think the day has come."

"I'm very proud of you. What happened to turn you around?"

"I had a bit of a meltdown this last weekend, nothing big, but a few years ago, I would have been on the phone to you, but suddenly I realized I knew what to do. I didn't need to call. What happened was not that big of a deal."

"How did the rest of your weekend go?"

"Once I figured out what I needed to do, I was fine."

"How is everything else?"

"Surprisingly good."

"So how do you want to handle this?"

A part of me wanted to tell him, I didn't want to leave the safety of his door, but I knew better. It was time to let go. He had been my savior and I loved him. I knew I would never forget him, but I would find a new life.

"I'm ready to let go of you, but never forget you."

"You have all the tools."

"As many as I can carry, for now."

We both laughed and I watched him watch me. I was a success story. I had not ended up like Donna. I had survived my demons. I had survived two psych wards, three seizure episodes, and my return to the real world.

"So how will you fill the hour of my time?"

"I've been reading and writing. I'm going to apply again to the graduate program."

"You wanted it so badly."

"Yes, and as we well know, it wasn't the best of time. I think I'm ready for it now."

"Look what you've accomplished. I don't get a lot of chances to say this. Ten years, you've been with me. You came out whole."

"A few scrapes here and there, but yes, I believe I'm finally whole. I've also made a decision. I'm going to look for her again. I can search on the internet and I am determined to find her, or at least learn more about her. I went so far before, I just can't give it up, not at least until I learn more."

"And your family?"

"You gave me the tools to deal with them. It is my life, as you always said I just had to grow into it. I think I've done that."

"You've done your homework."

"Yes, I have."

"So do we say good-bye?"

"No, not ever, you will be in my heart always, without you I couldn't have moved forward. I will be indebted to you forever."

We stood up and as I reached for the handle, he reached out for my arm. "Now it is my turn to ask you. Can I have a hug?"

"I would be honored." He reached around my shoulders "You saved my life."

I sat in the car and felt such a sense of relief, not that I was leaving him, but that it was my choice to go. I had been afraid all those years that he would kick me out, that I wasn't loveable. He helped me believe I was.

For the first time, I drove home free of challenges. I drove past work, grateful that I'd had the opportunity to return. I drove past my parent's house and knew I had a chance for a new beginning. I stopped in front of Sally's and saw that she was doing well, with her garden, as beautiful and as cherished as the first time I met her.

I was moving forward.

36

The call came in at five-fifteen, according to the answering machine. I heard sadness in my sister's voice. She said to call her back right away.

I didn't.

It had been a long day. I wanted a glass of wine and just not think about anything.

I could tell something had happened. Something that would change my world.

I fiddled with the handset, then finally began pushing the buttons. It rang and I took a deep breath.

"Hey, what's going on?" I tried to stay calm.

"It's Dad." There was a hesitation like she was choosing her words.

"He died this afternoon."

I didn't say anything. I didn't know what to say. I always wondered how I would feel when the day came.

"Did you hear me?"

"Yes..."

"What happened?" Somehow, I heard in her voice a smugness, that she relished the responsibility of being the one to tell me.

I understood, she was his daughter.

"He was at the church. Can you come over...right now?"

"Of course. I'll leave Carl a note." I hesitated. "Where's Mom?"

"She's here. After Monsignor called, I went and got her. Would you hurry?"

"Are you OK?"

"Yes—No... I have to stay strong. I can't let her see me break down."

"You have every right. He was your father."

"I know... just right now she needs me to be strong."

"OK, I'm on my way."

I left a quick note for Carl, and went into the bedroom to change clothes. I hung up my work slacks, then slipped on a pair of jeans and sweater. I stared into the mirror.

Portland was over five years ago. I had come so far, I was completely off all my meds, I had bid Dr. Benning good-bye and never even called him. I had grown my hair out and put on a few pounds, more filled-out, as a friend had said.

I pinched my cheeks and added a dab of lipstick and blush to bring more color back to my face. Then I wiped it off. *Where was I going?*

To weep with my mother and sister.

* * * * * *

I started the car and headed toward Route 30. I waited to feel something, some tug that told me I had loved him. That he had loved me.

It didn't come. There should have been tears, lots of tears—he was my father.

I didn't know the man. I didn't know his favorite

color or flavor of ice cream. I didn't know his favorite sport.

I knew he adored his church… his roses… his natural born daughters.

I thought about calling Dr. Benning, but it had been a long time. What would I say? Hey, my dad died, what am I supposed to feel?

Dr. Benning taught me how to handle myself, but he didn't teach me what to feel.

I had spent half my life trying to please my father and the other half angry that I never could. I remembered something Dr. Benning had said. "People come in to your life for a reason. Maybe to teach a lesson, provide an insight you might not normally have. Maybe to teach you something about yourself."

Was that what my dad had done? Given me some insight?

Bullshit. He was my father, not someone I met on the street corner, or someone who opened a door for me.

So what lessons did he have for me? Love harder? Show more feelings? Maybe I learned things not to do. Especially to someone you promised to love.

Did he do that or was I the one who built our wall?

Christ— I'd known Dr. Benning so much better than I'd known my own father.

Now, they were both gone.

Once on Highway 30, I drove the ten miles to my sister's. I rolled down the window and turned up the radio, hoping to drown out the voices in my head.

Then a Reba song came on, *The Greatest Man I Ever Knew*.

Was that what we had? Was it all on me? Had I

been the one to misunderstand him the whole time? Had I never tried to know him?

Shit. I pulled over and banged on the steering wheel. *No, I wouldn't let that be the last thing I got from him.*

There were no cars in the driveway, except my sister's. Had she called the rest of the family? Were they on their way?

I opened the back door and found Mom sitting at the kitchen table, a cold cup of coffee sitting in front of her. "I'm so sorry, Mom. Are you OK?" I sat next to her and took her hand.

"Yes, dear, I'm fine. Just a little tired. I've got a lot to do."

I rubbed her wrist with my thumb. "We'll help, you don't have to do everything."

I looked up and saw my sister at the counter. Her eyes red and swollen. "What happened?"

"Monsignor said Dad was finishing up in the garden. He was deadheading the roses and sweeping the path. They had a wedding earlier today and there was rice everywhere.

"Anyway, he said he had checked on Dad about a half hour before and he was fine, even complaining about the rice. When he went back outside, Dad had collapsed near the gazebo. He called the paramedics, but there was nothing they could do."

"He died in the garden. He would have liked that," I said.

"Yes, he would have," Mom agreed.

"Mom wasn't home, so he called me. He wanted to know what we wanted him to do. The police had to be called, but because of his age and heart history, they would most likely call the funeral home instead of the coroner."

My sister spoke very matter-of-factly. Some people react to death with hysteria, some with strength. I could tell by her eyes, she had had her moments, but her words were almost business-like.

"Will there be an autopsy?"

"Weren't you listening? I just said the police would call the funeral home.

"He was old... he had a heart condition. Why would they do an autopsy? There'd be no need.

"Tomorrow, we need to go down to O'Reilly's and make arrangements. She can't do it," she said staring at our mother.

"I'll call in and take the rest of the week off school. What would you like me to do?"

"I don't know, I guess we should call people."

"Do you want me to make a list?"

"No, we can go through Mom's address book."

We sat for the next few hours making phone calls, telling people of his passing.

Susan wanted to do all the talking and that seemed appropriate. She was his real daughter... his blood daughter. She had to do it. Her mother couldn't. It was her place.

As we sat there, we should have been sharing memories, stories that would make us laugh, make us cry.

We just sat there. I had no memories to share. There were no times I could say, "oh, remember when..."

The next day strangers filled my sister's house.

People I barely recognized from church, from his work, some mere acquaintances.

People poured out their stories; his kindness, his generosity. Everything anyone would have wanted in a friend, a man, a father.

I noticed though, as everyone was talking, my mother just sat there. She didn't nod, she didn't comment. She had no stories. Maybe it was the grief.

After the arrangements were made, my job was to write the obituary, which would appear in the paper three days later. I wrote nothing from my memory, but what I had heard from strangers. I wrote about a kind man who people loved, admired, and revered. I did my job. It was a work of art. It was a work of fiction, at least for me.

The night before the funeral people lined up for his viewing. I sat and watched as they wept. They continued to greet us with stories of how he had touched their lives.

As requested, there was a funeral mass. The pews overflowed. We sat in the second row behind Mom, Susan and her family. Roses of every color filled the altar. I listened to the eulogies praising my father. I watched the people file out of the church, grieving for their loss. I couldn't grieve.

Three days after the funeral I went to his grave site. I thought it might be a good idea to try to talk to him. Maybe he and I could finally find peace. Maybe even shed some tears.

I knelt on the wet ground and dropped my head into my hands.

I guess I'll say to you all the things I never could say when you were alive. First, I am so sorry you lost you daughter, but more importantly I am so sorry you couldn't find it in your heart to give just a little more, not to the people outside of your world, but the people in it, the people who tried to love you.

I could feel the moisture from the wet lawn come through my jeans.

I don't understand, I wanted to love you. More than anything. But I couldn't find a way in. There was no place for me.

I get it now, I really do. You never stopped loving her. I wouldn't have either. She was your world, and now you're together.

In the strangest of ways, his death freed me. It was over. I could move on.

I think we were both free to move on, he to Teresa, and me to the rest of my life.

37

The rain fell for three days in St. Helen's, which was nothing unusual. The freeze had killed plants on patios and under porches. In the houses that lined the streets, lights glistened through the moonlight. Santa Clauses spun around, reindeers pivoted from right to left in synchronized movement. I had googled her name for as long as the internet was available. Every time, I typed her name and watched where it took me. Usually it took me to endless sights about Ireland that told me everything about the country, but nothing about my family.

A week before Christmas I received a letter from Dr. Banardos. I had not written to Carol, the social worker, since 1994, and then only to trade updates. In our letters, she had provided me condolences. She tried harder to be nice, rather than provide me with information. I opened the envelope and a single card came out. Inside the note I found four hand written lines:

Alice Brennan
Alice and Aidan Leary
—Aidan Leary Deceased—August 20, 2005
Dublin Ireland
<u>whitepages@erie.com</u>

I turned the card over, and there was a note.

Dear Claire,

I hope you are well. I'm leaving Dr. Banardos
and I needed one last correspondence to
provide you an update that Sr. Helen may not
have given you. Use this with care.

Carol

I opened my computer and googled the website. It was Ireland's white pages. I typed in Alice Leary. There it was an address and phone number, something I had never had access to. Now it sat in front of me on the screen, like a birthday cake a week late.

This was the exact moment I had waited for. I was paralyzed. I choked up and couldn't breathe. I had fallen from a mountain and was still falling. I called Devon and gave her the website.

After 23 years of searching, there were no words to explain the feeling of seeing her name in print, knowing that she was still there. I was giddy, excited, terrified, anxious, but above all, relieved. She wasn't a dream.

I walked into the living room and handed Carl the card and took a seat on the couch.

"Who sent this?"

"Carol, the social worker from Dr. Banardos. How could she have remembered, it was over twenty years ago? And he has passed away? That was her reason for not seeing me in 1990, because he was still alive. He's gone. She can see me now."

"What are you going to do?"

"I want to go back. I want to find her. What do you think?"

"Would you go alone?"

"No. I think Devon would like to go. Adam is starting his new job. It would be right in the middle of his season."

Carl looked over at me. Ran his hand across his forehead and settled his fingers on his chin. "Take her, you need to go. You've been doing this for twenty-five years. You need to finish it."

"Are you sure?"

"If it was me, wouldn't you tell me to go? It's just the two of us. Do this, take Devon, resolve it, once and for all."

It was decided on a cold winter night sitting in the Corner Cafe looking at our reflections in the window, twenty years later, Devon and I would make a pilgrimage back to Ireland, for a second chance. I'd allow myself two weeks to get some trace, some small piece of evidence. I was older, wiser, but more importantly, stronger than I had ever been.

We'd go toward the end of July, when the weather would be more pleasant. This time there would be no hunt. We would know exactly where to go, but first, I'd send her a letter with pictures. I'd let her know what to expect.

* * * * * *

On a warmer Saturday than it should have been for January, I met my mother for lunch at a small cafe close to her house. We had been spending every Saturday together having lunch and talking about the news of the day, since Dad passed away. She sat in the back corner of the crowded café, as usual. She hated the draft from the door opening all the time. My sister was with her and they appeared to be in deep conversation, their hands wrapped around white, restaurant coffee mugs.

"Hey, everyone," I said as I sat down. I unwrapped my scarf and tossed it on the back of the chair.

"Did you order me coffee?"

"No, sorry, didn't know what time you'd be here. Didn't want it to get cold."

"No worries," I motioned to the waitress to bring a coffee. "So, how is everybody doing today? Little warm for January, don't you think?"

"How is work, Claire?" My sister asked, somehow knowing I was anxious to take the conversation in a different direction.

"Good, busy as usual, you know how it is, always something going on.

"I want to talk to both of you about something," I said putting sugar in my coffee, plunging right into the conversation.

"Oh, look Mom, there's Sandy, we haven't seen her for a long time," Susan said, as she anxiously waved down the woman with the floppy hat.

"Hey, I need to tell you guys something."

"This is not the time, Claire." Mom motioned, waving at a waitress for a refill.

"It will never be the time. Mom, I found her. I searched on the internet and found her name. She's alive. Her name is Alice Leary. She lives in Dublin. Her husband passed away three years ago and she has daughters, all grown now. Devon and I are going to go to Ireland and try to meet her. I think we'll be going this summer."

"Well, that is news. I must say. You have been looking for her for a long time. Are you sure it's the right family?" She asked, taking a sip from her mug.

"Claire, Mom doesn't need to know this."

"Why not? I've been talking about it for a long time, I thought I could share when I finally found her?"

"You don't need to upset her," Susan said.

"Mom, am I upsetting you?" I asked, staring at Susan.

"No, Susan it's fine. It doesn't bother me. She has wanted this for a long time. I just hope you don't get hurt again."

"I won't, Mom."

We ate our lunch in silence. Susan threw darting glances my way, as she took bites from her salad. I wanted to believe she was worried for me, but it was all about Mom, what it would do to her. I understood her need to protect her.

There was something about delving into my past that didn't sit right with Susan. I never understood. It was my life, my past, but I had to respect her feelings. I did the best I could.

"Does she know?" Susan asked, "I mean about your coming?"

"No, not yet. I'm in the process of composing a letter."

"What about Carl?"

"What about him?"

"Where does he stand with all of this? It's been going on an awfully long time, I would think he would be kind of tired of it, by now."

Was she speaking for Carl or herself? Was she the one who was tired of hearing about my past? Then it hit me, between the bites of salad and gulps of coffee. She was right. There was no reason she needed to hear every detail about my trip. I didn't need to announce every step.

"No. Actually he's been amazing. I'm so thankful for his support." I smiled directly at her. I wanted her to see that I understood her, maybe for the first time ever.

"Well, whatever you decide, I'm sure it will be great," Mom said.

We didn't spend our usual hour. The waitress cleared our table and before long we were off in different directions.

As I approached my car, Mom came up and tapped my shoulder. "Claire, I know this is important, so do what you need to do. It doesn't bother me. I know why you have to do this. I really do understand."

"I never meant to hurt you, I just need to find her so I can let it go. I might never get another chance, besides, nothing may come of it. She might not see me, but I have to try." We stood in the parking lot looking at each other. I could tell she did understand, maybe better than anyone. But I was still self-conscious.

"I won't be talking about it so much anymore. I know how Susan feels, so I'll keep it private. You can ask if you want to know."

I reached over and put my arms around her narrow shoulders, and for a few seconds, we embraced. She kissed my cheek and walked off to her car. I watched her back out and took a deep breath with a sense of relief. Everyone who needed to know, knew. I could go to Ireland with no worries.

There was a sadness though, I couldn't explain it. I felt I was in the throes of a depression. It felt bigger than me. I had gained so many tools in my years of therapy, whenever something came up, I pulled out my bag of tricks and I made it through. But there were no tricks for this, nothing that I could explain. It dropped over me, I could feel the weight.

* * * * * *

Everyone knew about the trip except Adam. He was on his own, working hard to make a name in his career. Though he knew I had been looking, he had not been involved in the process.

We met for breakfast at his favorite restaurant. He was late so I ordered coffee and tried to figure how I would tell him.

I saw him coming through the doors with his broad shoulders slouched forward. He was dressed in workout clothes and sat down announcing that he was starved.

"How you doing? Have you ordered yet?" He asked, reaching over to give me a kiss.

"No, I waited for you. I'm good, busy with work and all. How about you?"

"Oh, you know, always planning for next season. Worked with my players this morning. All right Mom, what's up? You only invite me out when you have something going on. What do you have to tell me?" He asked.

"Wow, we haven't even ordered, you're getting right to the point."

"You know me," he laughed.

"I found her, Adam."

"Found who?" He asked, looking up from the menu.

"Alice, my mother, in Ireland."

"Oh my God, really?"

"Yes, I received a card from one of the agencies I worked with years ago. They gave me her last name. I have her address and phone number."

"Are you sure it's her?"

"As sure as I've ever been."

"You're going back, aren't you?"

"Yeah, I have to. I have to try one more time."

"Good. I think you should. You've had this dream a long time. You can't give up now."

We ordered our breakfast and Adam went on and on, about his new job. The restaurant was almost empty. I watched my son when the waitress set our plates on the table, he began eating, moving the eggs around the plate, and then drowning it all with a root beer.

"Are you OK? With my going back?"

"Mom, I'm a big boy. You don't need to watch over me anymore. You need to go."

"I'm taking Devon with me."

"Of course." He looked up with a big grin.

"That's OK with you?"

"Of course, stop asking. You need to go, and you need to take Devon. She has been in this with you from the beginning. It would be silly not to take her."

"What about you?"

"What do you mean? I'm fine I don't need to go."

He went back to finishing his breakfast and I went back to observing my son. I couldn't figure out why I was so uncomfortable with how our visit was going. He was fine and I dragged on about it.

"Are you going to give her anything, you know make her an afghan or something, like you always do?"

"Yes, but not an afghan. We've put together a picture album. Do you want to see it?"

"Sure."

"Here," I said, as I handed it over across the table. He laid it flat and flipped through the pages, grinning at pictures he had forgotten about, laughing out loud at pictures he remembered from the past.

"You did a good job, she'll like this," he said handing the album back to me.

I couldn't explain why I felt so guilty about leaving him behind, like I was making a choice and he was not it.

"Mom, I'm fine, I know what you're thinking, and you need to stop. There will be another time. This is about finding her, not a vacation. I know the difference."

As he slurped the last of his root beer, I slipped a folded paper across the table until it touched his fingers. "What is this?" he asked.

"A little something."

"A payoff?" He laughed. "Mom, you don't have to do this." He slipped it back, but I stopped him.

"Mom."

"Not another word."

I paid the bill and we stood in the parking lot, each waiting for the other to say something. He reached over and hugged me.

"This is going to be great," he said. He slowly let go and moved toward his truck.

"I know. I'm just sad for you."

"No reason to, just keep sending pictures and texting as much as you can. I'll be fine."

He got into his truck and slowly backed out while I stood there.

38

I was heading off once again for Ireland, only this time Devon was along for the ride. As we drove, we had long conversations of how the countryside would look, avoiding the massive elephant in the back seat. Then came the scenario of how it would be when we finally met her. We each imagined how it might go.

"I have to tell you Devon, no matter how it goes, I'm not going to give up this time. I won't settle. I let them treat me like a child, last time. I won't let that happen again."

"What exactly are you saying?" She asked.

"I'll call them, show up at their doorsteps. I'll do anything to be heard."

"Do you really thing that is such a good idea?" Devon looked over at me, with a tiny smirk on the edge of a smile.

"Well, I'm hoping it won't come to that."

As we passed through the green countryside, we fell silent. There was too much going on to share, too many fears, that it would all come to nothing.

"I don't want to hurt her," I said. "I just want to see her face, to find myself in her eyes. Everywhere I look, I find someone else. When I look in your eyes, I know what I helped create. I just want to look into her eyes and see myself."

"Am I doing the right thing?" I whispered into my cell phone when I called Carl.

"You can't be questioning yourself now. All you have to do is find her. You can do that, but what you can't do is control how she responds."

"I know. I just don't know where to start."

"You've already started."

"But she didn't write back. Maybe she didn't get the letter."

"Claire listen, you have her address, her name and her phone number. What more could you want?"

"OK. I'll call again when I can."

He was right. I had more than I ever had, and I was clearly not the same person. I was stronger, smarter, and I didn't have to defend myself. There would be no Sisters stopping me this time.

Throughout the plane ride, the anticipation was impossible to put into words. It was so different, this time.

I had control of how the events would unfold. It would make all the difference in the world.

It took twenty minutes to get from the airport to the hotel. We passed multiple roundabouts and wildly colored doors. We were here, the journey would begin.

"Well safe and sound, we are," the driver said, as we pulled up to a modern five story hotel, just outside Dublin Center. He hopped out, popped the trunk and set our suitcases on the curb.

"You be all right here?" he asked.

The door was a few feet away. "Yes, we'll be fine." I paid the fare, added a tip and watched as he pulled from the curb.

After checking in, we took the elevator to our room and plopped down on our respective beds. We both started laughing. We didn't know what we were laughing at, maybe just the fact that we had made it. Devon took a few minutes and called home to check on her babies and I left a text message for Carl.

We made it. At the hotel. Miss you.

We closed the drapes, and after unpacking, pulled back the covers for a quick nap. Four hours later, I pulled open the curtain. The sun had set, but it was still light out. We washed up and went down to the café for dinner. The clerk told us it was still early, if we wanted to take a bus ride into Dublin Center, but we declined, deciding to have a light dinner and walk around our private little part of the world.

The next morning, we were up early and down at the desk before seven. I gave her Alice's address, but she looked back at us with a blank stare.

"I'm sorry, ma'am. I have no idea where that address is. If you take the bus into Dublin Center, the Information Center would be able to help you."

"Where do you catch the bus?"

"We have the bus passes here and they will take you all around Dublin. You can get a pass for seven days."

"Perfect."

"I'll have them ready for you by the time you finish breakfast."

We went into the hotel restaurant, ordered our meals and mapped out our day. We would go to Town Center, ask about finding her address and get a feel for the city. We both agreed this was not a time to be tourists. We had to find her. She had not responded to my letter, but it had not been returned, so I felt sure she must have gotten it. I had to learn if she would see me.

Alice Leary, on Thomas Road in Filgas.

Our first stop was to the Service Center to find Filgas. Everything seemed turned around. We asked two people and got two different sets of directions. One told us to take the Stephen's Green bus and that would get us there, but when we asked the bus driver, he looked as confused as everyone else.

He suggested we take the Temple Bar bus, but again, the same confused look. By the time we had ridden through two full bus routes, picked up sim cards for our phones, and got back to the hotel, we were ready to call it a day.

We had dinner in the hotel, and decided to ask a clerk one more time. We waited for a young man as he tugged at the copy machine.

"Be right there ma'am."

We waited as he continued to tug. "Oh, be damned," he said just enough under his breath for us to hear. He left the copier and came over to speak with us. He gave us a wide smile. "What can I do for you?"

"Could you tell us where this address is?"

"Oh, that's the Whitehall area, all the way on the other side of Dublin."

"Are you sure?"

"As sure as I can be."

"What bus would we take?"

"Bus 8 would take you right there. You'll be able to pick it up across the street. Do you have a pass?"

"Yes, a seven-day one," Devon said.

We walked toward the door and I turned back for just a second, he had gone back to his nemesis, and began tugging at the paper, once again.

The next morning, we stood in the rain and waited for Bus 8, which would come at 7:45. As we got on, we found what seemed to be the last two seats. Devon asked where the Whitehall stop would be. He told her we had plenty of time and he would call it out when we were close.

The city was busy, people coming and going everywhere. Cars and buses turned without notice. Women with brightly colored scarves hurried along. Young girls no older than Devon rushed along to work, carrying brief cases and shoulder bags.

In no time the driver called out "WHITEHALL."

Before stepping off, Devon showed the driver her paper with the address. He took it in his stubby stained fingers, turned it over, then handed it back to her.

"Go up four blocks, turn left, another three. Should be on the right, maybe four or five houses down."

"Thank you so much," Devon said, brimming with excitement.

Twenty minutes later and Thomas Road was still not to be found. We walked round and round, after the third time we realized we were going in circles. The houses looked alike, except for the painted doors. But no Thomas.

We walked back, looking for the bus stop, which seemed to have become just as elusive as Thomas Road. We were still going in circles when we saw a woman sweeping her driveway.

"Ma'am can you tell us where the bus stop is?" Devon asked.

"Down at the end of the corner. Are you lost? You've been walking around for quite a while."

"We were looking for Thomas Road."

"You'll find no Thomas Road around here."

"Do you know where it might be?" I asked.

"On the other side of the thoroughfare, M50."

"Our hotel is on M50," I said, looking over at Devon. "Thank you," I said, turning toward the street.

The woman dropped her head and continued sweeping. We took a seat on the bench without saying too much. A day wasted was all I could think of. I looked up when the doors to the bus opened. We had a different driver, but I wasn't about to ask for directions again. It was just past noon. We stepped off the bus on O'Connell Street.

We went into the café on the corner and took a seat by the window. It had just started to fill up. I realized that things were no different than the corner café on Washington Street, in St. Helen's.

"Well that was a wild goose chase," Devon said, looking up at the menu on the wall.

"No, not really. We were able to see a regular old Irish neighborhood, where life is what it is. I'm OK."

"Are you sure? We wasted a whole morning."

I smiled. "We had three bus rides, we walked through an Irish neighborhood, and now we know where to find her. I believe the old woman more than anyone. Let's have lunch and start over. She might be closer than we think."

The tenseness slipped from my body. I knew now that we would find her. The search would soon be over.

39

"Maybe we should ask the clerk at the desk again."

"No. Let's just head down across the street and see what we find."

"I think we should ask." Her tone pleaded, so I relented.

I watched the crowd while she went inside. People seemed to be everywhere, getting on the bus, riding past on bikes, some just strolling around the street.

"OK, I think we have it. He said Thomas Street is about two streets behind the hotel."

After about forty-five minutes and going in circles, a man with a woolen cap and short-sleeved white shirt, finally noticed our distress.

"Miss, are you lost?" He asked, addressing my daughter.

"Yes, I'm afraid we are. We are looking for Filgas. Is that a street or a town?"

"It is a small town, actually a county area of Dublin, about two miles south of here," he said pointing away from the hotel. You need to go back the way you came, and head in the other direction. You just came the wrong way that's all. Go the other way on the round-about." He didn't even blink as he gave directions. He bid us good-by and wished us luck.

It took twenty minutes to get back to the hotel and headed in the opposite direction at the round-about. It was the same route we had taken Saturday evening. We saw the Burger King and passed the Tesco. Across the street we saw the Filgas sign and froze in our tracks.

We just stared at each dumbfounded. How could we have missed it?

It was just after two o'clock, when it started to rain.

We were here. In her town.

I looked around at the beautiful flower baskets hung from the street lamp. We passed a bar, a florist, and three restaurants; everything open for business. As we came up the hill, we saw a church, and walked up the long driveway as the rain began to pound down. We went inside to get out of the rain. Orange flowers bordered the double doors contrasting the gray stone of the building.

The church stood empty, but there was a distinct feeling, the last of the parishioners had just filed out having lit the final candle or saying the concluding prayer.

It was nothing like St. Patrick's in Dublin Center. Though tall pinnacles reached to the sky, there was a simplicity to it, almost dowdy.

Surprisingly there was a statue of St. Teresa surrounded by tiny glowing candles. It looked as if a great many prayers had been offered to her over time. I walked up to the altar and genuflected slowly to the God who had brought me this far.

I dropped three coins in the receptor, adding my own to the prayers, I prayed to her and to Him, to whomever I thought would listen to find her, to have her open her door.

You know I made it here, for that I am so grateful, but we've hit a bit of a wall. We can't find her. Please don't make me leave here before I hear her voice or look into her eyes. I don't think I could bear it. We've come so many miles, gone in so many directions. Please help me find her.

I bowed my head and turned back to where Devon stood. Suddenly a stillness came over the church, even the candles stopped flickering, and it made me wonder if my prayers might not have had been answered.

After a few minutes we walked outside and found two women standing by a car chatting. I wanted to ask if they knew Alice Leary, or if they could take me to her house. Instead I asked them if they knew "Thomas Road."

"Why yes, Miss. It's just a bit down the way. Turn to the right when you see the antique shop. What is the name of it? Sorry I can't remember, anyway, go down a few blocks, but I think it is Thomas. Is it street or avenue?"

"I don't know, just Thomas, that is all we have," Devon said.

"Well, they actually go into each other, so just look for your number."

"Thank you so much, I appreciate it," I chimed in, watching as they got in their car, pulling down the brims of their hats.

"Are you visiting family?" The older one asked, adjusting herself behind the wheel.

"Uh," we paused and looked at each other, then Devon spoke up. "We're from the States and looking up some friends we met."

"Best of luck on your search. Would you like a ride?"

"You wouldn't mind?" Devon asked.

"No bother. Come on dears, it's not far at all, and I am going that way anyway, and with the rain coming down, you'll catch a death."

She tossed some papers about, and we quickly climbed into the backseat. She drove down the same route we had taken earlier.

The passenger turned toward us and smiled.

"Have you been here long?" she asked.

"No, we just arrived the other day."

"Friends on Thomas Street, do you?"

"Yes, as a matter of fact," Devon said.

"Where are you ladies from?" The lady with the over-sized hat asked, looking into her rear-view mirror back at us.

"Oregon."

"Didn't think you were from here, could tell by the accent. Who might you be looking for?"

We looked at each other quickly and Devon suddenly replied, "A friend," she paused. "We met in the States and we told her we would visit when we came to Ireland. And, well, here we are." Devon laughed.

"I've lived here for over 10 years, what is her name?"

There was a long pause. "Alice Leary." I took a deep breath.

"Sorry, don't know that name, but I live on the Westside. She must be in the other parish. We usually don't cross paths."

We passed the elementary school and the produce store. We were two blocks past where we turned around, when we saw the sign for the antique shop. If we had only gone a little farther.

"Well here we are. I can drop you at the corner or I can take you to the door."

"Oh no, we're fine here. They're expecting us."

I looked over at Devon with quite a shock. No one expected us, least of all Alice. As we got out of the car and waved our gratitude, I saw the sign on the low brick wall. "Thomas Road." We had arrived. I looked up at the number on the first house. She was only a few houses away.

"Thank you so much."

"I can take you to the door if you like."

"No, we'd rather walk, but thank you."

"Well ladies, have a grand trip. Be safe." We waved to them as they swiftly turned back the way they had come.

It had stopped raining and the sun was desperately trying to break through. Devon took a picture of the street sign and we slowly walked the curves. We turned left, then right. It was a small cul-de-sac. Her house stood dead center. There was a tiny car parked inside the front yard.

I stood there like a fool, taking pictures of her house. I walked closer and took more pictures. There were no words.

I walked up to the door and peered into the polished windows. Everything was neat and orderly, flowers... yellow roses, stood in a vase on the dining table, an afghan hung over the back of the couch.

I stood for a long while in front of her door. I walked back to the driveway but stopped and quickly pulled a note pad from my purse and scribbled a note.

We're at the Legend Inn, arrived Saturday, anxious to see you.
Please call. 013-241123
Claire

As we walked out of the cul-de-sac a man stood behind his gate, sweeping. He looked up at us, then went back to his work.

"Good afternoon," Devon said.

He nodded and went back to work.

We walked back to the church with a light sprinkle following behind.

There was something about standing in an empty church. It reminded me of the massive church in St. Helens. It wasn't all that big, just when you're seven... and alone, a church with high ceilings can make you feel very small.

I was seven again, as I walked up to the front, genuflected and knelt once again at the same altar, this time offering thanks and begging for His attention in the disguise of a prayer.

Dear God,

It's me Claire, I was here earlier. I just wanted to thank you for the two ladies in the parking lot. They took us to her block, and I think we found her. I left a note. Please let her know that she needs to call. Let her know I don't want to hurt her in any way. I just need to meet her and then I'll go home.

I bowed my head and stepped away. We left the church and headed to the bus stop.

Everything had taken place in less than an hour. It was just past three when we returned to the hotel. Too early for dinner; too early to go to bed; too early for pretty much everything. We sat in the hotel café and had a glass of wine. I wondered how it would be when she saw my note.

We decided to shower and go back into Dublin Center. We spent the evening on Grafton Street, catching dinner in a small Italian restaurant and ice cream at Stephen's Green. We had been walking all day and I was exhausted. Ready to call it a day, even though there were still a few more hours before day's end.

By day three we knew her town by heart. We had gone to mass, walked the streets and even bought souvenirs. I called her house phone, but no one answered, and I wasn't comfortable leaving a message.

On our second visit to her house, I rang the bell and knocked, but again no one was there. I could see that mail had been slid through the slot. I took a note pad out of my purse and left her another note.

Sorry we missed you today. Hope you are well.
Please call.
013-241123
Claire

We walked back to the church and I decided to see if I could find a priest to help with my dilemma. I knocked on the rectory door and a delightfully sweet looking man, with deep set blue eyes and rosy cheeks, answered. His collar was turned, and he had a wool cardigan over his shoulders.

"Come in, come in. How may I help you, child?"

I proceeded to tell him an abbreviated version of my story to see what advice he might offer.

"By all means search for her," he said. "But I don't think I'd call her daughters. This is about you and her. You need to allow her to be the one to tell them, if she chooses." His words reminded me of Ruth. "Remember Lass, those were different times."

"Thank you, Father. I think I know what I need to do."

"Would you like a blessing?"

"Yes. Thank you."

He blessed us both, then shook our hands, and walked us to the door.

"Mom, what do you want to do?"

"Besides, go back to her house?"

"Mom, we left a note. Let's do something today to get your mind off everything for a while."

"Isn't Glasnevin just down the road. We could take the bus. I saw it on the internet. It's remembrance for the Magdalene's."

"Settled," Devon said. "We can spend the afternoon there. Besides, it will be a great place to get some pictures."

In fifteen minutes, the bus pulled up and we were on our way to Glasnevin.

The sun broke through the clouds, just as we arrived. We asked about the Remembrance, and were given directions to the memorial. As we strolled through the cemetery, we were caught up with the aged headstones, some that had fallen over, simply due to age.

While Devon roamed the grounds, I found the Marble wall of the Remembrance, a list of women's names who had spent time in the Laundries had been carved in the stone monument. The names dated back to 1878.

Women who died at the hands of those who used the name of God to justify their actions. Many, with their families having no idea. They were never told what happened to daughters, their sisters. It was truly reason to pause.

I stood alone reading the names and felt compelled to do something I had promised I wouldn't. I pulled out my cell phone and dialed the number I had found in the Irish white pages.

"Hello."

"Could I speak with Alice, please?"

"She isn't here right now. This is her grandson. She's in London. Would you like to leave a message?"

"No, thank you. I'll call back later. Do you know exactly when she'll be home?"

"Yes, Sunday night," the soft voice replied.

"Thank you."

I snapped my phone closed. She wasn't ignoring me.

Then I stopped for a moment. She knew the date we were coming. I had written, I even sent pictures.

She left on purpose. *Why would she do that?* I stared at the names of the women who had been forced to work in the Laundries; a place where I was sure Alice had lived for a while. The Magdalene section had three white headstones across a graveled area surrounded by small pea-sized rocks. I looked for Brennan and Leary. A Mary Leary, died in 1898.

Just as I turned away and walked across the gravel to find Devon, I went down. It happened so fast, it took my breath away. My camera went flying across the gravel, and my cell phone slipped from my hand. I didn't fall on anything except the small rocks, but I went down hard. The palms of my hands were bleeding along with deep cuts on my right knee. By the pain I knew I had bruised my thigh, because it hurt as I tried to walk across the gravel.

I thought it ironic that I had gone down in the cemetery.

I understood why. I had lost myself over finding Alice. It should have seemed like nothing, but it was my whole world. I had surpassed all my attempts when I came to Ireland in the 90's. Actually, I was surprised I hadn't gone down sooner.

I found the camera that had flown across the gravel. With the broken camera I knew I would have to tell Devon. It had been an early birthday present, now I would need to replace it.

She saw me coming and knew immediately what had happened. My face was drained of color and I shook as I moved across the paths. I held out my camera to show her the damage. She took hold of my hand.

"Are you all right?"

"Yes, it came so fast, I wasn't ready. I need to wash my hands, and my knee and thigh ache. I am sure I will be quite bruised by the time we get back to the hotel."

"Do you want to go back now?"

"No. I really want you to read the names on the wall."

She stared at the marble, even running her hand across the names. She didn't turn back at me, so I came up behind her and put my hand on her shoulder.

"Let's find someplace to eat," she said. "We could go to the Botanical Gardens, I think they're close, maybe a few stops down. We can eat there, and you can rest."

"No, let's go back to the hotel. I'm really tired."

I was relieved to be able to get off my feet as we waited for the bus. Within a few hours my bruise had blossomed. Devon ordered room service and we called it a day by five. I drifted in and out of sleep, seeing visions of Alice... in her house, on the couch, reading the notes. I couldn't see her face, but I saw gentle hands holding the paper.

* * * * * *

Of all the places I had wanted to go, I was desperate to return to Castlepollard.

I needed to go there.

I had read everything I could. I had read about the nails in honor of the infants who had lost their lives, buried without sacrament, wrapped in blankets and stacked on top of each other.

We took the bus out and walked up the path in the rain. The rows of gray buildings stood in sharp contrast to the lush green of the lawns.

It was a prison. They had been detained for a sin that could never be forgiven by God. I could only wonder whose God could not forgive.

I thought of Alice who had committed no sin at all but had been sinned upon.

We stopped at the gate. The lawn, lush and green, no sign that we were about to walk into a cemetery. It was called Angel's Plot, a suitable name for those buried here.

I went to the wall, feeling for the worker's nails, and they were there in mass. Each one placed in remembrance of a child, a baby that didn't survive. I moved my hand along the crevices of the stones, and each inch stopped me with another nail.

Purple, white and blue ribbons adorned them. They were wet and soggy, but they were a rainbow of color.

I had read about the ribbons, placed in remembrance by the survivors.

I was one of them, a survivor. I wasn't one of the nails.

I placed both hands against the wall and wept. Not for me, for them, for the ones who never had a chance. I walked the length of the wall not taking my hand away.

This was no Angel's plot. It was a garden, a garden of nails.

40

We took the final bus out of the city. I was filled with a sense of melancholy. We had come to the end of the ride, literally.

We proceeded to our room through the stillness of the halls. Devon opened the door and noticed a red light blinking on the phone.

We looked at each other. Throwing the bags on the bed, Devon walked over to the phone, then looked back at me.

"There are four messages," she said, trying to hide her excitement.

"We don't know it's her."

"We don't know it's not."

"You listen, and then tell me." She picked up the receiver and followed the directions for collecting messages. She held the receiver in her hand, moved over and sat on the bed. Tears came without a word. It was her. She pushed another button and continued to listen, this time she smiled through the tears.

"Mom, you need to be listening to this. She is talking to you, not me."

"No, you finish." It was like getting a letter, but you're afraid to open it, so you hand it off to someone else. She hit another button. By the time she was done, she had listened to all four messages.

"What did she say?"

"You need to listen for yourself."

"Just tell me."

"Mom, you need to hear her voice." I walked over and picked up the phone. "Dial '7' and listen to the directions."

"Hello, this is Alice. I received your notes, when I returned from holiday. I will ring you later."

"This is Alice, I am home from London. I hope you are well. I'm sorry, I missed you. I'll ring again."

"I'm calling again. Yes, I'd like to meet with you. I could come to the hotel. I'll ring one more time this evening, hoping to reach you." That was her third message, one left.

"This is your Mum. I hope I have reached Claire Hamilton. I read your messages, and I can come to the hotel Monday at one o'clock, if that works for you. Please don't come by the house again. So sorry I missed you, hope to see you soon."

The phone went dead. There were no more buttons to press. My tears didn't come as fast as Devon's. It was her voice. She called herself Mum. She would meet me.

"Mom, are you OK?" She came over and hugged me and took the receiver from my hand. I fell apart. We slid to the floor and I buried myself in my daughter's arms. Of all that had been said, I heard "this is your Mum" and "don't come to my house anymore."

* * * * * *

There was no rain in Dublin.

I wanted the rain. I wanted the safety of the clouds wrapped around me. Both my children had been born on rainy mornings.

I had dreamt of this moment. I had lived it. So many times, I woke up believing it had already happened. I had my lines memorized and I promised myself I would remember every detail.

We were to meet at one o'clock in the lobby of the Legend Inn. I had the picture album that traced every fragment of my life that truly meant something.

Finally, at one-fifteen, the call came. I walked to the table and waited for it to ring two more times, before picking up the receiver.

"Hello."

"Yes, this is the front desk, your visitor has arrived. She'll be in the restaurant."

"Thank you. I'll be down shortly." Slowly, I placed the receiver back in its cradle. Stepping over to the window, I watched gray clouds move across the sky.

Devon came up behind, giving me a hug. "Mom, you can do this. This is what you have waited for." I turned into the arms of my daughter and smiled.

I looked back into the full-length mirror before I stepped out the door. I realized it didn't matter what I looked like, what I wore, or how I combed my hair. After worrying for so long, it only mattered that I would see her face and hold her hand in mine.

We were on the second floor, so the elevator ride was quick. When the door opened, I leaned back against the rail, bracing myself. My daughter had been right. I had been waiting forever.

I stepped off the elevator, paused, took a deep breath and walked into the restaurant.

Straight ahead, a very refined woman sat at a table with files spread before her. She wore her hair in a short bob showing off gold hooped earrings and bright red lipstick that matched the tiny flowers on her blouse. I reached out for the leather bar stool so I wouldn't fall. She read from papers spread out across her table. I stared at her, wanting to believe we resembled each other. But there was something about her. There were no freckles.

She didn't look like an Irish mother who couldn't tell her family about a bastard child. This woman had no secrets. She looked up for just a moment, then went back to her papers.

She looked at her daughter. Didn't she know that? Did I need a sign?

I had the album clutched to my chest. Absolute fear draped my face. The waitress tapped my shoulder and pointed to an occupied booth in the far corner of the room.

Looking over, I saw a small gray-haired woman, in a purple jogging suit standing in the aisle, watching me. She stood with her arms by her side, smiling half a smile. She waited for me to recognize her.

"Alice?"

"You must be Claire." I looked at her and reached out my hand, she pulled me in for an embrace.

We stood together, mother and daughter, for the first time. Tears came before I even realized.

"Don't cry, dear one," she whispered, as she pulled me close once again. She held on to my hands.

"I'm sorry."

"Let me look at you. Oh, you are lovely," the tiny woman said, as she stroked my hair.

"As are you," I said, too stunned to know what else to say.

"You have freckles. You look much like I did at your age, but of course you would, you're my daughter." Alice blushed as she put her hands to her face.

"I've had them as long as I can remember. Someone told me they were kisses from the sun," I said, with an uncontrollable grin.

"Oh yes... and they make you look so Irish." Alice grinned.

"They've been my distinguishing trait," I said.

"Come, sit down." She guided me to the booth.

"I just can't believe that this is happening," I said, taking a seat across from her. Cups and saucers were already on the table, with a plate of sliced cake, in the middle. Once we were settled, the waitress left us alone.

As she sat in front of me, I saw a sadness move into her eyes and she reached across the table to take hold of my hands.

"I want you to know what happened. It is important that you understand." She bowed her head, as if in prayer.

"You don't have to do this right now."

"Yes, I do. I want you to understand why things turned out the way they did. Why I couldn't keep you." She began to talk, slowly and methodically. Staring straight at me, only turning away to take a breath. I could tell with each sentence how delicately she picked her words, her phrases, so that I could know her truth.

"It was late March. I was tardy getting home from school. It had been raining. It was the same path I took every day. I heard a noise as I walked, but I kept going, I didn't want to stop or turn around. I walked faster. Someone pushed me down. I tried to fight. He covered me. He tore at my clothes, and I smelled stale alcohol. I almost threw up." She stopped and looked at me. "I'm sorry. I tried so hard to get away."

She grasped my hands tighter. I didn't pull away.

"I saw his face for just a second. He was older, I didn't recognize him. I'd seen him in the village, but I didn't know who he was."

Between each sentence, she took a long pause, and the words slowly spilled from her. It didn't seem real.

I fingered the silverware on the napkin. I brushed my hair away and continued to fiddle like an anxious child. I didn't know what to do with what she told me. There was an ache in my chest, a tightness in my throat. I was proud of this woman sitting before me, allowing me to know the truth she had hid for so long.

"I was immature, too scared to even breathe, only fourteen. I didn't understand any of it. He left my clothes torn and my body bleeding. I waited alone, hiding in the bushes to be sure he was gone." Her voice was clear with no stammer or hesitation.

I felt there was something I should say, but this was no place to intercede in the events of her life, so I listened.

"I pulled myself up from the bushes and tried to wrap my coat around me. I was alone, and so scared."

It was hard to watch, overhearing a secret so terrifying. I didn't know if she said it for me or for her, but as I listened, it didn't matter why she told me, just that she had.

"In spring, Mum noticed my body changing. I was getting plump. When people asked about my weight, I laughed that I was a growing girl." She tried to smile, almost making a joke, but her smile dropped, her face went sad again.

"Finally, Mum took me to the doctor. She asked if I had been with any one. I lied at first because I didn't know what to say; then I told her what I'm telling you now." Her face turned red. "The doctor confirmed her fear, and she swung me around, yelling, "what did you do, girl?"

I didn't know what to say as she unraveled her story. I wanted to take her hand and tell her to stop, but I knew this was a truth she had to tell.

"While I sat outside his office door, Mum told him that I had never been with a boy. I waited while they decided what would happen."

There was a long pause before she started up again. Eventually, she took a sip of tea and a bite of biscuit. The sadness returned, as she carefully set the cup down.

"She told him that I was to blame. She said if I had walked home from school on time, nothing would have happened."

There was nothing I could say.

"That night Mum talked to Da, but he only said he would have none of it. After two weeks, they woke me in the wee hours of the morning, telling me I'd be leaving. Da wouldn't look at me," she said. "I had been his favorite, but now I was invisible."

She reached to her purse for a hankie. "I never told anyone until now."

She took off her glasses to clean them. "They came on a cold day in June before the sun came up. The local priest drove me to St. Peter's, at Castlepollard. Four parishes away. When I arrived, they took my belongings and took me to Mother Superior's office. I was told, to be kept in God's good graces, I needed to repent, every day." She looked at me with a weak smile, perhaps relieved that it was over, that after all this time, I knew.

"I worked up until the day you were born. You came in the morning with a matte of black hair, and wrapped your finger around mine. On the same day they took you, they sent me away," she said.

For the first time since meeting, tears filled her blue eyes, but she looked away, wiped her cheeks, and dropped her head in her hand.

"They told my brothers and sisters I was sent away to school. At that time, if you were poor and sent off to school, everyone knew it meant you had gotten yourself pregnant."

"After you were born, I wanted to give you your heritage as I had been given, but Mum refused, so in desperation, I gave you the only thing I could."

Her truth was my history. She had told her firstborn daughter her most private horrors.

"My mother came after nine days but, the Sisters told her I needed to be sent to the convent school in Dublin." Then she stopped. She had nothing more to say.

"That is enough about me. Tell me about you, dear one. What happened after we were separated."

And then it was my turn to tell what I knew.

How the years in the orphanage had not been so

good. I had been fostered out and brought back. I was sick and couldn't leave for a while. I told her about the woman who brought us over, and the reason I was adopted and the sadness that my new family had been through.

Her face changed when I told her about my condition, that I had not walked or talked. She could not show her face, burying it in her hands, but her eyes couldn't lie. She had no idea, I had been sick. I could see the guilt in her eyes, they narrowed and drooped.

"But you're good now, right?"

"Yes, I am good, I have my own family and we're happy."

"Where is your daughter? Is she here? Can she come out?"

She wanted to see Devon. Now it would be complete, we would be together, the only thing missing was Adam. He wasn't here.

"I have something for you." I laid the album on the table, moved it in front of her and went to call Devon. She smiled as she flipped through the pages.

Devon answered on the first ring.

"She wants to meet you."

I watched as Devon approached. Suddenly Alice turned around, and stood to greet her. Neither could contain their emotions; the sadness, joy, anticipation, the pure acceptance. Devon leaned into her arms and she held her granddaughter for the first time.

We sat back down and the conversation pulled from the intimacy it had held moments before, to the tenderness of a woman to her granddaughter. Alice touched her hand, caressed her in ways that broke my heart in a very good way. Alice asked about her life and family and Devon was proud to share her world.

The hours passed and both histories were divulged sacredly and intimately. Had someone walked by, they would have been embarrassed by the intenseness of the body language.

We learned about her children as they grew and her life. There were times her eyes clouded with tears, memories that she had promised herself she had forgotten.

In the album she came upon a picture of me holding Devon as a newborn, she had a flock of black hair.

"You had the same hair." She had remembered a moment with me. She captured that moment, keeping it locked away in her heart. Now, it would never be gone. She had a face to give it to.

She closed the album and held it to her chest.

"You know, I can't keep this out. No one can know about you."

I didn't know what to say. With everything we had been through, all her pain, our separation, even after telling me the horror of her rape, it was not enough. I was still separate from her life. Our worlds had collided, but they would never come together. I saw that now.

"I've hurt you." She reached over and took hold of my hand. "It has to be this way."

I brushed away tears and smiled. "No, I understand. You have to protect yourself. "I'll be going home, and you'd be left to explain."

A part of me wanted to run. Nothing had changed. I was still a secret. How could I have been so foolish to think I could have meant more to her? How could

I have thought this moment would have made a difference?

No one wanted the time to be over, when there was a silence, someone would say something to pick it up again.

Her cell-phone began to ring. "Will I see you before you leave?" She asked, not even responding to the call, as if it meant nothing.

"We would love to see you before we go," Devon said.

"I could come by the hotel. When are you leaving?

"We leave early Sunday morning," I said.

"Yes. We have to be at the airport by 6:00," Devon said.

"Then it's settled," she said, reaching over and patting Devon's hands. "I'll come Saturday night, before it's too late."

I kissed her on the check and wrapped my arms around her, not wanting to let go. I ran my fingers down her cheeks and brushed the hair from her face.

She turned and walked out the door. Our time together had ended. I watched her cross the street.

41

We had arranged to meet in the hotel lobby, as she wanted to give the children presents. We spent our last full day in Dublin shopping and saying good-bye to what we had grown to love in a short time.

She said she would be at the hotel by 6 o'clock. I was afraid of missing her, so I made sure we were back from the Center by five. The joy of shopping on our final day was bittersweet. I wanted to remember every moment, but I knew there would be things I'd forget; pictures that would get lost in my mind's eye.

Soon it was six o'clock, then seven, then eight. I looked out the window to avoid my daughter's disappointment. *She wasn't coming.* I couldn't look at Devon's face, so I looked out the window, watching the children play in the streets and old couples walking hand in hand.

I called down to the lobby, but there were no messages for either of us. By nine, Devon took a shower, and I changed into my night clothes.

"Mom, are you OK?"

"I knew she wouldn't come."

"She still might," Devon said.

"No, but I'm ok. Hey, I got to meet her, you got to meet your grandmother. Yes Devon, I'm OK."

Just as she was about to reach over and hug me, the phone on the table rang. It had to be her. A woman named Alice was in the lobby waiting. Would we be coming down?

She looked as young and fresh as the first day I had seen her. Her cheeks red from her walk to the hotel. She had a gift bag in one hand, and her windbreaker in the other.

"I'm sorry I'm late. I was watching the football game and my daughter was there. I couldn't tell her where I was going, so I do apologize." Again, she reminded me that I was still her secret.

"It's OK; I just thought you might not come."

"Of course, I'd come. I have gifts for the children. Devon, I want your children to have these. And I have a present for Adam, and then both of you. So, did you have a nice visit?"

"Yes, it has been an amazing trip." Tears ran down my cheeks.

"Oh, dear one, don't cry." I looked over and Devon was crying, too. "Oh, I've made you sad. I am so sorry."

"I'm not sad. Just the opposite, I don't want to leave. I've just found you and I don't know when I'll see you again."

"Well maybe, I'll come to America."

"I'd love that."

She opened the bag, so we would not have to talk about saying goodbye. It was too hard to know, I might never see her again. She had a truck for Devon's son, a bead kit for her daughter. She had a wallet for Adam, with Dublin written on the bottom.

She sat with her hands holding mine, and then slowly reached down in the bag again. She handed

Devon a book called <u>Irish Tales and Sagas</u>.

"I wanted you to have something so you wouldn't forget me."

"We could never forget you." I could no longer pretend that finding her was secondary to coming here. I searched for her and found her... and now I would have to leave. Reluctantly, I pulled away trying to regain my composure, to wipe the tears from my cheeks.

"The rain is coming down harder, I must be going soon," she said softly. She turned and looked out the plate glass window.

"We could call a taxi, if it's too late," Devon said.

"Oh no, dear, I'm fine."

We stood and she reached for Devon, embracing her one last time, after that she came to me, taking my hands firmly into hers.

"Thank you," she said looking straight into my eyes. She cupped her hands around my face grinning as though she had found a treasure.

She reached one last time into her bag. "This is for you she said, handing me a set of journal books. This will help you understand everything, why I may have hurt you even more than I ever thought I would."

"I can't take these."

"You must. It will answer your questions. then you'll know I've always loved you."

"I really...." I paused, "I don't want to let you go."

"It's OK, I'll always be here, just like the swans in the Liffy."

I watched her walk out the double doors. She turned to me and smiled, pulled her parka up over her hair, opened her umbrella and walked away.

I stood, holding on to Devon's arm, hoping Alice would turn back, just once more.

42

Years pass and time gets away. Day to day tasks fill the voids. Life moves on and you live it the best way you can.

One afternoon everything changed. A message was left on my cell phone.

"My name is Catherine, I'm calling from Dublin. My mother is
Alice Leary. I believe we are sisters. Please call at your convenience."

Not just one message, but three, over and over they said the same thing. I set my phone on the counter and played the messages again. I hadn't heard from Alice in over three years. She hadn't answered my letters, or acknowledged the gifts I sent, the pictures... nothing.

Carl had gone fishing, so I had the house to myself. I walked from room to room, replaying the messages just to hear her voice. Catherine, Alice's middle daughter, born sometime around 1965.

I called Devon and asked her to meet me at Starbucks, after work. She seemed the one to tell, the only one who would understand. She was off work at two, so we had an hour before she had to pick up the kids. I ordered her favorite drink and sandwich and had everything ready when she arrived.

I watched her walk up to the patio, her hair pulled up into a ponytail and her scarf loosely wrapped around her neck. She had both hands stuffed in her pockets.

"Hey what is going on?" She asked, taking a seat at the metal table.

"I have something I want you to listen to." I pulled out my phone and set it on the table.

Devon leaned into the phone and watched as I pressed the button. There it was. What I had been waiting for since the day she asked me to stop going by her house.

"What do you think?"

"Are you kidding? Is that really your sister?"

"Well, I can't imagine anyone else claiming to be a Catherine from Dublin."

"What are you going to do?"

"There's more." I took the phone and tapped the different areas.

"This is Catherine, she lives in Boston. Her daughter's name is Isabelle."

"How do you know all this?"

"It wasn't hard, she was right there on Facebook."

"I don't believe you," she said laughing. "She wants you to come now?"

"Yeah, I think something terrible has happened."

"Not necessarily. Maybe she's calling for Alice, for everyone to get together."

"Maybe... I can't just drop everything."

"Why not? You said you'd go, if she ever called. "

I put my phone away and took a bite of the sandwich. Devon drank her latte, and we were silent. We kept our words hidden from each other, but I knew my daughter well enough to know what she was thinking.

"I never told you this, but a few months ago, I got a nasty letter from Rose, followed by a phone call."

"What did she say?"

"Basically, to leave Alice alone. She wants me to stop the presents, the cards, the texts, everything. She said her mum wanted nothing to do with me."

"What did you do?"

"I stopped."

"It's different now, Catherine called," Devon said.

"I don't know..."

"You have to go. Did you call her back?"

"No. That's why I called you. I don't know what to say."

"Tell her you'll do everything in your power to get there."

"If I go, you'll come?"

Devon put her cup on the table. "You think something is wrong with Alice, that's why she's calling. You have to call."

"Should I call now? It is almost nine-thirty in Ireland. Is that too late?"

"No. Do it now."

I placed the phone back on the table and rubbed my temples. Suddenly, the phone began to ring, almost jumping off the table. Devon looked down, then up at me.

"It's her. Look, an Irish number."

I pushed the button.

"Hello."

"Is this Finn, I mean Claire Fischer?"

"Yes." I reached out and took hold of Devon's hand, then set the phone on the table and hit speaker.

"I'm Catherine. I believe we are sisters. I'm calling from Dublin. Our other sister Francie is standing next to me."

"Hello." There was a long pause.

"Claire, please don't hang up."

There was no way. I had waited years to get this call, so terrified it would never come.

"No, I'm not. I just don't know what to say."

"We found your number in our mother's phone. We found your

text messages."

"Oh my, you must think me a crazy lady."

"No, not at all. She got them all, she just, well, I guess she couldn't answer them." There was a silence. "Are you still there?"

"Yes, of course I am."

"Our Mum must have cherished those texts, she never got rid of them. Without them we never would have found you."

"I never thought I'd hear from anyone, again. I received a call from Rose a few months ago. She made it very clear that I should stop calling and bothering Alice."

"Rose never wanted us to find out about you."

"Why?"

"I don't know, Claire. The reason I called is that Mum, Alice is sick. We're hoping you'd come to Dublin to see her and ..." She paused. "You could meet all of us."

"Catherine, Rose was very clear."

"Rose was wrong. She had no right to speak for us.

We want you to come. It's important. We don't really know how much longer she has, and well, Francie and I think she would like to see you. You are her daughter."

"She sent a letter, as well. She said Alice didn't want to hear from me."

"Rose did that on her own. She never told Mum, or us. I hate to say it, but Francie and I never even knew you existed, until just a couple of days ago.

"Mum took a fall. We don't know how things are going to go. You need to be here."

"Are you sure?"

"We're very sure. If Rose doesn't like it, well, this isn't about her. Francie and I can't wait to meet you." Her voice was soft and pleading.

Then a new voice came over the line, "Finn— Claire, this is Francie, we would really like you to come. Please. Do you think you can make arrangements in the next few days?"

"I guess so. I'll have to take care of some things here at home. Can I call you?"

"We'll pay for your ticket. She had money set aside, and we are positive this is what she would want it spent on."

"Can I bring my daughter? She's met Alice and become very attached. We can pay our own way."

"Of course, she can. No discussion. We will pay for both of you. There's plenty of money. Call back with all of your information."

"Thank you. I will call back in a few days."

"You'll come?" I could hear the begging in her voice. Something happened that changed everything. I was finally real. I brushed the tears away.

"Yes. Let me check my calendar and I'll text all the information."

"Perfect. We'll make all the arrangements. You have my number in your cell, right?"

"Yes, I'll make you a contact." I laughed out loud at that. She must have heard me.

"Who would have imagined this day would come?" It was Catherine, her voice still a bit on edge. "We had no idea you even existed."

"I don't know what to say."

"There is nothing to say, just come as soon as you can. How long can you stay?"

"I don't know."

"Why don't you just make it one way? We can figure out a return flight after you're here."

"I'll call you in a day or two."

I needed to take it all in. Up to an hour ago, I had almost given up on any of this, and now I was being begged to come home.

"Please realize, time is of the essence. We're not sure how things will go."

"Yes of course. Thank you. I'll be speaking to you soon."

"Good-bye."

Devon clicked off the phone and we sat in silence. "My God, it happened. We're going back to Ireland."

"As good as that sounds, it might be the worst thing ever. It must mean she's dying."

"Maybe she isn't that sick," Devon said in protest.

"Yes, she is. I could hear it in her voice."

"Are you going to ask Dad?"

"I don't have to ask anyone. He has known all along this day would come."

"Did you tell him about Rose calling or sending the letter?"

"No. I kept it to myself."

"She had no right to tell you that you couldn't write your own mother."

"I may well have done the same thing, if I thought I was protecting her."

"I could see that happening," Devon said.

"Are you sure you're up for it?"

"Oh, thank God, I wasn't sure you meant it."

"Of course, I did. You were very attached to her. I just wish Adam could come."

"He'd never leave, not with the baby so young, and work."

"What do we do now," Devon asked, brushing long strands of hair from her face.

"I guess you talk to your husband, and I talk to your dad, and we set a date, and call them."

"How about the first week in November." Devon drank from her cup, then looked up.

"That's a little over a week away. Can we get everything together by then?" I asked.

"Haven't you always known exactly what you would do if that call came?"

I laughed to myself. I had everything together, all her letters, the certificates, pictures, and the journals that would show, without question, that I belonged.

"Yes, I have everything together. I just have to put them in the suitcase."

"A week should be more than enough time, if they can make the arrangements."

"We still have to deal with Rose," I said, twirling my empty cup between my fingers. "She is not going to like this."

Devon, sat back, and fiddled with her purse. "She had no right. You belong there as much as any of them."

"Not in her eyes. She is the oldest, and she's been protecting her mother all this time. I understand that."

"From what? Her daughter?"

"She has her reasons."

She looked at her phone. "Jeez... Mom, I gotta go. Call me tonight."

"I'll call you."

I hugged her tight and watched her walk across the parking lot. The wind picked up, but the rain had stopped. I tossed everything in the trash and walked to my car. My keys fell as I unlocked the door. I crumbled as I reached for them.

I cried. I was going home, again.

The journey was coming to a close.

I had spent almost half my life trying to be a part of her life and now I was being let in. It terrified me.

43

On the fourth of November, I sat with Chelsea curled at my feet, reading the latest Patterson thriller. I put the book down and picked up my cell. I couldn't wait any longer, there was no reason not to call. Everything was in order.

"Catherine, this is Finn/Claire. I thought it was better to call than text."

"I've been waiting. When can you come?"

"The eighth. I just want to be sure that it's still all right. I can't seem to get Rose's words out of my head. I don't want to come in the middle of anything."

"You'll be in the middle of everything, but you need to be here. We know that Mum thinks about you every day. I won't try to explain Rose or her actions, but I know in my heart, how much Mum needs you," Catherine said.

"The first time I met Alice she gave me a set of journals. They explain a great deal. Would you like me bring them?"

"I'd be lying if I said we wouldn't want to see them. There is so much about her life that we don't know."

"Good. I'll bring them. I found a United flight #311 on the eighth. It arrives in Dublin at ten o'clock in the morning. Would that be all right?"

"Wonderful. Let me take a look, I have my computer right here. I see it. I can book it right now, two seats, for you and your daughter. I need your information to book the flight."

I gave her the information and in a few minutes it was over. I set my phone down and stared out into the garden. It was beginning to fill out; to grow into its own. I had the one piece of Sally that I could keep forever—her garden.

I stepped outside and began to pinch off buds, and pick up dead leaves, all the things Sally had taught me to keep my garden in shape. When Alice and I had met, she had talked about a garden where she spent a great deal of time. I wondered how it might look, and how it was that we both loved gardening. I heard Carl as he came through and stepped outside.

"What's going on?"

"I called Catherine. We are leaving on the eighth." I looked up at him. He had taken this trip with me so many times before, from my sessions with Dr. Benning, to each trip, coming home just a little more broken, like a china cup, repaired again and again.

"You want to go, don't you?"

"Of course. This has been the trip I've waited for forever, even after Rose called, I still thought there would be a chance. I just didn't want it to be because she was dying."

"Maybe she isn't that bad."

"I don't know. They said she fell. No fall is good. She was so strong when I saw her last. I wish it could have been different, you know, that she would have let me in, meet her family, then maybe this wouldn't be so dramatic."

"Just be glad you get the chance."

"I know... grateful."

"I don't mean that."

"I know you didn't. It just stings when I hear the words."

I kissed him and we hugged in the garden. I didn't want to let go, so I held tight, leaning my head on his chest. "I love you."

"I know, I love you, too. Now go on, you don't have much time."

I went to the bedroom and pulled the suitcase from the top shelf. Item by item, I packed everything I would need for an indefinite stay. Before closing it, I reexamined everything I had put inside to be sure nothing was missing. I zipped up the suitcase and placed it on the floor by the door. I opened the top drawer of my dresser and dug down for the journals, still tied together.

I untied the ribbon, and laid them on the bed, then picked the one in the middle, and opened it.

The title read

Howth Beach

I found my shoes sinking deep into the sand, I took them off to free my feet of their confines. The sand melded between my toes, like clumps of oatmeal. I reached down, taking hold of this newfound gift, mushy in my hands, I had never felt such a sensation, watching as the sand trickled through my fingers, dropping to the ground. I seemed drawn to the water. The constant movement of the waves beckoned me, pulling with a promise of rebirth. A moving, ever-changing force.

So, is that where it came from—my love for the beach, the ocean?

I put all three books together, retied the ribbon and brought them into the extra bedroom, with my passport, and all the legal papers I needed to take with me.

I had spent the last few days prepping, after Devon and I had confirmed the dates. I had told everyone I was going except Adam. Everything had come so fast and in the past few years his life had made drastic changes. He had traded in his bachelor pad for a house with a tricycle in the front yard. He had been busy.

Since I'd taken Devon the first time, it only seemed right for him to come along, or at least be offered the invitation.

"Hey, are you busy?"

"We're always busy. What's going on?"

"Can I come over for a bit?"

"Sure."

"I need to talk to you."

"What did I do?"

"Nothing, more like something I did."

"Come on over."

As I drove across town, I wondered how I would explain taking Devon again. I pulled up in front and saw them through the open curtains. Adam was wrestling with Mia and Maggie was folding clothes.

"Okay, Mom, what do you have to tell me?"

"I'm going back to Ireland. Alice has fallen and she's very sick. I got a call from one of her daughters."

"I'm sorry, why are you telling me this. You certainly don't need my permission."

"I'm taking Devon, again. I feel bad that you aren't going this time."

"Look around Mom, I pretty much have my hands tied. I just started a new job, and I couldn't leave Maggie alone with the baby. Don't worry. I understand."

"Are you sure?"

"Don't worry. I don't need to go, but take pictures with you, of all of us, so they know you have another child."

"Of course. I know they would love to see you, Maggie and Mia."

"Mom, don't worry about me. You need to go. We'll talk when you come back, and you can take us out to dinner."

I smiled but felt a sadness that I was leaving my son behind again.

"When are you leaving?"

"The seventh."

"You've got a lot to do. Go on now, kiss Mia good-bye."

I hugged her as tight as I could, then went over and hugged Maggie and Adam together.

"I'm sorry. I hope she'll be okay," he said.

"I don't think they would have called if she was going to be okay."

"Be safe Mom, we love you."

"I love you, too."

44

I would have thought meeting Alice would have been enough to send me over the edge but meeting my 'sisters' after so much drama set me into a tailspin. I had nausea the whole flight, unable to keep anything but water in my system.

"Mom, come on, you have to relax. You've done the hard part, this is the icing on the cake."

"You really call this icing. I should have let you read her letter. Rose definitely does not want me here."

"Maybe she doesn't, but Catherine and Francie do, and they're convinced Alice wants to see you. She's been asking for you. That's what counts. Besides, you know, if she is that angry, she might not come around at all."

"That would be a blessing, in a way."

The pilot announced we'd be landing in Dublin, in a few minutes. I took a deep breath and looked out the window at the landscape, as green as I remembered. No matter my fears, I was coming home.

Devon stood up, but I remained seated. I felt frozen and couldn't move.

"OK, is this how you're going to do it?"

"What do you mean?" I asked looking up at Devon.

"Fine. We'll wait for everyone to get off."

"I'm sorry. I know it is ridiculous, but I just can't move."

"You've talked to Catherine repeatedly, in the last couple of days, right?"

"Yes, and she's been delightful."

"And they've invited you, so they're all you have to worry about. Screw Rose."

There it was my very logical, strong-willed daughter telling me how to stand up to anyone. I looked back out the window. She was right. It had been their call that put everything into motion. I pulled my backpack from the floor, stuffed my Kindle inside, and stood up.

"Let's go find Catherine," I said, finally giving Devon an honest smile.

"That a girl, that's the Mom I know." Devon squeezed my hand.

Though still the last passengers off the plane, the attendants greeted us respectfully. I heard the last one say, as she waved us off, "Have a grand time."

It would be a while before we would see anyone, as we had to go through customs. We were guided into the room and moved along at a steady pace. I held my documents, to be ready for the attendant. I placed my passport and boarding pass on the counter in front of a red-cheeked jolly man, with an Irish cap.

"Morning, Miss."

"Good morning."

"Let's see that you have everything here?"

"Yes, sir."

He looked at the documents, then up at me, and smiled. "Welcome home," he said.

"Thank you."

I waited and watched with Devon, then we moved along. "Mom, he welcomed you home. That was so amazing."

"Yes, he did. I guess I am home." I took hold of Devon's arm and we walked through the gate.

As the people in front of us fell into the arms of their loved ones, I searched for Catherine's face. She had texted me a recent picture. I stopped and turned in all directions, then I heard my name.

"Claire?" I turned and saw an older woman with short silver hair. She didn't look like the picture, but I didn't know who else she could be. I knew it wasn't Alice, much taller than I remember Alice to have been.

"Catherine?"

"I'm Catherine," a much younger woman stepped forward and said. "This is Claire, she held you in the nursery, when Mum couldn't."

"So, I'm your namesake?"

She reached over and took me in her arms. She held me so tight I couldn't breathe. This was *the* Claire, the one Alice had spoken of, who had helped her and been so kind.

"I'm Claire."

"As am I. I held you when you were a newborn. Look at you. I thought about everything I would say to you if I ever saw you again. I promised her I…. You look so grand."

I tried to smile, but I couldn't stop the tears. I felt Devon take hold of my arm, as if she were holding me up.

"This is Catherine and Francie, your sisters."

"And this is Devon, my daughter."

"We are so pleased to meet you, my dear," the elder Claire said.

I stared at the women in front of me. I could see myself in them, Catherine's eyes, Francie's eyebrows. I couldn't stop looking at them, back and forth. Then there was Claire, who intrigued me the most.

"I never thought I'd meet any of you. She was so afraid," I said.

"Well, there was a lot for her to be afraid of, but not anymore," Claire said.

"We're all here," Francie said. She pulled her scarf around her neck and took hold of Devon's hand.

"I've waited for so long, but I knew coming here would mean something terrible must have happened."

"Mum's been having a time with things, but seeing you will surely help," Francie said.

"I never called her mum, or mother or anything like that. It seemed wrong. When we met, I called her Alice out of respect. I don't know what to call her."

"Call her whatever makes you comfortable. You know you belong, regardless of what you call her," Claire said. She took hold of my hand and I looked down at the freckles and patted the wrinkles. I couldn't take my eyes off her. She had held me first, as Alice had said, protected me from all the evil in a place that had brought my mother so much sorrow.

"Thank you. I've worried about offending everyone, calling her something I had no right, or being some place, I wasn't wanted. How will Rose be?"

"We called you, remember? Believe me, you're wanted," Catherine said.

"We are so glad you came, both of you," Francie said, still hugging Devon, as a youngest aunt might. "We didn't know that you actually existed until a few weeks ago."

"I know. I'm sorry for that," I said. "I've known about all of you for...I guess it's been nearly ten years, now. Alice gave me pictures."

Catherine took hold of my hand while Francie clung to Devon and we walked toward the baggage area. "Rose didn't come?" I asked.

"No. She won't be joining us," Catherine said.

"I'm not surprised. Her letter spoke volumes. There was so much anger."

"She's been very protective of Mum, and to be honest, she doesn't believe you're real." Catherine blushed when the words came out. "I'm sorry."

"Don't be, Rose said the same in her letter and phone call. She's going to be the tough one to face."

"Come on," Catherine said, pointing toward the escalator. "We'll go this way. It will take a while for them to bring the luggage down."

"I want to thank you," I said. I stopped and turned toward everyone. "You have no idea how much I have wanted to meet you—all of you. I was so afraid I'd never hear from her again, and that we would go the rest of our lives isolated from each other."

"I think I can speak for all of us," Catherine looked around. Francie and Claire nodded. "We've waited a long time to meet you as well, we just didn't know it."

"How is she doing?" I asked, a bit anxious to change the subject.

"It's been touch and go. All we can hope for is a good day," Catherine said.

"I called the hospital earlier and they said she was awake and having a good morning." Francie had let go of Devon and had moved over to my side.

"Don't be upset," Catherine said, reaching her arm

around my shoulder. "You know, they were all about you. She was so afraid of losing you."

"They were all about me? What do you mean?"

"Her episodes," Claire said. "She keeps going back to when she was in the Home—when she had to give you up. She never forgot you."

"I know, she told me that the first time we met."

The ride from the airport left me stunned, just thinking about meeting everyone, but I was really here. The wait was over. I kept quiet in the car and Devon and I sat close. I didn't remember too much of the conversation, a bit about Alice's fall, about Rose refusing to be a part of anything. In no time Catherine drove into the hospital parking lot. We all walked through the doors together. Claire took hold of my arm and Devon walked between Francie and Catherine. I wondered if this was the same hospital Alice had written about in her journals, where she worked, delivered her children and lost her beloved Aidan. In the elevator we were quiet, even as we approached the nurse's desk.

She came around the corner, looking rather stern. "You can't all go in at once."

"We won't. We promise. Her daughter is anxious to see her," Catherine said.

The nurse glanced at us all, then moved in close. "Your Mum is still very fragile. We can't be upsetting her."

"Her daughter and granddaughter are here from the States. She hasn't seen them for a very long time."

I watched the interaction going on between the nurse and Catherine. I appreciated Catherine's determination, but also understood the need for the nurse to protect her patient.

"Just two at a time."

"I understand," Catherine said. "We promise not to upset her. Thank you."

Suddenly, a group of young people came out of her room. They were Devon's age, so they must have been the cousins who kept a vigil by her bedside.

"Paddy, Izzy, this is Finn. She just arrived from Oregon, with her daughter, Devon."

"So nice to meet you. My mother is Francie and she has told me so much about you," Paddy said.

"Thank you." He was taller than anyone else in the group. He had a mass of reddish-brown hair and wore a leather jacket. He gave a shy smile and stepped back.

"And this is my daughter, Isabelle, but we call her Izzy," Catherine said.

Isabelle stepped forward upon her introduction and reached across for my hand. "You are lovely, so much like your mother."

"We are going to step in for a few minutes," Catherine said. "You and Devon can get acquainted."

Her room was white and cold, nothing identifying the frail woman lying in the bed. I stood back and waited, but Catherine gently touched my back, moving me forward. A nurse was still in the room, folding over the covers and pushing buttons on the machine that stood behind the bed. Wires came from under the covers. Her eyes were closed, but I recognized her immediately.

"Mum, are you awake?" Catherine asked, leaning in and touching the blanket.

"Yes, of course dear. Oh Catherine, it's you." She moved her hand from under the covers and patted Catherine's fingers.

"Mum, someone's here to see you." Catherine

stepped aside and nudged me forward. I began to cry, realizing that this might be the last time I would see her. I was overjoyed to meet my sisters, but it was for her we had come. I brushed away the tears and leaned down.

"Alice, it's me, Finn. I'm back."

She opened her eyes and looked over at me, then smiled. I could see the veins just below the layer of her skin, her thin hair fallen to the side. There were bruises up and down her arms. I reached out and took hold of her hand and knelt down at her side.

"You're really here."

Catherine moved a chair over to the edge of the bed and motioned for me to sit down. I sat, still holding her hand, taking a deep breath to hold back the tears.

"I'm going to step outside," Catherine said.

"No, please stay. You belong. Can you bring Francie in, just for a few minutes?" I asked.

Catherine stepped out, but I kept my eyes on Alice. It had been over six years since I had seen her last, remembering her turning and going out the hotel door. I hadn't heard her voice, but she had sent a few notes, over the holidays and one for my birthday.

"Lean in closer, so I can see you." When she spoke her mouth barely moved, and I leaned in to hear her words. I didn't even realize when Francie and Catherine came back. I felt alone with her, free to say anything I wanted.

"How are you?" I asked, brushing the side of her cheek.

"Oh, don't cry, girl. I am so glad you're here."

"I am, too."

For the first time, I felt Catherine come up behind me as she sat on the edge of the bed. I looked up as Francie moved over to the other side.

"Here are my girls." She looked over at Francie, then back at me, then her eyes moved over toward the door.

"She wouldn't come," Catherine said. I knew at that point who she was looking for and wondered why Rose had not come. "We tried, but it was too much for her. It will take some time."

"I don't have time," Alice said so softly; it was a whisper.

I reached back and took hold of Catherine's hand, as I watched tears stream down her cheeks. We were stopped in our moment, as the door opened, a nurse closed the door behind her.

"I'm sorry, she needs to rest, now."

She said the words softly; as if she were hoping the softer they came out, the better we might feel. I looked back at Alice and she had closed her eyes, such a peace had fallen over her, a smile spread across her face.

We stepped out the door and Devon stood just outside. Claire must have guided her, knowing it was important for her to see her, hoping it would not be too late.

"I'd like to see my grandmother, if it's all right?" Devon said. "Claire said it was okay."

"She fell asleep, but, go ahead," Catherine said. "I am sure the nurse will let you in."

Devon moved toward the door, without saying anything to anyone. She had made a connection from the first time she handed her the flowers, to the last time she saw her as Alice handed her gifts for her children. I wanted to wait for Devon to come outside, but Catherine and Francie guided me toward the elevator.

"She can meet us downstairs. Her cousins will bring her down, if that's okay with you," she whispered as we moved down the corridor.

45

As we moved toward the chairs to wait for Devon, Claire grabbed hold of my arm and pulled me down on the chair. Francie and Catherine moved over to the nurse's station. Claire began, her voice soft, but with a bit of a scratch.

"How have you been getting a long?" She asked in a whisper.

"I've been good, my life is full."

"That is all anyone can ask for."

"Alice told me about your kindness."

"She never gave up on you. She even went to a private detective to find you. Did she tell you that?"

"No, but she did say she went to talk to Reverend Mother, but it was quite a disaster."

"Yes, that woman was a bitch, may she rest in hell…. I'm sorry, that was cruel."

"What did the detective find out," I asked, curious to learn how I was seen through someone else's eyes.

"He returned your Mum's money, and told her that from his search, you had died due to a complicated surgery."

"Oh my." I wondered what she must have thought after all of this, to think I had died before she could meet me.

"She buried all her documents in the yard so no one would find them. She tried to bury her feelings as well, but I don't think it worked. She couldn't get you out of her head."

"We found everything she buried," Catherine broke in. "We dug up the box after she told us about it, and that was how we were able to bring you and Devon here."

"Tell me about your life in Oregon," Claire pleaded, as if hearing about it would satisfy her fears.

"I really don't know what to say. It's all I know, the only place I have ever lived, I imagine, like you, being in Dublin."

"It is on the coastline, right?" Claire asked.

"Close, about an hour and a half away. It rains a great deal, like here. Everything is green and it allows almost everyone to have an amazing garden."

"Mum had, well she still has her garden."

"I know she told me about it. We compared plants. I can't wait to see it."

"You will in all good time," Francie said, leaning in. "And you will love it, like Mum does."

"I just want to stare at you, if that is all right?" I said, taking hold of Claire's weathered hand.

"And why would you want to do that?" Claire asked.

"Because she spoke of you so endearingly, and wrote about you with such love, how you were there for her, protected me from everything. She said you loved me so."

"I did. I was young and your mum, well, she was even younger. She had no one to stand up for her, the poor dear, too young to have any backbone. She needed someone to watch over her. I had no power in the rooms of the Home, but I did in the infirmary. The Sisters never went there."

After a few minutes Devon came with her cousins to the waiting room. The sadness she wore worried me, but I realized she had just seen her grandmother and knew that might be the last time.

"I didn't stay long, she was sleeping, but she woke up a couple of times."

"Did she remember you?" I asked, turning away from Claire.

Devon smiled. "Yes, once she recognized my face, she called me by name."

"Did you get to talk at all?"

"She asked how I was, but I mainly held her hand. That was enough. I was just glad to see her."

"There is so much to catch-up on. Let's go meet everyone else," Francie said. "Devon, you have a couple more cousins who are eager to meet you."

"That would be lovely," I broke in, fearing that Devon might be getting a little overwhelmed.

"Great. We have reservations for six at a quiet little Italian place,"

Catherine said. "We'll have just enough time to stop by the house and drop off your bags. You'll get to meet Connor, your uncle and his wife Jenny. Izzy and Paddy will be there as well."

"My husband, Colin is coming, too," Francie said. "Even Jean and Marie, Rose's daughters' will be there."

"Are you sure you're up for this? You must be exhausted from the flight," Catherine asked.

I was exhausted, I was saddened and enlightened, but I didn't know when it might end. I had waited my entire life for it, I would not let a weakness settle in.

"I wouldn't want to miss a minute," I said.

Catherine left a number with the nurse where we would be, and her cell number. We went down the elevator and out the door without too much conversation, but Claire did break in. "We have all night to get to know each other."

Everyone filed into different cars. Catherine following Claire. In a few minutes both cars pulled into parking spaces, we were inside the foyer of the restaurant, before we knew it.

Catherine led us to a table. I held on to Devon, while Claire hung on to me. Before we sat down, we were introduced to the rest of the family. Paddy and Connor stood out, both of them replicas of each other. They stayed standing until we all sat down. Claire took Devon and I to the head of the table, while Francie talked to the waitress. I took the chair next to Connor and Claire sat on the other side. Devon found herself between her cousins, who wasted no time asking about Oregon and the States in general.

We did look like them. I had Francie's hair, Devon had the girl's long fingers. I looked around and wished we could have done this years earlier, Alice would have been here. It would have made a difference, but I was grateful for now.

"What happened after you left Ireland?" Claire asked.

"I stayed in Dublin for almost five years, in an orphanage, then they sent me to Oregon, where I spent the rest of my life." I looked over at Devon, and she nodded.

"When did you learn about us? Paddy asked.

"I learned about Ireland when I was ten, but I didn't learn about you, or Alice until I was thirty-five."

"Why so long? Did they forget?"

"No. They told me she died. I guess they thought it was easier."

The room fell silent. They had their secrets, I guess I had mine as well.

"When did all this start for you?" Connor asked, taking a sip of his wine.

"I met Sister Helen in 1990...."

"You met her? She's the devil that locked your Mum away," Claire said.

"At first she wouldn't tell me anything. She told me to go home and hug my kids, but for whatever reason when I was getting ready to leave the convent, she said she remembered her."

"Of course, she did. God forbid she offer any help for a family to be reunited."

"You came back again, didn't you? You met Mum? That was when she gave you the journals. What brought you back then?" Catherine asked.

"A card from a social worker at Dr. Banardos. On the card was Alice's full name and address. It also gave me the date of Aidan's passing. That was why she wouldn't see me. He didn't know about me, and she was afraid of what he would think."

"So, you met with her?"

"Yes, Devon and I came. I decided that we wouldn't leave until we found her, and we did."

"How was it for you?"

"Everything I could have dreamed, and more, except for you. She kept you all so hidden, protected you with her life. She told me I couldn't go inside her house. She asked me not to call any of you. I didn't, but I did look you up on Facebook."

That one comment eased the room. Francie laughed, Paddy shook his head.

"So how did we look on Facebook?" Francie laughed.

"You looked like everything I could have imagined. You have no idea." I felt my voice quiver as the words came out.

"I wish she could have let you in then. We've missed out on so many years," Francie said.

"I've waited such a long time to meet you. I had hoped she'd have been able to tell you. I was always hoping she would be here to share it."

"It means a great deal to all of us, as well," Francie added.

"They shamed her into never telling anyone," Claire said, taking hold of my hand, and seeming to speak for all of them. "Not even her own husband or children. For what? Something she had no control over?"

"The year we met, she came to the hotel. She wouldn't allow us in the house," I said, turning toward them all.

"We never knew about you at all, but Rose must have learned something then. It took a while for the rest of us to put the pieces together. Once we did, we realized that she was afraid we'd stop loving her," Catherine said.

"I never meant to hurt anyone. I needed to learn about my heritage, especially since I found out she wasn't dead."

"Why weren't you satisfied with your life the way it was?" Jean asked, as she took a sip of her wine. I sensed she was asking what her mother might have, had she been here.

"Jean, why would you ask such a thing?" Marie, nudged her, but Jean just stared at me.

"No, that's okay. I don't know how to explain it. When I found out she was alive, I knew I had to find her. I didn't know what I would find, but I had to see her face. I had to know where I came from. It had nothing to do with my family, I think they understood my need." I looked over at Devon.

"My mother talked about searching for all of you for as long as I can remember," Devon broke in. "It consumed her life. I knew who I was when I looked in the mirror, but she didn't. I think that's what drove her."

Encouraged by my daughter, I picked up where she left off. "I needed to fill a hole in my heart," I said, looking around. "Something was missing, that is the only way I can explain it."

"Mum kept her secret well. I'm sorry we never knew about you. There had been Da and the three of us, and Mum. We were a family," Francie said.

"The Sisters said she never wanted her family to know. So, I stopped, but I continued to write hoping they might try to contact her again."

"It must have been hard to go home empty-handed," Marie said.

"I think it was one of the hardest things I ever did, but I left a letter. It wasn't until twenty years later, that I learned they never sent it. I went back to my life, but I never forgot her."

"I wish my mother would have known these things," Marie, Rose's youngest daughter, said. "She'd have come to meet you. She wouldn't have been so angry if she had known. I'm sorry she isn't here."

"She knew about me. She called and told me to leave your grandmother alone. She told me I was bothering the family."

"My mother wouldn't do that," Marie said.

"She did. She also sent a letter, telling me to stop all correspondence because I didn't belong to the family." I shrugged. "I did what she asked... until Catherine called."

"To put it bluntly," Jean chimed in, "she doesn't believe you exist. She was very protective of our grandmother. She told me a long time ago about a letter from a woman in the States. She made me believe you wanted to hurt our family."

There it was, the betrayal that Rose had passed on to her daughters. So many things could have been different, if Rose had taken the time to listen. It was over. I had to forget it.

"You should have told us," Francie said, her eyes hard on Jean.

"I promised I wouldn't."

"This family and their fucking secrets," Francie said.

"Maybe, she'll see me before I leave," I said. "I would like to meet her. I don't want anything. I'm not here to hurt any of you. I hope you understand."

I was too exhausted to even finish my meal. I picked at the pasta, moving it around on the plate, drinking more wine than I should. Just as I pushed my plate back, Catherine stood, and laid a plastic medal attached to a string on the table. I gasped at the sight of it.

"I gave that to her when we met, the first time. She was surprised that I'd kept it."

"Why did you give it to her?" Paddy asked.

"I can answer that," Claire said. "I promised your Mum that I would make sure it stayed with Finn," Claire said. She reached over and touched the medal, then ran her hand along the stained string.

"She said she wanted her daughter to have something she could remember her by."

"I held you as your mother put it around your neck," Claire said, "then hid it from Reverend Mother, so she wouldn't rip it off of you.

"I guess wherever you went, they kept it for you."

"My adoptive mother gave it to me when she told me my birth-mother had died."

Claire sighed. "Alice thought if the chance ever came to find you, if you had it on, she would know you. The medal is how she knew you were you."

The table fell silent. I held the medal that Francie had dropped in my hand.

"It was with this medal that she remembered everything about you. She told us, Catherine and I, without realizing it. She wept for you, so terrified that she had lost you. We knew, right then, we had to call and bring you home."

"I am so grateful that you did." I handed the medal back, but Francie folded my hand up and pushed it back.

"This is yours. You have earned the right to keep it."

Yes, I was home. I clutched the medal and slipped it into my purse.

There was a silence and soon Izzy turned to Devon asking about her photography. I watched as the others slipped easily into a natural flow of conversation. For a while I tried to forget that we had been separated for so long. I enjoyed watching Devon take part, she fell into place, like she belonged.

"I'm afraid I have to be going," Connor said, standing up. "Early morning, tomorrow. I must say Claire, Devon, it has been a delight to meet you. I am so sorry my sister had to keep her secret for so long, but hopefully we can put this behind us."

"Thank you. I think we've already begun. I know it's been hard for everyone, but I do understand...I don't hold it against her. I would be lying if I said it was OK. It broke my heart, but we are here now."

"Well ladies, good night, and no worries, the tab is taken care of."

I watched as Connor stood and left the restaurant with Jenny. I had a family, parents, sisters. I was greeting strangers as family, sharing deep dark secrets. I looked hard to see a piece of myself in each of them. But it was Alice. She was the commonality. I could see her in every one of us.

"Devon," Izzy said, "you should stay with me tonight. It would give our moms a chance to catch up, and I could get to know my new cousin."

"My suitcase is in Catherine's car."

"No problem, we're all parked in the lot, we change everything then. Paddy has room in his car for your luggage and he can drop us off. We'll meet up with everyone tomorrow."

"I think that is a great idea, Izzy," Catherine said, staring at Devon.

"I'm sure you both have lots to share."

Catherine looked over at me, as I took in everything. "Would that be OK, Claire? Francie and I would like to spend some time with you."

"Sure, whatever works," I said.

46

Catherine pulled into the driveway and I flashed back to the day I stood on the steps, writing the note that would bring us together. When I looked through the window at yellow roses on the table.

Francie opened the door and stepped to the side. I walked in and found myself mesmerized. Everything I saw through the window on that day was the same.

"When I was here," I said, looking at Francie, "I peeked in the window." I found myself smiling. "After all this time it was still the same, the sofa, the afghan, even the dining room table with yellow roses."

"Oh, the roses," Catherine said it under her breath and smiled.

"She's always loved roses. For as long as I can remember she's had them in the house. Now that she has been gone, we've tried to replace them every few days," Francie said, "just because... well, we're hoping she'd be home soon."

"They're beautiful, just like I remember."

"What would you like to do?" Francie asked, seeming to watch my every moment.

"I know I should be tired, but so much has happened." I placed my purse and jacket on the couch.

"Would it be all right if we just talked for a while? I have so many questions, especially after tonight. And I have some things I'd like to share. Maybe if everyone knew, it might make things different."

I looked around, touched the couch, the tablecloth, and the rim of the lampshade. *I was really here, in my mother's house.*

"The last time we talked, she said she had a garden. I'd love to see it."

"Of course, I'll take your luggage upstairs. Can I get you something to drink? Wine?" Catherine asked.

"No, I'm afraid I've had too much, but some water would be good, if that's all right?"

"I'll get a bottle from the kitchen," Francie said.

"Please don't let me stop either of you from having anything of your choice."

"I'll be down in a minute. Go on out to the yard. The light is right by the door." Catherine grabbed her suitcase, along with my carry-on and took it upstairs.

I followed Francie to the kitchen and just kept staring at everything. I didn't know how to explain what it meant just being here.

I touched the edges of the china cups with tiny purple flowers that sat on the counter and fingered the doilies on the table. I ran my hand along the tile, wondering if it was real.

I picked up the glass on the counter and turned toward Francie. "Is this hers?" I asked.

"She hasn't changed a thing since Da died. Claire, it's okay. You belong here, maybe more than any of us."

"It's been so long... I never thought it would happen." I felt the tears on my face. "I'm sorry. This is ridiculous. There is no reason for me to be doing this."

"Oh, my dear. I can't begin to imagine how you

must be feeling. I have always had her. We all have. I think that's why Rose is so angry. Being the oldest she never wanted to share, even with Catherine and me. Now she has you, as well. You're turning her world upside down. You're real. It's that simple."

I brushed the tears away and turned away from the window.

"Her home is really lovely. I often imagined how it would look... beyond the front window. I love the roses," I said, looking around as I leaned against the counter. "I came here every day, walking up the driveway, terrified she would abandon me, again."

"Did she know you were coming?" Francie asked, coming over to stand by me.

"I wrote her before I came and gave her the dates. I called once and, I guess it was Paddy, said she had gone to London to visit her sister."

"I remember that," Francie said. "How ironic."

It didn't seem ironic to me.

"The garden?" I asked.

Francie flipped on the lights and all I could think of was Sally's garden. I walked in circles. It was beyond magnificent.

"Da did this for her, a little bit each year. It became her sanctuary," Francie said, standing behind me. "It's where she learned about all the different plants."

Francie continued talking, but I was so taken by everything I stopped listening. I walked around, touching each plant and vine, as I had done at Sally's.

"After that I came to understand her passion." Her voice trailed off.

"So, what do you think?" Catherine asked, joining us.

"It's lovely. I can see why she loved it so."

"It's been her pride and joy, along with Mittens. Have you seen her yet?"

"No, A cat?"

Francie nodded.

"She never mentioned her. Hmm, something else we have in common. I have cats as well."

"She's around here somewhere. Don't worry, she'll show up. Just look for a fat, fluffy-tailed old girl," Catherine said.

"It really is lovely."

"Mum took great stock in it, always kept it livable. In the winter, the smells of her stews and soups filled the kitchen; then in spring, all the flowers."

I watched as Francie and Catherine put her house on display. They were saying everything they could to get me to like it. They succeeded. I loved every inch of it.

Francie went on about Alice, sharing everything she loved. I lapped it up like a puppy. Everything she loved, I wanted to love as well.

"Let's go in. I don't know about you, but it's getting chilly. We'll have lots of time, while you're here," Catherine said, turning toward the door.

I didn't want to go in, in fact, I never wanted to leave the garden. The only other place I wanted to be was by her side. "Sure."

"Let's go in the living room, it's much more comfortable. Do you need more water?" Francie asked, looking more nervous than I would have expected.

They had grown up in this house. It was their home.

"So, Catherine, you live in Boston?" I asked, taking a seat on the couch.

"Lived — now I live here. I left Dublin when Michael started a business in Boston. When Mum got sick, I came home."

"Did you like Boston?"

"It's was nice, I think more Irishmen live in Boston, than here. But it's not the same. There's something about Dublin. I missed my home dreadfully, and everyone," she said looking over at Francie.

We talked on, while Francie came back with another bottle of water. She and Catherine drank wine. I stared as they told me about Alice, what it was like growing up.

I liked Francie's brave Bohemian style, Catherine was a bit more sophisticated. With my long hair and jeans, I was more of a hippie, I guess.

"What are your passions?" I asked Catherine, abruptly.

She took a deep breath and looked at her Francie. "Finding you."

I blushed at the idea of that. I never imagined anyone looking for me.

"I can only imagine what you must have thought of me. I assume you found the picture album along with the text messages?" I blushed at the idea. "I just wanted Alice to know what she had missed."

"We found everything," Catherine said.

"Mum cherished everything from you," Francie added.

Those words stopped me, I didn't hear anything else she said. My head was still spinning from the wine at dinner; even the water hadn't helped.

The evening had turned into much more than I could have ever imagined.

"I'm sorry. I didn't mean to..."

"The album is beautiful, and it deserves to be on the coffee table.

"I never meant for her to keep it out on display. I just wanted her to see my life, what it was like. What I accomplished. I just kept thinking, if it had been me, I'd want to know everything." I looked back and forth between them, not sure I was making any sense at all.

"You seem to know everything about us, but we really know nothing about you, except the pictures. Did you live in Oregon your whole life?" Francie asked, abruptly changing the subject.

I nodded. "I never left the area. It's the only place I've ever known."

"And the orphanage?" Catherine asked.

"I don't remember anything about the orphanage."

"Did you think you'd ever come back?" Catherine asked.

"I never stopped thinking I'd come back," I laughed. "Every minute of every day."

"So, now that you're here?"

"I hope to see Alice every day. I'd like to try to work through things with Rose, if I can. It's important. I can't imagine how she must feel knowing someone came before her."

"How is it you understand?" Francie asked, setting her glass on the coffee table. "It's a quandary to me."

"I went from being the oldest to the youngest, in the oddest way. I had no say. It changed me, as I'm sure it changed her."

"I have a question for you," Catherine said, not looking up.

"OK, I hope I can answer it."

"What do you want us to call you? Is it okay that we call you Finn? I know it's the name she gave you, but you've lived your life as Claire."

I took a deep breath. It was a fair question, but not one I had expected. Claire was all I knew.

Without knowing why, I began to talk about my name. "I didn't even know I had another name until I was a grown woman. My adopted family changed it right away. They thought the middle name was simpler." I took a sip of water.

"I wish I'd known sooner," I continued, not even looking at them. "I'd have given it to my daughter. It means a great deal to me, now that I understand. It would be confusing with Claire, so, yes, please call me Finn. At least I'll know that name for a while." Even as I said it I believed it. "You'll have to give me a few minutes if I don't reply right away."

"That would be grand." We giggled like schoolgirls.

"Then Finn it is. You must be exhausted," Catherine said as she rubbed her eyes.

"Yes, but I'm afraid if I go to sleep, I'll wake up at home."

"It's a lot to take in," Francie said, leaning in on the couch.

"To be honest, I didn't know when, or if, I'd ever see Alice, again."

"I guess you have our dear Claire to thank for that. It was her idea that we get a hold of you," Catherine said.

"It was Claire?"

"She'd seen Mum in her episodes. She said they were all about you.

"She would cry out for you," Francie said, with the saddest of eyes.

"What do you mean?" I asked.

Francie continued to tell me about Alice's episodes in the home. Episodes where she fell to the floor and cried out. As heartbreaking as it seemed, it filled my heart to know even in the depths of her illness, I was in her heart.

"Do you know who Sara was?" Francie asked.

"Yes. She wrote about her in her journals."

"That's right. She gave those to you," Catherine said.

I felt like the journals were my ammunition. If no one believed I had a right to be here, I had her journals to prove I was important.

"And where was Rose in all of this?" I asked. It had been Rose who didn't want me here. I remembered the tone in her voice over the phone, the bitterness that I had dug into her family and taken her spot. I didn't want her spot. I wanted my own place. It was that simple.

"Oh, we approached her, repeatedly, but she would have nothing to do with you. That was when we found out she wrote you," Catherine said.

"Mum needs you here, Finn," Francie said.

"Do you think she's going to die?" I asked, finally allowing myself to take in that possibility.

"From what the doctors have said? Yes. The tumor has grown rapidly since her first fall," Francie continued.

"She's getting worse every day. I was surprised she was so clear this afternoon. She must have known you were coming," Francie broke in, looking back and forth between us.

"I hope you know I never meant to come between anyone. When I got the letter from Rose, I decided to back off completely, I tried to understand."

"Rose told us about the letter when we told her we had found your pictures and text messages. We didn't know she knew about you."

"How did she find out?"

"Years ago, she was at the house when Sr. Eleanor came to tell Mum that you had made contact."

"And?"

"She made Mum tell her what Sr. Eleanor wanted, but Mum didn't tell her everything." Francie composed herself.

"I found her once, but she turned me away, because you—Francie, it must have been you, were still living at home. Your Da was still alive. She didn't want me to hurt her family, so she refused to see me.

"We left letters for each other with the Sisters, but they wouldn't forward them."

"Our mum thought of you every day. You need to know that," Catherine said.

"Thank you. I'm sorry. I used to dream about standing in this very room. Now, here I am on the threshold of losing her."

47

I didn't sleep that night, maybe it was the wind and the rain, or maybe it was being in the room where my sisters grew up. I had dreamt about this room, what it would've been like. In the dark I pulled the covers over my head, wondering if I had done the right thing by coming home.

When the light came through the window, I got up and went into the bathroom. There was a set of towels on the sink, with a note.

Make yourself at home.

Turn the faucet all the way to the right for hot water.

Jiggle the sink faucet for cold water.

Francie

After a shower I went to the bedroom and pulled on a clean pair of jeans and a sweater from my suitcase. I made the bed, fluffed the pillows and wondered what the conversation was after I went to bed. I went to the window and looked down at Alice's lush garden. I was in my mother's home.

I slipped downstairs to a very quiet house. I searched through the cupboards and found coffee, bacon and eggs in the refrigerator, so I decided to pretend I belonged here. I started coffee, peeled off strips of bacon and popped them into the pan that was already on top of the stove.

I took a steaming mug of coffee and gravitated to the garden. It was more luscious in the light of day. I walked around touching the vines and buds from winter blooms. I liked the alone time.

I called Devon from my cell, unable to take my eyes off the swan planter buried among the vines.

"Hey Mom," she said over the line.

"How are you doing?" I asked.

"Grand. Isn't that what they would say?" She laughed.

"I suppose so. How was everyone? Did they treat you well?"

"Oh, yes. They've catered to my every whim, if I had any. Seriously, they've been beyond gracious."

I let her go on, telling me how they had taken her to another pub after dinner, then to Izzy's apartment. It was small, and she slept on the couch, but she didn't mind.

"What are your plans today?" She asked.

"No one is up yet. I imagine we'll go see Alice," she said in a low whisper.

"We are too, later this afternoon. We'll catch up there. Gotta go."

I tapped off the phone and took a seat on the bench.

"We didn't have this garden when we were little," Catherine said, standing in the doorway.

"I just love it. It takes my breath away. I have a friend, well I did. She passed away, but she taught me everything there was to know about gardening. I've cherished every moment in my garden."

"You and Mum would've gotten along well." She took a seat on the bench.

I thought how it would have been to grow up in this home. It saddened me to think that if someone had stood up for me, things would have been so different. I brushed the tears away, went back to the kitchen and returned with a steaming cup of coffee for Catherine.

Just as Catherine took a sip from her mug, Francie sprang through the door, looking much more refreshed, than she had the night before. Her wavy curls flopped around on the top of her head, and when she slipped her coat off, I saw a beautiful necklace with different color stones hanging from her neck.

"OK, I just got off the phone with Rose." She reached over and hugged me, like no time at all had passed between us. "She is in a tizzy."

"Because of me?" I asked.

She laughed and looked over at Catherine, knowingly. "You don't get all the credit, our sister is in a fit most of the time."

"Usually of her own making," Catherine chimed in.

I went back to the kitchen and poured another cup of coffee, this time handing it to Francie. I watched as she and Catherine settled in at the table, still trying to figure out why my presence caused so much of an uproar.

"How was your first night? Did you sleep in our room?" Francie asked, looking directly at Catherine.

Catherine immediately broke in. "Yes, and she slept in your bed."

"And?" Francie asked, her face beaming and curls falling around her face.

"I could see your personalities, and I think I even figured who's who." I looked back and forth between

Francie and Catherine. "Rose had the dolls. Francie, you had the posters, and Catherine, the books? Right?"

"That's a little scary," Francie said, looking at her sister.

"We know each other better than you might think. We're sisters."

I went back to the kitchen to finish preparing breakfast. I set the plates on the table and together we all sat down. We ate and chatted about being middle-aged women in this day and age. I let them babble on. I wanted to learn as much about them, as possible. As Francie refilled the coffee, we bragged on our children. I wasn't sure why, but I was surprised that Devon actually had a great deal in common with her cousins, they were all in the arts. Izzy painted, Paddy worked at the newspaper and Devon had her photography.

"What time should we leave for the hospital?" Francie asked taking the last sip of her coffee and picking up the plates to take them to the sink. At the sound of her phone Catherine flipped it on speaker. It was Connor and his voice tense and strained.

"Are you girls together?" he asked.

"Except for Rose," Catherine said.

"You need to come now."

I sat up straight in my chair, starting to feel nauseous. This was the moment I dreaded most of all. I hoped I'd have had more time. We could have walked in her garden, sat among the vines. We wouldn't even have had to talk to each other.

I wasn't ready to let go, but time had stolen her from me, once again.

"I'll call Rose." Connor's voice broke my thoughts. He sounded solemn, no gaiety, like the night before, laughing.

"Where is Claire?"

"She's here," he said. "Came early to spend some time with Alice."

I listened to the conversation, sat back and realized what the words were saying. That in any moment she would be taken, I'd never hear her voice again. Would she know how much I loved her, how long I had waited to stop being her secret?

Suddenly everyone knew what to do. Francie cleaned up the kitchen, while Catherine nudged me upstairs. In a few minutes I was back down, coat in hand and going out the front door, watching Catherine pull it shut.

"Did you call the kids?" Francie asked, opening the gate and going toward the car.

"Yes."

I didn't hear the rest. I just knew that Devon would be devastated.

The radio buried our thoughts. We didn't talk.

Connor and Claire met us at the doorway. Claire patted the shoulders of both Catherine and Francie, but she reached out and took hold of my hand, then pulled me close to her, wrapping her arms around my shoulders.

"You should have had more time," she whispered into my hair and kissed me on the forehead.

She was kind, but more importantly she loved Alice, I realized that now, watching her move between us. We were her girls, as well. All of us.

"Maybe, it isn't too late," I whispered to her.

I kissed her and held tight, not wanting to let go. "Can we go in? I whispered.

Suddenly, Claire stepped back and looked up past me. Her once soft touch suddenly hardened. I turned back and a lady with a short bob and pearls stood a few feet away.

"All right, I'm here, but I don't want to meet her, so don't even try."

I reached out my hand.

"I have nothing to say to you. Step aside please, so I can go in and see *my* mother."

"What the hell, Rose?" Connor said.

They all looked surprised, especially Catherine. I could tell, regardless of everything that had happened, she wanted to believe in her sister. It broke Catherine. I saw it.

"I am so sorry," Claire said.

I could feel Catherine's fingers under mine. They were trembling.

"Don't pay any attention to her, she doesn't really mean it," Catherine said, wanting with all her heart.

Rose knew exactly what she was doing.

48

They tried to convince me I should go in by myself, but I told them that we were sisters. We'd do it together. We walked arm-in-arm and stood at the foot of her bed. I listened to the hum of the machine that kept her with us.

I moved to the side and took hold of her hand, but didn't notice what was going on behind me. Rose had slipped in, but stood in the corner

I took a seat on the bed and brought her hand up to my lips. "Alice, it's Finn. Can you hear me? I just want you to know I'm here." I caught my breath. "I met my sisters. I've seen your house, been in your garden."

I held on to her hand and I could feel the beat of her heart. I waited for her eyes to open, for her to see me one last time.

"I've wanted to be here for so long, but," I continued, "your daughters told me how you held on to my memory. I'm so sorry for your pain."

I no longer worried about who paid attention to me, I realized watching her that my time was limited. I wanted her back.

I stepped away so that Francie and Catherine could have their time with her.

Catherine came over and took hold of my hand.

"Come back to the bed," she whispered, "You need to be here with us..

Suddenly there was a blur in the room, nurses began to move back and forth, getting us out of the way. They said nothing, just slipped between us and guided us out the door. She was slipping away, and they didn't want us to watch.

We stood together outside, but I was not comfortable. This was my separate loss. They could never know what it felt like to lose her, because they had never had to find her.

I watched as Francie and Catherine talked to the nurse. I heard what she said, but remained separated.

"They want us to go downstairs and wait for a while. They need to adjust some things."

"If it's okay, I'd like to go back in, just for a minute. I'll meet you downstairs."

They looked at each other, then Catherine and Francie nodded. They would deny me little, least of all having time with her. I watched as they walked toward the elevator. I walked back down the hall and sat in the chair, waiting for permission to go inside.

I had said good-bye to my father, a friend in college, even Sally, but this was different. She was my mother. I had missed so much.

In a few minutes, the nurse opened the door, and stood to the side as I stepped inside. The tubes had been removed. She looked peaceful now. Calm.

"Why was everything removed?" I asked.

"It is doing her no good," the taller of the two nurses said.

"What does that mean?"

"Your mother is dying. There is nothing more we can do. We want her to look peaceful for you. Families are often stressed to see all the wires, especially when it is so close to the end."

"Is she really gone?"

"It will come very soon."

"I was just hoping for a few more minutes to be with her, alone."

"You have them now. She probably won't know you're there."

"Thank you. Can I stay?"

"Yes, of course."

I took the seat by her bed and sat down. I picked up her hand and held it close, hoping she would wake and smile at me. Of course, she wouldn't open her eyes. I was helpless.

Losing Alice brought me a sorrow I had never experienced. Her blood flowed through my veins. She had held my heart next to hers. I had never really been so close to anyone.

"Alice, this is my last chance. I stepped into your world and now it will always be part of me. Your garden, the roses on the table, the afghan on the couch, The chipped teapot, even Mittens. I am so grateful to have the memories. I will never forget you. But more than anything, I have the journals you gave to me, so I could know you."

Then I stopped. I leaned down and kissed her lips, something I had never done before. I had hugged her, kissed her cheek, but never so intimate, so personal. I'd let go of the moment, but I'd never let go of her. I knew, that once I left the room, it would be over. I was overjoyed at the peaceful look on her face, no more strain of heartache. I left her alone for the last time.

The hall was empty, and the elevator seemed miles away. I leaned against the wall. I didn't cry in front of her, once outside the room, I couldn't stop. A nurse came over to my side.

"Can I help you?"

I didn't say anything at first, then looked at her. "Can you bring her back?" I asked.

"No, Ma'am. I sorry, I can't, but I can call someone."

"No. I'm okay." I brushed the tears away and made my way to the elevator.

When the door opened to the lobby, I saw Francie gathering papers from the floor.

"What happened?"

"Michael. It's a long story."

* * * * * *

I stood and watched as everyone tried to pull things together. I went over and stood behind Devon, talking with the cousins. I touched her back and she immediately turned around.

"Mom, are you all right?" She was crying, as she turned and took me in her arms.

"Did you get to see her?" I asked.

"Yes, we came in early. Each of us spent time with her, until the nurses said we had to leave.

"Did she know it was you?"

"I think so. I mean, she looked at me and squeezed my hand. I wish we could've had more time."

"I know, so do I."

Alice's death left me in shambles

"We're taking Devon with us today," Izzy said, coming to my side with Paddy.

"That would be a good idea," Claire said, "and I am taking your mother. She'll be fine."

"I'll be there to watch over both of them," Francie broke in.

"You all go on. I'll stay and finish up the details," Connor said. He stood with his hands shoved into his pockets, his cap sitting just above his eyebrow. Jenny stood at his side, clinging to his arm. He was crestfallen. It was written in his eyes, in his every movement. He had been Alice's rock— Jenny was his.

49

I had barely been in Dublin two days and I was overwhelmed. My mother had died and I felt guilty grieving for her. Catherine, Francie and Rose had lost their mother as well. I felt absolutely helpless.

I had still not spoken with Rose. Every time she was supposed to show up, it never happened.

The next morning, sitting on the patio, I heard the door open. I half expected it to be Rose, but Catherine came in alone.

"I'm sorry, I shouldn't have left like that," she said, taking the only empty chair on the patio.

"Michael was crazy," Francie said. "What were you supposed to do?"

I looked back and forth between the two, and felt like I needed to pitch in. "I'm sorry about what happened."

"I told her about Michael and all the mess surrounding it. I hope you don't mind," Francie said.

"No." She looked over at me and smiled. "It's been a bit of a mess for a while. If it's OK, this is not the time to be talking about it."

"Fair enough," Francie said and we got lost in a conversation of details of Mum and her garden.

Eventually, it came back to Rose. For a woman I had barely met, her presence was extremely powerful in our family.

I heard the front door open again, this time it was Claire. She hugged Catherine and sent kisses to Francie and me. I could see the grief. Her eyes were narrowed and her shoulders slouched.... Alice had been her friend longer than any of us had been alive. She had protected her, cared for her and gone above the call of duty by keeping her friend's baby safe. Her love for Alice was on display.

I followed them into the kitchen and watched as Claire laid a stack of envelopes on the table. Everyone encircled her. I still felt like the outsider. *Who was I kidding, of course I was.* In a few days I would leave and they would go back to their lives.

Catherine called Rose, and by the look on her face, I didn't have to hear her words. She wasn't coming, and it was because of me. *I didn't belong here.* Catherine hung up and walked over to the counter and poured a cup of coffee.

"She doesn't want to help with anything. She may not even come to the funeral...." She paused.

"As long as I'm here, right?"

"Yes."

"Maybe I should go home. I can't come between you. This was a really bad idea."

"No." Claire insisted. "That's out of the question. You and Devon aren't going anywhere. Rose had issues long before Alice got sick. I refuse to tolerate this behavior, I don't care who she is. She is acting like a child." Claire glared at us. She folded her arms across her chest. "Enough is enough."

The rest of the morning we spent planning Alice's funeral. Claire had all the details. Phone calls were made and after about an hour, the church had been secured, flowers had been arranged, and Monsignor had agreed to the service.

"See what happens when we work together?" Francie asked.

"I'm going upstairs to freshen up, if no one minds," Catherine said.

"Is she all right?" I asked.

"She's been going through a lot. Michael's been a real bastard. With the divorce and all. It would have broken Mum's heart."

"No," Claire said, "Your mother was smart. She wouldn't have wanted her daughter to stay with someone who abused her. Catherine is doing the right thing. She deserves to be happy."

"You're right. Everyone deserves happiness." Claire came up behind Francie, gave her a hug and winked at me.

"I have an idea, ladies. Everything's done—your mother would love this. Let's go to lunch. Go upstairs and change," she looked over at me, "something casual, but chic."

I smiled. "I don't know if I really have anything chic."

"Francie help her. I'm sure there is a scarf up there where she can add some color. I'll clean up down here and tell Catherine to move it."

Francie drove into Dublin Center, and in a few minutes, pulled to the curb of a busy street. A valet came, opened the doors and Claire stepped out first, with a massive grin. We followed behind her as she strolled into the restaurant.

"Claire, we don't have reservations for a place like this."

"We do, when you know the right people."

Catherine gave a wink. Francie lifted her eyebrow and waited to be led to a table.

"Holy shit, Claire what have you done?"

Claire smiled when we all took a seat. "We'll need another chair, if you don't mind," she instructed the waiter.

We watched, all in awe. "So, what's next?" Catherine asked.

"This chair — is for your Mum. I'm sorry that Rose can't be here, but it's important that you are, my dear girl." She patted my hand. "We're going to have lunch in honor of your mum. We'll talk about the times she made us laugh, the times she made us cry. The times she was everything we could've imagined and more. We will honor the memory of her. And then tomorrow we will bury her with the love she deserved."

And so we ate and drank. Each of us told our stories of Alice Leary whom we had loved in so many different ways. Francie told the story of Alice sticking up for her and Paddy and not allowing them to be sent away.

"She loved him so much, and she stood up to him, but I really don't think he would have sent us away. I didn't know what it meant to her then, but I understand now. Every day I am grateful."

"And you Catherine?" Claire turned toward her.

"I called her one night after Michael had beat me and she told me to come home. To leave him... but I couldn't, not then. It took me a long time to realize I had the right to be strong. Mum knew it all along."

"It is your turn, dear."

"When she gave me the journals. When she said her story was my story. When she told me I was her angel."

"Claire, you started this," Francie said. "What's your memory?"

"I have to choose just one?" We laughed. "It is the day she entrusted you to me, so long ago. She put the medal around your neck and told me I had to watch out for you. And I did, the best I could, until I couldn't anymore."

A long silence took over, then Claire lifted her glass. "To Alice, a woman, a mother, a friend, someone who will never be forgotten."

We clicked our glasses.

"I wish Rose could be here."

"Be careful what you wish for," Francie said.

"No, I am serious. I want to meet her."

"We're serious, too." Catherine added. "Rose has spent her entire life being angry, and no one really knows why. To be honest, I am dreading tomorrow. If, she even decides to come."

* * * * * *

Just after three, we arrived back at Alice's. There had still been no word from Rose. We drank champagne and toasted Alice a few more times than we should have.

I stepped out onto the patio while Francie and Catherine went into the kitchen.

"I don't know about you, but I need some coffee. Anyone else?"

"Sure," I called out.

"I can only imagine what you think of us," Francie said coming up behind me.

"What do you mean?"

"Cocktails at one in the afternoon?"

"Well, yes…No, it was just what I needed."

"You need to understand Claire. That's how she is. Always has been, as long as I've known her. Loves to celebrate, never misses a chance to go out. But she loved Mum… more than anyone in the world. She was always here. She'd take us to her work, out on picnics. If we were out and about, it was usually with her."

"You don't need to explain anything. I've loved every minute with her. When Alice told me about her, that first time, her face lit up, like she was talking about an angel. There's no question she loves you all. To be honest, I'm worried the most about Rose. How long does this go on?"

"How long does what go on?" Catherine asked, coming out on the patio holding two mugs.

"She's worried about Rose," Francie said, taking her mug.

"I've been worried about Rose since the day I was born. There is nothing we can do about her. She'll do whatever strikes her fancy. All we can hope is that she will respect Mum enough not to do anything stupid."

We spent the rest of the darkened afternoon in quiet conversation, slowly each sister left, needing time to prepare for the next day. With the house empty I fixed a late dinner and tossed myself on the couch, still imagining myself on the outside of the house, on the outside of their lives.

50

I had plenty of time to get ready for the funeral. I changed clothes twice, feeling stupid that I couldn't decide on anything. I remembered I had done the same thing on the day I first met her, changing sweaters like I was going to a party.

It was early, I slipped my jeans and a sweater back on and went down stairs, started coffee, and stood on the patio, as I watched the rain. It was fitting she would be buried in the rain.

I called Devon and we chatted for a good long time. She had spent every minute with her cousins and loved them all, even Marie and Jean had been much different than she expected.

"Marie really warmed up to me," she said, "but I think it was because of the photography."

"I'm glad you're making connections."

"Mom, how are you? How are they treating you?"

I sipped my coffee and thought for just a second about their treatment of me. "Like royalty," I said.

"What about Rose?" she asked.

"We still haven't formally met. Today will be the big day, if she even shows. Francie and Catherine seem to have their doubts. I think Claire expects something big."

"I guess I'll see you at the church."

I clicked off the phone and placed it on the table. I took in her garden once again, knowing this might be the last time I would be able to take in its beauty with no one around.

I heard the door open and Catherine called from the living room. "Hope you're dressed, I'm coming through."

"On the patio."

"Why aren't you dressed?" Catherine asked, already decked out in a simple black number that made her look quite beautiful, her hair pulled back, and small drop earrings to set everything off. She looked truly lovely.

"Just relaxing," I replied. "Am I late?"

"It's almost twelve. They'll be here soon. Go on now, take your coffee and finish up."

"Do I have to? It is so relaxing down here."

"You'll have plenty of time tomorrow, go on, now."

Connor and Claire came in together. Connor dressed in a blue suit, with his hair slicked back. I smiled. He was nothing like Alice. He ran his finger between his collar and his neck.

"Come on now," Claire said waving his hand away. "It's not that tight."

"Fine for you to say. You'll not be wearing it yourself."

We all laughed, and Catherine gave him a hug. "Francie will be here in a bit, then we'll be off. You girls can go together, and Connor and I will be right behind you."

The door literally burst open and Francie stepped through, her curls flying in every direction.

"I'm so sorry, come on now, Colin is in the car."

With the rain still coming down, Colin drove out onto the thoroughfare. Francie turned toward the back seat and complimented our dresses, then turned back toward Colin. We all wore black dresses, only different colored coats and scarves, as if what we had on made any difference at all.

"Did Claire take you to this church?" Francie asked.

"No. I have no idea where we're going."

"It's where they were married, and we were all baptized here," Catherine added.

Suddenly as we pulled into the drive way the clouds parted and the sun broke through. We stepped out from the car, careful to miss the puddles from the storm.

I felt odd. I was no longer a stranger. I walked in with the family and would be introduced as family, as would Devon. I took a deep breath and Catherine took hold of my hand.

"You'll be grand," she said.

We went in a side door and were greeted by the Monsignor.

"Father, this is our sister, Claire. From America."

There was a long pause, then he reached out and shook my hand.

"I am so glad you can all be together during this difficult time. You're Mum was... well, we all loved her."

"We all know what my sister was, and we loved her for it," Connor said.

"Any sign of Rose?" Monsignor asked.

"We're on pins and needles. You know that girl," Claire said.

"Would you like to see the altar?" Monsignor

asked. "It is really lovely. Her friends out did themselves."

"We specifically said no flowers."

"Well, I'm afraid no one listened. Come and see."

"Holy shit," Francie whispered. "Sorry Monsignor. I've never seen so many flowers."

It was quite a display. Flowers of all sorts, potted plants, sprays of roses and gladiolas seemed to float across the altar. It was truly the most beautiful thing I had ever seen.

Devon and the cousins came through the back door and immediately came to our sides, each moving to stand by their family. I took hold of Devon's hand as we moved to the first aisle below the altar.

We took turns watching, as people filed in. Anticipating Rose's entrance.

Suddenly Francie tapped my leg and leaned over. "Don't turn around, she's here."

At this moment I didn't care about Rose. I took hold of Devon's hand and together we listened to the young woman sing *Amazing Grace*. I couldn't hold back the tears. I heard the words and realized for the first time, that she was now free, free of it all. She was no longer lost, no longer afraid.

I felt her, her presence as she seeped through me. Alice was here. Her fingertips touched mine. She was home. I cried for myself and what I had lost.

Devon put her arm around me. We were there with our children, honoring the woman that we had all known so differently, but loved with all our hearts. I had to believe that, even Rose loved her, and it was that love that drove her madness.

As quickly as it started, it was over. We filed out, holding hands. I genuflected at the altar, as I left the tiny church she had called home. I prayed that she would always be there for me.

We all stood in the sunshine, waiting to go to the cemetery.

Suddenly, in a flash, she stood in front of us. "Rose..." Catherine whispered."

She didn't say a word, just stood there and stared.

"Hello, I'm Claire." I reached out my hand and my greeting was answered with a sudden slap.

The sting on my cheek burned, I didn't hear anything around me. I couldn't take my eyes off her.

"I had no idea," Rose barely mumbled.

I looked around, not sure what to say or do.

Her voice came out cracked and broken. "You have no right."

"She's our sister. She has every right." I heard Francie say.

"Why did you come here? We were doing fine without you. You had no right to try to claim our mother."

"Rose, stop, what are you saying?" Francie reached for her, but she jerked away.

"No, I mean it. Why did she come?"

"She came because Mum wanted her here, Rose. She wanted all of us here. She knew her time was short and she wanted all her girls to meet before she got so sick she couldn't remember," Catherine said.

"I don't believe you."

"Why?"

Everyone seemed to be talking at once. I couldn't tell who was talking to whom, but I knew what the look in Rose's eyes meant. I held back the tears. I had never in all my life been treated with such bitterness.

When I looked up, I could see Rose walking toward the parking lot. She didn't turn around or say a word, just got into her car and left everyone wondering what had just happened. Connor came up behind me and guided me with his hand; Claire came to the other side.

"Never you mind her," Connor whispered. "You belong here. You'll always be family." Devon came from behind and we all walked to the car.

So that was my sister. She didn't believe I had a right to be at my own mother's funeral. *Would I have done that to her?* I sat in the back seat with Devon, watching as Connor made his way through the cemetery across the street to the burial site.

We stood huddled together. The sun had disappeared, I couldn't listen to the prayers, all I saw was Rose's face and her hatred. *What had I done?*

"Mom, there is nothing you can do about her. Don't let her ruin this."

I took hold of her hand and we stood together. I let the rage slip from my face. Connor was right. I should be here. I would always be family, no matter what she thought.

51

The house remained quiet. None of the mourners had come from the gravesite. No surprise there, at least not for me.

I slipped out into the garden, telling Devon I needed to be alone. I had been drained of every possible emotion. I thought about telling Devon that we should go home, but I decided it was better not to make any decisions, just yet. We only had one more day before we were leaving anyway. What kind of sister would I be if I couldn't take flak from Rose.

I lingered along, hoping her garden would bring me strength. I told myself I wouldn't let anyone see me cry. What was the point in crying? It was over and done with, and as Sally had once said, you can't change anyone who doesn't want to be changed. And Rose didn't want to change. She wanted her mother back. We all did.

I looked up and saw Catherine watching me. I waved and gave her a smile. She came over to the bench and took a seat.

"I'm fine," I said, looking over at her.

"Just checking."

"I'm a big girl." She went back inside.

A few minutes later Claire stuck her head out,

then came and took a seat on the bench.

"Are you all right?"

"Oh, my heavens. I'm fine. Do I look that bad? First Catherine, now you."

She patted my hand. "I've been around long enough to know when I see heartache. I'm sorry." She smiled. "I keep telling you how sorry I am for what other people do."

"You don't have to do that. I'm a big girl. I really do understand."

"Come inside, the rain will be here soon, don't want you drenched."

I smiled at this dear woman who reminded me of Alice with every word. I took the hand she stretched out to me. We walked back into the house and mingled with the family.

Devon and I were talking when suddenly everything stopped. I looked around and saw that Catherine had moved to the front door, and there she was. *Shit, hadn't she said enough? I got it. She didn't want me here. Fine.*

"You can't stop me. I have something to say, and you're all going to listen." Rose stormed into the dining room.

Devon and I sat down and watched as Rose almost lunged toward the table.

"Okay, I'm sorry. It was wrong." The color drained from her face. "It was a disgrace and I never meant to do that." She took a breath and stood up straight. "I never meant to do that to Mum's memory."

Her words were like whispers. She apologized. Not to me, but for the disgrace she brought to Alice. *Was that what I heard?*

"Sorry? That's all you have to say?" I heard Catherine ask. I think it was Catherine.

"Yes. I said I was sorry." She didn't look at me; instead she set her eyes on her daughters who had gathered around the table. Jean cried and Marie stared in disbelief.

"That isn't enough." I turned and looked at Francie. "You owe Finn an apology, not just walking through the door saying I'm sorry. After what you did, you owe us all an apology, but especially her."

"You're right. I was wrong to do that. I know that saying I'm sorry doesn't make up for any of it." Rose bowed her head and I saw her hands shaking as she held on to the chair. "I can't give you a reason for what I did. I don't even think I know. It was all too much, too soon..."

I stopped listening, until I heard, "I hate that you came back. I hate that she might have loved you." She stared at me. "And she thought of you every single day, even while she was with us."

I didn't need to hear any more. I was tired of her excuses, tired of being blamed for the things she hated.

I heard the front door slam, and when I looked up, I realized the kids were gone. Claire was coming in from the living room. "I have something for you." She walked to the bureau and pulled a stack of manila envelopes from the drawer.

"They don't need to hear all of this," Claire said as she turned around. Her voice softened as she talked about Alice. Her strength and determination. "I know you're angry that she didn't include you in her decisions, but that was your mum. Quite simply, it was her right."

I folded my hands and waited to see a change in Rose's face, something to tell me that she really understood. Nothing changed. She wasn't getting it. I had a pretty good idea what was in the envelopes.

"I have four envelopes that were given to me by your mother. Before she died, we were able to talk. She was coherent."

"How would we know that?" Rose blurted.

"Because I'm telling you. I have no reason to lie. I have no hidden agenda. Before I let you read these, I want to tell you, one more time, of how we met. Then I'll go. You've all heard it before, but it's important. After, if you want to tear yourselves apart, it won't be my doing."

Rose fiddled with her ears, Francie brushed back strands of hair. Catherine folded her arms in front of her. None of us took our eyes off Claire.

"Okay, here goes. I met your mum at Castlepollard, on my first nursing job. Her parish priest brought her in after she became pregnant from a rape. Your grandfather sent her away and your grandmother did nothing to stop it. When the time came, I delivered the baby.

While in the home she experienced tremendous abuse. Besides me, she had Sara. You all remember Sara. After nine days they sent the infant off to an orphanage and she and Sara were sent to a Laundry in Dublin."

I stopped listening. I knew the story, probably better than anyone, except for Claire, who lived it.

She unfolded the story as Alice had done in her journals. I knew about Jonathan, the priests and what they had done. I knew about her time in Howth where she reinvented herself.

Rose stared at Claire. "I don't believe you."

"It is not my job to make you believe. Whatever you do with it, is up to you."

"She would have told us," Rose said.

"You think so?" Francie asked.

"We were her daughters," Rose said.

"And that was why. Don't you understand Rose, how much your mother loved you. She never wanted to hurt you. She never wanted you to think the worst of her, because of what she had been through."

Rose fought every word, as if her legacy was being torn apart. She had no intention of listening to what anyone said; not Claire, not Connor, not even her own sisters and certainly not me. She had her mind set.

Then Claire got to something, no one knew about. She brought up the medal, my medal. The Miraculous Mary medal.

"I have something to say," I said.

"No one cares about what you have to say," Rose shot back, finally looking over at me.

"You have every right to speak," said Claire.

"I have something that I don't think any of you know about, well, Claire and Catherine know. When I met *my mother* for the first time, I returned a medal on a string that she had given to me when I was born. I wanted her to have it back."

Silence filled the room. Everyone sat back and Rose lit a cigarette in her impatience.

"She gave me something else, too," I said. "I have it upstairs, and if you want, I'll go get it. I can prove I'm not lying. I belong here. I am your sister." I stood up, then turned back toward Rose. "I never wanted to hurt you. I had your phone numbers, I knew where you lived, I knew your children's names. Catherine, I knew you were in Boston, but I never contacted you because she asked me not to. I kept your mother's secret for almost ten years."

"I can't do this anymore. I need to leave," Rose said.

"Sit down, girl," Connor said.

"Why don't you just wait to see what Finn has? If you want to leave after that, then you can go with our blessing," Catherine broke in.

"We can't keep beating this dead horse. We can't make you do something you are dead set against doing," Francie said.

I went upstairs and pulled the medal from the box, clutched it in my hand. I also grabbed the journals. That would prove I belonged here, more than anything.

When I came back another envelope lay on the table. I assumed it had been from Claire. She seemed to be the keeper of the family heritage. I placed my belongings on the table.

"I have three volumes of journals our mum wrote," I said. "I learned all about you and your life as a family. I learned about her life in the Home and the Laundry. She wrote about the abuse, her fears, and her hatred for what her parents did to her. How she would never let any of you experience what she had gone through."

Rose reached for one of the books, but I saw the look in her eye. She didn't believe me any more now than she had an hour ago.

"Mum never kept a journal. You're lying," she said.

"I'm not lying. They're in her handwriting. Look at them. They're her words. She gave them to me so I would understand why she signed me away. Maybe she had to write it down for herself, so when she went back for it, she knew that it really happened. I don't think she ever wanted to forget."

Rose flipped through the pages. Her mannerisms were gentle. She touched the pages, feeling the texture between her fingers.

"Please remember, they're mine. She gave them to me. They're going home with me. You have your real memories, all I have is the words she wrote on these pages."

I handed a journal to each of them, and even pointed out the hand written cover, *"The Swan Garden."*

Each of the girls held tight to their books, neither Catherine nor Francie opened theirs, but Rose kept thumbing through, like she was examining them for something to call me on.

"You said you had something else, Claire. What is it?" Francie asked.

"I have the letter your Da left for your Mum when he died, telling her how he learned about everything and how much he still loved her. I think you should all read it. So, you really understand your Da."

"That's private, I don't think we should be reading that. It was between them," Catherine said.

"It was your mum's idea. She asked me to be sure to have each of you read it."

"I don't need to read a stupid letter. I'm going home. Connor leave me be." Rose pulled away, stood up, and moved from the table.

"I'll have the letter when you're ready to read it. If you think you need to go home, we aren't going to stop you anymore," Claire said, watching Rose.

"She was our mother as well, Rose. We are all devastated by her death, but why do you refuse to accept the truth," Francie broke in.

"She doesn't know her," Rose screamed. "She has no idea what our life was like. She is not her child."

"You are wrong, Rose," Claire said.

"She was every way her child. It wasn't Mum's choice that she was taken from her. How can you be so cruel?"

"I don't have to put up with this." She was gone, just like that.

I didn't have to put up with it either. I wanted to scream. What the hell? I got up and went outside. I tried to take deep breaths, but I couldn't.

One by one they came out to help put me back together. I didn't want to be fixed.

52

Claire was taking everyone out again. She had said it was a goodbye for Devon and me. I had come to learn that Claire had been the fixer of everything. Broken dolls, broken hearts, and once again broken families. We met for brunch at the Alex in Dublin, to say our goodbyes as best we could. We laughed, traded phone numbers and took pictures with our cell phones. No one talked about Rose.

To be honest, I wanted to go home, too much had happened in the last few days. I didn't think I could take much more. The drama with Rose had worn me raw and angered me beyond what I could have imagined.

Just as we were ready to put on our coats, Claire stood and tapped her glass.

"I know that everyone's busy, but I'd like you to indulge me, one more time." She paused, looked around, then continued. "I'd like you to spend a few more hours with me. I promise to have everyone back by two."

Jean was the first to protest, but with a few looks from her aunt, she agreed to go.

Catherine and Francie both looked over at me. "I have no problem with that, as long as we're back by two. We need to be at the airport by three."

"I promise you'll be at the airport by then," she paused for a moment. "Your Mum would have wanted this. There's a place she'd have liked all of you to see, together."

"Where are you taking us?" Izzy asked.

"It's all been arranged. Paddy will drive the cousins. Francie, you'll drive the rest of us to Castlepollard?"

"You know I will."

"Okay, what is going on here?" Marie asked looking around the room.

"I knew if I just asked you to go, everyone would have an excuse, so I sort of planned it. I got some assistance from Paddy and Francie in the planning."

The rain poured down as we reached the hills surrounding Castlepollard. I had been here. I knew what Claire had planned. We were going to *"The Angels Plot."* I leaned back and closed my eyes, remembering when Devon and I walked up that long, gray hill. Suddenly Catherine took hold of my hand and squeezed it.

"You all right?" she asked.

"Just anxious, I guess. We've been here before."

"I might have thought as much. You seem to know so much more about our history than we do."

"Don't feel bad," I said. "You had no reason to know. You had your life, your mum, everything was right here. I didn't, so I kept searching. You do that when pieces are missing. I can't explain it. You just keep going until you have all the pieces. It just took me longer than usual."

"I'm so glad you did. We all are."

It was the first time anyone had acknowledged what I had done.

"Claire brought Francie and I here a few months ago," Catherine announced. "That's where I learned about everything, about you, about what happened, Mum's secret." I leaned in even closer. "I don't think this is for us. I think Claire wants to pass Mum's story to the kids."

I thought about what Catherine had said. Claire knew exactly what she was doing. She had probably even planned it with Alice when they lunched together in Dublin. I had shared their heritage with my daughter, now it was here for all of us to share together.

Claire gave the final call when Francie neared the turnabout. It didn't take long to reach the winding gray driveway. It rained like it had done on the day Devon and I came.

It looked no different than it had years before. The memories of those gray prison buildings would never leave me. I stood back as the others walked around the buildings, touching the doors and peering in the windows.

"This was a mother baby home, where girls, no, where babies were sent to have their babies," Claire said. "I was here. I helped them deliver. This is where I first met your grandmother."

I headed up the path to The Angel's Plot.

It was like a forest here, everything hidden behind lawns and gardens. Hidden, so no one would ask. I waited at the gate of the cemetery, staring into the tiny plot where so many bodies had been buried. The gate felt cold to my touch. I waited for the squeak as it opened, but there was nothing to mark its movement. It began to rain, again.

"This is a cemetery," Claire said, "for the babies who didn't survive." I heard her say as she stepped through the gate.

"If it's a cemetery, why aren't there any gravestones?" Izzy asked.

"The babies were buried in mass graves," Devon answered.

There were no more questions. The stillness spoke for itself. The rain continued, softened to a mist, steady but light.

Suddenly Claire stepped forward out from under Paddy's umbrella. "Jean when you ran your hand along the wall, did you feel anything?"

Marie put her hand to the wall. "What is that?"

"Worker's nails."

"They cover the entire wall," Paddy said, running his hand across as well. "You can see them sticking out."

"There must be hundreds of them," Marie said.

"Actually, there are over five hundred on this wall alone." Devon knew her history. "After the 1930s, for every baby buried, a nail was placed in the wall. The worker who started this said he wanted the babies to be remembered."

"What are the ribbons?" Jean asked.

"A few years ago, survivors started holding annual remembrances. They put ribbons on the nails to honor those who died," Claire said.

"I just can't believe this. I had no idea grandma was here. She was so... so happy all the time, she loved us so much." Marie fingered a tattered ribbon.

"She probably loved you even more because of this place. The hatred she experienced brought out the love she had for her family. I don't know if this makes sense," Claire said, "but sometimes you take love from the darkest of places."

"So, this is our heritage? This is where Grandma came from?" Izzy looked around, running her hand across the ragged edges of the wall.

"No, your heritage is in Meadow's Glen. This was a stopping off point for her, a place that changed her life forever, but she took the bad and turned it around. She carried it with her everywhere," Claire said.

"You're sure babies are really buried here?" Jean asked.

I walked past them, to the only gravestone in the whole plot. It read:

IN MEMORY OF
GOD'S SPECIAL
ANGELS
ACCEPTED IN THIS
CEMETARY

Paddy nudged me quietly. "Why is cemetery misspelled?"

I smiled and looked up at him, "most of the workers didn't know how to read or write, but their intentions were good."

Claire pulled Paddy down and whispered in his ear. He smiled and nodded. I didn't know what Claire had planned, but it had to be something special.

One by one, we came together in a circle. The rain fell around us. This was to be Claire's final honor for Alice.

In slow motion Paddy handed the purple ribbons to Claire.

"I brought ribbons for everyone." She handed one to each of us. "I'd like you to choose a nail and place a ribbon around it for whatever memory you hold dear." There would be no responses to her requests. I imagined that one by one we would all dedicate a ribbon to someone special.

Paddy went first, reaching as high as he could. He reached for what looked like a rusted twisted nail. "This is for the child no one came back for."

Marie tied her ribbon, then bowed her head. "This is for my mother who never found her way back."

Francie wrapped her ribbon around the nail she had chosen. Paddy came next to her and put his hand on her shoulder. "This is for my boy, and my mum, who had the strength to spare us."

Izzy walked away from us, then bent down and tied her ribbon. "This is for my grandmother, who found the strength to survive."

Jean wiped the moss from her nail and tied her ribbon tight. "That someday my mum will stop being so angry.

When it was Catherine's turn, she took her ribbon and rambled down the wall, waiting for the one that called out her name. I couldn't hear what she said, but she bowed her head for a long time.

Claire added hers, moving farther down the wall. "This is for my friends, Alice and Sara, who fought so hard to be free."

Devon and I had done our own ribbons in the silence of rain without anyone looking. There was no question where our hearts were. We had watched our family come together and we could go home, even if we never came back, everything I had set out to do had been accomplished.

I looked back one last time as we left *The Angel's Plot,* I wondered how I survived. How I had found a way out?

53

Paddy drove us back to Alice's house, where we spent the afternoon. Our flight had been delayed until ten that evening.

It was the first time that Devon and I had actually been alone there. Paddy left his cell number and told us when we were ready, to call him.

Devon went to the kitchen to make some tea, and I stepped into the garden. Of all the places I could be in Dublin, it was Alice's garden that grounded me. I felt her at every turn. I found myself drawn to the swans draped with ivy and vines, buried deep within the plants.

I'd love to take some of her plants home, but with customs and all....

Devon stepped into the garden, "Mom, hey, come here." Her voice sounded funny, almost hushed. "Someone's in the living room."

"What are you talking about? Did Paddy come back?"

She kept looking at me like I was supposed to understand, and then I saw her. I looked at Devon then back at Rose. She stood, as she had earlier in the living room, with jeans and the same sweater, no make-up.

Her face swollen with tears.

I met her in the living room. Devon excused herself and went upstairs.

"What do you want? You made yourself very clear early on. You know I am going home. I will be out of your life in a few hours."

She took a cigarette from her purse lit it, then took a seat on the couch. I watched her, not sure what to do.

"What do you want from me Rose?" I held my anger in my fist, so it would not show on my face. I was tired of apologizing.

"I want you to accept my apology."

She had to be kidding. She had ridiculed me, insulted me and basically told me I had no right to be here. Now she sat on the couch with a cigarette asking for my forgiveness. I went into the kitchen and pulled an ashtray from the cupboard. I went back and placed it on the coffee table.

"You know what Rose, let's just call it even. I get it and I am sorry, not for coming here, but for Alice never being able to tell you herself what happened."

"No, you need to listen to me. I have something to say, and I'm not leaving until I say it. You can do what you want with it."

"Okay, fine. I took a seat in the chair across from her.

"I was cruel."

Suddenly Rose got up and headed toward the kitchen. "I'm going to get a glass of wine, I'll need one to do this. Do you want one?"

"No. We have to leave for the airport in a few hours. "

She came back in the living room, sat down and placed her glass on the table.

"Okay, you have your wine and your cigarette. What do you want to say?" From the chair I could see Devon sitting on the last step of the staircase. She put her finger to her lips. I nodded and turned back toward Rose.

Her eyes blinked, then dropped, and she took a deep breath. She took a sip, then a drag, and finally got up, and walked behind the couch, still holding her glass.

"Oh my God, Rose, just say it."

"I didn't want to meet you because I was angry. I was angry that you looked for her. That you had found her. My own daughter never looked for me."

I heard the words and by themselves, I knew what they meant. Together they made no sense. "What are you saying?"

"She didn't write about it in her journals? Her eldest daughter going off to London?"

"No. She wrote about you taking care of your sisters, going off to university and how proud she was of you."

"She said that?" Rose asked.

"Yes. She wrote about how you loved your dolls and how you always kept her on her toes. What was it that you thought she told me?"

"I went to London for a year before I married Charlie. I worked for a while and stayed with my aunt."

"I don't know what this has to do with me?"

"I had a baby. It wasn't Charlie's and I never told him. I gave her up for adoption, but I left a letter for the Sisters, hoping they would give it to her, if she ever came back. I never heard from anyone, then I found out about you. You didn't give up. Why did you want to meet her so bad?"

'Rose, times were different. Maybe her family
...₁ told her she was adopted. Maybe the Sisters
never gave her the letter. They never gave me Alice's.
There are too many variables. You can't compare us."

"But you kept coming back."

"It was different for me."

"I wanted so much for her to come back to me,
but I have no idea where she is. It just made me so
angry, and I took it out on you, and even more so when
you came back here. I didn't know why my daughter
couldn't love me the way you loved our...your mum."

"I don't know what to say." I had hated that she
had been so cruel, but I understood her heartbreak.

"You don't have to say anything now, but if you
could think about it and then maybe down the road,
you could....forgive me?"

I looked over at Devon, and she had both hands to
her mouth.

"I don't need time down the road. I understand
and yes, I forgive you. I'm sorry about your baby, and
that she hasn't contacted you, but please believe me
when I say it doesn't mean she doesn't love you. There
could be so many other factors. She may not know
about you. Maybe you could go back to the Sisters and
try to find out where she is, then send your own letter
to her, that was what I did."

Rose brushed the tears away and took a long
drink from her glass, then came around the couch.
"Everything I did was wrong. I just wanted someone to
feel for me the way you felt for her."

"It all takes time, Rose." We hugged and I felt her
tears on my checks."

"Thank you." And then she wept and it came from
her soul.

"Rose, I don't mean to be rude, but we have to go to the airport. Our flight will be going out at ten, and it is already half past six. We need to be getting on our way."

She brushed the tears away. "Let me take you. That is the least I can do, after being such a bitch."

"You weren't a bitch."

"Yes, I was."

"Okay, you were." We both laughed. An honest, sincere laugh.

＊ ＊ ＊ ＊ ＊

One day, as Mia and I fussed in the garden, we heard the doorbell and she ran immediately to the front door and called my name. By the time I had washed the mud from my hands, the porch was empty. A box sat on the mat.

Inside were six clay pots. On the bottom was an envelope. I slipped it open and took out the note.

> *Finn,*
> *I wanted to share these with you. I thought the jasmine, heather, and roses, would help remind you of us.*
>
> *R.*

Mia helped me carry the pots back to the garden.

We carefully planted each cutting, mixing them with the ones from Sally. I watered them with tears of love, as I watched her tiny hands bring our garden together.

CPSIA information can be obtained
at www.ICGtesting.com
Printed in the USA
BVHW071229270519
549345BV00001B/58/P